PHILIPPA

Netta Muskett

HOUSE OF
STRATUS

This edition published in 2014 by House of Stratus, an imprint of
Stratus Books Ltd, Lisandra House, Fore St., Looe,
Cornwall, PL13 1AD, UK.

www.houseofstratus.com

Typeset by House of Stratus.

A catalogue record for this book is available from the British Library and the Library of Congress.

ISBN 0755143027
EAN 978 0755143023

Netta Muskett was born in Sevenoaks, Kent, and was educated at Kent College, Folkstone. She had a varied and interesting career, at first teaching mathematics before working as a secretary to the then owner of the 'News of the World', as well as serving as a volunteer during both world wars – firstly driving an ambulance and then teaching handicrafts in British and American hospitals.

It is, however, for the exciting and imaginative nature of her writing that she is most remembered. She wrote of the times she experienced, along with the changing attitudes towards sex, women and romance, and sold millions of copies worldwide. Her last novel 'Cloudbreak' was first published posthumously after her death in 1963.

Many of her works were regarded by some librarians at the time of publication as risqué, but nonetheless proved to be hugely popular with the public, especially followers of the romance genre.

Netta co-founded the Romantic Novelists' Association and served as Vice-President. The 'Netta Muskett' award, now renamed the 'RNA New Writers Scheme', was created in her honour to recognise outstanding new writers.

AFTER RAIN	A MIRROR FOR DREAMS
ALLEY CAT	MISADVENTURE
BLUE HAZE	NO MAY IN OCTOBER
BROCADE	NO YESTERDAYS
CANDLE IN THE SUN	NOR ANY DAWN
CAST THE SPEAR	OPEN WINDOW
THE CLENCY TRADITION	THE OTHER WOMAN
CLOUDBREAK	PAINTED HEAVEN
CROWN OF WILLOW	THE PATCHWORK QUILT
THE CROWN OF WILLOW	PHILIPPA
A DAUGHTER FOR JULIA	QUIET ISLAND
THE DURRANTS	RED DUST
THE FETTERED PAST	THE ROCK PINE
FIRE OF SPRING	SAFARI FOR SEVEN
FLAME OF THE FOREST	SAFE HARBOUR
THE FLICKERING LAMP	SCARLET HEELS
FLOWERS FROM THE ROCK	SHADOW MARKET
FROM THIS DAY FORWARD	SHALLOW CUP
GILDED HOOP	SILVER GILT
GIVE BACK YESTERDAY	TAMARISK
GOLDEN HARVEST	THIRD TITLE UNKNOWN
THE HIGH FENCE	THIS LOVELY THING
HOUSE OF MANY WINDOWS	THROUGH MANY WATERS
HOUSE OF STRAW	TIME FOR PLAY
JADE SPIDER	TODAY IS OURS
JENNIFER	THE TOUCHSTONE
LIGHT FROM ONE STAR	THE WEIR HOUSE
LIVING WITH ADAM	THE WHITE DOVE
THE LONG ROAD	WIDE AND DARK
LOVE AND DEBORAH	WINGS IN THE DUST
LOVE IN AMBER	WINTER'S DAY
MIDDLE MIST	THE WIRE BLIND

Chapter One

'Oh, Phil, you look too, too lovely – doesn't she, Mrs. Joliman?'

Philippa's mother could only nod speechlessly, bending to adjust a fold in the shimmering slipper satin. She had no words with which to clothe, or to cloak, her admiration, her pride and joy and delight in the achievement of her only child which today's ceremony was to perfect.

Philippa turned to them, her mother tightly corseted in blue which was not the right shade for her but on which she had insisted until Dior washed his hands of her, her bevy of bridesmaids in shell-pink-with little Juliet caps of silver lace, one or two admiring, excited maids hovering in the background now that the bride was 'finished'.

'Please, dears,' said Philippa, 'will you all go and leave me alone for two or three minutes?' her voice not quite steady, her face determinedly smiling but with a look almost of fear in her eyes.

Everybody else gave instant, smiling acquiescence. Only Mrs. Joliman stood her ground and was left alone with her daughter.

'Now, Philippa, whatever's the idea?' she asked anxiously. 'Not going say anything's wrong now, at the last minute, are you?'

Philippa shook her head beneath its veil of precious old lace lent by her future mother-in-law.

'You mean am I going to change my mind and leave Justin waiting at the church? Of course not. I just wanted to have a last minute alone. When Daddy comes up for me. I'll be ready. I don't seem to have belonged to myself for weeks, and after today I suppose I never shall again – but everything's alright.

Ella Joliman heaved a sigh of relief. All the time that was the thing she had feared, that Philippa would do another of those unexpected unpredictable things and call off this stupendous marriage. Not that her mother would for one moment have put worldly considerations before her daughter's happiness, but she was satisfied that nowhere in the world would she find a man more calculated to bring happiness to Philippa than the man who must at this very moment be waiting at the altar for her.

Philippa heard the door close softly after that sigh and turned back to her mirror in a last attempt to recognise herself in this pale, frosted, shimmering princess of the fairy tales into which they had transformed her.

The fear that had shown in her eyes was beating unevenly in her heart. She knew what they all thought, and who could blame them? Everybody thought that she was marrying Justin for what he could give her, for being made the Countess of Hollmere Abbey and of a grim, old-fashioned, dilapidated house in London.

Lady Hollmere – she, Philippa Joliman!

A cold hand seemed to be squeezing her throat and automatically she put her own hands to it – and felt there the pearls which Justin had sent the day before.

'Pearls? Oh, he shouldn't ought to have sent pearls, not for your wedding day,' her mother had said, her careful gentility slipping a little temporarily in her shocked voice. 'Pearls for tears, they say.'

Philippa had laughed and fingered the lovely things.

'I expect all the Hollmere brides have worn them before me,' was all she had said, but now she was remembering.

Tears? Well, of course, every life must have its share of them, she told herself impatiently, and so far she had had only a very small share.

But, with a sort of panic, she tried to think of Justin and could not even remember what he looked like – or so she thought, looking at her unfamiliar self in the mirror. Here in this house, in her familiar bedroom which had only changed with her as she had grown from childhood into girlhood and now into womanhood, her real self had lived. Now, in a few short minutes, she was to go from it and it would never be her own again, not in the same way. They would still call it Philippa's room but the Philippa who had belonged to it would no longer exist. She would have disappeared in the unknown personality of the new Lady Hollmere. Philippa Joliman would be gone forever.

Philippa Joliman.

How she had hated that name at times! She could feel a shrinking into herself even now as she recalled her first introduction to the expensive, exclusive school which had at last been forced to accept 'daughters of tradesmen' through sheer lack of a sufficient supply of daughters with money from the 'upper classes', the professions and the even then declining nobility.

Joe Joliman had with difficulty been prevailed upon by his wife to let her go alone to the first interview with the pale, thin, aristocratic, scholarly woman who was the principal of the school.

'You know, Joe, you slip up in your grammar and your aitches when you get excited,' his wife had told him, 'and we don't want to let Phil down. I'm more careful and I don't get excited.'

She had no idea that her painfully acquired accent, her very correct manners and the style of her expensive clothes were every bit as revealing as Joe's uncertain grammar and aitches would have been, but Miss Eckton had been told plainly by the Board of Governors that she must no longer refuse pupils on the grounds of their parents' shortcomings if the girls themselves were presentable, and Philippa stood up well to her critical scrutiny. Her speech and manners were natural, and the slight flamboyance of her clothes would disappear with school uniform.

But Philippa (she had been fourteen then) soon discovered that her background was known and despised and though she had always previously accepted it as an unimportant part of life, now her father's advertisements, the picture of the fat, jolly red-faced little man in the butcher's striped apron, sharpening a carving knife as he contemplated a royal sirloin, became the ruling factor and the source of unutterable misery in her life.

'Jolly Man Turned Meats. You can eat 'em but you can't beat 'em', ran the slogan which was known in every household all over the country and ever a large proportion of the outer world as well. Joe Joliman had never, within Philippa's knowledge, worn a butcher's striped apron and quite certainly when the first of the pictures of the bald red-faced, smiling little man had begun to appear in newspapers, on hoardings and on the tins themselves. Joe Joliman could not have looked like him. But there was no doubt he closely resembled him now. Possibly, over the years the picture had figured so largely in Joe Joliman's life that he had unconsciously grown like it, as people long and happily married are said to grow like one another.

The picture was made to haunt Philippa at school, appearing mysteriously in all sorts of unexpected places, on her pillow, pinned to the wall of her cubicle, slipped between the pages of her text books and even sent up in her exercise books, though she was quite certain they had not been there when she handed her book in for correction. It was so easy to get such pictures. Joe Joliman had built up his reputation and his huge fortune by two things – the excellence of his wares and the extent of his advertising. The highly coloured picture could be cut from almost any magazine, and Philippa suspected that her tormentors collected the paper bands from tins used in their own kitchens to bring back to school.

She accepted her position with silent, bitter resentment under an appearance of calm indifference, and gradually they tired of the sport, especially as Philippa made her own indisputable place in the school life, being good at games and able to shed lustre from her position in the lacrosse and hockey teams. She was also a fearless rider, and though she had her own valuable thoroughbred mare in the school stables, she was always ready and willing to let less fortunate girls ride her.

But she was never popular and never entirely happy during her school-days. There were other girls whose fathers were 'in trade', but none of them continually threw the fact in the face of the world as did 'the Jolly Man', and the story of her father's wealth, turned by rumour into fabulous millions, set her apart in the minds of most of her schoolmates. She always felt herself to be an interloper, and she made no close friendships during the whole of her four years at Leaway.

Her *bête noir* from the first had been Susan Therne, the *Honourable* Susan Therne, born of a long line of Thernes who were now as impecunious as most of her particular social class, people who, according to Joe Joliman, were 'dead but they won't lie down'. Philippa hated Susan Therne for her petty tortures, her contempt, her bitter, gibing tongue, the skilful ways in which she could point and emphasise the difference between her own background and upbringing and that of the daughter of the Jolly Man. It was all done cleverly, with outward smoothness and good manners, and it made the other girls giggle at Philippa's expense.

Only once was there an actual open show-down between the two, and during the course of it Philippa's slow, terrible temper, which had smouldered for years, burst into flame. With her tongue and her blazing eyes, with words and phrases which she had not even known she knew, she had scourged her tormentor, whilst the little crowd that had collected round the pair watched and listened, fascinated and delighted. Philippa was not popular except when she played for the school, but Susan was generally disliked and feared.

Susan could find nothing to say, and feared actual physical attack, for Philippa was taller and stronger, but though fists were clenched, the attack did not go further than words.

'What are you and your class but parasites?' was Philippa's final thrust. 'What do any of you contribute to the growth or welfare of the state? We have to keep you by our brains and our work and I'm glad I don't belong to your so-called upper class, and one day we shall be on top and you'll be nobodies. You're dead but you won't lie down,' on which note of bathos, which she regretted at once as a weak ending, Philippa marched away, head in air, her heart thumping almost audibly as the blood raced through her veins.

After that, Susan left her alone, and though both girls remained at Leaway for more than a year longer, they never spoke to each other again and averted their eyes when they met.

Philippa, standing before her mirror in those last moments of her life as Philippa Joliman, saw as many of her twenty-two years as she could remember, pass in review before her.

From Leaway she had gone to be 'finished' at a small, select school in the north of Scotland, not in France or Switzerland as her parents would have wished because the war was on. Here she was not subjected to the indignities and small torments of school life, but she had lost the art of making friends and she lived for the most part as a solitary individual.

Just before the war came to an end, with her education regarded as finished, she went into the W.R.N.S. for what was probably the happiest and most carefree eighteen months of her life. Though her parents had assured her that she could easily be kept out of the services, she had insisted on joining up and again refused the assured suggestion of getting her a commission.

'What's the good of having all this money if I can't make my only child a bit comfortable?' protested her father. 'You don't have to *work*.'

She had laughed and gone into the ranks, but as she had from her earliest memories been able to handle almost any kind of boat and quickly proved herself strong and adaptable, she became a member of a boat crew, and it was in that capacity that she met Justin, who was then merely Lieutenant Breane of the 'Wavy Navy'. His two elder brothers were then still alive.

Justin could never forget the first sight he had of her, in her trim uniform of navy-blue suit and white blouse, her Jack Tar cap set at a jaunty angle on her short, thick brown curls.

His commander was standing beside him on the deck of the launch at whose side the girls were manoeuvring the dinghy which they had rowed out to bring the two officers ashore.

'Y'know, Breane, those girls handle their ship jolly well,' said the commander. 'Look at the one standing up now. Wonder whether she'd be as handy at anything else as she is with the boat-hook?' and at that precise moment Philippa lost her balance at a sudden roll of the choppy sea and went in head first. Justin caught sight of her face as she felt herself falling. There was mingled horror and laughter in it, but no fear, and when she reappeared, her cap gone, her curls dripping water, she was still laughing. There was no need for the watching men to do anything about it, as her companions were fishing her out expertly with her own boat-hook, and she shook herself like a dog, managed to reclaim her floating cap, gave it a shake and perched it again on her curly top and proceeded with her job.

As she came aboard the launch and saluted smartly, undaunted by her bedraggled condition, the two officers smiled.

'Well, you're in the navy now, Wren ...?' said the commander.

'Joliman, sir,' said Philippa, standing correctly to attention.

'H'm. Very apt,' he observed, turning away, and Philippa caught Justin's eye and something intangible but unmistakable flashed between them.

She was aware of his eyes on her as she pulled her oar on the way back to the shore, where the commander jumped out, nodded briefly to his subordinate and strode away.

'Are you going to get a chance to change into dry clothes?' asked Justin when the girls had drawn the boat up on the beach and were preparing to leave.

Philippa made a grimace.

'Dry clothes and few dry words, sir,' she said with a sort of cheerful dismay.

'Well you know what the commander said. You're not in the navy until you've fallen in at least once,' he said and turned away, but he took with him the memory of her laughing face, her grey eyes, her sunburnt skin and her mop of wet brown curls. It was only after considerable thought that he realised she had been lovely. Her expression and her sense of fun had made mere beauty seem of secondary importance.

Philippa did not think of him consciously at all until after their second meeting, which took place the next evening at a dance held in H.M.S. *Dimrose*, the official name given to the shore establishment where the W.R.N.S. lived.

Justin went for the express purpose of seeing her again and he saw her almost at once, picking her out unerringly from the groups of uniformed girls and making a bee line for her.

'Do we dance?' he asked. 'I take it you're dry by now?'

She laughed.

'I really need not have changed,' she said. 'The blistering telling-off I got burnt me dry in no time!'

She was fairly tall for a woman, and he an inch or so taller, and their steps suited each other's exactly. It was an odd sensation to him every time a curly end of her brown hair touched his cheek, and he found himself moving his head to make it happen, just as he searched his mind for things which might call forth the delight of her laughter.

By the end of the evening, Justin Breane was in love for the first time in the thirty-four years of his life, and all he knew about her was that her name was Joliman and that he wanted her forever.

He had told her his name, and she had given him an odd look, as if she had a private joke, but she did not offer an explanation of the look even when it was time for him to go, and he summoned up sufficient courage to speak of meeting again.

'I'm due for leave,' he said, 'though with this final offensive on, heaven knows whether there will be any leave. I wonder if you will be here when I come back? Or if I may write to you if I'm moved?'

'I'm quite sure it isn't done,' said Philippa.

'The people who never do what isn't done are very dull,' he said. 'May I write?'

Again she gave that odd little smile.

'I'm going on leave myself,' she said.

'Then I'll wait till you come back – unless you're going to give me your home address?'

She shook her head.

'Better wait,' she said, 'and the name, by the way, is Philippa.'

'Thank you. I told you, didn't I, that I'm Justin Breane?'

'Yes, sir,' she said demurely, and with 'Ma'am's' eyes on her severely, she slipped away, her smile turning into a chuckle.

She would have remembered who he was even if he had not told her. She had been struck by something familiar about him the first time she had looked at him, though not until he spoke his name did she realise that she had recognised him.

Justin Breane of Hollmere Abbey.

Of course. She should have known that at once. He and his two older brothers had been familiar to her by sight for as long as she could remember, though they had been grown-up all the time. This one, Justin, had been at home less than George, the eldest, who had inherited his father's title some years previously, and it was probably this fact, coupled with the unfamiliarity of the naval uniform, which had prevented her from recognising him at first.

The Hollmere people did not, of course, meet the Jolimans socially. Indeed, Philippa thought it more than likely that they were not even aware of their existence, though The Beeches was barely two miles from the great iron gates of Hollmere Abbey. The gates were no longer kept closed, and it was common knowledge that when the old gatekeeper died, Lord Hollmere decided to save his wages by keeping the gates open and letting the lodge to a paying tenant who was a relation of the family. Yet in spite of the open gates, Philippa had never gone inside, and not a glimpse of the old Elizabethan house could be caught from any point outside the park. Her knowledge of it was merely from postcard views, and until she met Justin Breane, she was not particularly interested.

She wondered, amused by the thought, what would happen if, as seemed possible, they were both on leave at the same time and met by chance in Sloworth, or along one of the village roads which were used by the inhabitants of The Beeches as well as of the Abbey.

She had not to wonder for very long. On the second day of her leave, she met him face to face at the door of the one chemist's shop.

Automatically standing aside for her to leave the shop before he entered it, he glanced indifferently at the girl in tweed suit and green beret and then stared unbelievingly.

'Why, it's—you!' he said, startled. 'What on earth are you doing in Sloworth?'

She smiled, but was aware that the girl behind the counter was staring at them, knowing both of them.

'Much what you're doing,' she said, 'except that I don't expect you're going to buy lipstick.'

'But why here of all places?' he asked, bewildered. 'I suppose you really are here, and haven't just materialised out of my thoughts?'

'I'm really here. I happen to live here.'

'Here? ' he asked, frowning and looking at the chemist's shop.

She laughed and edged farther away from the door, though out in the street there would be even more curious eyes to discover them.

'Well, not actually in this very spot,' she said, but not far away. You probably don't even know there is such a house as ours. It's called The Beeches, mainly because it is surrounded by poplars.'

His face showed complete enlightenment.

'Why, of course! Philippa Joliman! How idiotic of me never to have guessed it, wasn't it? But I always imagined that your father's best production was his very excellent tinned meat that's saved my life more than once – and a good many other lives as well. Where can we go to talk?' – beginning to walk along the pavement beside her, his business with the chemist forgotten.

'What about your lipstick?' she reminded him.

'Oh – it was some stuff my mother wants. Do you mind if I just pop in with the order and ask them to send it? Will you wait?'

She nodded and walked slowly along the straggling row of village shops, knowing and being greeted by everybody going about their customary affairs. There was no one in Sloworth who did not know the Jolimans – no one, it seemed, except the people from the Abbey.

Where could she and Justin go out of the sight of these curious and, she knew, tremendously interested eyes? None of the three sons of that majestic autocrat, Lady Hollmere, had ever been known to walk and talk with any Sloworth girl, and the story would run round the village like wildfire.

Justin was either unaware or supremely indifferent to the fact for, when he rejoined her, he walked beside her in full view of all who were about that morning, returning with his usual automatic courtesy the respectful greetings given to him.

'I simply can't get over my stupidity,' he said. 'Of course I ought to have known you at once, but I suppose it was the uniform, and the sailor's cap – and then you fell in and came up like a drenched kitten. Remember?'

They laughed together, and she seized the opportunity afforded by the path through the fields to turn off the main street.

She could net help it if he thought she was arranging a setting for a flirtation. Anything was better than running the gauntlet in the village, and her home lay in this direction.

'I usually go this way,' she said. 'Do you mind?'

He was also out of uniform and looked comfortable in shabby tweeds and brown brogues. He detached the leads of the two golden cockers and let them rush ecstatically away to smell out real or imaginary rabbits, and Philippa made a little sound of protest.

'Won't they—oh!' she began, pulling herself up short with the sentence unfinished. 'These are your fields, aren't they?'

'My brother's,' he said. 'You know, Philippa, this is the most amazing luck to find you here, right in my own homeland. Did you know?'

She nodded.

'Of course,' she said.

'But you didn't tell me. Why not?'

'Isn't it obvious? I couldn't claim acquaintance with the Honourable Justin Breane,' she said, the faintest touch of derision in her voice.

She regretted that touch as she saw the colour run swiftly to his face, staining even beneath the sunburn. It would not have occurred to her that one of his clan could be so sensitive. From earliest memory, she had regarded the Breanes as too much wrapped up in their own importance to be pricked by far sharper darts than that.

'That's rather absurd – and quite unjustifiable,' he said in a low voice.

She was quick to apologise. She hated to hurt anything or anybody.

'I agree. It was also ill-bred – but then I am,' she said.

He turned to meet her grey eyes with his brown ones, eyes so much like those of his spaniels, she thought.

'You are what?' he asked.

'Ill-bred. How could I be otherwise? The daughter of Jolly Man Meats,' but her tone was smooth and held no suggestion of inferiority but rather of amusement.

He laughed and their friendship was subtly restored and strengthened.

'You don't really mean that that is why you didn't tell me we might meet in Sloworth?' he asked.

'But of course. Your family would certainly not want to know mine, and I didn't want to make things awkward for you if we met.'

'Well, we did meet and what was awkward in that? As for our families not knowing one another, that's just nonsense. In these days, all that sort of thing has gone. If the wars have done nothing else, at least they've cleared that away.'

'You know you don't believe that. What do I call you, by the way? Mr. Breane? Or do I say "sir" to my superior officer?' her eyes teasing him.

'I think you say Justin to a friend,' he said.

'How familiar!' laughed Philippa. 'If I ever do such a thing, it is to be hoped the village never hears of it or our reputations will be gone like chaff in the wind.'

'Perhaps I shouldn't mind sharing anything with you, even a bad reputation,' he said. 'Us naval types, you know! How long have you got, by the way?'

'Seven days. And you?'

He nodded.

'Presumably – though I was warned to keep myself available. This thing's clearing up, isn't it?'

'The war? Heaven knows it should be. Everybody in the world, even the financiers who make wars, must be tired of it. If only things could be arranged so that no one could make money out of war, there would be no more war.'

There was a weariness and a bitterness in her voice which he felt was inconsistent with his conception of her. What lay behind it? Yes, of course. Her father must be making money out of war, a vast amount of it whether he intended doing so or not.

'I suppose people can't always help making money, even if the war itself is not of their makings,' he said gently

She gave him a quick, half-startled look.

'You read my thoughts, don't you? You get inside people's minds,' resenting it a little.

'Not the minds of people in general. Yours perhaps at that moment. When I suggest that you're transparent, it isn't meant to belittle you, but – I think you're very honest, Philippa.'

She hesitated and then laughed to break the embarrassing tension. How had they become so serious? Like most people, she was not averse to hearing herself analysed by a member of the other sex, especially one as gentle and kindly as Justin, but her sixth sense warned her to take flight.

They had come to the field path which led to her home. His lay straight ahead. Just beyond the open fields lay the outer density of the Abbey parklands, guarding the sanctity of the great house itself.

'I turn off here,' she said, and stood still.

'Come home to lunch with me,' he said.

Her eyebrows went up above startled eyes. Then she smiled.

'For a moment I thought you meant it,' she said.

'Of course I meant it. Why not, Philippa?'

'But you know all about why not. Your mother would have ten thousand fits. Besides, there might not be enough for an extra guest – oh, Justin, I didn't mean it that way!' distressed and ashamed of the clumsiness of her speech. 'I only meant that the rations won't stretch to provision for unexpected guests.'

His smile was a little grim.

'Don't feel you have to explain. I knew what you meant,' he said, and they both stood silent for a moment, aware of the thing that had come between them and might always be there – his family's position and the wealth of hers.

'Well?' he asked, breaking the silence. 'Will you come?'

She shook her head but smiled as she did so.

'Better not,' she said. 'Don't let's go into that, though.'

'Then won't you ask me to lunch with you? I'm quite a small eater.'

They both laughed, and without waiting for her to refuse the self-invited guest, he whistled the dogs.

'Is it alright for them to come too?' he asked. 'I can't truthfully say that they're small eaters, but they don't eat at this time of day and they can go to the stables.'

'What makes you think people like the Jolimans have stables?' she asked, helpless now to avoid the sensation his appearance was going to cause in the household and keeping her tone light.

'For one thing, you have already told me you ride and I don't suppose you hire hacks. For another, the Jolly Man must get his meat from somewhere!'

She laughed again, enjoying his intentional impertinence and the libel. Most of the people she met outside her own social circle studiously avoided any reference to the source of her father's wealth, treating it as something to be ashamed of.

'Better not let Daddy hear you suggesting that horse ever goes into his tins,' she said. 'Do you know him at all, by the way?'

'Very slightly. We've met on a board or a committee or something. The new hospital scheme, I think it was.'

'Did you fall out with him? His ideas are slightly different from yours, you know.'

'How do you know what my ideas are?'

'I don't, but as one's ideas must come out of one's form of life, one's background and upbringing and environment, how could yours be anything like his? He calls himself a working man, as of course he is.'

'And you think I'm not?'

'*He* wouldn't think anything your family does is work.'

'So he despises us?'

'Well—let's not go on with this. It won't help us anywhere, and if you really are coming to lunch, it won't help to ease the situation. We go through here and cross the road. There's a gate that takes us into the lower end of the garden, though of course I'm going to take you in by the front door.'

'Why not by your usual route?'

She gave him a look of mock dismay.

'Take the Honourable Justin Breane in by the back door the first time he pays a visit to the Joliman ancestral home?' she asked. 'Have you any idea what a stir and commotion you are about to cause?'

He stopped, his hand on the gate which he had held open for her, the dogs sitting obediently beside him, waiting to be told to cross the road.

'I say, do you mean that? That it's going to be horribly inconvenient?' he asked.

'You know – you *must* know – what I mean,' she said 'Don't be naive. Everybody is going to be thrilled to the marrow at the condescension of a member of your family in coming to lunch with mine.'

'I wish you would stop talking like that,' said Justin, frowning. 'You know neither of us really thinks like that – nor does anybody nowadays.'

She thought of his mother, whom of course she had never met socially, of the few members of his family whom she might have met, and though she smiled at his remonstrance, she kept her own views.

They were chatting amicably again by the time they had skirted the tennis courts, still superbly maintained in spite of the war, and were crossing the immaculate drive between shaven lawns and weedless flowerbeds to the ugly, pretentious, redbrick house which showed no sign of mellowing though it was getting on for twenty years now since Joe Joliman had caused it to be built. Justin felt a sick envy and fury at the thought of all the money which must be spent on this atrocity, and the pitifully little that could go towards the upkeep of his lovely and beloved home.

Inside the house it was the same. Everything had cost a lot of money; in fact its value in money was the only claim of most of the furniture and pictures and carpets to merit a place there at all. There was no sign of cultural appreciation anywhere. Priceless antique and modern horror were cheek by jowl, and all were polished and shining to the glory of the Jolimans.

Philippa, taking him into the drawing-room whilst she sent a maid to find her mother, gave him an amused look and went across to open an enormous cocktail cabinet which revealed a further galaxy of winking lights from bottles and glasses.

'What will you have?' she asked him. 'We've got everything.'

'Needless to say—everything,' he said, but though he smiled, she could not detect what she had feared and had been certain she would find, scorn and derision. He was merely gently amused, and she realised that gentleness was the keynote of his life. There was nothing aggressive about this son of a long line of blue-blooded earls, nothing that was conscious of superiority, nothing condescending. His very naturalness made her feel ashamed of her own approach. It had been cheap and ill-bred. This perfect composure of his was something probably innate in people like the Breanes.

He asked for beer rather than spirits or a cocktail, and she was taking a bottle from the ice-cooled section of the vast cabinet when her mother came in.

'You got the proper message, Mummy?' she asked. 'One can never be quite sure with Annie. I've brought Mr. Breane to lunch. Mr. Justin Breane—my mother.'

She realised that in the very short time between Annie's message and Mrs. Joliman's appearance in the drawing-room, her mother must have torn off the dress she usually wore in the mornings and got into an afternoon dress of rose-pink marocain, the colour too bright for her henna-tinted hair, the dress too tight without the 'best' corsets which she had not had time to put on. She would have looked so much nicer, Philippa thought regretfully, if she had kept on the loose grey woollen suit she had worn at breakfast.

The girl found herself watching critically the meeting of these two, her mother flushed and breathless and almost speechless with gratification at the amazing appearance of one of the Breanes in her own drawing-room, Justin revealing nothing at all of what Philippa felt certain must be passing through his mind. She knew that if he had shown the faintest hint of patronage, of condescension, of amusement, she would have been ready to fly up in her mother's defence and whatever fragile thing might be growing between her and Justin Breane (though what could grow, however fragile?) would be destroyed forever.

He showed no such sign. His manner was perfect, and he found exactly the right words to set Mrs. Joliman at her ease, continued to find them through the meal at which her father appeared late, having telephoned that she was not to wait for him. Joe Joliman stared at his guest, as he might well do, and then clapped him on the back and took his seat and began to help himself generously to the very good fare arrayed on the table. After a hurried private consultation with Philippa whilst Justin washed his hands in the elaborately fitted cloak-room off the hall, Mrs. Joliman had decided against getting Annie to wait at table.

'She'd never get through without dropping things,' said Philippa firmly. 'Have things as usual, with the food put on the table. That will be quite as much as she can manage.'

'Well, and how's life in the navy?' asked Mr. Joliman with his beaming smile that was so much like the one known all over the world on the Jolly Man tins.

'How did you know he's in the navy?' asked Philippa.

Joe winked at his guest.

'Old Joe Joliman knows a lot of things,' he said. 'And how *is* life in the navy, Lieutenant?' pronouncing it army-fashion instead of navy-fashion.

Justin smiled.

'Made much more comfortable by you, sir,' he said.

His host slapped another slice of prime ham on the plate in front of him.

Ah, that's what I like to 'ear,' he said. 'People say I'm making a lot of money out of this war, and so I am. So I am. A lot of money. But I'm giving value for it, and I'm making things a bit easier for them as 'as to get the rough side of it. Do you know 'ow much stuff the Red Cross has just ordered from me?' and he went into vast figures and details. 'You see? All that stuff's going to our boys in the prison camps – or let's 'ope it'll get there. And my orders to my packers are that only the best is to go into them parcels, only the tip-top stuff – not that anything that's not tiptop ever goes into my tins, but some's bound to be better'n others, so I say that's what's to go out to our boys in the prison camps. People guzzling at 'ome can make do with the rest. Now the other day there was a man from the Argentine in my office, come with someone from the Food Ministry ...'

'Joe, the Honourable Mr. Breane isn't *interested* in tinned meat,' put in his wife reprovingly.

Justin turned to her.

'Oh, but I am,' he said. 'I'm most *interested*,' and Philippa knew that it was his exquisite manners which prompted him to accent the word in the same way as his hostess had done, but though he had pleased Joe by declaring his interest, he managed to turn the conversation into a channel more acceptable to Mrs. Joliman and they talked with animation about such things as Rhode Island Reds and layering carnations.

When he had gone, Joe Joliman giving him and his dogs a lift to the Abbey gates in his Rolls-Bentley, for which he received an adequate supply of petrol coupons, Mrs. Joliman sank into a chair with a sigh of satisfaction, relief and pride.

'Now that young man's something like,' she said. 'Fancy me and your dad being so against you going into the Wrens, and you picking up with the Honourable Mr. Breane there!'

'Mummy, that isn't correct,' said Philippa mildly. 'You say either Mr. Breane or the Honourable Justin Breane but don't combine the two. Besides, he did suggest that you call him Justin.'

'Oh, but I couldn't do that!' she said, aghast. 'I'm sorry, dearie, if I called him wrong though. I've always been afraid we might let you down in front of your nice friends, and your dad just don't seem able to get his aitches right.'

Philippa put an arm round her mother's shoulders for a moment in an affectionate hug.

'Don't worry, Mum. I don't think it matters a bean nowadays. Why should it? If they've got something we haven't got, we've certainly got something they'd like to have – all this money!'

'Yes,' said her mother, again, thoughtfully. 'Yes. That's right.'

Her daughter laughed.

'Now don't go getting ideas into your scheming head,' she said. 'Justin and I happened to meet through both being in the navy and because the war's still on, but as soon as it's over, back we go into our right pigeon-holes, the Honourable Justin Breane into his and Philippa Joliman into hers, and there won't be any mistake about that!'

But of course there had been.

Within six weeks of their first meeting, Justin was asking her to marry him and she was bewildered and thrilled and frightened all at once.

They had to meet surreptitiously, since it was not done for a naval officer, even a Wavy Navy officer, to be seen about with a Wren ranker except at some officially organised affair such as the dance at which they had had their second meeting. They met now in a room at the back of the Dog and Duck, actually in the private sitting-room of kindly, romantic Mrs. Bond who put it at their disposal and showed them the private entrance when Justin confided in her the difficulty in which he was placed.

'You must have known from the first that I was going to ask you, darling,' said Justin as Philippa sat there and simply stared at him speechlessly.

'Not to marry you. No, of course not,' she whispered.

'But, good heavens, you didn't think I'd want anything else, did you?' he asked.

'I thought you might.'

'Then I've made a rotten impression on you. Of course I want to marry you. I wouldn't insult you by wanting anything less. How could you think so? I've never even kissed you, or tried to make any sort of love to you.'

'I know, but—Justin, be sensible. Of course we can't marry. I'm not in your class at all.'

'Of all the idiotic and—*cheap* things to say!' he said hotly.

'You see? You've condemned me yourself. I'm not an idiot, but I belong to the people who think and do and say things which you would consider cheap. But it's not cheap to look things squarely in the face, and you know quite well that I should not fit into the pattern of your life once the war is really over.'

'You would not only fit into the pattern of my life. You *are* my life, Philippa. I'm a good bit older than you, but I don't think that matters. What matters is that I've never married, never thought seriously about any girl until I met you, and have waited for life to bring you to me. I knew that somewhere you existed, which is why I've waited till I'm thirty-four instead of putting up with a second best. There's only one thing that worries me seriously, and you know what that is, don't you? It's all that money your father's got. I'd far rather you had nothing so that we could live on what I'm able to make. I've got a bit, of course, though all investments have gone to pot and will take years to recover, if they ever do recover. My brother Tony and I got bits out of my grandmother's estate and some of the houses and one of the farms at Sloworth belong to me, but of course the Abbey and the actual estate, for what it is worth now, went with the title to George. I haven't told you much about myself and what I propose to do when this beastly business is over and I'm free again, but I have always been more interested in the estate than my brothers, even though I knew it could never come to me, and during my father's lifetime I studied estate management, farming and all that sort of thing. George doesn't like living at the Abbey. He's got a fly-by-night for a wife, half French and half Irish, and if she can't live in Dublin, her only idea of life is in Paris. They'll have to settle down at the Abbey, of course, especially as they've got two sons to come after them, but when my father died, George asked me to take over the management of the estate as he would have had to employ an agent in any case, and I was only too glad. Of course it's a heart-breaking business in many ways, seeing the old place going to ruin and not being able to do much about it, and heaven knows whether there will be anything for George's sons to inherit when the time comes, but I'd rather plod along there, putting my heart and my strength and my knowledge into doing the best that can be done, than earn twice as much anywhere else as old George can afford to pay me. Couldn't you be happy at the Abbey, darling?'

She had listened, fascinated, seeing something she had never experienced before, the deep love, the passionate reverence, which lay in his heart for the land of his fathers, for the fields and the woods and the distant hillside, for the crumbling old house, for all the things which had been owned and known and loved and cared for, guarded, fought for, by generations of men who had borne his name. She caught some glimpse of the bitterness which the loss of these things must bring. She remembered that her father had bought the land on which The Beeches was built from Justin's father. She recalled things Joe had said from time to time, pleased with himself for having struck a hard bargain over the land, for having haggled and argued until he got the little copse included in the purchase.

'Kept 'arpin' on some silly nonsense about it 'aving been the scene of some little battle or other a couple of centuries ago. Who cares today what happened then? Anyway, I got it out of 'im. Told 'im I wouldn't buy the rest without the copse, take it or leave it, and o' course 'is lordship took it in the end. 'Ad to. I told 'im I might, only *might*, I said, buy another lot when 'e wanted to sell. You should've seen the look on 'is face! You'd've thought I was suggesting 'im 'anding over his lady wife – though nobody in their right mind would want that bag of rags and bones!'

Philippa, remembering that whilst Justin was speaking winced. It had never occurred to her that the sale of that land had been anything but a business deal between two men trying to best each other. Now, listening to the son of that man, watching the expression in his face, she began to realise that it had not been just fields and a wood that the old earl had sold, but a portion of his heart, cut from the living flesh, the wound never to be healed whilst he lived.

'Couldn't you? Philippa, darling?'

She heard him repeat his question and pulled herself back into the present.

'It isn't that, Justin, though I certainly could never imagine myself living at Hollmere Abbey. It's the whole thing, your mother, your brother, Lord Hollmere, his wife, the whole family – can't you see? They'd resent me and I shouldn't fit in. I've no background, no traditions. Even my politics, if I had any serious ones, would be opposed to theirs.'

They were sitting before the fire in two of Mrs. Bond's best armchairs. Now he rose and took her hands and drew her gently to her feet and held her, their linked hands swinging lightly.

'Suppose you stop thinking along those ridiculous lines and talk sense?' he said. 'All the old order, the background and the traditions that made it, is passing away, has actually passed. I won't pretend I'm not sorry, because I know what it means to people like me, born in those traditions, to lose their homes, to give them to the nation because they must not sell them even if purchasers could be found, or to struggle along for a few more years by turning them into show places, letting anybody who can afford to pay half a crown come rampaging into them, poking and prying, grumbling because the half-crown does not include the right to go into the private rooms, bedrooms, bathrooms, the one small sitting-room where the family has taken refuge. If they're not watched some of them carve their initials on the panelled walls, and steal "souvenirs" about which they boast afterwards to their friends. We haven't come quite to that at the Abbey yet, but we may have to, though my mother says she would rather die – and she probably would. Do you know my mother, Philippa?'

'I've seen her, of course,' said Philippa, and had a mental picture of the tall incredibly thin, incredibly haughty woman whom it was increasingly difficult to associate with Justin as she now knew him.

He smiled at her tone and guessed her thoughts.

'She's really terribly kind underneath,' he said, 'though I admit it's quite a long way underneath and we've all been rather afraid of her. You wouldn't need to be though, my beautiful Philippa. She's a mother, after all, and what else could any mother in the world desire than a girl like you for her son's wife?'

Philippa made a grimace.

'Oh, my dear, a whole lot else!' she said. 'I should be terrified of her. Justin …'

'Yes, my darling?'

'Justin – how do you know if you're in love? How can you tell? You say you're in love with me. How do you know it's love?'

He smiled, his kind face, distinguished by its look of fine breeding, of unconscious pride which held no arrogance, rather than by any actual good looks, filled with the enchantment she held for him.

'I am happy only when I am with you. I want always to be with you, to share my life with you, to look after you and protect you and give you, to the extent of my powers, all the things you want. I love your mind with its healthy outlook, its complete honesty, its queer questions and doubts even. I want you to bear my children. How can I feel all that about you and not know that it is love? Do you love me at all, Philippa? For anything there is about me?'

She nodded her head slowly, but there was still that doubting question in her wide, fascinated eyes.

'For a great deal that is about you, Justin,' she said slowly. 'Your kindness most of all, and your – is it silly to call it your gentleness? I don't mean that to make you sound unmanly, but most men are afraid to be gentle. They try to be so smart and clever and amusing, and it's so boring. You never bore me, Justin.'

His smile deepened. His brown eyes wore the look she thought of as their spaniel look, an unnerving, disarming look against which she could not protect herself.

'Well, that's something anyway,' he said. 'If I'm kind and gentle and I don't bore you by trying to be clever and amusing, can't we call that a basis for future happiness? I'll promise you never to be clever or consciously amusing. I'll remain the very dull dog I am.'

She laughed uncertainly and wished she could feel that any of this was real, but she could not.

This was Justin Breane, a member of the family whom for as long as she could remember she and her own family and friends had regarded with something like awe, a race apart. Even her school years, when she had been thrown into contact with a good many girls of his world, had not been able to rob her of that inherent awe. And he was asking her to marry him! The thought frightened her, and yet she knew she was dazzled by it.

She knew by his face, the kind eyes, his slight, puzzled frown, that he was trying to guess her thoughts, trying to think of the right things to say to persuade her. Almost unconsciously she smiled, and he took it for a good sign and drew her a little more closely by their linked hands.

'You're so beautiful,' he said. 'I've never seen anyone like you before and I never shall again.'

'You really love me, Justin, don't you?' she asked wonderingly.

'Why else should I ask you to marry me?' he asked, and it was a symbol of her own honesty and simplicity that it never occurred to her that there could be other reasons for a scion of an old, crumbling house to want to marry the Jolly Man's heiress. When, much later, the thought did occur to her, she knew it was unworthy and untrue. Neither then nor at any other moment of their lives did she doubt Justin's love, nor that it was for that reason alone that he asked her to marry him.

But, for herself? She was twenty-two and would have been lovely even if her father's money had not made it possible for her to aid that loveliness in every way possible. Inevitably she had had many proposals; inevitably she had had many 'affairs', gay, light-hearted things which had meant little or nothing to her. She had supposed that she would marry someday. Once or twice she had even seriously considered a proposal but in the end had rejected it. Now, for the first time, she felt the solid ground beginning to shake beneath her feet. She knew she was enormously attracted by Justin Breane, attracted and flattered and a bit dazzled.

He watched the changing expressions on her face and felt that he was reading her thoughts.

'Dearest Philippa, why should you be afraid of marrying me?' he asked in his quiet, restrained way.

'Is it that? Am I afraid of marrying you, or just of getting married at all, Justin? Marriage seems to have failed modern civilisation. Is it marriage or is it us? People getting married don't take it very seriously nowadays. It used to be for better for worse. Now it's until we get tired of each other, or until one of us finds someone we like better, or for a thousand trivial reasons which never seemed to crop up out of marriage a generation or two ago, not really even in our parents' time. The thing is, how does one *know* that it will last? I wouldn't want to make a mess of my marriage.'

He smiled affectionately at her serious, troubled face, its expression so unlike its usual cheerful, gay acceptance of all life had to offer.

'Dear, I expect that's what every girl feels. Don't you think I am feeling something of the same myself? Rather afraid of the step we may take together, if I can persuade you to take it?'

Her face cleared a little. After all, he was *nice*, she thought, really nice right inside him and not just on the surface, and the niceness had nothing to do with the fact that he was the Honourable Justin Breane and belonged to the unapproachable Hollmeres.

'Oh, Justin, do you feel like it? Even though you love me?'

'Perhaps because I do, Philippa. I want above everything else in the world to make you happy. Are you going to let me try?'

And, after another moment's anxious uncertainty, she nodded her head.

'I think so. Yes. Yes, I am, Justin. I'll marry you,' ending up in a breathless little rush of words.

Then he kissed her and she felt vaguely disappointed and then glad, for the kiss was a rather solemn affair, a close pressure of her lips, his arms about her, but as if she were something almost too precious to be touched. She had never been kissed like that before, and after that first moment of feeling that something was missing from her own reactions, the gladness came because, of course, this was not in any way to be confused with those light-hearted, exciting affairs which she had known would end in nothing more than kisses. This with Justin Breane was for life.

'We'll be married as soon as we can both get out of uniform,' he told her. 'We don't want a hole-and-corner affair, together only for a few days' leave when we can get it. But let's hope we shan't have to wait long, my dearest.'

She agreed, of course. It was so much more sensible than rushing into the sort of thing so many of her friends had made shift with, a semi-detached affair satisfactory to no one.

They had had to wait less than a year, thought Philippa in those few minutes of memory whilst outside the redbrick house, faintly audible, was the bustle and laughter of her bridesmaids going to the church, and downstairs her father would be waiting uncomfortably, trying not to be too much aware of his immaculate morning coat made by the most expensive and exclusive tailor in London, although, as he had said when he put it on: 'I should look the same, and feel the same, if I'd hired one from Moss Bros., and saved meself a deuce of a lot of money. I've only got one daughter, so I shall never wear this silly get-up again, thank goodness.'

During that year of their engagement, so much had happened which, like this wedding, would never happen again.

She had met, and been chillingly approved by Justin's mother. Calls, strange and terrifying to Ella Joliman, had been exchanged between the two mothers.

And during that year, Justin had become Lord Hollmere when the plane bringing his two brothers and George's wife and two sons from Dublin had crashed and left no survivors.

Philippa had offered to give Justin up.

'Everything is altered now,' she said. 'It was never intended that I should be Lady Hollmere and the mistress of the Abbey.'

The dowager countess had previously announced her intention of leaving the Abbey when George brought his wife there to live.

Justin's face was grey with the grief of his loss, the shock and the fatigue of his journeys to and from the scene of the disaster, the bringing back of whatever was recognisable of his brothers, of gay, life-loving Maria, of the two little boys.

He held Philippa closely, as if to his only sheet-anchor, laying his face against her breast.

'Don't make me lose you as well,' he whispered. 'You're all I've got left.'

And so, today, in the little village church which could accommodate only a carefully selected few of the number of people, relations, friends, villagers, or mere sight-seers, she would be turned for good or ill into a countess.

Lady Hollmere of Hollmere Abbey.

Her eyes widened under the veil beneath which so many Hollmere brides had bowed their heads. Had any of them been as unworthy as hers? she thought. Had any of them been led up the aisle by a man who tinned meat for a living?

There was a soft knock at the door and her father's voice asked cautiously, as if intruding on holy ground: "Adn't we better go, Phil? Yer mum's gone and all them chattering gals.'

She flung the door open and, regardless of her ivory satin and the billowing veil, caught his tubby form in her arms and pressed her cheek against his.

'Darling Daddy, bless you. Bless you forever,' she said. 'Thank you for being you, for being my father rather than any other girl's in the world. Thank you for everything.'

Her cheek against his was wet.

'Goodness me, Phil, you're never crying, are you?' he asked in consternation. 'Wot's up, girlie? Changed yer mind or anything? Because if you don't want to marry 'im, nobody's going to make you do it, not if there's fifty bishops waiting for you and you'd 'ad a million presents. You've only got to say the word and yer old dad'll go to the church and tell 'em straight they could all go 'ome and they'd get their presents back when we'd 'ad time to pack 'em up. Nobody's going to make you marry anybody you don't want to marry, not if 'e was a royal prince or the King of Persia.'

That made her laugh and she rubbed her cheeks and dusted them with powder again and picked up the bouquet of white orchids which had been sent to her from the famous orchid house at Hollmere Abbey.

'Of course I want to marry him,' she said brightly. 'It was just a moment's jitters. I expect all brides have them. Shall we go?'

He chuckled and patted her hand.

'I expect you're right. You should've seen yer mum coming up the aisle to me on our wedding day. White as a sheet she was. And scared? She was scared alright. So was I, but we both stuck it out and 'ere we are – and 'ere you are, girlie. Going to be a ladyship! Well, well, well. 'Oo'd 'ave thought it? Me as the father of a ladyship! 'Ere goes. Give me the flowers w'ilst you get in. John,' to the smiling chauffeur who stood at the open door of the car, 'look after 'er ladyship's train and if you let it so much as touch anything, I'll sack you on the spot,' with one of the wide affectionate grins which made him adored by his personal staff.

'Well,' he said again as the car door closed on them, ''ere goes.'

Chapter Two

Justin had been ready for a long time on the morning of his wedding-day – too long for his peace of mind or for that of his best man, Jock McNault, who had served with him in the navy, a large, raw-boned, cheerful Scot who was more than half in love with Philippa himself and said so openly.

'For the love of Pete, can't you sit down and take it easy, mon?' he asked. 'If ye mess up yer nice new suit, you won't be able to go to the wedding, but why should I worry? I'm ready and willing at any minute to take yer place at the altar.'

'I'll go into the library and finish some letters off,' said Justin. 'Can I trust you not to let us be late at the church? Philippa would never forgive me if I were late.'

Jock pushed him out of the room.

'I'll not let ye be late. Go and do your letters whiles I make up what I'm going to say in ma speech aboot the bridesmaids, God bless 'em.'

But Justin sat in his chair before the great library table and did nothing.

Nothing, that is, but think.

His mind, like Philippa's, went back over the past and tried to peer into the future.

He smiled at his first memory of her, slim and straight and workmanlike, her curly brown hair round the sailor cap, her arms reaching out with the boat-hook – and then her total loss of dignity as she went overboard, to come up dripping and laughing and being hauled unceremoniously aboard with her own boat-hook.

He had loved her from that moment, her laughter and her capable strength and her womanly softness. He had loved her when they danced together, loved her when, with a stab of exquisite delight, he had come face to face with her that morning in the village and knew that Fortune was giving him this marvellous chance of getting to know her better.

He remembered that first lunch at her home, the awful furniture and gruesome pictures, the over-padded chairs, the many little tables of black glass and chromium-plated steel. He thought of Mrs. Joliman, so nervous and flustered and anxious, and of tubby little Joe for whom he had by now such a warm regard and who, he knew, liked him and was glad to have him as a son-in-law.

Justin frowned as he thought of the private conversation they had had only a few days ago, in the atrocious room, at The Beeches which Joe referred to as 'me lib'ry', confessing to his guest that he had bought up the bankrupt stock of a bookshop to fill his empty shelves.

'I'd like you to take this, son, and do something with it, anything you like,' said Joe Joliman, and almost sheepishly pushed a folded paper into Justin's hand.

He opened it and looked at it, flushed hotly and tried to give it back. It was a cheque for ten thousand pounds.

'I—I couldn't possibly, you know,' he said. 'It—it wouldn't be right – and the wedding present you've already given us – well, it was magnificently generous. I couldn't take this as well. I really couldn't.'

The present to which he referred had been a car which he would be able to use as soon as the petrol ration returned, and a cheque for five thousand pounds. Philippa already had her own car, stored in one of the garages of The Beeches.

But Joe refused to touch the cheque again, waving it aside with an embarrassment equal to Justin's own, both men avoiding the eyes of the other.

'Of course you could, son,' he said almost testily. 'I call you "son" because that's what you're soon going to be, ever though you *are* a lord. My daughter's husband. My son. The one I've never 'ad and that all my money couldn't buy. Take it. Please take it so as to make believe as I'm giving it to my own son. Don't tell Phil if you don't want to. Better not. Might make 'er—well, women can be that silly at times ...

Justin knew what he meant, knew why he suggested that the gift be hidden from Philippa, It might have savoured of paying in cash for the honour of his title, for making her the mistress of Hollmere Abbey. No one knew better than Justin how touchy she could be about her father's money, the only thing which so far seemed to make her touchy.

In the end he had to take the money, though he hid it furtively in a deposit account at his bank.

He did not reveal that gift even to his mother, that proud autocrat who had bowed her stiff neck before what she saw as inevitable, namely the marriage of her one remaining son to a wealthy woman. Since the death of her other sons and her grandsons, there was nothing left to her but Justin to whom she had never been close, and the Abbey which she loved as much as she could love anything.

For one thing she could be thankful, and that was that, though the girl came from impossible people, their wealth derived from vulgar sources, their name screaming from every point of vantage in the country, Philippa herself gave no sign of vulgarity or ill-breeding. Also she was beautiful, healthy, young, and Justin was infatuated with her. It was impossible for Lady Hollmere to believe that Philippa returned his love. The girl was, of course, marrying him for his title and position, and was justified to some extent in doing so by the fact that she brought with her not only that specific five thousand pounds, but also a dowry in the form of a substantial income from blocks of shares in his various companies made over to her by her father, and the certainty that when he died she would be even better provided for.

So, the necessity as bitter as gall within her, Lady Hollmere had paid a state call on Philippa's parents, advising them first by letter that she intended doing so.

Poor Ella Joliman was in such a state as the time of the visit drew inexorably near that Joe, himself almost as nervous, gave her a stiff, neat brandy and stood over her whilst she drank it. Then, terrified lest it linger too obviously on her breath and give her daughter's future mother-in-law the impression that Philippa had a brandy-drinking mother, she rushed to the kitchen and burnt her mouth and throat with a spoonful of cloves, which she chewed feverishly, spitting out the residue and rushing back to the drawing-room when she heard the sounds of horses' hooves in the drive. Since the petrol ration had been taken away, Lady Hollmere had returned, not without secret pleasure, to the ancient barouche and the pair of greys of her earlier married life, though they were not the same greys, and her old coachman was long since dead.

She closed her eyes for a moment at the impact on them of Ella's drawing-room scheme, but opened them again and faced the horrors with the serene composure of her kind, contrived to set almost at ease the parents of Philippa (Joe had remained for the afternoon to support his wife in her hour of trial) by finding sufficient suitable subjects of conversation to fill the traditional twenty minutes, and did not refer to the forthcoming marriage until she was at the point of departure. Justin was not, at that time, Lord Hollmere, so that all she was being called upon to accept was the wife of a not very important third son.

'It has been charming of you to allow me to call on you, Mrs. Joliman,' she said just before she left. 'We shall, of course, have a common interest in the marriage of your daughter Philippa to my youngest son, Justin. I hope it will be a happy and successful marriage. She is a charming girl.'

The two parents flushed with pride and gratitude.

'I'm sure we 'ope so too, my lady,' said Ella, flustered into losing an elusive aitch. Joe, conscious of the straying propensities of his own aspirates, had left as much of the talking as possible to his wife, but now he felt it incumbent on him to add his quota.

'We like your Justin too, my lady,' he said, beaming. 'A fine young feller, if I may say so, not but wot 'er mother and me thinks as 'e isn't getting as good as 'e gives in our Phil. A good girl she is and never bin one for runnin' 'ere and there, as you might say, though with 'er looks, e isn't the first as 'as bin after 'er by a long chalk – not by a long chalk, eh, Mum?' putting an arm round his wife's waist and giving her a squeeze.

'I'm quite sure of that,' said Lady Hollmere, with that mixture of condescension and affability which only the years and her position and experience could have given.

They shook hands with her as she prepared to bow herself out, and though Joe went bare-headed to help her into her carriage, the coachman who had been her chauffeur was already there and forestalled him, so that all he could do was stand and watch the carriage out of sight.

Then he went back to where he knew he would find his wife in a state of near-collapse.

'Well, Mum,' he said, plumping down on the over-stuffed couch beside her, 'that went off O.K. Did you see 'er face when she come into this room? Fair dazzled, she was. It must've looked fine after all them dull things she lives with. Remember the day they opened the Abbey to the public in aid of something or other? It'd give me the willies to live with all that stuff, and everything so shabby, the curtains falling to bits and the chair seats all faded and not a bit of comfort anywhere and not a bit of colour. I like a bit of something bright about me. You've made this place a real 'ome, Ella, everything spankin' and bright and comfortable. Good job Phil won't 'ave to live at the Abbey. It'd send 'er crazy.'

His wife looked suspiciously round her drawing-room. She, too, was having a mental picture of the rooms they had seen at the Abbey, vast, dim rooms with painted ceilings and all those little bits of glass in the windows that must make them so hard to clean – not that they looked as if they ever were cleaned. The enormous, heavy furniture too, a dining-table that would seat forty without having to squeeze them, chairs with narrow seats and straight, high backs and no cushions, cabinets with flat glass tops so that you could look at the collection of rubbish in them, bits of old books, torn embroideries, medals, pieces of stone and rusty iron. What was the use of keeping such rubbish? One thing, they had the sense to keep them under glass to save the dusting, though who could ever even begin to dust some of those rooms?

Yet, remembering them and looking round at the polished splendour of her own home, Ella Joliman found herself wondering whether there was not something she had failed to understand about the Abbey, something which had made even the naturally noisy young people in the sight-seeing party lower their voices and walk on tip-toe. Perhaps those shabby old things had got something, after all, though she did not know what it was.

Philippa had been away at school on that occasion, and as that had been the only time when the Abbey had been open to the public, she had never been inside it – not, that is, until last week when Justin had taken her there to meet his mother.

Philippa had been very quiet about it when she returned, and in answer to her mother's question had said: 'Yes, everything went off alright. Lady Hollmere didn't frighten me as much as I thought she would, and of course the house is wonderful – what I saw of it. Justin says he will take me all over it one day.'

'Have you been inside the house you're going to have?'

'Yes, though of course the Duttons don't like being turned out for us. At least, Mr. Dutton doesn't, though I rather think Mrs. Dutton and the daughters are looking forward to being in a modern house. Teazlewood Farm is Elizabethan, you know, about the same period as the Abbey.'

'Well, there's one thing about it,' said her mother comfortingly, 'you won't have to do any of the work yourself, and once the place is yours, you can put away a lot of that old stuff and get some nice new furniture at Maples. I only went inside once, but I remember it was furnished something like the Abbey, though of course not so much of it, and Lucy Dutton told me that all the old stuff belonged to the Hollmeres. What a good thing you haven't got to live at the Abbey!'

Philippa nodded absently. There was no point in trying to tell her mother what she had felt about the Abbey, that indefinable atmosphere only created by great age, bringing with it a feeling of reverence, a strange tenderness. She understood as never before something of what people like the Hollmeres and the Breanes felt at having to give up their homes, at admitting strangers who paid to be allowed to peer and pry, at best shutting up most of the rooms and leaving them to rust and decay whilst they themselves eked out some shadow of their former existence in a few small rooms which had probably at one time been given over to the servants.

Lady Hollmere had received her in one of the enormous drawing-rooms which she guessed, rather than knew, had been opened expressly for that purpose. Wood fires roared in the two huge grates but had had no power to warm the mildewed chill of the unused room. The long brocade curtains had been drawn back from the range of the floor-length windows and the autumn sunshine seemed rebuffed and driven back by the faded yellow satin on spindle-legged chairs and comfortless sofas, and there were stains and spots on the parchment-coloured brocade panels set between the windows, and the tarnished gilt frames of dingy paintings of long-dead Hollmeres who looked indifferently upon the ruins of what had been their splendour.

Lady Hollmere herself might have stepped from one of those frames, thought Philippa, stepped out of it and been cleaned up and put into a gown which, though conforming to modern fashion, had much in common with the painted brocades and velvets and satins of those other women, who had briefly borne her name.

Philippa had been bidden to dinner on that first occasion, not to lunch as she would have expected and preferred, and she was glad that Justin had warned her to wear an evening gown for the occasion.

'Better dress up like a dog's dinner, darling,' he had said when presenting her with his mother's formal, written invitation. 'She will expect it – this first time, anyway.'

'You mean you don't always dress for dinner?' she asked.

'Well—we do, as a matter of fact. It's one of the unnecessary but rather nice things my mother clings to. After a day out of doors, working or playing but getting pretty messy anyway, I rather like changing into something very clean and formal.'

He spoke somewhat apologetically and Philippa smiled.

'Darling, you don't have to apologise for being what I suppose you would call civilised. People like us don't dress for dinner, which my mother still calls supper, but I'm quite adaptable and I expect I shall slip into "civilised" ways easily enough. You'll have to educate me, though.'

He drew her closely and kissed her.

'Darling Philippa, why should I want to change you in the least respect? I adore you just as you are, and if there's any changing to be done, I'm the one who must change, not you.'

'Let's agree to be a mutual admiration society of two and stay as we are then,' she agreed laughingly. 'But about the terrible ordeal tomorrow night. Evening dress, you say. Long or short?'

'Oh, long. What about that green thing you wore at the Helstons'?'

'That got something spilt on it and I had to throw it out,' she said.

'Throw it out? Wouldn't it clean?'

'Oh, possibly, but why bother? Come upstairs with me and look over the long frocks I've got and help me choose,' and they went up arm in arm to her bedroom and she opened the long range of fitted wardrobes built into one wall and took out dress after dress, each with its protecting long muslin wrapper.

Mrs. Joliman saw them go, heard Philippa's bedroom door open and knew that they had gone in. She was faintly scandalised. She had been nearly forty when Philippa was born, the only child out of the six she had borne which had survived infancy. She had been young in an age when girls did not take young men into their bedrooms, unless they were girls of a certain type and the purpose was a specific one. Thinking of the haughty correctness of Lady Hollmere, she was anxious about the effect of Philippa's modern ways and the free-and-easy attitude of girls to their boyfriends in these days.

With laughter and friendly argument, the dress was chosen, a young girl's frock of white organdie embroidered with pink and silver roses. Philippa had protested that it was too young for her now, a frock which she had worn before going into the W.R.N.S.

'I'm not an *ingénue* any more, Justin,' she said, shaking out its billowing folds when it was released from its wrapper. 'Why, I wore that when I was eighteen. I don't know why it's still here, and only the war has kept it in fashion. Think of the coupons that must have gone into all these yards of material!'

'It must have taken your whole year's supply.'

'And then some! Not that we worry much about clothing coupons,' said Philippa gaily.

'Why not? Everybody else seems to be worried.'

'But, darling, one can always buy them! Mummy buys whole books at a time. There are always people to whom the money is of more value than the coupons as they can't afford to buy clothes, mothers with big families and so on.'

'You mean you *buy* clothing coupons? Other people's coupons?' asked Justin, plainly shocked.

'But of course! How can one keep clothed otherwise? Why, shoes alone exhaust all our own coupons,' said Philippa unconcernedly, her brow furrowed over the problem of whether or not she could get anyone to do certain alterations to the frock in question before tomorrow night, since Justin wanted her to wear it.

'But it's dishonest, dearest,' said Justin, and she was caught at last by his tone and turned to look at him.

'Oh no, not really, is it?' she asked. 'After all, they only issue coupons enough for the clothes and materials they can afford to let us have, so what does it matter who uses them? It doesn't mean that any extra clothes or materials have to be provided.'

'That's a specious argument, dear. If it were found that more coupons were being issued than were actually required, stocks of materials could be made to last longer so that less would be needed and the saving would have gone towards the general war effort. Don't you see that?' His manner was faintly pompous.

'Well—I suppose you're right, though everybody does it. You're a bit rigid, Justin, aren't you?' but her smile took off any edge there might have been to her voice. 'It's to be hoped we have finished with clothing coupons by the time we get married, or bang will go all Mummy's dreams of a slap-up wedding. Do you want a white bride, by the way?'

His arms closed about her.

'Any colour in the world so long as it's you inside it, my sweet,' he said, and the faint rift closed as if it had never been.

Philippa realised that he had made a wise choice. There was approval in Lady Hollmere's frosty eyes of the little-girl white frock, and Philippa's nervousness kept up the illusion that she was very young and inexperienced, even below her twenty-one years.

'I shall be able to manage her,' thought her ladyship calmly. 'I can mould her into the right pattern so that we shall not have to be ashamed of Justin's wife, and in time we may be able to forget that her father is a meat-packer or a butcher or something equally vulgar.'

Later had come the shock of the air disaster, with its complete revolutionising of the Hollmere family position. With Justin acceding to the title and the ownership of the Abbey, the question of his marrying Philippa Joliman needed further and more careful consideration according to Lady Hollmere and the host of near and distant relations who regarded it as their affair.

His mother raised the question with him. Justin had always been the most amenable of her three sons, easily persuaded into a course which she thought desirable, though he had refused to allow any process to be set in action which might keep him out of the war, the proposed plea being that he was needed to work the estate and the home farm.

Now she found him quite calm, as courteous as ever, but as adamant as he had been over that.

'There is no reason at all, Mother, why I should not marry Philippa,' he said.

'But the circumstances are entirely altered, and instead of merely being married to a younger son, your wife will be a peeress, a most unsuitable position, charming though she is.'

'Whatever the position, Philippa would grace it,' said Justin.

'I suppose she would withstand you if you suggested breaking the engagement? An unfortunate feature is that we are not in a position to—er—recompense her for what she would naturally feel a keen disappointment. It is unusual for a meat-packer's daughter (or whatever he is) to be able to marry into a good family, and unprecedented for one to become a Countess of Hollmere.'

Justin's face did not appreciably change from its habitual expression of courteous attention to what his mother was saying, but she heard the note of determined opposition in his voice.

'I am sorry, of course, if anything in my marriage does not meet with your wishes, but there is no possibility at all of my engagement to Philippa being broken.'

'You mean she would not give up the idea?'

'Not at all. She has actually offered to set me free for the very reason you put forward, namely that it is not usual for a girl with her background to marry into a family like ours.'

'Well, she is a sensible girl, it seems. She evidently realises how unsuitable she is for such a position.'

'She is quite mistaken if she thinks that,' said Justin evenly. 'With her looks and her youth and her superb health and her inheritance of strong, healthy forbears, she is doing an honour to this family in uniting herself with it – and you notice I have not included the family fortunes of both sides. I have no doubt that some people will consider that I am marrying for money and she for position. The simple fact is that we are in love with each other.'

'Love? Nonsense!' said his mother harshly. 'That sort of thing does not exist outside romantic novels. You could care equally well for a suitable girl as for this one. You know the girl you ought to be marrying, and who has reasonably expected to marry you.'

He faced her steadily, aware that in his love for the young, free, vital Philippa, he had acquired a new bulwark against his mother's dominating personality.

'There is no girl other than Philippa whom I either ought to be marrying, or who has any reason at all to expect that I will marry her,' he said, and finally she had had to give in, and with a good grace so that she could face the family without showing a loss of pride or any defeat.

Now, sitting in the village church, stiff and regal in a beautifully designed and executed grey gown which eventually Philippa would find herself paying for, her grey head held high beneath its close-fitting hat of parma violets and soft, drooping feathers, watching the nervous movements of her son as he stood waiting for his bride, she was ready for the imminent meeting with the rest of the Hollmere family. She would never lower the pennant of her pride in their eyes. None of them should be able to guess how bitterly she resented the necessity of this marriage, the secret humiliation she experienced at the thought of appearing to accept on equal terms these new relations, the unspeakably common little man always associated with advertisements for tins of meat, and the woman sitting as uncomfortably as she herself on the other side of the aisle in her dress of over-bright blue and her not quite matching hat.

And then, as the organ changed into the processional hymn and there was a general rustle and stir of turning heads, the bishop and the clergy and the choir began their slow journey up the aisle, and behind them, pale as a pearl, her head bent under the lace veil so that she seemed no taller than her tubby, perspiring little father, came Philippa.

Chapter Three

As Philippa came down the aisle on her husband's arm, the dreamlike feeling persisted, though she was vaguely conscious of the heads all turned towards her, the smiling faces, the eyes that reflected almost every emotion, admiration and envy the most predominant.

Behind her came her bridesmaids, her mother on the arm of the oldest of the Hollmere men. Justin's mother barely touching the arm of the radiant Jolly Man, and behind them the trail of important people who had been crowded into the tiny vestry during the signing of the register.

And Philippa did not realise that one face of all those watchful faces, one pair of those envious eyes, had been registered on her mind until she was in the car with Justin, her train of satin and lace swirling about her feet, the white orchids in her lap.

As the face detached itself from the rest of the blurred memory, she spoke unexpectedly and quite inappropriately to her husband.

'Susan Therne! What on earth was *she* doing there?'

'Susan Therne? Do you know her?' he asked after a pause.

'We were at school together. Why is she at my wedding?'

There was an unusual sound of irritation in her tone and he looked at her in surprise. Only afterwards did she realise he also looked a little embarrassed.

'Well—she was invited, of course. The Thernes are amongst our oldest friends. They sent the silver candelabra. Remember?'

'Oh yes—yes, I do. Somehow I hadn't associated the name with Susan. Silly of me. It was quite a shock to see her in the church just now.'

'You don't really mind, do you? About Susan, I mean?' he asked
then. 'There's nothing about her that really matters, you know, not
any more, not now.'

She laughed, easing the odd tension.

'No, I suppose not. She can hardly go on throwing it up at me
forever, can she?'

'Throwing it up?' he queried.

'Yes, she was an absolute beast to me at school, taunting me about
my father, about the meat. I got used to it in the end, but she never
got tired of trying to bait me, used to cut those beastly labels off tins
and haunt me with them. I found them everywhere, in my bed, in my
books, even in my prayer-book when we went to church! How silly
you can be when you're young – and how cruel!'

'Oh, is that all?' asked Justin, and her eyes widened at his tone.

'You sound relieved, almost as if I might have had something much
worse against her,' she said.

He laughed and slipped his hand into hers.

'Did I? That was unkind of me. What could there be worse than
giving my darling a moment's unhappiness? I haven't had a chance to
tell you yet that you're the loveliest thing I or anybody else has ever
seen. When you came up the aisle, I was terrified in case you melted
away. You looked like a perfectly wonderful ice maiden, frosty and
quite unreal.'

She smiled and leaned towards him and kissed him.

'I'm no ice maiden,' she said. 'Does that feel real?'

'Yes – though I'm afraid to touch you. You still might melt away.'

'I shall melt – but not away,' she told him, in her voice the teasing
note of happiness that added the last perfection.

'I'm still horribly scared, you know,' she said. 'All those people.'

'If you had the faintest idea what you look like, my darling, you
couldn't possibly be scared of anyone. Besides, don't forget that you're
now Lady Hollmere, and they just don't get scared.'

She made a grimace.

'That's just it. I'm wearing that imposing name, but inside me I'm
just the same, just Philippa Joliman. Oh, Justin, what if I make a mess
of it? Of being—Lady Hollmere?'

'My darling, you won't,' he said comfortingly, but she was not so sure.

There had been moments during their engagement, and since his accession to the title, when she had been frightened enough to want to call it off, amazed at her temerity in even contemplating such a marriage. Why couldn't she have accepted one of the many other proposals she had had, remained in her own comfortable way of life? What presumption and sheer stupidity to imagine for a moment she could live the Hollmere way!

Yet here she was, irrevocably committed to it, wearing a wedding ring, turned in those few minutes of unreality into Lady Hollmere of Hollmere Abbey!

'I'm terrified,' she said again, as the car turned in at the Open gateway and made its way up the drive to the front of the Abbey. She half rose in her seat as if she would have got out and fled if she could.

Again his hand quieted her.

'Darling, don't get into this state. I shall be with you all the time, and there's nothing on earth to be frightened of. Everybody loves you, or they will when they know you.'

'I'm not so sure about that,' she said grimly, leaning back again. 'Those aunts of yours in the vestry. They looked at me as if I'd come out of cheese – or probably they were remembering I'd come out of tins of meat!'

He frowned. He wanted her to forget that, or at any rate not constantly to be forcing others to remember it. He had never been foolish enough to think she would be accepted into his family without question or objection, but it lay within herself to live down her unfortunate origin.

'I'd rather you didn't say things like that, sweetheart,' he said uneasily.

'Alright, but you know it's the truth. Justin, you really will stay with me? Today, I mean? Don't cast me loose amongst them for a single moment, will you?'

He reassured her, and called her attention to the little knot of village people who had come to help with the reception, but were gathered outside the front of the house to be the first to welcome them.

Philippa's eyes grew dim and her throat ached a little as she caught sight of first one and then another of the people she had known nearly all her life – girls and boys, now young men and women, with whom she had played in her school holidays with no thought that her father's money and the great redbrick atrocity made her any different from the grocer's children, the boy at the local garage, the girl who served in the baker's.

Since her engagement to Justin, circumstances and not her own wish had kept her apart from them. She had not long been home from the W.R.N.S., and the few weeks had been spent in a whirl of visits to the Abbey, of meeting Justin's family and friends, of shopping and fittings. Her conscience smote her about these older friends of hers. She had neglected them. What might they not have thought of her?

When she got out of the car, she paused a moment and turned to them, her face flushed and animated now, her eyes glowing.

'How lovely of you to be here,' she said to them. 'Can you believe this is me, Philippa, done up like this? Fenny, how are the rabbits? Don't forget the black and white doe's mine. Oh, Mrs. Dove, you're able to walk again! Is your leg quite alright now?'

The grocer's wife moved a step forward, red-faced and plainly embarrassed. She had come to help in the kitchen that day, but did not expect to be spoken to or she would have found time to take off her overall.

'Thank you—My Lady,' she said awkwardly. 'I'm quite well now.'

Philippa stared at her and then laughed. It was the first time anyone had called her, seriously, by that title.

'My Lady!' she repeated gaily. 'Doesn't it sound funny? But you don't have to call me that, Mrs. Dove. I've been Philippa to you ever since John dragged me out of the pond and brought me to you to be dried. Remember? The awful part was that he'd left Annie still in the pond to struggle out by herself. Do you remember?'

The tension which had held the whole little group relaxed. One could feel as well as see it. Fixed smiles softened, and there was a pressing forward to see her better. She spoke to most of them by name, exchanging little jokes with them whilst Justin stood beside her, frowning a little and looking uncomfortable. One of the things he had always loved about Philippa was her complete lack of affectation, but surely this was carrying it too far? There was such a loss of dignity in this procedure, and just beyond them, the double oak doors thrown wide, two men in the specially resurrected livery of the Hollmeres stood waiting for the bridal pair to enter the Abbey.

'Come now, dear,' he said quietly to her, touching her hand, and she looked at him and smiled. She had come to life again through her own people after having been almost frozen to death by his. He realised it better than she did.

'Sorry, darling, but it was so exciting to see them here. Now let's go in in great style!' and with her hand in his, whilst a footman gathered up her train and held it tenderly over his arm, she entered the Abbey for the first time as its mistress.

The first time Justin had taken her there had been for the official meeting with her future mother-in-law, and she had been too scared to register any detailed impression of anything but vastness and dimness, but he had taken her there the next day, when Lady Hollmere was out paying a round of visits.

She caught her breath then at the sheer beauty of the great house, two wings set at right-angles to the long, many-windowed centre portion which it enclosed within protecting arms. In that central portion were set the great doors of massive oak sweeping up to the high arch above them. A small door was inset to provide easier entry since it took the full strength of the two men to operate the ancient chains and locks which opened the main doors.

At either side of the door ran a line of windows reaching to the flagged terrace, and above them another line of long mullioned windows, and above these, carved in stone, the coats of arms of those families which had been united by marriage, or by conquest, with the Hollmeres for more than three hundred years. The stone figures and heraldic signs were blunted now and broken, some of them indistinguishable – symbol of an age which spurns the old way of life and is bent on destroying without being able to create anything beautiful and enduring in its place.

Justin stood looking at them for a moment after he had explained to Philippa what they were, pointing out the arms of this or that forbear, describing their significance. There was a tenseness in his look; his eyes and his mouth were narrowed and bleak as if indrawn by the thoughts that pierced his soul.

'The old order changeth – giving place to what?' he asked, seeing her questioning look. 'No chivalry any more, no need for kindness nor sympathy, no need to feel for others and be constrained to help. The State do everything – oh, forgive me, darling. I know it's got to be accepted, but necessity doesn't make a thing any more palatable.'

'Time can't stand still,' she said gently. 'Something must always be giving way to the next thing or there would be no progress in the world.'

'Progress? Do you call what is happening to England progress?' he asked bitterly. 'Whilst we fought a war designed to enrich some and enslave others, we could delude ourselves into the belief that we were fighting to save civilisation in Europe. When we get to the peace, we shall be able to see just what we have saved – nothing.'

Philippa could not find the answer she knew must be somewhere. Her father, she felt, would have found it. He was on the 'other side'. Though the ineradicable peasant in him could not help being pleased and flattered by the marrying of his daughter with the Hollmeres, the sense of revolution, the new stirring of the country to its very depths and in its very depths, found approval in him. In almost every country but his own, the old order had gone already. The war had not caused the revolution in Britain; it had only hastened it and provided it with fresh impetus. It had to come. All this, this beauty, this reverence for tradition, this age-old hierarchy founded on the mere accident of birth – it could not live.

Yet, faced with one of these things doomed to die in the sacred name of Progress, Philippa had taken a step over the threshold of Justin's mind and understood the bitterness with which he and his kind watched at the death-bed of most of the things they had been brought up to love and preserve.

She slipped a hand into his and for a moment leaned against his shoulder.

'Hollmere will not be lost just yet,' she said. 'I can do a little towards that – even if I haven't got a coat of arms to be carved over a window up there. If I had, I suppose it would be a couple of tins rampant on a field sanguinary!' laughing as she said it.

He did not join in her laughter, but frowned a little and did not look at her. He loved her for being just what she was, light-hearted, gay, full of courage and good sense – but he hoped she would not always push before the public eye what, in spite of his absorbing love for her, he must continue to regret.

She saw the look on his face and was quick to interpret it correctly.

'Darling, I'm not making fun of your traditions. In a way, I love them and am sorry to see what is happening to so much that has made you what you are. But—oh well, let's not talk about it. Can you bear to have *me* as I am? Nothing of yesterday in me? No forbears at all, as far as I know?'

He held her closely and kissed her many times. At such a moment, she was everything any man could desire.

'My sweet love, I want you just as you are, always—always,' he said fervently.

Well, that had preceded her first tour of Hollmere Abbey, a tour which both excited and oppressed her. These enormous rooms, their painted ceilings almost lost to view, the huge grates which, even filled with vast fires, could surely never warm the rooms? Against walls panelled with oak or with worn, faded satin, or with tapestry, hung pictures at whose value she could only guess by the varying depth of tone in Justin's voice as he pointed them out to her. Some of the names of the great painters she recognised, of some she had never heard, though she did not risk shocking him by saying so. In the long gallery, whose other use she could not imagine in any age, were the portraits of his ancestors, fierce-looking men, cow-like women, with here and there some pictured face that stood out from the rest, a man with a humorous twist to his lips and a glint in his eyes caught by the painter, a woman who dared to let something of herself, something not entirely subdued by being a Hollmere, lurk in a rebellious mouth.

'Well, at least people don't have fierce portraits painted of themselves to adorn their walls nowadays,' she said, relief apparent in her voice.

'But of course they do,' said Justin. 'This is the last one that was painted,' and he took her down to the end of the gallery to stand before a portrait which, though in a modern setting, the figures in modern dress, in no way jarred with all these other Hollmeres.

Philippa stood looking at it – at the cold, proud face of Justin's mother, thin and elegant in black velvet with a collar of pearls about her neck and diamonds glinting on her bare arms, on her long, slender fingers which had certainly never done a day's work, diamonds set in the careful waves of her hair which had been grey even then, though it was obvious from the surrounding group of her three sons that the portrait had been painted some twenty years ago. Justin had been a schoolboy in an Eton suit.

Philippa smiled tenderly at it.

'What a dear little schoolboy you were,' she said.

'Unfortunately there wasn't time for a real portrait of George, but I suppose we shall have to see about ours soon,' said Justin, the faintest pomposity in his voice.

'Good heavens, do you mean that?' she asked, between fright and amusement. 'Don't make me wear black velvet and diamonds, though. I could never live up to them!'

'They're not, of course, necessary, though you will have to wear something suitable.'

'Darling, I'm not suggesting rushing off to the nearest portrait-painter like this,' said Philippa, looking down with laughter at the scarlet pullover and grey slacks which she had put on for comfortable walking. 'Believe me, I have got some decent respect for the position I'm somehow going to occupy – though heaven only knows how!'

And now, for good or ill, she was actually in that position – Lady Hollmere of Hollmere Abbey.

She passed, her gleaming train rustling as the footman set it gently down on the floor, into the great, dim hall – dim still in spite of the fact that every light was on, all the galaxy of new lighting which was part of Joe Joliman's wedding present.

There had been some little altercation, some of it acrimonious, about the reception. It was only right and proper, Joe said, that the after-wedding festivities should be held at the bride's house.

'I know we mightn't 'ave the big rooms you've got at the Abbey, son,' he said to Justin, who had come from his mother with the command that he should overrule such objections as the Jolimans might make. 'That's soon got over. There's plenty of room outside, and wot's the matter with a darned great marquee on the lawn? A covered passage can go right up to where the cars stop so's nobody'll get wet if it rains. You can 'ave a dance floor laid over the turf so's the youngsters can keep things goin' to the next day if they want to. Lyons can do a slap-up job of the caterin' and no expense spared. Phil's our only child and if I can't make a splash w'en she gets married to a lord, my name's not Jolly Joe Joliman.'

It took Justin a long time and a great deal of patience and perseverance, and it was not until Philippa chipped in at last with a weary request to her father to let the Hollmeres have their way, that he finally capitulated, though with a bad grace.

'It ain't right, Phil,' he complained afterwards. 'They may be a big noise, these Abbey lot, but it's my daughter as is doing them the honour of marryin' one of 'em …'

Though Philippa was tired and not too well pleased herself about Justin's victory, she laughed and, after a moment's hesitation, her father joined in and they rocked together with mirth. Their shared sense of humour had always been a saviour to them both.

So, here she was, in her bridal enchantment, walking on her silver slippers into her new, age-old home within the first half-hour of her married life.

Under the great bell of flowers on which her father had insisted, though Lady Hollmere had opined that it was 'vulgar', Justin kissed his bride before any of the guests arrived.

'Thank you forever,' he said softly, and her grey eyes were dewy and her mouth trembled against his.

'I'll make you happy, Justin. Oh, darling, I will!' she whispered. 'I'll be everything you want me to be.'

Sublime, impossible promise!

Then the guests came in – Lady Hollmere with the bride's father, both ill at ease in the other's company, her ladyship showing it only by increased dignity and self-possession, Joe hot and flustered and vociferous – Jolly Joe Joliman to the life.

Lady Hollmere touched the cheek of her new daughter-in-law with frosted lips.

'Welcome to your home, Philippa. I hope you will be happy here,' she said without warmth.

'Thank you. I'm sure I shall,' said Philippa before she was engulfed in her father's arms and could forget, in his loving warmth, the complete lack of it in Justin's mother.

She had only a confused memory afterwards of that day of days, with so many new faces, such a conglomeration of names, some of them known to every reader of newspapers and magazines, some quite unknown. Many speeches, some long and involved, some mercifully (Justin's amongst these) short and well prepared.

One of the strangest memories of the day was the meeting, face to face and without the protection of the village church, with Susan Therne.

Susan came up with the lines of guests to pay their respects to the bride and bridegroom, and though Philippa had smiled mechanically and said the right things to all the others, when she was faced with Susan Therne she felt tongue-tied, awkward, as if in a second she had been whisked back to school, back to her uncomfortable girlhood there, back to school uniform and desks and inky fingers.

'Well, well,' said Susan in an amused, lazy drawl as their hands touched, but Philippa stood silent.

'Oh—hullo, Susan,' she said at last, angrily aware that she had betrayed herself to this entirely self-possessed and *soignée* young woman. 'I hadn't realised you—that we—I mean, it was quite a surprise seeing you.'

Susan gave a small, amused laugh.

She was wearing a colour which few people, even with her dark hair and faintly sunburnt skin, could have worn with effect. It was a colour between rose and cyclamen, and in complete accord with her small hat of grey feathers was an exquisite wrap of pale platinum fox skins. Though she and Philippa were almost exactly the same age, there was a maturity about Susan, an air of self-assurance, which made the bride feel years younger, infinitely unsophisticated.

'A surprise, was it?' asked Susan in her quick, high, amused fashion, so bitterly well remembered. 'But surely you knew that Justin and I are very old friends? Or no—I imagine you never confessed that to her, did you, Justin?' glancing at him with a smile in her eyes which did not reach her mouth and which had the effect of shutting Philippa out.

To Philippa's surprise, Justin looked uncomfortable. His face flushed.

'I don't know why you use the word "confess", Susan,' he said. 'What was there to confess, either to Philippa or anyone else?'

Susan shrugged her thin shoulders and drew her furs more closely about her, though the day of early summer was fine and warm – too warm, one would have said, for even light furs.

'Oh—nothing, my dear,' she said, giving the words a subtle denial by the pause in them. 'You see how carefully I have kept these?' rubbing her cheek against the fur.

'Yes,' said Justin curtly, and turned aside as other guests came to greet them.

Later, in a momentary lull, Philippa turned to him.

'Do we have to go on knowing Susan Therne?' she asked.

'Oh—she's ... I suppose we shall meet her at people's houses,' he said a trifle uneasily.

'What did she mean about the furs? What's it to do with you?'

'Just a bit of catty nonsense,' he told her. 'I gave her the skins a long time ago.'

'Oh,' said Philippa, and again had to break off because of the approach of yet more guests.

It was a bit odd, she reflected, that a man should give such a valuable present to a girl in whom he was not interested, but perhaps people in this new world of Justin's thought nothing of it. She decided it would be sensible to forget it, which she proceeded to do.

The long, exciting, tiring day came to an end at last, came to an end rather surprising to Philippa in the corner of the drawing-room of the

Paris hotel in which they had decided to spend their first night instead of going straight to the South of France where a friend of Justin's was lending them a villa for their month's honeymoon.

They had flown over, and a taxi had hurled them from Le Bourget to their hotel with far more incident and danger than the aeroplane, after which their small suite, high above the noise of the city, seemed a haven of quiet peace.

Philippa did not know quite what she had expected from this, their first moment alone together after their marriage, but she tried not to feel that this was anti-climax, this gentle holding in his arms, kisses more restrained than those of their engaged days, a gentle but definite withdrawal from her though within herself she had been aware of the leaping of her desire for him, a desire which now need no longer be withheld.

'What is it, darling?' she asked, her voice quivering with her excitement, her eyes warmly ardent. 'You're not afraid of marriage and of me, are you?' a teasing note in her laughter.

But his answering smile was grave and he did not accept the challenge of her eyes which plainly invited him.

Instead, he moved about the room for a moment and then opened one of the two doors leading from the tiny, stiffly uncomfortable room and took into the room beyond the dressing-case which was all she had brought with her for the one night, the rest of the luggage going on by train.

'I think—this will be—the better of the two rooms for you, darling,' he said as he came back to her.

She looked bewildered.

'Two rooms? You mean—that we're going to be as formal as that?' she asked.

He came close to her and set his hands on her shoulders and stood holding her, looking into her face, his eyes serious.

'Dearest,' he said very gently, 'when you asked me if I were afraid of marriage, I didn't answer. I'm trying to think of the best answer now, to explain myself to you without giving you a wrong impression. I love you, darling. You know that, don't you? With all my heart and soul, I love you forever.'

Her bewilderment increased.

'Justin, what's all this about? Of course I know you love me. And I love you. Isn't that why we got married?' she asked.

'Yes. Yes, of course. Only—I don't want you to misunderstand what I'm going to say. I *am* afraid of marriage, Philippa. I'm afraid of the awful power it has to alter two people. It's like some dreadful magic potion which, once drunk, turns people from the nice human beings they were into—monsters. I've seen it so often. So must you have seen it. Of all the people who get married as we have done, for love and because each thinks the other wonderful and perfect, how many keep those illusions? How many married couples do we know who are happy? Really happy and contented with each other, who haven't changed each other out of all recognition?'

'My dear, sweet Justin, have you gone suddenly mad?' she asked, between laughter and astonishment. 'What's all this about? You don't mean you're regretting having married me already?'

'No, of course not. Haven't I told you that I adore you? That I shall love you forever?'

'Yes. Yes, you did say that,' she said slowly, looking away from him but otherwise standing quite still between his hands. 'With all your heart and soul, you said, but—but you didn't say anything about the other part of you, the part that usually counts for quite a bit in married life, especially at this stage of it. Did you mean to leave out your body, Justin?'

'Yes. Yes, I left it out,' and he set her free and rambled about the room again, though there was little space between the stiff, dusty furniture. 'I have wanted to talk about this before, but—to be quite honest, I couldn't bring myself to it, and I decided in the end that this was the best way.'

She swallowed a difficult lump in her throat. She was virgin but she was of her age and generation and by no means ignorant.

'Justin, are you trying to tell me that you're—impotent, I think they call it?' she asked, her face scarlet. It was not easy to talk like this to her bridegroom of less than a day, not easy to understand exactly what this would mean to her.

He reassured her on that score instantly.

'Good heavens, no! What an idea! If it were that, I certainly wouldn't have married you or anyone. It's that—that the thing I so want us to avoid, both of us, is putting too much emphasis on the physical side of marriage. That side has to have its place, of course. I want children, Philippa, a son to inherit my name and the Abbey. But it must keep its place, an unimportant place in comparison with other things.'

'I see. Or do I? It's rather a facer to me, this. I've always realised that we're different, Justin, not only in our backgrounds and upbringing but also in our minds. I'm so much more frivolous than you, less thoughtful and serious-minded. I know that. But—darling, when a man and woman get married because they're in love with each other, are they usually in different minds about *that!* I'm trying to get down to what you really want, or don't want, out of marriage. Are you telling me that you don't want to sleep with me?' the colour flooding her face again.

'No, of course not. Haven't I said that I want so desperately to make our marriage perfect, not to spoil ourselves and each other, to let that completion of our love develop gradually from a continuance of the friendship we have had and that we enjoy so much.'

'I can't pretend to understand,' she said with a touch of irritation in her voice, the effect on her of the humiliation she was suffering, 'but if you don't want to sleep with me, well, of course, that is perfectly alright with me.'

'I'm so clumsy, Philippa,' he said humbly. 'I have thought and thought about this and felt so sure that you would understand and agree. It's to *save* marriage for us, darling, to keep a proper and sensible and enduring balance, not to let everything else, the more important things, get swallowed up by the one thing that we know won't endure.'

She laughed, a hard and reckless sound.

'I have a feeling that what you really ought to be saying is something about loving me more as my hair grows grey and my waist-line expands.'

He caught her hands.

'That's just it,' he said eagerly. 'It's because that's what I want most of all – to be sure not to spoil for us now the chance of loving and being loved then. Don't you see? Let's keep all the other things we have, our friendship, our happy comradeship, our faculty for sharing things, all our new interests and our old as well, and when we know that these are secure for us for all time, then we can take our fill of all the other joys of marriage without imperilling the more important things.'

Her hands made no response to his. She merely stood there, her face calm, her eyes remote, her voice cool. If he did not know how he had humiliated her, how bitterly she resented this extraordinary attitude, she would die rather than show him.

'I see,' she said. 'Is there any particular term to this sort of trial run? I've heard of trial marriages when two people live as married people without actually being married so that they can see whether they're likely to make a successful marriage. This is the first time I've heard of a trial friendship, if that's what our marriage is going to be. Do we set a definite term to this sort of prolonged engagement after marriage?'

She kept her tone so steady, her face so smoothly unemotional, that he felt with relief that she understood and concurred.

'Well, I thought about three months,' he said.

'Alright,' said Philippa, slipping her hands from his and turning away. 'I'll go and have a bath and change. What time shall we have dinner?'

'I thought about eight?'

She nodded and went into the bedroom he had said should be hers, closed the door and, in a moment of exasperated anger, turned the key in the lock. She found a bathroom at the other side of it. She neither knew nor cared whether his room was similarly equipped. She rather hoped it was not.

Tears stung her eyes but she forced them back fiercely, and stood for a few moments holding her throat with her two hands, unconsciously trying to ease the aching which tears might have relieved.

What had she done? Had she made a horrible, irretrievable mess of her life? Inevitably the vile thought came to her that perhaps, after all, Justin had married her for her father's money, because with it he could keep Hollmere Abbey, his beloved home, for at least one more generation, his own – possibly his son's, too.

His son!

Her eyes grew stormy and she began to get ready for her bath in order to give her hands something to do. Unoccupied, they might, she felt, break and tear things from the rage and frustration and humiliation of her thoughts.

Justin's son – that son she would be allowed graciously to produce for the benefit of the Hollmeres. Her frantic imagination drew all sorts of pictures. Justin, with that pomposity of which so far she had seen only the slightest hint, would come to her room one night, impeccably attired for the surrender of his blasted principles and would graciously intimate to her that he was prepared to seduce her that night – ladies and gentlemen, positively for One Night Only – in order that she might do herself the honour of bearing in her body, for nine months of ugliness and probable discomfort, one of the God-given of the earth, a new Hollmere!

Yet when she heard him moving about again in their sitting-room she went out to him showing no sign of the turmoil through which she had just passed.

His relief at the calmness of her entrance was obvious.

'Darling, how wonderful you look!' he said tenderly.

'Rather too bridal, but this is the only dress I brought and I thought it would be far more suitable than it is,' she said, and almost in the same breath, 'Shall we go down?' sweeping in front of him and giving him a view of her beautiful, bare back and shoulders rising out of the ivory satin of her exquisitely cut gown.

'Not wearing the pearls?' he asked.

She laughed carelessly.

'Aren't they for Hollmere brides?' she asked, and without giving him a chance to reply, sailed down the corridor and pressed the lift bell.

Over their dinner she was apparently as she had always been, and he took heart and chatted with her, his only surprise that she drank more champagne than he had known her to do. It was not a wine she liked, but tonight she had asked for it.

'What would you like to do now?' he asked over their black coffee with cognac – again something for which she had asked.

'I should think the Opera House,' she said calmly.

'The Opera House? But I though you hated opera?'

"Well, what's the alternative? The Folies Bergères or the Bal Tabarin might not be quite suitable in the circumstances.'

His assurance crumbled at her tone.

'We'll do whatever you like,' he said.

'Then if you really mean that, I'll go to bed with a good book,' she said, and rising from the corner of the drawing-room where their coffee had been served, she went past him and out of the room without another glance at him.

She had been lying awake for a long time, restless, unhappy, completely bewildered by Justin's unexpected attitude, when she heard him come to her door, softly try the handle and then finding that she had turned the lock, tap hesitatingly at it.

She sat up in bed wondering what to do and whether any other bride had ever been in like quandary.

'Philippa, will you say goodnight to me?' he asked, and she caught the desperate misery in his voice. Her heart always too quick to soften, gave its own response, but she still sat there motionless.

'Are you asleep, my darling? The light's still on.'

'No, I'm not asleep,' she said.

'Please unlock the door. Please, darling.'

She slid out of bed and opened the door to him. Her brown hair was childishly tumbled, her face very young without its make-up, her eyes red from the tears she had not been able to hold back. Standing there in the gaily embroidered satin kimono which only partially concealed the chiffony nightgown, she looked far more child than woman. He felt his bones turning to water at the sheer enchantment of her – Philippa, his wife, his bride of so few hours.

He pulled her into his arms and held her.

'Is it your heart that's making all the noise, or mine?' she asked in an unsteady whisper.

'Philippa—Philippa ...'

He was kissing her, and her ardent body was aflame, all her desire for him and for the fulfilment at last of all the muddled, thrilling, rather alarming dreams of her girlhood.

And then his arms slipped from her and, walking like a blind man with stumbling steps, he left her and closed the door behind him.

Philippa was alone. On her wedding night, dressed in the chiffon and lace which yesterday she had looked at, wondering whether she would ever dare to appear in it – she was alone.

She sat down on the edge of her bed and stared down at the pattern her toe was tracing in the carpet. Justin, her husband, her bridegroom, had left her, just like that. She thought suddenly of his mother, the proud, arrogant face the eyes which had told her that she, at least, would never in anything but outward show accept the Jolly Man's daughter as a Hollmere.

Philippa wanted to cry, to beat at the door with her fists, to dress and run away, back to her parents and her home and all the familiar, loved and loving things.

Instead, she got into bed and eventually went to sleep.

Lying sleepless in his own room, Justin, Lord Hollmere, thought anxiously of himself, of his young wife, of all that today they had undertaken. It had cost him a tremendous effort to leave her just now, but not for one moment did he feel it had been anything but right to do so. There would be other nights, but tonight was sacred, something set apart, an offering and an oblation.

Chapter Four

Philippa paused on the staircase to look down at her assembled guests for a moment. She had gone to her room for a minor repair to the hem of her lace gown and had realised what a relief it was to be able to do so.

'Don't hurry, Brownie,' she said to her maid – dear Lizzie Brown who had been imported into her nursery when she was able to walk and had been with her ever since as nurse, companion, friend, and now, in spite of Lady Hollmere's attempts to replace her by a smart young French girl, her personal maid.

Lizzie Brown looked up affectionately as she knelt on the floor with needle and cotton.

'Are you tired, dear?' she asked.

'Not tired really. What do I do to make any woman tired? But a bit fed up, Brownie, with always having to be a ladyship, always having to remember Who and What I am with capital letters. It was much more fun being Philippa Joliman – and most of all, I think, when I was Wren Joliman. Heavens, what years ago that was!' stretching her arms and yawning.

On her arms there winked and shone diamonds and emeralds, treasured possessions of a long line of Hollmere women, though Justin had had them reset in modern fashion. Since this was one of the really grand occasions, the annual Hollmere ball, revived after years of desuetude by the insistence of the dowager countess, Philippa wore all the jewels she called 'the regalia' so that from head to toe she sparkled and glittered. The gown of fine Mechlin lace was in itself an heirloom, discovered during one of her raids on the contents of the many closed rooms and remade into this garment of gossamer and priceless loveliness.

'But, dearie, surely you're having fun?' asked Brownie. 'Why, every girl in the county must envy you. You can have and do anything you like – the title, and all that money of your dad's, and this house – and a husband who worships the ground you walk on! If anybody's lucky, it's you.'

Philippa stood still whilst the older girl sewed, looking at her reflection in a long mirror.

Lucky? Yes. Yes, of course she was. She had all those things and a lot more. Everything, in fact, that the heart of any woman could desire, and at the centre of all the material things, Justin with his adoring love, his unchanging devotion, his utter faithfulness. For three years she had had all these things, three breathless, crowded, successful years, years in which she had been admired, sought after, flattered, envied, adored.

The experiences of those years had brought her a new beauty, had softened the hardness of her early youth, had given her poise and self-assurance, had completed her always a good dress sense and taught her how to flatter her faultless lines, her warm colouring which needed so little assistance.

Yes, she had everything in the world – and at twenty-five that was perhaps the saddest reflection she could make.

She sighed a little.

'I suppose that's just it,' she said. 'I'm too lucky. There's nothing left to wish for, nothing to look forward to.'

Brownie bit off the thread from the finished repair.

'There. That's as good as new,' she said, 'and tell those men to keep their clumsy feet off it for the rest of the evening. As for nothing to look forward to – how long is it since you were married?'

'I know what you're going to say – that after three years, it's high time I produced an heir. I know it is, and I suppose that my next step, always in keeping with the divine tradition of the Hollmeres, will be to produce one.'

Brownie looked at her with quick, loving scrutiny.

'You don't mean ...' she began, and Philippa laughed. There was a faint hardness in her laughter.

'No, not yet. I had to get certain events over first, but I suppose any minute now. The Hollmeres expect it!'

'Don't you want one, Philippa?'

When they were alone, the maid slipped unchidden into the easy familiarity of the old days.

'Yes, if it could be mine, but it won't be. It will be just another possession of the family which I have been privileged to bestow! Don't look so woebegone. Brownie, I'm just a beast, ungrateful and dissatisfied. Forget it. I'll go down now and be the beautiful and fascinating and popular Lady Hollmere again!' And she dropped a light kiss on the cheek of her faithful friend and left her.

And now she stood for a moment looking down at her guests.

Her guests! The guests bidden by her secretary, the estimable Ena, herself a poor off-shoot of the family tree act until Philippa remedied it, grossly underpaid because of that privilege. Ena had presented to her the list of guests but Philippa had barely glanced down the names.

'Same old crowd, I suppose?' she asked. 'Nobody new and exciting? Nobody who's done anything they shouldn't have done? Gone off with somebody else's wife or cook or anything?'

'I'm afraid not,' said Ena, who loved her quite apart from her gratitude for her much improved status.

'Shall I ever be as beautifully balanced as you, Ena? You seem to accept everything without question or anxiety.'

'Nobody could say you haven't done well, Philippa,' said the secretary, fortyish, plain, good-tempered, tranquil.

'So far, but someday I may break out, and then watch!'

Ena had been right, she reflected on the stairs. Nobody new or exciting, certainly nobody about whom the slightest scandal had ever circulated. As a result of the exclusiveness of Hollmere Abbey, parties there were dull in the extreme, composed of elderly or, at best, young middle-aged people, wives with their husbands for the most part, with just a sprinkling of unmarried girls and men carefully vetted to meet them, men who left their vices and their fun outside the sacred precincts and seemed even to wear different faces when they were bidden to Hollmere Abbey.

She saw one head raised, one pair of eyes looking expectantly towards her – Justin's of course. He always knew when she was not there, was always waiting in a sort of suspended animation until she came back.

But she smiled and continued her slow descent of a great staircase to find, of course, that Justin had woven his way through the little knots of people to reach the foot of the stairs when she did.

'Could Brownie mend it?' he asked.

She smiled, nodding.

'You know what happened, then? You always know everything that happens to me, don't you?' she asked.

'Isn't that what I'm for? Not tired, darling, are you?'

'Heavens, no! It isn't exciting enough for that, is it? Shall I ever be tired again, I wonder?'

She regretted the light speech as soon as she saw the little frown that for a moment furrowed his forehead. Dear, darling Justin, it was so hideously easy to hurt him!

'You have such wonderful vitality, my dearest,' he said. 'When we can get away, would you like to do something different? Go somewhere fresh?'

'May I?' she asked ironically.

When they went away from the Abbey, it was always to move in a narrowly prescribed circle, going at the right times and for exactly the right period to Scotland, to the South of France, to the big, gloomy house in London which Philippa's money had enabled them to reopen and make habitable.

'We'll talk about it,' he said easily, and she knew what that meant – that he would discuss it with his mother and come to her with some idea, by no means new or exciting, planted there at such an interview.

She moved amongst her guests, gently but firmly breaking up the conversations to get everyone into the long gallery, and seated.

'Kerslik is going to play for us,' she said, putting into her tone exactly the right note of reverence and pride, infusing it with gratitude as if the violinist, a Polish refugee, were not being paid to provide an accompaniment to their continued conversation.

Whilst he was playing, his emaciated body swaying as if bent and bowed by the force of his own music, Philippa happened to glance at Ena Blackthorne and found her interest caught and held.

Ena's plain face was transfigured, her eyes hidden behind their thick glasses but her mouth softened, her nostrils dilating, whilst her capable hands, with their large knuckles, kneaded each other in her lap as if under the stress of some great emotion. Then, as she watched, Kerslik bowed his last, almost fierce, drawn-out chords and at the same time looked towards where Ena was sitting, and Philippa knew the amazing, undreamed-of truth.

These two were in love with each other!

How and where had they met? How on earth could there have been any opportunity for them to get to know each other? And whatever did they see in each other, Kerslik who must have been at least fifty and looked rather like a half-starved crow with his thin face and body and unkempt straggling black hair, and Ena Blackthorne?

She had given Ena the cheque for the violinist earlier in the day, and she remembered now that when she had, on an impulse, added another five guineas to the agreed fee, Ena had showed a disproportionate appreciation of it.

'I know he'll be glad of it, Philippa,' she had said. 'It isn't easy for him to make a living, though in his own country before the war he was recognised and regarded as a great musician.'

Now how had she known anything about that? reflected Philippa. And, thinking back, she realised that it had been Ena's idea to have a violinist, and Ena who had picked out Kerslik and engaged him.

A small ante-room leading off the long gallery had been set aside for his use, with chairs and a table, and refreshments provided for him and his accompanist. Philippa saw Ena going there and when presently the pianist reappeared to play without Kerslik, there was no sign of the secretary.

After the guests had gone, Philippa found some excuse for going into the room which was used as an office, guessing that she would find Ena there. She was industrious and conscientious and, however late the party had ended, would remain to make notes of items which by the morning she might forget.

She glanced up in surprise at Philippa's entrance.

'Ena, how long have you known Kerslik?' she asked without preamble, and the swift flush told her how right she had been.

'Why do you ask?' she stammered defensively.

Philippa leaned on the table, smiling with a strange look of pity and envy in her face.

'My dear, I'm not your enemy. You should know that by now,' she said. 'Is he in love with you? You are with him, aren't you?'

Behind the spectacles, Ena's eyes filled with tears. She bent her head and nodded, her bony, unlovely, capable hands opening and closing on her round ebony ruler.

'You look as if there's a tragedy in it,' said Philippa. 'Is he married?'

'No.'

'Then what's wrong?'

Ena looked up.

'What's wrong?' she asked, shocked. 'He—we—it would be most unsuitable – impossible ...'

Philippa laughed.

'My dear Ena, how unsuitable? And why impossible? You don't mean because you belong to this family, do you?'

'Well—yes—in a way. We—we've never actually discussed marriage,' said Ena hesitatingly.

'Yet you know you love each other? You're sure? Sure he does, I mean?'

It seemed odd to her to think of people like the gaunt Pole and Ena Blackthorne suffering the pangs of love, and yet why not? Most love, she reflected with a faint bitterness, is only skin deep, but does that mean that all love is as shallow?

'Yes. Yes. I'm quite sure.' said Ena simply. 'I'd like to tell you about it, Philippa. May I?'

'Of course! I do hope there's a breath of scandal in it. It would so much relieve the tedium of being a Hollmere,' laughed Philippa, sitting on the corner of the table.

It was, as Ena told it, quite an uneventful, even a dull little story. She had met Paul Kerslik during the war, when, escaping from Poland, he had been amongst the bunch of his fellow-countrymen whom it had been part of her business to house in one of the various places requisitioned by the government for that purpose.

'He seemed so solitary, did not make friends, found it very difficult to settle down though he learned English quickly – I suppose being a musician made that easy. It helps, you know. We found him a job until the war ended and then he took up his music again, and though actually he works in an office, this is what he wants to do, become a great violinist – though I think he is that now,' she ended simply.

Are you going to marry him if he asks you?'

No, I—I couldn't,' whispered Ena, looking away.

'Because you belong to this wonderful family?' asked Philippa ironically.

No. I—I told you that he's not married. That isn't really true. He had a wife in Poland and for years he didn't know if she was alive or not. Now he knows she is – but she went out of her mind. They were caught separately when the Germans invaded, and he couldn't get back to her. Somebody told him she had escaped and reached England so he managed to get here, but it wasn't true. She is still there, but she is in an asylum.'

'In Poland?'

'Yes.'

'What is he doing about it?'

'What can he do? He couldn't get permission to bring her to England, and if he went back to Poland, he would be arrested by the Russians. He gets word every so often about her. Apart from her mind, she is quite healthy and strong and she's not being ill-treated. She is with some nuns who will look after her until she dies. He sends money when he can.'

Philippa sat in silence. How different her own life had been, how easy and simple and pleasant!

'It's late,' said Ena at last, getting up from her chair. 'You'd better go up, hadn't you?'

'I suppose so. Thank you for telling me, Ena. Isn't there anything anyone can do?'

'What is there?'

'I don't know, but surely there's something? Would you marry him if you could?'

'Oh yes. Yes, I would.'

'And he'd marry you?'

'We don't talk about marriage, but he loves me—and—yes, he would. I'm sure he would,' said Ena simply.

'Are you having an affair with him?'

Ena flushed.

'You mean—are we more than friends?' she asked.

'Yes. Are you? You need not mind telling me. I'm safe, and I'm a sacred Hollmere only by grafting, not by birth!'

'We're only friends,' said Ena in a low voice.

'Why don't you go off and live together?' asked Philippa.

The other frowned and fidgeted with some papers.

'You make it sound so easy and possible,' she said.

'Are you shocked, Ena?'

'No. After all, I'm forty-two and I've nobody belonging to me nearer than Justin and Lady Hollmere, and though they'd never forgive anybody who caused a scandal in the family. I'm too unimportant to matter much. They'd be able to cover it up.'

'Then why don't you?' asked Philippa.

Again Ena hesitated and then looked up, with a shy, dawning smile that seemed to take years off her and made her almost attractive.

'The chief reason is that Paul's never asked me to,' she said. 'You see, he has an exaggerated idea of my birth and importance, as an offshoot of this family, whereas even in his own country he was nothing and nobody except a violinist, and he hadn't got to any real position even with his music. After all, he was only just getting known when Poland was invaded. And of course he hasn't anything but what he earns in the only job he could get, as a sort of office boy. He's not much good at anything but playing the violin!'

'But you could get a job quite easily,' said Philippa.

Ena stared at her, flushed, not quite able to realise what was happening.

'Philippa, what you're suggesting is—is—well, you're Lady Hollmere!' she said at last, between laughter and tears. Philippa slid off the table and smoothed down her lace skirts.

'How terribly right you are, of course,' she said. 'Good night, Ena dear. I wish I could make things come right for you,' and with a thoughtful smile, she went slowly upstairs to the rooms she shared with Justin.

He had lit the gas fire and, in his dressing-gown, was sitting in front of it reading.

The thoughts with which she had left Ena crystallised at sight of him. Here they were, she and Justin, husband and wife of three years' standing, so well used to each other that it was difficult to realise they had once been friends beginning to fall in love with each other, that their blood had ever quickened at sight of each other, that it had been odd and exciting for him to be in her room.

He looked up with his unvarying smile.

'Hullo, sweet. Glad it's over?' he asked. 'Do you want Brownie in here or can I help you?'

I told her not to wait up,' she said. 'It's cosy in here. Just some hooks somewhere, and then a zip, darling,' turning her back on him so that he could find the fastenings in her dress.

'It's a most successful dress,' he said. 'You looked lovely – but then, you always do.'

She let the lace gown and its slip of soft, thin satin fall to the ground and stepped out of it, alluringly feminine in the scantiest of lingerie, and something that had become unusual entered her mind suddenly and she looked at him over her shoulder provocatively.

'I think perhaps I'm tired enough to be put to bed tonight,' she said, her laughing eyes and the mocking lilt in her voice intentionally giving the lie to her words.

Instantly she saw the faint fear she knew so well leap into his own eyes, the momentary widening of them, a wary lift of his head.

She laughed and went across to the door of her bathroom.

'Don't worry,' she said. 'I was only teasing you. I'm going to have a very long bath, so don't wait for me if you're tired.'

'You won't have it too hot, darling, will you?' he asked anxiously.

'No, dear mother,' she said and turned on the taps, leaving the door open between the two rooms.

'I needn't be afraid you'll come in,' she added.

He sat upright in his chair, laying his book down. He knew that she wanted him to come in, was inviting him to make love to her, that she liked him to sit on the edge of her bath and see through the perfumed steam her lovely, seductive body.

Why couldn't he go? What was it in him that always held him back from the complete surrender to their love-making which she herself could give? He loved her with a deep, abiding worship. Perhaps that was it. There was that unconquerable element of worship in his love. To love her so utterly, with all that was in him, and yet always to leave her unsatisfied because she had so much more to give, so much more than he wanted or could take!

With a little helpless gesture of his hands, he got up from the chair and went towards the open door of her bathroom.

'Philippa,' he said.

'Mm?'

Her voice was drowsily contented.

'May I come in?' he asked.

'Not unless you really want to,' she said, and again he stood undecided, with that strange, unconquerable reluctance against which for three years he had fought in vain.

And whilst he still stood there, nervously fingering the things on her dressing-table, with a swish of water and a swirl of steam she was there beside him, lovely, warm, utterly desirable, laughing at him as she shook the water from the tightly curling ends of her hair.

'I'm nice,' she said. 'I'm all clean and scented and smooth, and wet – do you love me, my husband?' coming to him and linking her arms round his neck. 'Well? Afraid your very elegant dressing-gown will get wet?' as very gingerly his arms went about her.

In the next second she had broken away from him and gone back to the bathroom, wrapping herself in a huge, warm towel without looking in his direction. She was remembering, as she never failed to remember on such an occasion as this, how humiliated she had felt on their wedding night, a humiliation which she had thought had been wiped out by understanding and yet which was ever to be renewed at moments like this.

Why was she such a fool? Why, why, could she not by this time learn to control her senses and desires? What had happened tonight to make her feel like this? The discovery that Ena and her black-haired crow were in love?

She heard her husband behind her and felt his arms come about her as she stood wrapped in the towel.

'Philippa—my darling, my dear darling.'

She stood quite still, her hands holding the folds of the towel, her head high, her face expressing nothing.

'Forgive me. Oh, Philippa, I'm not good to you as a husband, am I?' he whispered. 'I don't deserve you. I can't give you what you want. I can only—love you most utterly and wholly and forever.'

'Please, Justin,' she said very quietly.

But he still held her, his head pressed against her back, his hands covering the ones with which she held the bath sheet tightly about her.

'I wish I could be different. I wish I had been made differently,' he said. 'You know that it isn't that I don't love you, don't adore and—and worship you.'

'I know,' she said evenly. 'Please go back into the bedroom, Justin. I won't be long.'

'May I stay in your room, darling?' he asked humbly.

'Of course, but please let me finish now,' she said, trying to keep the impatience out of her voice.

When she came to him again, she was trembling, and he pulled her chair nearer to the fire, brought her a footstool, took off her bedroom slippers and chafed her cold feet.

'I've made you unhappy,' he said.

'Because I'm cold? Heavens no. I expect I had the bath too hot. Has Brownie left something hot in the thermos jug?'

He investigated.

'Yes. Coffee in one and soup in the other. There are some sandwiches, too.'

'I'll just have some soup.'

'Shall I make you some toast? There are some slices of bread.'

'No, just the soup,' she said, and sat there when he had brought it, sipping it gratefully.

'I ought not to have married you, Philippa,' he said suddenly.

She set down her half-empty bowl.

'Oh, Justin, for goodness' sake!' she protested wearily.

'Are you sorry that we married? Tell me the honest truth, darling.'

She shook her head.

'No, I'm not sorry. I expect all marriages are like ours really – except the ones that come right apart. I think actually we're luckier than most people. We've each got something out of it that will last. I'm Lady Hollmere and you can keep the Abbey.'

He winced at the matter-of-fact tone, so different from the love and seductive laughter with which, only a few minutes ago, she had offered him all her loveliness, the enchanting wonder of her.

'Is that all we've got left, Philippa?' he asked in a low voice.

'No. We've got friendship, and—I suppose in a way we've still got love,' she said.

'Do you still love me though I'm such a poor travesty of all you really want and need in a husband?'

'Yes. Yes, I still love you,' she said, but she said it with a sigh, passing her hand over her forehead as if trying to push away the clouds that fogged her mind.

'Not as you did when you married me, though,' he said sadly.

'Well – things change. People change. I think there's quite a lot to be said for trial marriages, living together for a bit to find out if it will last.'

'If we had done that, you wouldn't have stayed with me?' he asked.

Almost against her will, a smile broke through.

'Oh, I don't know. I do still love you, Justin, and I've never met anybody I have ever wanted more than you, never anybody I could even have endured as a husband! I think the thing that's wrong with us is that I'm so much more earthy than you, that there's more of the animal and less of the spirit in me than there is in you. We may as well face it. If I could turn myself into pure spirit and let you worship me, you'd be quite happy – and so, I suppose, should I. Oh, why go on like this?' breaking off suddenly and stretching her arms above her head. 'Do you know it's after two o'clock? I'm for bed.'

'Your own or mine?' he asked.

She laughed.

'Poor darling, don't make a martyr of yourself!' she said.

It was soon after that night that she found herself, for the first time in the three years of their marriage, likely to be pregnant.

She told Justin when, a month later, the doctor confirmed it.

He knelt at her feet, her hands in his.

'Darling, do you want it?' he asked her.

'Of course I do. Don't you?'

Fancy asking me that! It's almost the most wonderful thing that's ever happened to me.'

'Almost?'

'The most wonderful was your marrying me, beloved,' he said, and she turned her head away so that he should not read what might lie in her eyes.

With part of her she longed for this child, rejoiced in the knowledge that it lay within her, mysterious, incomprehensible bone of their bone, flesh of their flesh. And yet – what would it do to her and with her life? It would hold her forever to Justin, to the Hollmeres, to this life she lived with them, with them but never really of them.

And would it be hers? Would anything about it be really hers? Would it not be from the very start, and throughout all its life, a Hollmere?

'May I tell my mother?' he asked. 'She's wanted it so much.'

'Alright,' she said indifferently, though she would have liked to keep it just hers and his for a little while longer.

Yes, Lady Hollmere would be glad. She would approve at last of the meatpacker's daughter, she thought resentfully. All through the three years of her marriage, she had been guarded, guided, taught, fenced-in by her husband's mother. Though she knew that it must have been galling to her to have Joe Joliman's daughter for her daughter-in-law, taking her very own name and her place, old Lady Hollmere had been scrupulously fair. Never for a moment had she shown that resentment, either in public or in private. Her attitude to the girl had been coldly correct, never in the least affectionate since she had no affection in her makeup.

But she had seen to it that the new Lady Hollmere paid to the full for the inestimable benefits of being elevated to that position.

'I think, Philippa, the orchid house should have attention, I have asked Routledges to call this morning to discuss what should be done. You will arrange to be present?' Or, 'I have been talking to Justin about the pedigree herd at Belton's Farm. The new strain he got after the deplorable attack of foot-and-mouth disease is not, I think, adequate. Perhaps we should get an expert down?' Or, 'The tapestries in the long drawing-room can, I think, be repaired again, but they should go to that firm in France, and meanwhile I should like you to look at some patterns with which Maple suggests the walls should be panelled so that the room can be used.'

Lady Hollmere always referred to a firm as if the actual or supposed head of it were at her personal service.

Philippa had been only too ready to fall in with these plans. After all, she had the money and it was like a physical hurt to her to see the lovely old house falling into ruins, and she spent money lavishly wherever it was needed, laughingly turning aside the occasional protests of Justin.

'It's my home, darling,' she would say gaily, 'and I don't like my curtains hanging in shreds or worms eating my chairs.'

'But other things then? You ought not to have bought that bull. Belton says you paid over three thousand for him.'

She chuckled, though actually the bull had been rather a sore point and she had yielded to Lady Hollmere's more than hints for the same reasons for which she yielded in everything else – for the sake of her pride, which would not allow her mother-in-law ever to be in a position to say that she, Philippa, had had the best of the 'bargain', which was how she knew Her Ladyship viewed her marriage with Justin.

'I know,' she said with that chuckle. 'It rather shook me! Fancy all that for a cow!'

'A cow indeed!'

'Oh well, same thing except for gender and I'm just as much scared of them all, whatever their sex.'

'Philippa, promise me something.'

'Depends what it is,' she said warily, though he never asked her for anything nor willingly let her incur any expense on behalf of the house or estate.

'Darling, please don't spend any more money on things like this bull, or on alterations or big repairs to the house or the farms or anything. They're my job.'

She slid an arm round his neck and laid her cheek against his.

'But I'm glad to do them,' she said. 'I'm always hoping that, in the end, I shall feel that I belong here, really belong.'

He gave her a startled look.

'But, beloved wife, of course you belong here. This is your home. You're its mistress. How can you talk of not belonging?'

Her eyes wore that inscrutable look that had not been in them before he married her.

'Silly, wasn't it? Of course it's my home. Of course I belong.'

That was just it, she thought on that day when she knew he had gone hurrying off to the Dower House to tell his mother of the coming child. That was just it. It was she who belonged to the Hollmeres, not they or the Abbey or even Justin to her.

She had been so right when she had wanted them to live in the Dower House and leave old Lady Hollmere in possession of the Abbey.

'It's such a cosy little house, Justin,' she had said when they went through it to decide on what must be done to make it suitable for occupation again. It had been requisitioned during the war and first troops and then foreign refugees had been housed in it. Now it was empty again and it had been simply assumed that when Justin was married, his mother would move into it. Lady Hollmere had shown no objection or resentment. She had accepted the situation as a matter of course. It was the thing that was 'done' and had been done from time immemorial.

'But, darling, it would never do,' said Justin. 'Of course we must live at the Abbey,' and when she had diffidently made the same suggestion to her future mother-in-law, again it had been brushed aside, this time with a cold glance of disapproval.

'Naturally, I shall move into the Dower House, Philippa,' she had said. 'No discussion of this is necessary,' and, of course, there had been none. That was the way things always were.

Philippa sat with her hands in her lap and thought of her child. If only she could have any hope that it would be allowed to be hers! But it would be a Hollmere and belong to the Hollmeres, body and soul. If it could be a girl, it might possibly seem to belong to her because the child, like herself, would be in disgrace as having transgressed the Hollmere law, which decreed that the first child must be a boy. Lady Hollmere herself had produced not just one boy, but three, and it was not her fault that only one had survived.

During the day, Lady Hollmere paid the expected visit and was graciously approving.

'Of course it is not usual in our position for three years to have elapsed between marriage and the birth of an heir and I must confess I was growing a little anxious,' she said, 'but now all is well. The child will, of course, be born here ...'

'I should prefer to go into a hospital,' said Philippa, greatly daring. 'I could have a private ward.'

'A hospital? My *dear* child,' said her ladyship, shocked beyond measure. 'That is all very well for the majority of people, but not for you. Why, there might even be some risk of mistake so that you would not get your own child!'

Philippa smiled a small, tight smile. What a shocking risk! What an awful thing if some other man's child, a man made of common clay and not of superfine Hollmere porcelain, should be elevated to the position of the Hollmere heir!

'I am quite sure that mistakes like that never happen nowadays in well-conducted hospitals,' she murmured.

'One hears of them. However, we need not discuss that. There can be no question whatever of the heir being born anywhere but here, though naturally you will have the best possible attention and one of the rooms can be properly equipped. I think Sir Adrian Fell should see you. He is the best gynaecologist, I believe. Ena can make an appointment with him. He will come here to see you, of course, and nearer the time I will arrange to have nurses and a doctor in attendance so that Sir Adrian can be kept exactly informed and will be here at the right time.'

Philippa had listened quietly, the smile deepening, veiled mockery in her eyes.

'I suppose it will be actually I who will have the child, Lady Hollmere?' she asked smoothly.

The older woman gave her a sharp glance.

'I don't understand you,' she said. 'You actually are with child?'

'Oh yes,' said Philippa, 'though it was only a quite ordinary doctor who told me so. *Sir Adrian Fell* may have a different opinion, of course.'

She had wanted to suggest, ironically, that in addition to all the other arrangements which would be made by her mother-in-law, Lady Hollmere might also arrange that she herself should do the bearing and production of the child, but she let it pass. Her ladyship had absolutely no sense of humour and would certainly consider any such ribald suggestion to be *lése-majesté*.

'I trust not,' said Lady Hollmere. 'You must, of course, be prepared to take every care of yourself now and not endanger the life of your son by behaving as so many young women do nowadays, rushing here and there and taking all sorts of risks.'

'I shall take care,' said Philippa evenly. 'After all, it is my child, Lady Hollmere – and it may not be a son.'

'Of course it will be,' retorted her ladyship. 'The firstborn of the Hollmeres is always a son,' and she sailed out, presumably to give Ena the necessary instructions to Sir Adrian Fell and to the Almighty.

Philippa's face relaxed into a grim smile.

She had heard that the sex of a child is determined at the very moment of its conception. In that case, if the determination had been so careless as to be female, she felt that the look and tone with which

Lady Hollmere had ordered it to be male would have the effect of changing it at once!

Justin came into the room and put an arm about her and drew her to him.

'My mother is very pleased about it,' he said.

'Yes,' said Philippa. 'She is making all the arrangements and has stated that it is to be a boy.'

He smiled and drew her more closely.

'Darling, try to be patient with her. She doesn't belong to this age and never will. She either can't or won't (I think it's "can't") accept the revolution. She feels that by shutting her eyes to it and pretending that it isn't going on, she can stop it as far as she is concerned. Try to be patient with her. She is actually very fond of you, you know.'

She smiled disbelievingly.

'Justin dear, you don't really think that, do you? She would never have let you marry me if she could have prevented it, and now that I know her so well, and know the Hollmeres and understand how things are here, I really marvel that you *did* marry me!'

'Nothing could have stopped me – only you, my love, and thank God you didn't stop me. Philippa, you've given me all the happiness I've ever had, and now you're giving me a child ...'

'That may not be a son, Justin.'

'I shall love your daughter just as much, and some day there will be a son. I'm not worrying. Darling, thank you, thank you. My whole life will not be long enough to show you how much I thank you and how much I love you. If only I were less—less ...'

She stopped him with her lips against his, caught by a sudden uprush of love for him, love and compassion and that intangible fear which always seemed intermingled with her love for him.

'I wouldn't have you any different, darling,' she said, and at such a moment she meant it.

'What's the matter with me?' she asked herself irritably. 'What more in the world could any woman want? I'm Lady Hollmere, I'm mistress of this wonderful place, I've got all the money anybody could possibly want, and my husband worships me, and I love him.'

Yet, for all that, that strange, secret fear persisted.

Chapter Five

'Well,' said Philippa, looking down at her son, who squirmed red-faced, angry, vociferous, his feet plunging about under the unaccustomed weight of the great mass of silk and lace in which countless other Hollmeres had been christened.

'Well,' said Philippa, 'so you've become George after all, have you? The Honourable George Trevor Justin Macaulay Breane. Poor mite. Poor little Honourable.'

The nurse, middle-aged, efficient, full of authority, rustled in. For just one moment Philippa and her son had been alone, but that state of affairs could not be allowed to continue. She was Lady Hollmere and downstairs she had guests, the gathering of the clans, as she had put it to Brownie, at yet another Hollmere celebration.

'Can't you get him out of all that clobber, poor chick?' she asked the nurse. 'He hates it.'

'He must put up with it for one day, My Lady,' said the nurse firmly. 'After all, it is an important occasion for him and he is an important person. He's never too young to learn that.'

'That's quite ridiculous, of course,' said Philippa icily. 'He is a perfectly ordinary baby and the occasion, as you call it, is only to please the grown-ups. Take those absurd clothes off him as soon as you can, please,' and she sailed out of the room, angry and yet half-amused.

Of course they would have their way with him just as they had it with her, and if he were to be cramped and squeezed and chipped to make him fit into the exact mould prepared for him, they might as well begin now, with those ridiculous robes of yellowed silk and exquisitely mended lace. Freedom to kick about was not for George Trevor Justin Macaulay Breane!

She had argued in vain against that George, but in the end had given way.

'The eldest son is always George,' said Lady Hollmere. 'It is only by tragic accident that the present Lord Hollmere's name is not George.'

'I don't like the name. I've always wanted to have a son named Trevor,' she insisted.

'It is not a Hollmere name,' said her ladyship calmly.

'Neither am I a Hollmere,' Philippa flung at her.

'I am well aware of that, my dear Philippa, especially at this moment,' was the icy reply as Lady Hollmere sailed regally out of the room.

And in the end he was George, though Philippa had announced it as her firm and unalterable intention that he was to be called Trevor.

She had known, of course, how it would be, and during the first few months of the child's life she came as near to despising her husband as she would ever be whilst one spark of love remained for him. Over this, as over nothing else, he showed his complete domination by his mother, and not even his adoring love for his wife had power to conquer that domination.

'I don't want to keep Cooper,' Philippa told her husband. 'She is old-fashioned and disagreeable, and I'm sure she's bad-tempered.'

'My dear, she is very efficient. She has the very highest credentials. My mother made sure of that before engaging her.'

'Do her credentials say anything about being loving and kind?' she demanded.

'Darling, as if she would be anything but kind to a small baby!'

'I don't suggest she beats him or starves him or anything like that, but she doesn't love him, and a baby needs to be loved.'

'Well, we love him, darling.'

'When we're allowed to! I'm not even allowed to pick up my own baby and cuddle him. It's never the proper time for him to be picked up, and I'm perfectly certain I could have fed him if I had been allowed to try. I suppose it was your mother who decided it would be unwise to risk polluting a Hollmere with milk from a Joliman?'

'My sweet, that's rather—an unpleasant thing to say.'

'Vulgar, you mean? Well, what if it is? I've never become one of your family, Justin. I'm still what I was born, a child of the people, and I'm none the worse for that – and I've produced something quite worthwhile! Darling, don't let's get angry with each other and quarrel, but please send that woman away and let me get a nurse that will love my baby and let me love him.'

'Well—of course—if you really do feel strongly about it, dear ...'

I do,' she said, and sailed off and gave the nurse a month's wages and sent her off then and there and triumphantly left Brownie in charge of her son until she could replace the trained nurse.

The gods seemed always to work against her when she tried to assert herself or claim her rights. Two mornings later the baby was taken ill, was obviously so ill that the doctor sent to London for two nurses, having diagnosed a mild attack of polio.

Philippa was frantic and refused to be consoled or reassured.

'I suppose if Cooper had stayed, this would not have happened,' she raged, though her common sense, as well as her husband and the doctor, told her that once the germ had taken hold, nothing could have stayed its course.

The child recovered and no trace of the disease was left, but the spirit had gone out of Philippa and when Lady Hollmere, with no more than a pretence at asking her opinion, installed another nurse of Cooper's type in the nursery, she made no comment.

Justin watched her anxiously, realising the change in her wrought by the baby's illness. Whereas before she had seized every opportunity of going to the nursery, of picking up and cuddling the child whenever the nurse's back was turned, now she seemed afraid to touch him, almost to go near him. She would stand looking down at him, smiling perhaps but not attempting to take him, and when the tiny arms started to stretch out towards a human being, it was to the nurse or to the devoted Brownie, never to his mother.

'You love him, Philippa, don't you?' asked Justin once, when the nurse had offered the child to her and she had shaken her head.

'Of course I do.'

'Then why don't you want to hold him anymore?'

They had drawn aside into the window embrasure, and the nurse, attending to the baby, was out of earshot.

'I don't want to make him too much mine,' she said in an expressionless voice.

'But, darling, he is yours.'

'Is he?' she asked enigmatically and turned away and went out of the nursery without another look at the cooing child.

She ached for him with all her body and heart. Such dreams and plans had gone into the making of him. She had been happier during her pregnancy than at any other time in her life. Even the pains of her labour had been more bearable because she suffered them for him, to give him life, to have him in her arms rather than in the secret shelter of her womb. When she saw him, the perfect little body, the tiny, exquisite hands and feet, the lolling, downy head, the vacant baby stare at nothing, her joy in him was almost pain. Hers. Her own. Brought forth from her body. A living part of her that could never be other than a part of her.

And then gradually they had taken him away from her, and her one attempt to snatch him back had been followed by such terrible disaster that, in the ensuing panic, she had surrendered him. And now she could not bear to try to take him back because he would never be allowed to be hers.

She had become very quiet, moving about on unhurried feet where formerly she had always been dashing from one place to another, from one interest to another. She took long walks, alone except for the dogs, and never had anything to talk about when she came back.

When the baby was six months old, and there was no apparent change in this attitude of Philippa's, Justin came rather hesitatingly into her room for the first time since she had told him she was pregnant, now nearly fifteen months ago.

'Do you mind, darling?' he asked, tapping first at her door. 'I'd like to talk to you and somehow we never get the chance, do we?'

To some extent it was true, for he was a hard worker and kept very busy during long days, acting as his own agent and keeping the whole of the large estate under his personal supervision. If Philippa had spent large sums of money in repairs and renewals, in replacing poor stock by pedigree herds, in installing the latest modern farm and forestry machinery, in employing good, knowledgeable men in addition to the local farm-hands, Justin had made that expenditure worthwhile, getting every ounce and every shilling possible out of the land. Instead of being a derelict and moribund area of waterlogged fields, or acreage being ruined by lack of irrigation, with tumbledown barns and unproductive cattle, everything was flourishing, and for the first time for many years the estate could support itself and pay a reasonable profit.

Philippa knew, and appreciated, that Justin was giving all his time and his energies to justifying her expenditure, and though at one time she had complained that unless she trailed round the fields and woods after him she never saw him, latterly she had felt his busyness almost a relief.

'I know, dear,' she said calmly. 'Not working too hard, are you? You seem to do two people's work all the time.'

'Well, isn't it the least I can do to show you how much I appreciate all you've done for me – and for Hollmere?' he asked, and she realised he was as much embarrassed as she.

She smiled. It was an absurd position.

'Anyway, come in,' she said, for he had remained in the doorway between their two rooms, the door never locked against him but not opened now for so long. 'What is it?' she asked, sitting down on the padded seat that ran round the wide window embrasure and inviting him with a gesture to do the same.

But he remained standing, looking down at her and thinking, with a catch at his heart, how lovely she was, lovely with the new, more restful loveliness that had come with the birth of her child, though restfulness was a strange quality to ascribe to Philippa.

'I've been wondering, dearest, about you,' he said. 'You've not been away for so long. I've kept you tied here except for the odd weekends we've taken, or the fortnight you spent with your parents before Trevor was born. That's a long time ago now. I've been wondering whether you'd like to go again, either to them, or perhaps away with your mother – or some of your friends …'

He kept his eyes from her as he spoke, and she knew that what he meant to offer her was temporary release from the Abbey and from his mother, whose domination since the birth of the heir was supreme.

'You mean not with you, Justin?' she asked doubtfully.

'I couldn't get away just now, or for some time,' he said. 'We're busy with those new reaper-binders for one thing, and as you know, when that's finished there are the hops, and we've got a heavy crop in the two new fields. I'm afraid it sounds as if you'd married a farmer, but that's what it's really come to. It's our only means of keeping our estates and the only justification for having them.'

She was silent for a little while, looking out through the open window over the lands that belonged to Justin, or, as he preferred to put it, the lands that were lent to him for his lifetime and then would be lent to his son. She had been able to understand, without actually sharing, his deep love for the Abbey, a reverence for the very soil itself and the carking grief it had been to him to watch it disintegrate, starved and impoverished, until, with his marriage to her, he had been able to bring back life and vigour.

It had all been so well worthwhile to him, but what had it been for her? It was difficult even to remember now what she had been like four years ago when, as Philippa Joliman, she had seen life as a grand and gay adventure, had married Justin with so few real misgivings because she had loved him.

Had loved him?

That question had beaten at the doors of her mind for months now, even before the birth of her child. Did she still love Justin or had the love she had had for him been satisfied and ended when her womanhood had been completed by motherhood? She knew that her feeling for him had undergone a change, that whereas her body had felt full of eager vitality, or lightness, of desire to love and be loved, now it was quiescent, not only content that he should leave her alone at night but gradually becoming apprehensive lest he should not do so.

She told herself that, to be at all consistent and reasonable, she should be glad that it was so. On more than one occasion when her young married friends had discussed married life with the frankness of their generation, she had heard wives say that their whole sex desire had gone after the birth of their children, and that the importunity of their husbands had become a nuisance, something to be tolerated when it could not be avoided on pleas of tiredness, headache or some other excuse. Well, if that was how it was with her, she ought to be thankful. She certainly ought not to have within her a sense of loss.

And now that Justin was offering her a holiday away from him, she would miss the friendship established between them, would miss his affectionate care for her, his thoughtfulness which always put her and her wishes first, his many little acts of selfless kindness – and yet to some extent it would be a relief to be away from him for a little while.

She hoped that nothing of this showed in her face or her voice as she replied to him: 'You wouldn't mind that, Justin? You wouldn't feel that I was deserting you if I did go away for a few weeks?'

'Dearest, of course not, though I need hardly say that I shall miss you badly and look forward to your return. Have you anything in mind or have I sprung it on you too suddenly?'

She hesitated.

'Nothing really—except—would you think it very strange if I went away alone?'

'Really alone? But, darling, would that be good for you? You need cheering up, to be with your friends or your people. You always say that your father is your best tonic.'

'I know, but I have a feeling that's hard to describe. Are you going to tell me that it isn't done for Lady Hollmere to go off on her own?' with a mocking note in her voice.

He smiled. One of the most likeable things about Justin, to her mind, was that he had conquered his original dislike of her light way of referring to his title and family, and now he could even share her little jokes about them, since they were not malicious.

'Well, of course it isn't done, my dear,' he said, his kind eyes crinkling in the way they had, 'but perhaps we need not tell anyone?'

She knew that by 'anyone' he meant his mother, and she nodded, some of the old mischief coming back for an instant to her face.

'I need not even go as Lady Hollmere,' she said. 'Perhaps that would be best, though as I'd rather like to go to France, my passport would be the difficulty.'

'Why to France? Paris, you mean?'

'Heavens, no! I wonder why to so many people France means only Paris? At the end of the war, after V.E. Day, we had to go over for something or other, and it meant waiting a couple of days, so we were given leave and two or three of us found an enchanting little place. What was it called? Something *sur mer*. Bonami? Bonavie? I believe that was it, but I could find it again, not far from St. Malo. Bonavie. I think it was that, but it wouldn't be on any map!'

'And that's really the sort of place you'd like to go to? And alone?' he asked with a frown of perplexity. He would never understand her, however much or however long he loved her.

'I think so. Would you let me?'

'*Let* you? We agreed once we'd never use that word to each other, sweetheart. Naturally I'd rather feel you were somewhere a bit gayer, able to feel sure you were having a good time and not feeling lonely, but if that's what you really want to do – well, at least you know your way home if it doesn't turn out to be quite what you expected.'

She closed her mind to his disappointment, to the knowledge that he would miss her intolerably. Once she had decided to go, she could not get away quickly enough, and he kept his word in not letting his mother, or anyone else, know where she was going. It was assumed that she was going to stay with friends, and so long as she left Trevor behind, old Lady Hollmere did not appear to be greatly interested.

On the day before she left, she ran into Susan Therne – still Susan Therne though her name had been linked with more than one of the eligible young men of their circle. There had never been any intimacy between the two girls, neither had there been any open or expressed enmity. Since it was clear from the first that Susan was of her immediate circle and could not be avoided, Philippa had accepted the position and merely avoided Susan when it could be done without causing comment. She had discovered very early in her marriage that

Susan had meant to marry Anthony Breane and had then transferred her affections and intentions to Justin, but the discovery had merely amused her.

Poor Susan! What a pity there had been no more of them left for her!

Now, meeting her as she came up the drive towards the house, Philippa could not do otherwise than stop to greet her.

'Hullo, Susan. Were you coming to call? Because I wasn't going anywhere particularly, only down to Belton's Farm to see if Justin is there. I've got a message for him, but it can wait,' and she turned to walk back to the house.

'It's really Ena I want to see,' said Susan amicably, 'but it, too, can wait. I hear you're going away.'

'Yes. Tomorrow.'

'On your own?'

'Without either husband or son, yes,' said Philippa lightly.

'The independent Lady Hollmere. What has Mamma to say to that?'

'It is hardly anybody else's affair, is it? By the way, didn't your cousin say she would like some cuttings of that blue thing that did so well in the centre beds? I asked Groom at the time, but I'll remind him. I should say it's nearly time to take them.'

Susan, left alone some few years earlier through the death of her widowed mother, had an elderly cousin living with her at the far end of the village.

'Thank you. I don't expect he's forgotten. He's like everything else at Hollmere – completely adequate and to be relied upon to do the right thing in any circumstance.'

The little speech was barbed, Philippa knew.

She smiled sweetly.

'Isn't that a relief?' she asked. 'You know where you are with people who can always be relied upon to run true to form.'

'You didn't, did you?' asked Susan spitefully.

'When? When I married Justin, do you mean? Did you know my form?'

The other girl shrugged her shoulders.

'Wasn't it obvious?' she asked.

Philippa laughed.

Well, don't let's quarrel. We've managed so far, and after all, what is there for us to quarrel about? We've both grown up. There's Groom now, weeding the path or something. We can ask him about those blue things,' and she walked towards the stooping figure with the poise and dignity which the four years of being mistress of Hollmere Abbey had given her. As she had said, they had grown up.

Susan followed her, angrily aware of what in her heart she had always recognised – Philippa's courage and self-respect which had always, even as a miserable small girl at school, kept her from doing mean or spiteful things such as Susan and her cronies did not despise.

But the slight prick of the meeting was not sufficient to pierce Philippa's bubble of joy, not joy at getting away or of leaving Justin so much as joy at the thought of being herself again for a short while, herself untrammelled by Hollmere Abbey and having to be at all times and in all circumstances Lady Hollmere.

Though Justin had wanted to make all sorts of reservations for her, a seat on the train to London, another to Southampton, a private cabin on the cross-channel steamer, to contact Cook's so as to make sure someone would meet the boat and see to her accommodation, she refused gaily.

'Just let me take pot luck,' she said. 'I'll be alright. As for the channel crossing, don't forget that I, too, have been a mariner. I'll keep you posted as to where I am and what I'm doing, if anything.'

When she called in at The Beeches to say goodbye to her parents, her mother viewed the affair with misgiving.

'I know I'm old-fashioned, dear,' she said, 'but somehow it doesn't seem quite right for you to be going off like that to a foreign country without your husband. It isn't as if he had to work either and couldn't take a holiday when he likes.'

Philippa laughed.

'Oh, Mum, if he heard you say he doesn't have to work! He works harder than any other man I know, and as for taking a holiday – I don't know when he'll ever be able to leave the estate. I've got quite different ideas about being a landed proprietor from what I used to have. Justin simply *has* to work.'

'Then it's your place to stay beside him, my dear,' said her mother. 'Can you imagine me ever leaving your dad all these years? I wouldn't trust another living soul to see that his shirts are aired and that he doesn't go to some important meeting with holes in his heels. Besides, there's your baby. How about leaving him, the precious lamb, and only six months old?'

He isn't my baby,' said Philippa bitterly.

'Not yours? Then I'd like to know who carried him all those nine months!'

Oh, I had him alright, but—you see, Mum dear, they do things differently in families like the Hollmeres. There's a nurse, a very capable woman, and she knows much more about babies than I could possibly do …'

'Don't bother yourself to go on, Philippa. I can see that you've changed a lot since you became so grand, though I never thought when you turned into Lady Hollmere that it meant you'd have no proper thought for your husband and child.'

Philippa was silent. It was so unusual for her to be at variance with her mother and yet she knew that she could not hope to make her see with the eyes of her mind and realise that in her own home she was a mere figurehead, a cypher without value or meaning. Also, there was that knowledge that she had indeed changed, that something had gone from her, making her feel quite a different person from the girl who had loved and married Justin.

'Is Daddy going to be late?' she asked after a pause.

'I expect so. He often is these days, with all the labour troubles and the men always wanting more and more money, and petrol and railway rates going up and the taxes so heavy. He can't seem to make them understand that if they force prices up, it's them as has to pay them, and the profits now are cut down to the lowest they can be to keep the factory running. I'm worried about yer dad, Phil. He isn't hisself. He's not been hisself these last months at all.'

Philippa's heart missed a beat.

'You don't mean he's ill?' she asked.

'Not what you might say ill, but not hisself. Now mind. Phil, not a word to him about you going off to France without Justin. If you don't tell him different, naturally he'll think you're both going and I won't have him worried by thinking as you're not.'

'But he'll know Justin hasn't gone,' objected Philippa.

'Let that be as may. If he gets to know before you come back, I'll have to think up something, but maybe, as they're both so busy, he won't know.'

Philippa left with the feeling that she was committing a crime by going away without her husband, but in what way could it be wrong? Justin himself had suggested her going, and heaven knew that nobody and nothing else at Hollmere needed her presence!

Chapter Six

'Fee-leep! Fee-leep!'

Philippa laughed and put her head out as far as it would go in the odd-shaped frame of her window.

'*Tiens! Qu'est ce que c'est que cela?*' she called to the group of urchins in the street below.

"*Le moteur! Ca ne passe pas!*"

'*Taisez-vous! Je suis fatiguee, moi!*'

They laughed up at her. When was Feeleep ever too tired to mess about with their motorboat and eventually make it go again, no matter what went wrong with it?

'Oh Fee-leep,' they besought her.

'Oh—alright. I suppose I'd better. I'll be down in two shakes of a lamb's tail,' she called to them in English, and though they did not understand the words, they were satisfied and repaired to the shore again to consider the question of the ramshackle motor attached, more or less, to their dilapidated boat.

The man who had watched her for several days from the window of the tiny *estaminet* opposite, or from the rocks on which he lazed whenever the sun shone, waited with interest for her to reappear and then strolled after her, his hands in the pockets of his disreputable khaki shorts, his lips pursed to emit a low, tuneless whistling.

Perched on the edge of one of the boats, he watched her as she undid screws and nuts, cleaned this part with a dirty rag, put a spot of oil on another part, hunted through a box of every kind of oddment to find what she wanted, meanwhile chattering away to the little knot of boys in French that was more fluent than correct, making them laugh when she searched her mind for the word and substituted one which she decided would meet the case, interspersing her French with scraps of good, round English and not a few 'damns'.

Either she did not know Fergus Wynton was watching her, or she chose deliberately to ignore him, for she did not turn her head in his direction once, even though his tuneless whistling still went on.

At last came the great moment when, the antique outboard motor put together again, the last bit of wire in place, she gave it to the boys to set into position in the boat whilst she herself scrambled in ready to secure it.

'*Prenez garde!*' she cried. '*Tenez ferme!* Hold it, you chumps! Louis, *cherchez là!* Now—careful—careful! *C'est ça! Le grand* moment has arrived. I pull the what's name and—*voilà!* She goes!'

'She goes! She goes!' they chanted after her as the engine roared into life and there was a wild flurry and confusion to get the boat pushed out far enough for the loose shingle not to foul the propeller.

Hatless, in short-sleeved white sweater over her workmanlike blue slacks, she sat on the side of the boat manipulating the motor and giving its fastenings a few more turns for security, laughing and talking to the pleased, excited boys, her voice with its enchanting mixture of bad French and good English coming clearly over the water to the watching man.

Who was she? What was she doing alone here? Where was the husband whose ring she wore? What was he doing to let anyone like her be alone like this? Or did he no longer exist?

He had been wondering about her for three days, ever since he had decided to move off from this one-horse place and, at sight of her, had decided to give it another chance. It intrigued him that she kept him wondering, that never for a moment had she appeared to be conscious of him, and his tentative inquiries of old Gaston who kept the *estaminet* had elicited nothing but the obvious fact that she was l'Anglaise', the Englishwoman.

She was staying in the crazy little cottage which, with its upper storeys jutting out over its lower, seemed ready at any moment to topple head first into the tiny harbour. His attempts to scrape acquaintance with the old fisherman and his wife who lived there, and must have let her the room, were just as fruitless as his questions to

Gaston. With a characteristic French shrug, they had indicated that who she was was her own business, and neither his nor theirs. She was l'Anglaise' and the only other thing he had found out about her was that she answered to the children's cries of 'Fee-leep' and was extremely knowledgeable about marine motors.

She had hired a small launch, a neat workmanlike little boat with an inboard motor, and she seemed perfectly contented to spend her days cruising about the little bay, either alone or with one or more of the small boys who followed her like faithful dogs. When she wanted to bathe, she shooed them off and went alone, anchored some distance out, stripped off her slacks and sweater to the swimsuit she wore beneath them, had her swim, climbed back into the boat (no mean feat, as he knew from experience) and lay on the tiny deck in the sun to dry.

In the evening, she was not to be seen, but the light in the window of her room suggested that she was there, again content to be alone, sublimely indifferent to whatever attempts he had made in the day to establish contact with her.

Philippa had been by no means unconscious of his presence. She could scarcely have remained in ignorance of it from the mere fact that he was the only other foreign visitor; was, in fact, the only other person in Bonavie who did not live there.

She had seen him soon after her arrival. The proprietor of the hotel where she had stayed for a few days at Dinan had sent her to the Laurents, since, to his incredulous dismay, she had insisted on going to Bonavie, and Marie and her fisher husband had accepted her as a gift from le bon Dieu just when their pig had died and they badly needed some money with which to buy another.

They asked no questions, did not try to master Philippa's name when she gave it as 'Mrs. Breane' but were content to call her 'Madame' and refer to her as l'Anglaise'.

The tiny room they gave her was spotlessly clean, its ceiling so low that had she been a couple of inches taller she would have had to stoop, its one window so much misshapen by the years and the many repairs necessitated by winter storms that it was now almost triangular, and, sitting by it, she could feel she was on a ship at sea, so far did it hang out over the water.

From this window she had seen Fergus Wynton, big, muscular, his reddish-bronze hair tousled, his legs bare below the tattered shorts, his great sunburnt arms helping to haul in the nets which had been set for a shore-catch of mackerel, his white teeth gleaming in his brown face as he called some chaffing remark to one of the fishermen.

'Is he a visitor?' she asked Marie unthinkingly.

'*Oui. Anglais. N'importe!*' and with that and a shrug, Marie had dismissed him.

Philippa was not quite sure what prompted her to snub his first advances, except that she felt he was too ready with them, and she still had that longing to be alone, to find herself again, to shift from her shoulders the heavy burden of being Lady Hollmere and of belonging to everything that was Hollmere. The children had discovered her – or rather, she had discovered them. She had hired her little motorboat, *La Colombe*, from St. Malo and on her first trip out on the bay she had come upon their dinghy, drifting with a broken-down motor and without oars.

She had not only taken them in tow and brought them safely back to the little sandy beach, but, to their admiration and delight, she had revealed a workmanlike knowledge of engines and had soon got theirs going again, careless of what the job did to her white linen suit and her immaculately kept hands.

When they asked her how she knew so much about boats and their motors, she laughed and told them she had been in the navy, at which they laughed uproariously, for even they knew that British sailors were men!

On his third day, Fergus Wynton felt it was time for him either to make her acquaintance or to push on. He had a small cabin-cruiser, just a one-man job sturdy enough for sea-going, and he slept on it, coming ashore for his meals at Gaston's *estaminet*. The *Sea-dog* drew too much water to be conveniently hauled up, so he kept her anchored and used a little cockle-shell dinghy which almost disappeared under his weight and bulk but which got him to and from shore in a tolerably dry condition.

When Philippa came back in the boys' dinghy, which was now behaving admirably, Fergus was crouching in the little cockpit of the *Sea-dog* and, apparently by chance, happened to pull himself upright just as the noisy outboard chuffed and clanked past. His brow was furrowed with anxious thought, and in his hands was some detached part of his engine.

The boys edged their boat farther away, eyeing him distrustfully. He had made several attempts to get them to talk about their English friend, and they did not intend either to lose her to him, or to be obliged to share her.

'I say!' yelled Fergus through his cupped hands, and then translated it into its French counterpart, following it by a fluent exposition of some trouble he was in.

They looked at one another and then at Philippa.

'*Quest ce qu'il a dit?*' she asked them, and they told her in the slow, careful simple French they used so successfully with her that he was having some sort of trouble with his engine and wanted to know if they could lend him a spanner.

'Have we got one?' she asked them. '*Quelle sorte de clef a levier?*'

They shrugged their shoulders, were inclined to refuse, and then gave in and, collecting their miscellaneous assortment of tools, steered their boat towards the *Sea-dog* and in silence handed them over.

'*Mille remerciements,*' said Fergus, and then, turning the tools over one by one, spoke directly to Philippa, who sat at the far end of the dinghy and said nothing.

'I say, do you know anything about these things? These small marine engines, I mean? I watched you doing a wonderful job on the outboard a little while ago.'

'Is it your launch?' asked Philippa calmly.

'Oh yes, only an old thing but it's fun having her.' 'Rather dangerous not to know about the engine, isn't it?' she asked in the same cool way, though beneath her half-lowered lashes there was a spark of fun in her eyes. She knew quite well that he did not need help from her or anyone, and that the spanner had only been an excuse.

'Yes – but I rather like a bit of danger,' he said, trying to get nearer to her than the position of the boats would allow.

'Well, you're quite likely to be pleased then, if you try to put that plug back with a spanner,' she said. 'We'll leave you the spanners, anyway, and you can return them to the boys when you've done with them. *Allons, mes braves!'* and, by no means unwilling, the boys, set their dinghy racing for the shore again.

She rather expected that he would try to intercept her again, perfectly well aware that he had invited the need for a spanner, but she did not see anything more of him until, cruising lazily about late in the afternoon in her own boat, she was hailed by another some distance away. She guessed, even without looking, that it was the *Seadog* and she chuckled, hesitated for a moment and heard him hail her again.

'Ahoy there! Ship ahoy! *La Colombe* ahoy!'

And with the laughter flecking her eyes, she cupped her hands and returned the greeting.

'Ahoy yourself!' she called, and was setting her helm over to put more distance between them when he called again.

'Ahoy! Shipwrecked mariner seeking aid!'

The words came clearly over the water and she could see in her mind the look there would be on his face, bold, laughing, impertinent without being offensive. She hesitated and then gave a little defiant lift of her shoulders and swung her boat round, chugging off towards him without hurrying.

He was sitting in his disreputable shorts and an open-necked, sleeveless jersey on the deck, his brown legs spread out, his strong big hands pressed down at either side to support him. His eyes, which might have been bits picked out of blue sky or blue sea and set in his brown face, square-jawed and rugged, looked at her with such lazy impudence as she drew alongside that she resisted the impulse to go back only because she knew his ironic laughter would follow her. Of what was she afraid? She could not have told even herself. Whatever it was, she knew she was not going to run away from it.

'Anything wrong?' she asked as casually as she could.

He lay face downward and stretched out a hand to catch the nose of her boat and slide the two craft gently together, holding them there.

'Come aboard, shipmate,' he said, and gay impudence was in his voice as well. 'I'm becalmed and waiting for a following wind to belly out me sails, bejabbers.'

She sat where she was, the slight sea making the two boats rise and fall gently together. She was sorry that she was obliged to look up at him. It gave him an additional advantage, and she tried to look and sound severe.

'If all you want is a spanner again, I haven't got one,' she said primly.

'I wouldn't be after knowin' if 'twas a spanner or what else, mavourneen,' he said in an execrable imitation of Irish brogue, and she was not proof against it, nor against his merry blue eyes and the engaging ugliness of his brown face, if one could think of ugliness where there was such strength and humour and laughter.

She remained where she was, looking up at him.

'Have you really broken down?' she asked doubtfully.

'Sure and isn't it meself that's pl'ading with yer to come and take a look, alannah?' he said insinuatingly, holding the boat with one hand and offering her the other.

She looked at it almost furtively, strong, brown, square fingered, a capable, workmanlike hand that could almost certainly do as much to the motor-engine of his own boat as she could do.

'I expect your breakdown is as phoney as your Irish accent,' she said severely. 'I'm not deceived.'

'I wouldn't deceive you for the world, beautiful,' he said, dropping his 'Irish' brogue, and suddenly his face became quite serious and all the banter went from his voice. He leaned nearer to her. 'You're quite the most beautiful thing I have ever seen, Philippa.'

She was startled.

'How do you know my name?' she asked.

'So I was right. It is Philippa. It was the only name I could get out of the eternal "Feeleep" which the children call you. Please come aboard, won't you?'

'I—no. No, of course not,' she said and looked away from the open admiration of his eyes, but her voice did not convey the intention of her words and he did not release his hold on her boat.

'Please. There really is something wrong with my engine, you know. You wouldn't leave me to drift here all night, waterless, foodless, hopeless, at the mercy of anything that might run into me in the dark? I'm not carrying riding-lights, as you can see.'

Face and voice were persuasive and she did not know for certain whether he had broken down or not, nor whether he could do the necessary repair if he had.

'I won't come aboard, but I'll tow you,' she said,

'All that way?' he asked, indicating the shore. 'Wouldn't it be better to tow me as far as the island, where I can land if necessary and perhaps get help if you remain so hard-hearted?'

'What island?' she asked.

'Don't you know the *Ile des Pirates*?' he asked. 'Haven't you been as far as that? It's just the other side of the point,' indicating the long narrow arm of land, rocky and barren, which formed one arm of the sheltered bay.

'I didn't know there was anything round there where one could land,' she said, eyeing the point doubtfully. 'Is it safe? Do you know how near one can go without running on the rocks?' for some distance out into the sea from the point itself there were little fountains and crests of water indicating rocks just beneath the surface.

'There's a safe channel. I know it quite well,' he said. 'May I come into your boat as pilot? I'll throw you a painter and you can make it fast while I up-anchor,' and without waiting for her to agree, he made his way with the quick, sure steps of the experienced sailor to the neatly coiled rope at the bow.

'Catch!' he called to her and she caught the rope neatly and made it fast to the stern with the correct naval knot, aware that her spirits were rising and that she was ready for this amusing end to her solitude.

He pulled up his anchor, hauled his boat nearer and jumped across the remaining distance, his weight rocking her smaller boat so that she laughed, reached her hands out automatically to save herself from falling and found them gripped strongly by his for a brief moment. Then he released her and went forward nonchalantly to the tiny cockpit in which there was only just room for the two of them close together.

'All set?' he asked her and started up the engine without any of the fumbling of the novice he tried to make himself out to be.

'I knew you were a fraud,' she said, as he handled the boat expertly.

'Oh, it's the repairs that get me down,' he said blithely, and though he did not glance at her as he sent the two boats scudding towards the point, she knew that he was as acutely aware of her as she was of him. Watching him covertly, she thought she had never seen anyone so vital, so intensely keyed-up to the joy of merely being alive. Energy and force seemed to flow from him in every movement. He held his head back so that the wind blew through his thick hair that was neither brown nor red nor gold but a blend of the three of them. Sitting close to him, she lifted her own face to let the salty spray prick it with a million tiny points, and when he increased the speed of the boat, she laughed.

For a moment he let himself look at her.

'I told you just now how beautiful you were, didn't I?' he asked, and then, in the same breath, 'but of course that's absurd. Nobody could tell you that. There aren't any words. Isn't this grand? Don't you love to feel the salt on your face and on your lips and the wind in your hair?' turning the course of his speech without an alteration of tone or any break.

She caught her breath sharply and turned away from him.

'Yes,' she said. 'It's wonderful. I'm so sorry for people who don't like the sea.'

'Are you an ocean traveller?'

'Unfortunately no. During the war one couldn't, of course, though—I was sometimes lucky even then.'

'You got about?'

She laughed.

'You know the song: "I Joined the Navy to see the World"?'

He grinned and started to sing it.

'I joined the navy to see the world.'

'And what did I see?' sang Philippa.

'*I saw the sea!*' they both sang together, and went on singing at the top of their voices, the boat scudding across the water throwing up spray, the *Sea-dog* following faithfully at the end of the rope, ahead of them the point with the frothing water warning them of the treachery beneath.

'*I saw the Atlantic and the Pacific*
But the Pacific isn't terrific
And the Atlantic isn't what it's cracked up to be!
We joined the navy to do or die.
But we didn't do – and we didn't die?' they sang.

Philippa chuckled.

'We are likely to correct that any minute now,' she said, as he appeared to steer straight for the submerged rocks, the waves swirling and hissing about them. Strangely, she felt no fear, no apprehension. Everything seemed unreal, the figment of a dream, she herself unmaterial, immune from harm.

'Have no fear, lady. Trust your pilot.'

For a brief moment their glances met again and then parted.

'I do,' she said, and he nodded and neither of them seemed inclined to go on with their singing but sat close together, his big hands comfortably at ease on the wheel, the boat answering to his light pressure as it turned this way and that amongst the surging waters and finally came out, the *Sea-dog* still following safely at the other side of the point.

Philippa exclaimed in surprise and pleasure.

'Why, it really is an island,' she said. 'Fancy my never having come round here to find it!' for only a few hundred yards ahead of them it lay, tiny and rock-girt, but with trees growing down to the water's edge and, just discernible behind them, the corner of a roof.

'Better not come without me,' he said calmly, 'but if you do, don't come through the rocks. Get farther out beyond the buoys. I come this way because it leads direct to the only place where you can land. There's the last remnant of a hard here, and the water's deep enough to take my *Sea-dog*. I'll land and make yours fast this side and then pull mine round to the other side,' and he shut off the engine at precisely the right moment to let *La Colombe* lie easily alongside the battered concrete of what had once been a hard, and sprang ashore.

Philippa followed without waiting for his help, left him to tie up the boats and made her way along what was left of the concrete pier till she was on the tiny sandy beach. It ended in a sheer precipice of rock on the top of which were the trees which had seemed, from the sea, to be growing to the edge of the water. Whilst she was looking for the best place for climbing up, she heard him come behind her, his feet in their old canvas shoes crunching the shingly sand.

'Want to explore or shall we bathe first?' he asked her.

'Bathe? Here?'

He smiled at her surprised face.

'Do you know anywhere better?' he asked. 'Got any rig with you? Or on you?' with a sly grin which told her, as he meant it to do, that he knew her habits.

'Alright,' she said recklessly. 'Let's,' and she looked about her, pulled off her jersey and slacks and stood up, firm and straight and beautiful in the tightly fitting black satin, tailored and workmanlike, which he had already admired from a distance.

She did not speak or wait, but ran across the beach and straight into the water, not stopping until it was deep enough for her to swim. She was conscious of exhilaration, new and vital, aware of her youth and her perfect health and vigour, her mind accepting nothing but that knowledge, nothing of past or future, only the magic of the present.

He joined her quickly and swam, as she had known he would, with power and skill, his strong limbs taking his magnificent body through the water as if born to it as its natural element, though, coming abreast of her, he slowed down to accommodate his speed to hers and they swam together, the late afternoon sun slanting down into their eyes, the water icy cold but invigorating.

'Had enough?' he asked when she turned and swam towards the shore, but she did not reply. She had turned as a defiance of the strange impulse she had had of going on and on, out into the path of the sun, to swim on and never return to the life that was waiting for her on land.

She swam to *La Colombe* to get a towel, and then lay on the sun-warmed beach, her hair damp and curling tightly, one hand shading her eyes, the other idly sifting sand through its fingers. He lay a little way from her, burningly aware of her, aware that in the short time he had known of her mere existence, she had come into the place which had waited, empty, for the twenty-seven years of his reckless, irresponsible life.

Philippa. Gloriana. Who called who Gloriana? he thought with a dim memory of something heard, or read, at school.

He asked the question aloud.

'Who called who Gloriana?' he asked.

She smiled without moving her head or her lovely, supine body.

'Shakespeare? Elizabeth? Or if not Shakespeare, one of those,' she said hazily. 'Why?'

'I thought perhaps it would be nice to call you Gloriana,' he said.

'I should dislike that very much.'

'You don't mind Philippa, then?'

'Well, it's my name.'

'Are you going to call me by mine?'

'I might. What is it?'

'Fergus.'

'Scotch?'

'Originally, but I was born in London.'

She said nothing and soon he spoke again.

'Aren't you at least going to ask me what I'm doing in Bonavie, so far from home?'

'No, I wasn't going to,' she told him indifferently.

'H'm. Disappointing. Don't you mind?'

'Not particularly,' she said, but he was looking at her and saw the tiny smile that belied her words.

He raised himself to rest on one elbow.

'Did I mention that you're extremely beautiful, Philippa?' he asked in a conversational tone.

'You did. Yes,' she said.

'Was it astounding news to you?'

'Oh, people have mentioned it before,' she told him casually.

'Are you pleased?'

'That I'm nice to look at and have all my bulges in the right place? Oh yes, I'm quite pleased. Why?'

'You should be astoundingly grateful to providence, which, or who, has so endowed you that you make light the heart of man when he beholds you.'

She chuckled.

'I'm going to get dressed before you get any more involved and biblical,' she said.

'I'm not feeling a bit biblical.'

'All the same, I'm going to get dressed,' and she went to the rocks where she had left her clothes and pulled her slacks and jersey over her wet swim-suit.

When she came back to him, having taken an unnecessarily long time combing the tangles out of her hair, she found him dressed.

'You should have got dry first,' he said. 'You've still got your wet swim-suit on, I suppose?'

She nodded.

'It doesn't matter,' she said. 'I often do it when I haven't time to get my suit dry.'

He caught her hand and held it.

You had all the time in the world, Philippa,' he said.

She would not meet his eyes. The old remembered thrill was in her body, inflaming her, making her tremble and want both to stay and run away. Only now she knew she must not stay.

Yet she let her hand remain his. He swung it gently to and fro and then lifted it and looked at her wedding-ring and twisted it slowly round her finger.

'Does this mean what it says, Philippa?' he asked.

'Yes,' she said.

'You're married?'

'Yes.'

'And your husband? You live with him? Not divorced or separated or anything?'

'No.'

For a moment they stood there in silence, Fergus looking at her, Philippa with her face resolutely turned from him. Then, before she could guess his intention, he had taken her in his arms, holding her closely against him, one hand turning her face towards his.

'I'm going to kiss you,' he said. 'I'm going to kiss you, my beautiful, adored and wonderful one. Give me your lips. Give them to me yourself, Philippa,' and there was no resistance possible in that tumultuous moment. She surrendered herself wholly to his arms and knew of neither time nor space whilst he held her mouth with his own, her heart beating against his breast.

'Philippa—Philippa—loveliest. I adore you,' he told her. 'I shall never let you go again.'

His voice broke the spell, and realisation came back to her. She tore herself from his arms and ran headlong from him, keeping her balance by a miracle as she sprang from one to another of the blocks of broken concrete of the hard until she reached the boat.

She heard him following her and, as she stooped to slip the noose with which he had secured the rope to a jagged end of iron, he was level with her.

'You can't go and leave me now,' he said, and his voice was quiet and even, neither fun nor passion in it now.

'I've got to,' she said. 'I must. Don't you realise it?' and she jumped into the boat and pushed off and felt for the starter.

'For God's sake be careful of the rocks,' he called and looked for a moment towards his own boat.

Then he decided to let her go. He saw that she was heading out to sea so as to make a complete detour of the rocks, and he had watched her now often enough to be sure she was thoroughly competent. He stood looking after her until she had rounded the point and was out of sight. Then, with a shrug and a half-sigh, he went back to the beach and lay in the sun again and thought about her, remembering as he felt he would remember forever her swift response to him, the tightening and then the utter surrender of her body in his arms, the ardour of her lips, the trembling of her whole being with the passion that shook them both.

All his life so far he had waited for her – and now she had to be married to someone else, though what the hell did the husband of a girl like that mean by letting her run footloose about the world?

Thinking of her, vainly dreaming of her, he fell asleep and did not wake until his chilled body warned him that the sun had gone for the day and that if he were going to do anything about getting back to Bonavie, he had better start doing it now.

He stretched himself and walked about to restore circulation to his cold, cramped limbs and then strolled down to the hard and looked at his boat. There was, of course, nothing wrong with her that he could not put right, and he had used a slight mechanical defect as an excuse to get contact with Philippa. The question now was whether he could put it right before the daylight had gone altogether, and, with another glance at the swiftly dropping sun, he saw that the question had already been decided for him. If he took the defective part of his engine to bits now, he certainly would not get it complete again before dark.

He grinned ruefully.

She had 'served him right', if only she knew it, for he could think of a great many things he would rather do than spend the night out here, supperless and without even a hot drink to console him.

He grinned again and decided that at least he might have a walk to warm him before he turned in and made the best of it. Perhaps, after all, it had been worth it to have her in his arms just for that brief moment.

He stretched them wide and lifted his face towards the sunset.

'Gosh!' he thought. 'What wouldn't I give to have her here now, tonight and all the night!'

A late bird jeered at him as it flew past to its own home,

'Yes, maybe you're right,' Fergus told him and fished his pipe out of his pocket.

At least he had tobacco and matches.

Chapter Seven

The fury of action which had sent Philippa headlong from the arms of Fergus to rush across the water to what now seemed the security of Bonavie had worked itself out by the time she had reached the little harbour and left her boat at the accustomed moorings.

She walked slowly across the cobbled path and up the uneven stone steps which, in the high tides of winter Marie had told her, were often submerged so that she and Pierre had to reach and leave their house by boats for weeks on end. The old woman was sitting where she usually sat when her work was done, on a stool placed on the narrow ledge which ran outside, between the wall of the cottage and the edge of the steep drop down to the cobblestones, A little wooden stand held her lace-making pillow before her, and her gnarled old hands worked unceasingly and with little need for the help of her eyes, lifting and passing with incredible speed the countless bobbins, the web of lace growing as if by magic as they clicked and rattled.

It was a scene of unutterable peace, at the centre of it this quiet old woman with a face like a withered russet apple, her white hair brushed neatly down on her scalp and knotted into a tight bun, a spotless white apron over her black dress with its voluminous skirts, her eyes with the blue almost washed out of them by the storms and the tears and perhaps the happiness, too of her seventy-odd years of life. She had told Philippa that she had been born in this cottage and that, except for the period of her girlhood when she had lived in England as maid to an English lady, she had never lived anywhere else. When she and Pierre married, her parents were dead and the cottage hers, so that it was only good common French sense for them to live there, and Pierre, who had been a blacksmith, learned to be a fisherman instead. With the coming of the motor car, people were giving up horses but they would not give up eating fish.

Philippa, pausing at the top of the steps, wondered if life would ever bring her to this peace. What would she herself be like at seventy, her problems solved, her questions answered, her only expectation by that time – death? Her thoughts flying instinctively to her home and her husband, she tried to picture them both after another half-century, the Abbey unchanged but Justin grown old, their children scattered and with children of their own – or perhaps, as the three sons of Marie and Pierre had been, killed in one of the world's unending, futile, tragic wars so that she and Justin, should, at the end of life, be alone again.

She could not picture it. Pierre, with his stolid, unsmiling, expressionless face and almost silent voice and this tiny inconvenient cottage, dark and damp as it must be for the greater part of the year – these seemed a poor harvest for the long years of work and poverty and grief, and yet there was Marie with her calm face and serene eyes and gentle voice, surely satisfied and at peace? It was very unlikely that her own life would ever bring her hard manual work or poverty, though no one can foretell or hope to avoid grief, yet how could she see herself at the end of life with the calm contentment of old Marie?

Though the bobbins did not pause in their click-clack, Marie looked up with the thousand creases of her smile.

'You have a good afternoon, Madame?' she asked, proud of her carefully preserved English and always glad if a summer visitor gave her the chance to exercise it.

'Yes,' said Philippa and sat down on the flagged path, her back propped against the cottage wall, warm with the day's sunshine.

'You meet with Monsieur Wynton, I think,' said Marie. 'He was at the anchor.'

'That's his name, is it? Wynton. Has he been here a long time? Does he live here?'

'No, but he rest here one month, two month perhaps. He puts himself back at Bonavie after that he is ill. He recovers himself.'

'Ill? I shouldn't have thought he was ever ill,' said Philippa. 'What was the matter with him?'

'Not ill in the stomach, you understand, but he is what you call—
the *aviateur* who makes to fly the machines which may not perhaps
be quite well. You understand? *Hélas*, Madame, my English she is not
so good now. It is very long time that I have not been in England.'

Philippa smiled encouragingly.

'I think your English she is very good,' she said. 'It's a lot better than
my French, anyway! You mean that Monsieur Wynton is a test pilot?'

Marie nodded vigorously.

'Yes. *C'est ça*. And his machine it fall and they say that he take a
long time in the full air, you understand, before he must fly again. He
has the bad dreams sometimes. Then he come into the *estaminet* of
Gaston and go to sleep well and when he has no more the bad dreams,
then he sleep in his little boat again, you understand. The poor
Monsieur Wynton,' and Marie's kind heart brought a little sigh of
sympathy to her lips whilst Philippa's heart, which she was trying to
make harder, gave a jolt at the thought that there might have been
something wrong with his boat which he could not put right, and that
therefore she might have left him stranded on the island for the night.

Oh well, she consoled herself, there were houses there. She had
seen the roof of at least one, just behind the trees, and where there
are houses, there are people, and where there are people there must
be help of some sort, even if only a cup of hot coffee, or a glass of
wine, or bread and cheese. Even if he could not get back to Bonavie,
he would be alright.

Marie lifted her lace-cushion off the stand to carry it carefully
indoors.

'Madame will have hunger,' she said. 'We do not wait for Pierre,
and soon all will be ready.'

Philippa was healthily tired, and on the previous evenings after she
had had her supper, she had watched the last of the sunset and then
had read or written letters in her room and it had not been long after
nine any evening before she had gone to bed. Tonight, however, she
felt too restless, too much keyed up, to sit indoors reading or writing,
and she put a woollen cardigan over the thin summer frock into
which she had changed for supper, and went down to the beach.
Looking at the darkening water which reflected the last streaks of red

and orange of the sky, she realised that she would have known, even without the events of the afternoon, that Fergus Wynton's boat was not at its usual anchorage. She must unconsciously have looked at it each evening.

She walked to and fro, her hands in the pockets of her cardigan, her head bent, her mind full of thoughts which were gradually sorting themselves into some order. What a mad, wild, incredible episode that had been on the little island! What had possessed her?

She leaned against an upturned boat and closed her eyes. For a moment that memory had been overpowering. A shiver ran through her though she was not cold. She must not let that happen again. Though how was she going to prevent it, other than by going away, running away from Bonavie and putting herself beyond his reach? A sick feeling invaded her mind at the thought. She knew that she wanted to see him again, that in those few swift hours he had become a part of her life, not so easily to be cut away and forgotten. And yet, until Marie had told her a few minutes ago, she had not even known his name!

The whole thing was absurd, fantastic, of course. It could not go on. She was not only the wife of a British peer, but she was also a very respectable wife and a mother and she had not the slightest intention of jeopardising her position or her calm, unexciting happiness in any way.

And yet – he was there on that lonely island, quite certainly unable to get back or he would have returned by now, and she knew (for he had told her) that though he liked to sleep in his boat, he never did any cooking for himself on her and did not even maintain the small galley in working order. Except for heating his shaving water over a spirit stove, he did not go into it, coming ashore for his meals at Gaston's.

"Allo Feeleep,' she heard at her side, breaking her thoughts.

It was Louis, her favourite amongst the urchins who haunted the shore and who owned jointly the dinghy and the outboard motor which always needed repair. He was fourteen and had recently started work in every known capacity for Gaston, being pot-boy, waiter, messenger, household help and clerk. Gaston did not pay him much, but he picked up a good many odd francs in tips and had confided in Philippa that he was learning all he could about the business because some day he intended to have a big hotel in St. Malo and cater for wealthy Americans.

'Hullo, Louis. How's business?' she asked, making room for him on the upturned boat.

'Oh, ver' nice and good,' he said, airing the English which, with the quickness and determination of his race, he was picking up from her and from his other English friend, Fergus Wynton.

Philippa was still unconsciously looking towards the vacant moorings where the *Sea-dog* should have been, but she would not ask the boy and arouse any curiosity he might have. Instead, her question was indirect.

'I went out round the point this afternoon,' she said. 'Do you know that side?'

'*Moi, non!*' said the boy and gave a little shiver as if the question evoked fear. 'What made you there, Feeleep?'

'I landed at the little island and had a bathe,' she said as nonchalantly as she could. 'Do you know the island?'

'*Ile des Pirates*' he said. 'No, I go not there not at all. *Moi*, I go never to the *Ile des Pirates*,' with another shiver, his eyes wide.

'Why not? Is there something to be afraid of, Louis?'

'*But yes, Feeleep. Des revenants. Il y a des revenants dans l'ile, assurément!*'

'What is *revenants!*' she asked.

He cast about in his mind.

'*Des fantômes—spectres,*' and he got up and pulled a rag of cloth that was lying on the beach over his head and flapped his arms, wailing dismally.

Philippa laughed but gave a little shudder as expected.

'Ghosts,' she said. 'Rubbish. I don't believe in them. *Il n'y a pas de spectre.*'

He nodded vehemently.

'But yes, Feeleep. *Assurément, assurément.* Peoples have see. Many peoples have see.'

'But how about the people who live on the island? Don't they mind the ghosts?'

'Peoples live? *Restent?* But no, no peoples, only *les revenants.*'

Louis was plainly shocked at the idea of people living on the island.

'But there are houses. I saw them,' she said.

'Not houses any more. All gone—broken—no one anymore.'

She frowned.

'You mean no one lives there at all? Quite empty? *Vide?*' she asked anxiously.

'*Mais oui, vide—vide!*' throwing his arms wide in one of his expressive gestures.

'Louis! Louis!' called a voice from somewhere down the village street, and he rose.

'*Zut! C'est ma mère. Qu'est ce qu'il y a maintenant?*' and with a shrug of irritation at yet another demand for his services, he sauntered off in the direction of the voice.

Philippa sat looking anxiously out at the empty moorings and the empty sea. She was remembering what Marie had told her, that Fergus was a test pilot who had crashed and though he had recovered from his physical injuries, he had not yet fully recovered his nerve. He was here at Bonavie to get quite well by living in the open air, but he had, Marie said, bad dreams, and when these came upon him, he would leave his boat and find refuge and the company of others at Gaston's and then he could sleep.

And she had left him marooned on a deserted island, people only by ghosts which, even if he did not believe in them, were apt to become fear potentials when one lay awake in the silence of the night. Like all old houses, Hollmere Abbey had its ghosts, some of them almost regarded as members of the family, their reputed appearances accepted as evidence that, whatever might be happening to other old houses, at least they still regarded the Abbey as worthy of their fidelity. Philippa, modern in her outlook, laughed at the stories of the visitations, and yet there had been nights when, unable to sleep, she had lain listening to the strange sounds of an old house, creaks and taps, the ancient oak beams and wide stair-treads appearing to come to life and groan after the work of the day, a tapping at her window which she knew in her heart was only a rose branch blown loose, but which in the night seemed an unearthly visitor seeking entrance.

And tonight Fergus, unnerved through no fault of his own but just because of the gay courage which took him into the clouds in machines which had to be proved safe for someone else – Fergus was going to be obliged to spend the night on the island of ghosts, or in the cabin of his boat from which he had more than once had to flee to escape his dreams, flee towards the sanity and security of a room shared, or a house at least inhabited, by some other human being. Tonight there was nowhere for him to go, no one to whom he could flee, no human hand or voice to help him.

Darkness had fallen now, and tonight there were clouds over the sky to blot out even the stars and the young moon. The sea looked black and menacing. Straining her eyes she could glimpse around the point the little flashes of white made by the waves breaking against the rocks. She shivered, drawing her cardigan closely about her, and quite suddenly she knew what she was going to do.

She looked back at the cottage. It was in darkness. Marie and Pierre had gone to bed and, by an arrangement she had begged them to make with her, they had not left a light burning. She had an electric torch, and she had said that she would always take it with her if she went out after supper so that she could find her way up the steps and into the cottage.

'If you never leave a light when you go to bed, you will not need to find out whether I am in or out, and if I have already gone to bed, there will not be the risk of a lamp burning all night,' she had told Marie.

The beach and the hard were quite deserted. Everybody in Bonavie went to bed early and got up early, and at this hour, half-past nine, very few of the cottages now had lights showing. One small lamp burned all night in Gaston's *estaminet*. She knew now the reason for that, but tonight Fergus could not reach its friendly assurance.

She unfastened *La Colombe* and used an oar to push her out to sea before starting up the engine so that no one would appear to make inquiries. No fishing boats went out after dark from Bonavie and the sound of a motor starting would cause comment by anyone who heard it.

Though she watched the shore, no one appeared to have heard her, and as soon as she dared, she opened up and made for the point. One of the annoying things was that she had not filled up with petrol again after coming back from the island, and the long detour she had made to avoid the rocks had left her tank too low for comfort. If she made the same detour now, she might run out of fuel and then her own case would be worse than that of Fergus, to whose rescue she was going. She calculated that she would have enough in the tank to take her to the island by the shorter and more dangerous route, and she could syphon petrol from the tank of the *Sea-dog* for the return journey.

As her eyes grew more accustomed to the darkness, she found she could pick her course with a reasonable amount of safety, though once she was committed to it, she felt a few qualms as the water frothed over her bows in the narrow passage between groups of the submerged rocks. By going slowly and leaning well out, keeping her hands lightly but surely on the wheel, she could just see the route she must take and eventually, little by little, she knew that the danger was passing and that she had made the passage safely.

She was shaking after the tension when she was out again at the other side of the point, but the needle showing her fuel supply proved how right she had been not to take the safer route. As it was, the engine spluttered and gave out with the last few yards still to go, and she stood up and propelled the boat expertly with an oar until it slid alongside the concrete blocks where she could see the *Sea-dog* still gently rocking.

Now that she was actually here, and there was no sign of Fergus, she was at a loss, not knowing just what she had intended to do. She had expected to see him when she reached the island. How and where was she to go in search of him?

She made her way to the beach, getting her feet wet now that the tide was high enough to cover most of the broken hard, and stood uncertainly in the eerie darkness. A faint wind had sprung up, and the whispering of the trees above her mingled with the sound of the water splashing against the rocks and the two boats conspired to make the island as if inhabited by the ghosts, *assurément*, as Louis had said.

She swallowed a lump in her throat and shivered, wishing she had taken the time to go to the cottage for a warmer coat before she started on what seemed to her now a mad errand. Before scrambling to the beach she had flashed her torch for a moment on the *Sea-dog*, long enough to show her at a glance that Fergus was not there. Through the open door from the cockpit to the one small cabin she could see the empty bunk, its blankets neatly folded, and the table and chair which made its only other furnishing.

But where on the island would he be? She thought of the roof she had seen amongst the trees at the top of the cliff. If there were the remains of a house there, he might have preferred it to the cabin of his boat. She looked for the best way up and found what might once have been man-made steps in the rocks, though they were rough and broken and more than once she had a difficulty in stretching from foothold to foothold before she came out on the plateau at the top, a plateau covered with rough, coarse grass and rank weeds, behind it the whispering trees and amongst them the ruins of the house whose roof she had seen.

That was all that remained of it now – just a few crumbling ruins, broken walls, holes where windows and door had once been, the roof sagging and beyond repair. Surely he could not have chosen that in preference to the neat snugness of his cabin?

As she moved gingerly forward, some ground creeper caught at her ankles and she stopped, her hand at her mouth. She saw what it was and bent down to tear it away, but she felt she could not go on farther into the undergrowth which might once have been a garden.

She decided to call to him. Surely in that silence, broken only by the wind and the waves, he would hear a human voice, wherever he was? She had begun to be vaguely afraid, not for herself but because of him. What if he had not been able to stand the island and the weird darkness? What if his nerves had given way and he had done something dreadful? And it would be her fault, hers alone. She had known he was there, marooned by his defective boat, and she had deliberately left him there with Louis's ghosts.

What was she to call? She had not called him by his name, but in her overwrought state she had to suppress a giggle at the thought of standing there and calling out: 'Mr. Wynton! Mr. Wynton!'

'Fergus!' she called, tremulously at first, but then encouraged by the sound of her own voice: 'Fergus! Where are you?'

Her heart seemed to stop beating as she heard a crash in the bushes, but the next moment she heard her own name spoken in tones of incredulous wonder.

Philippa! Good Lord – it really is you!' and the bushes parted to let him come bounding to her, stopping a few feet from her to stare at her, joy breaking through the wonder.

She stumbled towards him, her hands held out.

'Oh—Fergus,' she half-sobbed in her relief, and the next moment he had her in his arms, holding her closely, stroking her hair and her neck as she buried her face against him.

'Why, darling,' he said, and at the note in his voice, the warm delight and wonder in it, her heart lifted and she knew neither fear nor cold nor any other emotion but gladness at being with him, held in the close enfolding of his arms.

'I had to come,' she whispered. 'I couldn't leave you here. I thought at first that there were houses here, other people, somebody you could be with. Then Louis told me there is nothing here, nobody—nobody but ghosts, he said.'

He bent his head to kiss her hair.

'And you wouldn't leave me to their mercy?' he asked.

'I couldn't have slept knowing that you were here, that I had left you here. Are you alright, Fergus?'

'I've never been so much alright in my life, dear heart,' he said. 'You're cold, little one, cold and wet. How is it that you're wet? It's not been raining.'

'No. It was the spray. I had to lean out to see my way and I got wet, but it doesn't matter. I never catch cold.'

'To see your way? Philippa, you don't mean that you came through the rocks?' he demanded almost angrily.

'I had to. I shouldn't have had enough petrol to go outside them but I was quite alright – as you see,' laughing up at the anger in his face.

'Quite alright? My God, you might have been killed. Whatever possessed you to do such a dangerous thing?' he asked in the same tone.

'I think—it was you who possessed me, Fergus,' she said very quietly and softly, and after another searching look deep into her eyes, he gave a little strangled sound and held her to him again.

'Can I believe that? May I? Dare I, Philippa—Philippa, my dear beloved? No, don't answer that. Just let me believe it and hold you like this. Are you happy in my arms?'

'Utterly happy.'

'You came in the dark, through all that, so that I should not be alone and—afraid, didn't you?'

'I didn't think you would be afraid,' she said.

'Didn't you? Haven't they told you about me? That I am afraid to be alone in my boat some nights? That I crawl into old Gaston's kitchen and sleep with the cockroaches rather than be alone?'

She looked into his face with sweet, unhidden honesty. 'Yes, Marie told me. She told me all of it, or most of it. That you had crashed testing out a plane and had come here to get quite cured, as of course you will be cured.'

'Sometimes I wonder about that,' he said with a touch of bitterness. 'That's why I chose to come to France rather than hang about in my own country where too many people would know and watch me. The thing that haunts me now is, suppose I don't get over it? Suppose I'm a coward for the rest of my life, afraid to sleep alone?'

'You won't be, Fergus. Tell me the truth. Were you afraid here, tonight? Is that why you are up here instead of in your boat?'

He laughed softly.

'No. Oddly enough, I wasn't afraid. I intended to go down to the boat to sleep, but I came up here to collect some dry firewood to boil a kettle and save my methylated spirit for the morning shave. Of course if I had been marooned here for long, I expect I should have gone native and grown a beard, but as I had every hope of being rescued in the morning. I thought I might as well keep decent.'

'What was the hot water for?' she asked.

'Tonight? I've rootled about in my cupboard and found some tea and a tin of condensed milk and some slightly battered biscuits, so I was going to have them for supper. I proposed in the morning to catch some fish. What was your plan when you set out to rescue me, by the way?'

She flushed.

'I don't know. I really hadn't any plan, except ...'

'Except to make sure I didn't spend the night, alone and afraid? Bless you, dear love. Don't let's have any silly pretences with each other. I should have been alone and I might have been afraid, and in the sweetness of your heart you came to me. Thank you. Thank you, beloved.'

She closed her eyes and let the magic bind her with its spell. Nothing like this had ever touched her before. This was what she had waited for, hungered for, had come to believe in the end did not exist except between the covers of romantic novels. Now she knew that these things were true. She knew because romance had come to her, and deliberately she closed her mind to all the things she would have to remember and pretended that for just this enchanted hour they did not exist.

When he let her go, slowly and gently releasing her lips but keeping his arms about her and looking into her eyes, she gave him a sweet, drowsy smile.

'Is this really happening?' she asked.

'No. Probably one of the dreams you came to save me from,' he said with a chuckle.

'Did you want to be saved from this?'

'Did you?' he asked, and his face grew grave.

She shook her head and turned from him as the sudden tears filled her eyes. All her emotions were very near the surface.

'It might have been better,' she said unsteadily.

'If we had never known this?'

'Yes.'

He held her for a moment in silence and then turned, keeping one arm about her shoulders to lead her back the way she had come.

'It's cold up here, my darling, and your dress is wet. Let's go down to the boat,' he said quietly.

She walked with him as in a dream, unaware now of the damp, rank grass or the clinging weeds which caught her. His near presence made everything outside and beyond them vague and formless. She could not think. Everything seemed concentrated on the passion of feeling.

'Go carefully, my darling,' he said when they reached the rough steps. 'Let me go first,' and he guided her down, placing her feet safely in each pocket of rock until they stood again on the beach.

She followed him, his hand holding hers, along the slipway until they reached the place where the two boats lay, and then he stepped aboard the *Sea-dog* and lifted her off her feet and into the cockpit as if she were no heavier than a child.

'I'll light the lamp,' he said, releasing her and going into the cabin. 'It's a foul-smelling thing but it works.'

It was a moment of tension for them both, keyed up as they were and supremely conscious of each other, and he spent more time than the task warranted in lighting the small oil lamp which, as he had said, smelt foul. He placed it carefully in its metal ring and at last could no longer delay the moment she both longed for and dreaded.

'Sit down, my sweet, and let me wrap you in the blankets,' he said with infinite gentleness, his voice and his touch trying to offer her, she knew, reassurance and comfort. 'I'm going to be reckless and use the methylated spirit to boil some water for a cup of tea. Are you comfortable like that? Had you better not take off your dress and hang it up to dry?'

'I'll be alright,' she said, snuggling down into the blankets which smelt of tobacco and tar.

Watching him through the open door of the tiny galley fitted into the bows, she realised how safe she felt with him, how sure that whatever came out of this situation, she need have no fear. Once he glanced over his shoulder at her and smiled. It was the smile of a friend, familiar, companionable. It was difficult to believe how short a time it was since they had first met and spoken. They seemed to have walked into each other's lives and minds through an open door.

He brought her tea which was at least strong and hot, but they both rejected the biscuits after trying them and Fergus pitched them overboard.

'They'll do to feed the fish for our breakfast,' he said, and they were silent again, looking at each other.

He stretched out his hand to put it over hers and she curled her fingers round it.

'I know you haven't enough petrol to get back in your boat,' he said quietly, 'but there's enough in mine.'

'Hasn't this really broken down?' she asked.

'Oh yes, it really has,' he told her with a smile, 'but I'll be perfectly honest with you. I am and always have been quite capable of repairing it.'

'So it actually was a trick this afternoon?'

'It actually was. Are you sorry?'

The smile that edged her lips came to dance in her eyes.

'I think I knew all the time,' she said.

'Knew that I could have got back?'

'Well – perhaps not quite that. I guessed this afternoon that you were pulling a fast one when you asked me for a tow, but afterwards – later – when you didn't come bac – well, I didn't know quite what to think. Fergus, did you stay here *thinking* I would come back?' looking at him speculatively.

'It never entered my head,' he said quickly. 'There is a very simple explanation of why I didn't come back. I fell asleep in the sun. When I woke up, I realised that it would be quite dark before I could get the job done, as it entails quite a lot of taking to bits and I didn't want to be benighted with all the bits and pieces round me and only this lamp to work by. I decided that the best thing to do would be to make myself comfortable in here until the morning – in spite of the ghosts! Never in my wildest, sweetest dreams did I imagine that you would have the—courage to come back like this. And I'm not just thinking of the courage to make the passage through the rocks, my darling.'

She let him draw her close with an arm about her, still wrapped in the blankets. Their minds were in that accord which comes so seldom to two people and which, when it comes, is so perfect.

She did not speak but sat resting against him, his cheek pressed to the top of her head, the little curls of her drying hair brushing his lips.

When he spoke again, there was a new and urgent note in his voice, as if he would compel the thoughts from her inner soul.

'Philippa, you said just now, up there, that it might have been better if we had never known this. Did you mean it? Do you mean it now?'

She twisted her head, turned her face up to him and waited for the touch of his lips, her eyes closed, her breath coming softly and quickly.

'No. No, I don't mean it. This must have been meant to happen. I think I have been waiting for you always. Kiss me, Fergus. Hold me very tightly, my dear love. How can you be that, when I have known you so short a time? But it's true. Fergus my beloved, it's true.'

They were lost in the tumult of their loving. She shook the blankets from her with a little gesture of impatience and locked her arm about his neck and could only whisper his name.

'Fergus—Fergus ...'

Presently he reached up and unlocked her clasped hands and held them in his and sat looking down deeply into her eyes. They glowed with the light and the warmth that was in her, with all the ardour of her passionate heart and body.

'Sweet, you must either stay with me tonight or let me take you back now—now at once,' he said, his voice unsteady, his body tense with the tremendous brake he was putting on himself. 'I can, you know. There's enough petrol in this tank to put into yours and get us back. Only—only, my dearest heart, if you are to go back, you must go now. You realise that? I'm merely human, and I love you with all my heart and soul and my body longs for you, Philippa?'

A tremor ran through her but her eyes did not leave his.

'And mine for you, Fergus,' she said. 'I'm not a child. I'm neither ignorant nor inexperienced. I want and need your love desperately, Fergus. I'll stay here with you – and we can pretend that there's nothing else beyond this night,' and she closed her eyes again and gave herself wholly to his arms again.

Towards morning, with the pate dawn beginning to steal through the cabin window, she stirred sleepily, and then woke fully to find him sitting on the opposite bunk and regarding her with eyes that were half-amused, half-sad.

Realisation came to her at once of the madness of the thing that she had done and with it came horror at herself and yet, inextricably mixed with it, the knowledge that she had known complete happiness for that short hour, and that the man looking at her with that strange sadness in his eyes had become a force in her life forever.

'You're so beautiful,' he said very softly.

She lay back and closed her eyes.

'Only to look at,' she said. 'Inside me I'm ...'

He leaned forward and closed her lips with a kiss which she did not return.

'Beautiful in every way,' he said.

She shook her head and he moved away from her at once, divining her mood, knowing that she was no light woman to take love-making as a pastime, to be forgotten as soon as it was over.

Philippa,' he said, and now his tone was very grave and his eyes held no amusement. 'There's no love between you and your husband, is there? Darling, forgive me if I'm probing into your life, asking things which probably I've no right to ask, but—you know what's happened to us, don't you? Tonight has not been just an affair, one of those things of which people think nothing nowadays, a sort of "hullo, let's have fun and say goodbye". I'm no saint, Philippa, I've taken my fun where I could find it, and when it was offered to me, and I've not regretted any of it nor left, I think, any regrets. It's just been fun, a light-hearted affair, with nothing afterwards. It isn't like that with us, Philippa. You know that, my dear heart?'

'Yes. Yes, I know it,' she said quietly and gravely.

'I knew it last evening, before we made things irrevocable. If you had wanted to go, I wouldn't have tried to stop you and I should never have seen you again, though even then I knew that I had found the one woman, my woman, the only one. Can you bear to tell me about yourself? Whether there is an inextricable tangle in your life or whether there might be a way out?'

'You mean—divorce?'

'It's a beastly way out, but if it's the only way ...?'

She shook her head and he read the unhappiness in her eyes even before she spoke.

'That isn't the way,' she said. 'I don't think there's any way, beloved. You see, Fergus, Justin does love me. I know now, and I think I've known it from the first night of our marriage, that his is a different way of loving, more spiritual, caring so much less than I do for the physical side of love. He's hurt me and upset me and disappointed me and made me feel that there is no depth to the happiness I have tried to get out of my marriage and honestly tried to put into it. But he loves me and he's endlessly good to me and I couldn't hurt him, ever.'

'So that this is all there can be for us, for you and me, Philippa?'

'Darling, what else can there be?'

'It's going to be like the other ones then, "hullo, let's have fun and say goodbye"?'

There was a deep sadness rather than any bitterness in his voice and she kissed him passionately.

'Fergus, no! Not like that. Not like those others. How could it be? I shall never be able to forget, never.'

'You mean you'll want to forget?' he asked her sadly. She closed her eyes and the tears, those tears she so seldom shed, welled behind her lids and crept down through her lashes. He kissed them away.

'I can't give you up, Philippa. Oh, I know all about the ethical side of it. I'm not going to pretend to you that I think it right to be your lover any more than you yourself think it's right. I'm not going to talk a lot of highfalutin nonsense about twin souls and the divine right of the individual to take what it wants and so on. I know it isn't, right, and I'm going to have a good many twinges of conscience and I'm not going to feel particularly proud of myself – but if you will still come to me, even for a few hours, let me be your lover again, I know it's what I'm going to do, with a passionate gratitude to the fates that let me have even that much. How do you feel about it?'

'I don't know. Don't ask me, Fergus. Not yet, not now. Let me get a little farther away in time from this so that I can know what I feel about it. What you say is right. Of course it is. I'm not very proud of myself for having broken my marriage vows, for betraying Justin like this.'

For a moment he stood looking at her uncertainly, with unhappy speculation in his eyes. Then he turned from her abruptly and left the cabin and a few moments afterwards she heard the splash as he dived off the boat and swam, with vigorous strokes in the ice-cold water.

Philippa was in her own boat when he returned, manoeuvring it into position so that the petrol could be transferred from his tank to hers.

In spite of the dead weight of her conscience, her body felt tremendously alive and young, and she laughed and waved to him as he came near.

'I don't know how to get the petrol out,' she called.

'I'll do it,' he said, and pulled his lean, strong body up over the side with effortless ease.

It was difficult for her to believe that there could ever be a time when he could be unnerved, the victim of his own mind, needing anything from any other human being, and yet in that long talk they had had in the quiet darkness, he had told her things he had never told a living person before, not even his doctors nor the alienist to whom in desperation he had once turned.

Her heart ached for him, and because he must suffer this thing alone, because she could not, must not, be there to hold him in her arms and help him to fight back to the normal life which should be his.

It was not a difficult job to put sufficient petrol into the tank of *La Colombe*, and the day was still no more than a pearl-grey dawn in the east by the time they were ready.

For a moment they stood in the *Sea-dog's* cabin, where she had been making everything shipshape again for him.

'I dare not touch even your hand,' he said softly, 'but in my heart I am kissing and loving and adoring every little bit of you. I love you, Philippa.'

'And I love you, Fergus, with all my heart,' she said, and turned away and went past him and climbed into her own boat without another word or look.

He took the wheel and made for the rocks, steering expertly between them.

'I shudder to think of your coming through here last night, alone and in the dark, for the first time,' he said.

'But I told you I'm a wartime mariner,' she said, laughing, though her voice was not quite steady.

'Promise you won't do it again, not without me,' he said.

'I promise,' she said and again they were silent, wondering what that promise was worth, since it might never be tried.

He ran silently alongside the fishing-boat quay where they would be less likely to be heard, though it would mean that she must scramble up the flight of steep, slime-covered steps used by the fishermen.

'Will you be alright?' he asked in a whisper.

'Yes, quite alright,' she said, and paused for a moment, turned her face towards him.

'Kiss me just once,' she said, and their lips met and clung and then she went swiftly from him, and he waited until she had reached the top of the steps and then worked the boat silently round the moored fishing vessels to its own anchorage.

Philippa made no sound as she opened the door of the cottage, which had neither lock nor bolt, and she was just going into her own room when she heard old Pierre shuffling from the other bedroom, little more than a dark cupboard, which he and Marie shared.

'It is you then, Madame?' he asked. 'You go without doubt to see the sunrise?'

She usually found it difficult to understand his guttural *patoisée* French, but she got the gist of it and nodded.

'*Oui. Il fait beau,*' she said and went into her room and sat down on the bed and thought about the times he had entered that room for the first time. Could it be so short a time ago? She seemed to have lived a lifetime in those few days.

She knew how near to her conscious mind was the memory of Justin and soon she could no longer fight it back but sat, her hands pressed down on the bed at either side of her, her head bent, her very being torn in two between these two men who loved her and whom she loved.

Whom she loved?

Yes, passionately she averred it. Why should anyone say that the human heart can hold love for only one man or one woman when there were so many different qualities and causes in love, so many ways in which love can reveal itself? Why must it be assumed that because one loved one man for his essential goodness of heart, his tenderness, his gentle ways, his unselfish generosity, one could not be aflame for another who could set the pulses leaping, the blood rushing madly through one's veins and bring oblivion of all else to one's mind?

As if to test that conclusion, when presently Marie brought her *petit déjeuner*, there was a letter from Justin on the tray beside the Breton coffee bowl.

It was addressed to 'Mrs. Breane'. He had smiled at her request that it should be so.

'I want to have a very simple, natural holiday,' she said. 'If I go as the Countess of Hollmere, you know yourself that that is impossible. Somehow there will be people to pass on to other people who I am), and there will be visitors and invitations and I shall have to dress up and do all sorts of things I'm not interested in. You understand?'

'Of course. Alright, dearest. Have your holiday as you want.'

She opened the letter reluctantly and with a feeling of guilt, knowing the sort of thing it would say – small items of news about Sloworth, about the Abbey, particularly the home farm, bits of gossip that were never malicious and, put as Justin put it, not even amusing. He was not a good letter writer. He could keep the accounts and dictate to Ena Blackthorne the necessary business letters, but apart from that it irritated him to have to deal with such matters and he very rarely wrote a letter with his own hand.

This one began as they invariably did, 'Dearest wife' and ended 'All my love, Justin' and she skimmed what lay in between the two with a feeling that nothing of which he spoke was quite real. Had her life really been so circumscribed? Had she been contented by these little happenings which seemed so amply to fill Justin's days?

Then she put the letter to her lips.

'Justin, Justin,' she whispered remorsefully, 'I'm not worth your loving. I'm not worth anything – and yet how can I be too sorry?'

Having a bath was a complicated affair, but Marie managed it as she managed everything, without fuss even if she puffed and blew, stoutly refusing ever to let her guest drag the ancient tin bath into the kitchen, or lift the pot of boiling water off the coal range to add to the buckets of cold water already drawn for her before Pierre left. When Philippa had had her bath and emerged from behind the screen set modestly between her and the rest of the kitchen, she found a note beside her plate.

The envelope bore no name.

'Of course he doesn't know it,' said Philippa to herself, hesitating before she opened it, trying to postpone the moment when yesterday invaded today. Why had he written?

Marie brought more coffee and some fruit.

'Louis has brought it,' she said briefly and without curiosity.

Philippa nodded and slid a finger beneath the flap, drawing out the slip of paper slowly.

Will you come with me in La Colombe to collect my boat? (Fergus had written). I'll be down at the quay. F.

She was glad that he had not written her a love letter. After Justin's, it would have filled her with shame and possibly regret. Possibly? She hated herself and yet knew that she might not be able to feel actual regret for last night, no matter what happened.

The very sight of his small, unexpectedly fine handwriting and the touch of the paper straight from his hand set her mind whirling again.

'Is Louis waiting?' she asked Marie, but received a brief 'No. Madame' as the Frenchwoman went about her many affairs.

When she could delay no longer. Philippa went down to the quay to find him sitting on an upturned boat helping the fishermen to mend their nets. His fingers had become almost as skilled as theirs, and he talked to them in the mixture of English, pure French and their own patois which they seemed able perfectly to understand.

Though he had his back to her, he was instantly aware of her coming, for he stood up and came to meet her, his face alight, his eyes seeking hers, his hand engulfing and holding her own.

'Shall we go, beloved?' he asked her without greeting. 'I've put petrol in and also a can for the *Sea-dog* in case we can get her to go,' and he released her hand again and they went down together to her boat, aware that for a moment the busy fingers of the fishermen had paused whilst their owners watched the pair of them.

'They're interested,' said Philippa.

He nodded.

'Only that. Not maliciously curious as town people might be. They've probably been expecting us to get together, *l'Anglais* and *l'Anglaise.'*

She was relieved to find that his manner was friendly but did not suggest their intimacy. There was between them a feeling of great comfort and ease, and the look that flashed in their eyes when, both working to get *La Colombe* started, their glances met, was that of perfectly happy comradeship.

It was not until they had reached the island and repaired the engine of the *Sea-dog* and were ready to start back that his attitude to her changed. Then, wiping his grimed hands on a rag before he put the kettle on the spirit stove so that they could wash the oil and grease off, he spoke very quietly.

'What are we going to do, Philippa?'

She looked at him quickly.

'Now?' she asked.

'And afterwards, yes.'

She did not answer and he busied himself arranging the tin shield to guard the flame from too much draught. Then he came back to where she sat on a boulder, her feet in the water.

'Well?' he asked.

She averted her eyes.

'How can there be any afterwards for us, Fergus?' she asked.

'There must be something.'

'There can't be.'

'You mean you'll go back to him?'

She looked up, her eyes were troubled and unhappy but he read his answer there.

'I must.'

'But you don't love him. You love me.'

She did not answer and he asked her vehemently the question she had asked herself so many times that morning. 'You do love me, don't you? Don't you, Philippa?' Slowly she dropped her eyes and lowered her head and sat looking at the water rippling about her feet.

'Yes,' she said at last, but her voice was unhappy. 'Yes, I do love you, Fergus. You know that. But I love Justin too, and how can that be?'

'I don't know. I think you're probably still confused. My own mind is quite clear. There's no one in it or in my heart but you, my beloved Philippa, and there never can be. You think you love him because of your association with him, the memories you share with him, the fact that you married him in the belief that you really did love him. Now that you know me and know what love between a man and a woman really is – a man and a woman like us, Philippa – what you feel for your husband can only be a shadow and an echo ...'

'No no, Fergus, that isn't so. If you knew Justin, you would understand. He is so kind ...'

'Have I been unkind then?'

She shook her head confusedly.

'No, of course not, but—he is quite different from you.'

'That's why you love me and not him.'

'I won't have you say I don't love him, Fergus, though it isn't the way I feel about you. I am so confused. I know Justin through and through, but how can I really know you at all? And if I love Justin, it is because I know everything about him and know that he is in every way worthy of my love, whereas—how much do I know of you? No, please let me finish. I'm trying to sort myself out. I love what I know of Justin, and that is everything about him. I love what I know of you – but that is so little, only that you can give me physical satisfaction— transports—rapture—feelings I have never had before. Is that loving you or loving myself? Fergus, try to understand! Try to make me understand! I'm so unhappy and confused and—distressed.'

The kettle boiled over, and he rose to blow out the flame. 'You wash first,' he said. 'I'll put some cold into the bowl for you. I'll use the same water. There's some soap there.' They were both glad of the break in so emotional a conversation necessitated by the ordinary happenings of everyday life, but the end of the discussion could not be avoided and Fergus returned to it, holding her by the shoulders and looking into her eyes.

'Dare I hope that you will ever come to me, Philippa?' he asked.

'I can't,' she said in a low voice. 'It isn't only Justin. There's my baby, Trevor. I couldn't leave him ever.'

'You've left him at the moment.'

'I know, but only for a very short time, and at this age, whilst he is actually only a baby, he will not be missing me. I couldn't leave him for good.'

'I will take care of you both. You know that – and later there would be others. When we are married, he can take my name and there will never be any difference.'

She shook her head. She did not want now to tell him the truth about herself, and why it was so much more difficult for her to take her son away than if she had not been Justin's wife and Justin's son the heir to the title and to Hollmere Abbey. Her original reluctance to tell Fergus who she was had grown into something she only partially understood. For him she was just Philippa. She had seen so often the change that came over people when they discovered that she was the Countess of Hollmere, as if she were on a different plane, almost living in a different world. She did not want to see that change in Fergus—Fergus who laughed at social barriers, made fun of people he called 'high hats', was more than a little tinged with sympathy for the revolutionaries in spite of asserting that he had absolutely no politics at all.

'It wouldn't be possible,' she said sadly. 'I couldn't take him away from Justin as well as—everything else. There couldn't be any real or lasting happiness for us, trying to build on that sort of foundation.'

'So you're going to be content to let me go? To lose all that we've found?'

'Oh, not content! Not *content*, my darling!' she cried, and leaned her head against his breast and felt his arms come about her and felt she was knowing the bitterness of death.

He held her in silence for a few moments, trying to enter into her mind, knowing something of the conflict there and that there was truth and justice and decency in the decision she was making. Without knowing this other man, he yet knew that what he proposed to do was a thing he would himself have condemned, and had indeed condemned when others were concerned.

Yet to lose Philippa? To know that she was in the world and not only never to see her again, but also to know that some other man possessed her?

'I can't,' he muttered in a low voice over her bent head. 'I can't. Not yet. Not altogether. Not forever.'

Then he lifted her head and looked at her searchingly.

'Dearest and only beloved,' he said, 'I can't go on arguing with you. In my heart I know you're right. I know that even if I could hold you, you wouldn't be happy. I've got to give you up, but not yet, not like this, not until we've got something else to remember, something beyond just the one night I have had you in my arms. I don't want a hole-and-corner affair with you here in Bonavie, darling, running the gauntlet of all the eyes of the village folk, having our comings and goings watched all the time. And I don't want never to have anything else but this rather grubby, uncomfortable business of a bunk in my cabin. Sweetheart, if I swear to you that I won't try to hold you, that I'll let you go without let or hindrance the moment you say you must go – will you come away somewhere with me? Now, before you have to return to England? Anywhere you like. Will you, Philippa? If I swear that afterwards I will let you go back?'

She nodded her head, her eyes filled with tears which she dashed away so that she could smile at him.

'I want that too,' she said unsteadily. 'I'm not going to struggle with my conscience or try to count the cost or anything just now. There will be time for that later – and, like you, I'm not going to try to pretend that it's right. I know it isn't, but I'm going to do it just the same.'

He smiled.

'Good,' he said.

'No. Bad.'

'Alright. Good or bad, who's going to say which it is? Where would you like to go, darling? Paris?'

'No, not the cities.'

She was thinking that in Paris, of all places, she would be likely to be recognised.

'What about Switzerland? We could fly there.'

'Yes. Do you know, I've never been to Switzerland.'

'Then we'll go there. I'll get reservations. Your passport's alright?'

'Yes. How about money? I shan't be able to get any more foreign currency.'

'I can fix that. I get a special allowance. We'd better not set off from here together. Will you meet me in Paris? We can fly from there. I'll go into St. Malo and get a lift from there either to London or straight to Paris, fix up reservations and money, and meet you—when? Today's Wednesday. Saturday?'

Feverishly now, she was willing to agree to anything, pushing back all the inhibitions she had to defeat, blinding herself to everything but the overpowering need to have these memories, not to have to part with him yet, to stave off as long as she could that inevitable and poignant agony.

With at any rate surface calmness, they made her boat fast to his and she sat beside him as he steered the *Sea-dog* through the now familiar channel, neither of them speaking of anything but superficial things, the currents, the weather, the success of the repair they had done to his engine.

Back at the quay, she climbed from his boat to hers, moored it and was ready to join him when he had made the *Sea-dog* fast and rowed himself ashore in his tiny dinghy.

'I'll tell Gaston to keep an eye on the boat if we get rough weather,' he said. 'You'd better haul yours up above the water line before you leave. You understand the arrangements? When and where to meet?'

'Yes. I understand,' she said, and for a moment they stood looking at each other.

Then she turned away and went slowly up the steps to the cottage.

Chapter Eight

'Give me your hand for the last pull-up.'

Philippa laughed, looking up at the man standing on the top of the peak they had just climbed.

'What do you think I am? A fat elderly lady?' she asked, and gave a spring which landed her on the rock beside him.

'Either with or without your hand, am I to tell you what you are?' he asked. 'Come here, my chattel, when your lord and master commands you!' and he caught at her arm, bare, warm, sunburnt, and pulled her down with him on the flower-spangled grass that grew in some miraculous way seemingly from the very rock itself.

She tried to shake him off, struggling laughingly with him.

'I'm no one's chattel,' she said, 'nor are you my lord and master,' but her strength was of no avail against the splendid virility of his body and soon she gave it up and ceased to fight him and lay there at his side, her head propped up by his arm so that with him she could look out over the vast range of the mountains, tier on tier, receding it seemed into infinity, the tops of them clad in everlasting snow, their lower slopes hidden by great tracts of spruce and fir, and below them the grass and below that again the sapphire waters of the lake.

'I can't fight you anymore,' she said half-drowsily.

'You'd never win, anyway, you worm, you insect,' he said, biting her ear. 'And I'm not your lord and master? Well, even if I'm not, you're my lady and my goddess and my eternal beloved,' his voice losing its teasing note for the deep, quiet tones which had the power to turn her bones to water.

She turned to rub her cheek against his arm.

'Don't love me so much, Fergus,' she said in a low voice.

'I wouldn't lose one bit of what I feel for you even if I could,' he said. 'There just aren't any words to tell you, but I think you know.'

'Yes. Yes, I know,' she whispered and closed her eyes.

To be with him there, with all that awe-inspiring beauty spread before her eyes, to sit with him on the top of the world to hear nothing but the sound of his voice, to feel nothing but his nearness – it caught her breath in a sound that was half-sob.

'There's no need, you know,' he said quietly.

'No need?'

'To part from me tomorrow. That's what that sigh meant, wasn't it?'

'Partly. Well—wholly perhaps. Fergus, my dearest love, we agreed that we wouldn't spoil things here by mixing them up with either past or future.'

'I know, and I've kept to it. But now that it's nearly over, the most wonderful two weeks I have ever spent, how can we not think of the future? We were in love with each other when we came here. Now it's more than being in love. We love each other, and we know that it is for keeps. How can we part now? Now that we are one flesh, one mind, one spirit? Philippa—Philippa ...'

'Darling, don't!' and she lifted her head and pressed her lips against his to silence them, her arms straining him to her.

'Stay with me,' he said. 'Let me see Justin, tell him what has happened, ask him to set you free.'

'I can't. Fergus, my dear love, we've been through all that so many times and there's never more than the one answer. I must go back.'

'Even if he will consent to your having the child?'

'He wouldn't and I couldn't ask him. Please, please, Fergus. You promised. Don't spoil today. Let's have these last few hours, our last night together, without anything to spoil them.'

'I shall never willingly give you up or let you go back to him, Philippa. You're mine, mine only and altogether,' but even whilst he spoke, putting into the words all the vehemence of which he was capable, he knew that he battered in vain against that determination of hers. She would go back. There was nothing he could do to prevent it.

They sat in silence to watch, as they had watched on each of those enchanting evenings, the miracle of the sunset, touching the snow peaks with jewels that took their radiance and gave it back again, rose and sapphire and amethyst, the ruby and the topaz and always the glitter of a million million diamonds.

Even in the happiness of their first nights, the sunset had brought its touch of sadness. Now they sat with their arms round each other and all about them brooded the sorrow of the next day's parting.

Philippa shivered and he picked up the white fleecy coat he had carried for her and wrapped her in it. She thanked him with a smile but shook her head.

'It's not my body that's cold. It's my heart thinking about—all the tomorrows,' she said, and then put a finger against his lips so that he should not offer her again that solution impossible to accept.

'Let's go down,' he said, and they descended, hand in hand, their feet familiar now with the rough mountain path that led them down to the tiny village hanging on as by a miracle to the steep slope, just a half-dozen little wooden chalets, their overhanging roofs sheltering them in the winter, the great stacks of logs already piled against the walls though it was still summer, and the windows were flung wide and the doors seldom shut.

With a word and a smile for the children sitting on one of the wooden steps of the veranda playing with two puppies and a small kid, the lovers went into the house and to their room, bare and clean and shining, the floor, the walls, the ceiling all of the same sweet-smelling, polished wood which had also made the huge bed with its boxed sides, the table which held jug and basin and roughly framed mirror, the chairs which just now were set on the small private balcony from which they could look down at the lake below.

Their evening meal was served to them there by the smiling daughter of the house, a simple meal of soup, homemade rolls and goats' milk cheese. Then Gretchen brought them a pitcher of coffee, another of hot milk, carried away the used dishes and smilingly bade them good night.

It was a day as the other days had been, a day which had held nothing eventful, nothing memorable, and yet would live in their hearts whilst life remained.

They went in at last, and Fergus closed the shutters against the early-morning mist which, before they awoke, would wrap the village in its damp white veil. Philippa stood to watch him.

'This I must remember,' her heart was saying, 'and this, and this. Just how he looks now, the easy way he moves and lifts the heavy shutters, the way he stoops to fasten them. Now he will turn to me – and smile – and come to me …

That night, for the first time since he had become her lover, Fergus had a recurrence of the torment of those terrifying dreams which he had come to believe had gone forever.

Philippa, her own sleep troubled because, even in her moments of ecstasy, her conscience would not let her rest, woke to find him twisted and writhing in that agony of mind and memory which tortured his body in its futile attempt to find relief.

Broken, unintelligible words came from his lips as his head struck the pillow again and again and when she spoke to him in alarm, for a few moments he seemed not even to know her. Then, when she tried to get up, his arms clung to her.

'Don't leave me. Hold me. These frightful things. Things I've done – seen – Philippa!'

He was wet through with the perspiration which streamed from him, her own body chilled by it.

'I'm here, my darling,' she said. 'It's alright. It was only a dream. You're awake now. It was just a dream. Lie quietly, dearest, and rest.'

Presently he let her go so that she could do what little could be done for him, towels, fresh pyjamas, eau de Cologne for his head and cool, wet pads over his eyes which at last began to lose their look of frenzy.

Then he spoke normally again.

'Are you ashamed of me? You see me as I am, a coward, afraid of shadows,' a deep disgust and loathing of himself in his voice.

She rocked him in her arms as one seeks to comfort a child.

'No!' she cried, her heart torn with pity for him. 'You're no coward. Do you think I haven't heard by now something of your war record which you will never speak about? Of the things you've done since? The mad, outrageously brave things? Marie told me. They all know at Bonavie and you're a god to them – and to me, my darling. All this is because you've not yet completely recovered from that last crash. That's all it is. Do you think I can't understand?'

He let her talk, though she did not know even whether he was listening to her, his body still now, his face still grey and drawn but no longer twisting with hideous grimaces.

Then presently he began to speak again, unburdening himself of all that weight which so far he had doggedly earned alone, refusing to share any of it lest any other human being could call him the coward he called himself. In his stumbling phrases which gradually became more complete and coherent, he took her through those months of fear and anguish, the nights he had dreaded, the torture which linked the days to them in a jagged chain of horror. He made it so real to her that, holding him to her, she marvelled in a new torment of fear that he had gone on living at all, that he had not ended it for himself instead of struggling on, so slowly and so gradually getting back towards normality and safety and health.

He had been so sure that he was getting back. Whereas at one time he had had the dreams every night unless he were given the oblivion of a drug, by the time he had reached Bonavie they came only every few nights. Since knowing Philippa, he had been entirely free of them, nearly three weeks. His mind had been at peace when he went to sleep, and when dreams came, they were of happy things, of Philippa and of love.

He did not tell her what she knew, namely that this dream had come back because of tomorrow's parting. He kept silent because he would not become an abject pleader for what she would not give. If she would not come to him for love and because she could not endure life without him, he would not abase himself by begging her to come for pity. Not another word came from him about their parting, but she knew he was afraid to sleep again and he lay awake in her arms until the morning.

Philippa had not slept. She had kept vigil at the altar of her love.

They did not talk of intimate matters as they breakfasted for the last time on their balcony, packed their belongings, drove to the little station on the mountain railway after many farewells and compliments and thanks and promises had been exchanged with Gretchen and her kindly family. Their tongues spoke of all the things that were of no importance, of the sunshine and the blue lake, of the eternal snows, of the music of the cow-bells and the melodious cries of the cowherds, presently of trains and of meals, of tickets and passports and labels.

Philippa had contrived to keep her passport from Fergus so that he should not know her name and rank. At first it had been merely so that she might remain anonymous to him. Now it had become something different. It had been impossible for her to make him understand why she would not let him make any attempt to get her husband to set her free. She had told him that there were no religious principles at stake, that she did not disapprove of divorce or of re-marriage, but that in her own case she found the proposition impossible to accept.

He had persisted.

'You love me, don't you, Philippa?'

'You know I do.'

'And you are and know you always will be completely happy with me, as far as human beings can achieve happiness?'

'Yes, my darling.'

'And you know that your marriage was a mistake, undertaken in ignorance? That you married a man who can never be your real mate or give you a full and complete life?'

'I—I suppose so.'

'You suppose so? You *know* it. We live in a modern world in which we face facts sensibly instead of blinding ourselves with old, worn-out shibboleths. Don't you love that word, by the way? I didn't know I knew it. Philippa, we love and want and need each other. Come to me.'

'There's—Trevor,' she said slowly.

'I've told you. He shall be mine just as surely as if I were his father, just as the children I give you will be mine.'

'I couldn't ask Justin that. I couldn't take everything from him even if he would be willing to give it, which I know he will not be. He would never give up his son. I would never ask him to.'

And you couldn't give him up yourself? Not even for me? Not for all there is in life for us? Darling, you're putting too much into this parent and child relationship. Look at all the other mothers you know. They bear their sons in pain and agonise over them all through their early childhood, magnifying every little ache or sickness into a major tragedy, every time adding just a little to their own burden of life, another wrinkle perhaps, a little of their own vitality gone. As a rule the whole of the child's early days and adolescence mean self-sacrifice and self-denial by the mother so that they can have everything and she makes do with nothing but the bare necessities, sometimes not even those. And as soon as the need for personal giving is over, what happens? The son marries, goes off abroad perhaps, in any case leaves the home. And then? Well, if the wife is a good and unselfish wife with a little conscientiousness she nags at him until he writes, scantily and rarely, to the mother who has watched the post for weeks, months perhaps, and hugs the scrap of paper to her and feeds her heart on the few scribbled lines for the weeks or months that will pass before the next one comes. All the time, she makes excuses which may delude others but which never delude or comfort herself. He is very busy, she says. Of course he has a very important and exacting job with little time for writing. Or, desperate at last, she says brightly and gaily that of course she has heard, that he writes to her every week – oh well, nearly every week – and she gets up early to go to the door and get the mail herself so that no one else in the house shall know how many times she has told that lie.

'My dear, I know. How? Because I've been like that and by the time I saw myself through plain glass, it was too late. My mother was dead. I didn't have to write any more of those grudging little letters. I didn't even have to have all the bother of saying thank you to her for her many kindnesses, for gifts she could not afford to make. I wasn't bored any longer by her concern for me, her anxiety about my winter vests, the cough mixtures she sent me. I was saved all that bother – and how do you think I feel about my mother now?'

'No, darling, this mother business isn't right or fair or even decent, as far as the mother is concerned. If mothers kept their children, especially their sons, in the right perspective and made them assume their right proportions in their lives, there would be fewer unhappy wives, fewer aching hearts amongst the mothers. You are already one of those mothers in the making. You are prepared to sacrifice yourself now, all your happiness and your future, for the sake of a son who will turn out like most other sons, casual, uncaring, not really unloving but never showing any of the love for which you will hunger, having given up my love for it.'

She had listened without moving, listened not because anything he said could move her from her determination not to lose her child but rather because he was giving her yet more knowledge and understanding of himself, helping to complete in every detail her picture of him. She had not known there was this gnawing remorse because of his mother, though whenever he had spoken of her it had been with a lingering tenderness which she now realised had striven to pierce the veil that hid her from him and through which, for all his strivings, he could never now reach her.

She could not leave her baby, nor could she ever ask Justin to give him up to her, to bring up away from the Abbey, out of reach of the Hollmere traditions and heritage. Nor could she find it in her heart to leave Justin for the sake of her own happiness and that of Fergus. Justin had in no way sinned against her. He was as he was made, and he had given her all his essential goodness, his kindness, his infinite generosity of mind and of material things, never forgetting or allowing her or anyone else to forget what Hollmere Abbey owed to her.

No, she could not leave Justin, and by the time she and Fergus made that last journey of their stolen holiday together, an uncomfortable one because the crowded summer traffic had made it impossible for him, even by bribery, to get sleepers for them, the subject had been exhausted and dropped. He had accepted the inevitable and all he could do now was to care meticulously for such comfort as could be got her, and try not to let her see him counting the hours and the minutes that still remained.

It was necessary for them to go to St. Malo in order to reach Bonavie, and when they got there it was to find that there was no connecting train for four hours. Philippa, who had not slept at all on their last night in Switzerland, and only in brief, broken snatches during the long train journey, looked white and exhausted and Fergus brushed aside her half-hearted suggestion that they go into the town to find some place where, late as it was, they might be able to get some hot coffee.

'I'm not going to drag you round St. Malo at this hour or have you sitting on the benches in the waiting-room,' he said. 'I know where I can get a car of sorts. If we can also get coffee, well and good, but what you want is to get to your bed and sleep. I'm going to leave you here in this corner with our luggage whilst I rout out old Antoine and get his car. You won't move from here?'

She gave him a weary smile and shook her head.

'I don't think I could,' she said, and when he came back for her, an ancient and dusty car drawn up nearby, he found her asleep with her head on their suitcases. She was grubby and untidy, her suit in a thousand creases, her hat with its jaunty feather falling grotesquely over one eye, and a ladder in her stocking.

He stood looking at her, smiling with loving, aching tenderness. Then he picked her up in his arms and, scarcely rousing her, carried her to the car and laid her down on the back seat, padding the broken springing as best he could with his coat.

She scarcely stirred until, with the dawn still a long way off, they began to bump over the uneven road, little more than a path, which would take them to Bonavie. Then, waking fully, she spoke to him and he stopped and she came to sit beside him, rested but not greatly refreshed by her sleep.

'You will be able to get in alright?' he asked when they came within sight of the little harbour, and of Pierre's cottage perched above it.

'Yes, they never lock up and I sent a card to tell Marie I should be back today sometime,' she said. 'They get up at crack of dawn, anyway.'

At the last minute, though she had pleaded for no goodbyes, he strained her to him. They had agreed that what lay between them must end here, that neither of them could endure a sordid, squalid intrigue before curious eyes and sniggering minds. She would go home, she had said, and had refused to allow him even to return to England with her.

'Let it end here where it began,' she had told him.

Now, holding her to him for a moment and kissing her chilled lips which warmed beneath his own in spite of the grip she had on herself, he whispered only half-heard words.

'My darling, my dear beloved – the memory of you – all my devotion – my gratitude …

'Don't. Don't make me cry—Fergus—dearest …'

She pulled herself away from him and stood with face and eyes averted whilst he brought her case up the steps and left it at the door. Then, without another word or look, she went in and left him outside alone, the closed door between them.

With trembling finger's she felt for matches and her candle, lit it and set it on her dressing-table.

Some letters lay there. They would be from Justin and from her mother, or perhaps from Ena Blackthorne. Only those three knew where she was or that she was here as Mrs. Breane.

She felt no urge to pick up the letters. Justin's handwriting on the topmost envelope was a stab of her conscience. How was she going to endure it, as she must do?

Then at the other side of the mirror she caught sight of two more envelopes, telegrams, and she picked them up with a sick foreknowledge of disaster. What sort of disaster?

She turned them over in her cold hands and at last tore one open, wondering which had been sent first if both were from the same source.

As it happened, she had opened the second one, and she read it and sank down with bowed head and bursting heart on the edge of her bed, the paper dropping to the floor.

Dad died this morning. Mother, was all that it said.

The other one had been sent three days previously, and in it her mother had told her of Joe Joliman's sudden illness and had urged her to come home at once.

She sat there for a few minutes, stunned with shock and grief. Her father had been the most outstanding figure of her life for as long as she could remember. Firm and immovable as the mountains themselves, he had seemed to her, never failing her, able to understand her when she had not understood herself, someone to lean on in any emergency whilst never thrusting his support at her unless her dire need of it was certain.

Though they had never discussed Justin nor her marriage, she had felt sure that he had known what it was that made her marriage not quite the success it appeared outwardly to be.

'Never expect a man to be perfect, lovey, nor even made in your own image,' he had told her once. 'Don't try to treat any man the way I treat my meat, chopping bits off 'ere and pushing bits in there so as to force it into the exact size and shape of the tin. If there are bits missing as you'd like to see there, don't think about them too much but look at the extra bits you didn't even know was there to make up for 'em.'

It was a knife in her heart to know that he had been ill, dying, and that she had not gone to him, that he had probably asked for her, looked for her, tried to keep alive until she came – and had died without her.

Her mother's second telegram told her that this had happened. *Dad died this morning*, Ella Joliman had said, starkly, not trying to smooth it or wrap it up. If it shocked Philippa, her mother did not care. She could have been there and did not go.

Her anguish filled her heart to the exclusion of all other griefs and she did not even remember Fergus, except as the man with whom she had been when she might have been with her father in his last hour.

She dragged out her other suitcase and began to fill it with the things she had not taken to Switzerland with her, her mind too numbed to make plans. She only knew she must get away.

She had just finished packing when she heard Pierre stumping about, stirring the fire in the kitchen that never went out, filling the kettles, exchanging with Marie the few brief words, rarely complete sentences, which served them for conversation.

She went to him, showed him her mother's telegram, the import of which not even his scant knowledge of the language could mistake, and said in a queer, unfamiliar voice that she must go at once.

'*Oui, oui*' he agreed, and with a half-scared glance at the guest, shuffled off to fetch his wife.

Philippa had no tears. The hurt went too deeply, the shock had been too great.

'I most go home, Marie,' she said. 'Will you find me a car to take me to St. Malo?'

Marie did not hesitate. The best man to help was Philippa's own countryman.

'*Je vais chercher Monsieur,*' she muttered and Philippa realised without emotion of any sort that it was Fergus whom she had gone to fetch.

She had still one or two things to do, a couple of small bills she owed for a film and some powder at the one local shop, and for oil for her boat. There was the boat itself to be sent back, but she could do that by letter from England. She made a rough estimate of what she owed Marie, added to it the other items, jotted them down on a scrap of paper and left a heap of roughly counted notes to cover them amply.

Only half consciously she heard a car drive up and stop as near to the door as the road allowed. It would be Fergus, she thought with a throb of thankfulness that he had been so quick.

'I can't carry both cases,' she called out.

Pierre had already left everything in Marie's capable hands and gone about his day's work.

'I'll fetch them,' said a voice. 'Where are you?'

She started, drawing a sharp breath.

The next moment she was face to face with Justin.

'It's—you!' she said in a gasp of astonishment.

'We were worried about you,' he said. 'You know what's happened?'

'Yes. I've only just got back. I've been—away.'

His eyes went past her to the dressing-chest on which lay the envelopes of the telegrams and the little pile of still unopened letters.

'You've only just had the telegram asking you to return?' he asked gently.

She nodded mutely.

'Of course I would have gone,' she said.

She seemed like a lost child now rather than the practical, efficient Philippa and he put an arm about her briefly and kissed her cheek.

'Are you ready to come now?' he asked. 'I've got a car here, and the plane's being refuelled. I don't need to tell you how terribly shocked I am, do I, darling?'

She shook her head. She could not speak again but hurried past him and got into the waiting car. He followed with her luggage, stowed it in the boot and leaned into the car to speak to her.

'Is there anything to do? Bills to pay or anything?' he asked.

'No, I've seen to it,' she said, and sat bolt upright, her hands clenched in her lap, her eyes hard and bright with the tears they could not shed.

Not until they had reached the field where the little plane lay waiting for them and had climbed into it and were on their way across the channel did she think of Fergus.

Fergus.

She looked at Justin seated beside her in the tiny, cramped cabin. Except that he was very grave and looked tired, he was as he had always been, familiar, safe, unexciting, unable to stir her to the least emotion, and yet he was Justin, her husband, and she was caught back again into the known routine. The young pilot had looked at her respectfully and called her 'my lady'.

Fergus seemed to have gone infinitely far away, almost as if he had never been, as if all this tumult of emotion, of rapture, of laughter, of passion, had been something she had read in a book.

Justin turned to look at her and laid one of his hands over hers.

Special permission had been obtained for the private plane to land, and a customs official was waiting for them.

'I'd better send a telegram,' said Philippa. 'I had a boat at Bonavie. I didn't do anything about returning it.'

Justin nodded.

'Alright, my dear. Do that whilst I see to the luggage. I've got a car waiting.'

Somebody showed her where to go and she wrote her telegram to Fergus. She felt curiously impersonal as she did so … and she could not make him a real, living person to her. Her mind was concerned only with the purely mechanical matter of getting the hired boat back to where it belonged.

When the words had been written, she paused with her pen over the paper. Her forehead wrinkled with the effort at concentration. This was Fergus. If Marie did not find him. Louis would have told him.

'Feeleep has gone,' he would have said in the patois which Fergus had picked up so easily.

'Gone? Where? Why?'

She imagined the staccato words and Louis's interested reply, that some gentleman, an English gentleman, had come for her in a car and they had driven away and there had been an aeroplane …

Though her mind was still numbed with grief and self-reproach, she could not leave Fergus like that.

She added to the message she had written, *Country Women's Club. Philippa*, and folded the paper to give it, with some money, to the waiting messenger.

Justin had seen to everything.

'Ready now, dearest?' he asked in the gentle, affectionate tone he had used to her throughout the journey.

She nodded and got into the car. She was grateful to him for being what he was just then, affectionate, kind, unexciting, dependable. Later she would be able to feel again. Pain would come back and with it who could say what of remorse, fear, loss? Just now her husband was able to supply all she needed and she was grateful.

Chapter Nine

Life, the life of the Hollmeres and the Abbey, closed about Philippa as if the surface had never been ruffled, let alone tossed and lashed in the whirlpool of her experience with Fergus Wynton.

She had gone at once to The Beeches to see her mother, but the visit had shocked her almost beyond bearing, not only because the white-faced, hollow-eyed, composed woman was utterly unlike what she had expected to find, but also at her mother's uncompromising attitude towards her.

'He kept asking for you and you didn't come,' was all she would say in answer to Philippa's impassioned explanations and open grief.

'You know I would have come if I'd known, if I'd had any idea!' cried Philippa, the tears pouring down her cheeks whilst that other face was stony and dry.

'You would have had an idea before you went away if you hadn't been so wrapped up in yerself and doin' the grand lady act,' said her mother bitterly. 'Saying you was ill and needed a change!'

'Why didn't you tell me he was ill?' Philippa demanded, her hands clenched, making an effort to get control over herself, bewildered and lost in the presence of this strange woman with whom she could make no contact. She had run to her mother thinking of the outstretched arms, the cushiony breast for her head, their tears mingling for the man they had both loved. Instead she was thrust back on herself, cast out, made almost to feel she had no right here in this house of mourning.

'You could have seen for yerself if you'd got two thoughts in yer mind about anybody but yerself,' said Ella Joliman harshly, and

Philippa had gone blindly away, back to her great house, back to doing what her mother had called her grand lady act.

Was it true? Had she been thinking only of herself? Might she have seen her father's illness and need of her if she had been less selfish? Less concerned with her own affairs?

Justin proved understanding. His essential kindness was revealed in as many ways as his love could devise. He could not know that her conscience turned such acts of his into barbs to pierce her.

'Don't think too much about this attitude of your mother's, dearest,' he said. 'It is part of the reaction of her shock and grief.'

'I am shocked and grieved as well,' said Philippa.

'Yes, but not perhaps in the same way. She feels that her whole life has gone – as mine would be if I lost you. That's a part of happy marriage, the penalty one might be called upon to pay for one's happiness.'

'Yes. Yes, I—know what you mean,' said Philippa in a muffled voice. 'She feels she has nothing left, whilst I—have—still so much.'

Bereft of her father, always such a dominant factor in her life even after her marriage, and bereft, too, it seemed, of all she had come to look for in her mother, she felt herself tossed anchorless on a sea of desolation and storm. Even had it been possible for her to find comfort in Justin's fussy, rather pompous attempts at consolation, the knowledge that she had betrayed him would have kept her from taking advantage of it. In spite of her self-abasement, her attempts to scourge her memories with the whips of conscience and the knowledge of her unworthiness of Justin's trustful love, she could not keep the thought of Fergus from constantly invading her mind. She knew that she longed for him, and time, which of necessity made less poignant the loss of her father, did nothing to ease her of the burden of her aching need of the man she knew she most deeply loved.

Daily she had to force herself to accept Justin's little acts of thoughtfulness, of the protective care with which he sought to surround her whatever she did and wherever she went. Instead of making her grateful to him, she was made unhappier by the feeling of irritation such acts engendered so that there were times when she could scarcely bear his company and longed to get away from him, had to hold herself rigidly in check lest she let him see how passionately she wanted to be left alone.

With that part of her which she had acquired, like a shell to cover her real self, with her marriage, she went through all the motions of being Lady Hollmere, of carrying out the duties and obligations of her position. Some of the merely social duties could be discarded for the moment because of her recent bereavement, but other responsibilities had to be accepted. There were village activities which would suffer from her absence, her regular visits to the local hospital of whose committee she was an important member, church work which had always been undertaken by the Lady of the Manor.

In addition she tried to find solace and temporary forgetfulness in spending more time with her child, playing with him, taking him out, choosing his clothes, doing for him some of the things which most mothers do for their children but which it had not seemed 'suitable' for a Lady Hollmere to do.

At length something happened which, unconnected with her secret life, offered her temporary distraction.

Ena Blackthorne came to her with shining eyes and transfigured face, an open letter in her hand.

'Busy?' she asked.

'Only trying to fill time,' said Philippa. 'Have you been left a fortune?'

She was in the linen room, making a new list of the stocks of sheets, towels, cloths, everything of the finest quality and heavily monogrammed, the shelves fragrant with the sachets of lavender, orris root and pot-pourri which old Lady Hollmere made herself from flowers and herbs grown for the purpose in the Abbey gardens. Philippa could never see herself, when that austere lady had at length been vanquished by the one invincible conqueror, pottering about with scissors and pots and bottles and little bags, following the ancient recipes in the yellow-leaved book.

'I've just had this,' said Ena. 'From Paul. It says that his wife is dead. Oh, I don't want that to sound too crude, but—we can be married, Philippa. That's what the letter's about. He wants us to be married quite soon.'

Philippa came out of the retreat in which her mind had been wallowing in its own affairs.

Sue put out her arms impulsively and gave Ena a little hug.

'My dear. I'm so glad, and of course it isn't crude. After all you never knew her and she can't mean anything much to him now. You'll do it? Marry at once?'

Ena nodded. Her plain, homely face had become beautiful as the faces of all women who know themselves loving and beloved can reflect beauty. There was a soft radiance about her. Happiness shone in her eyes and danced in her voice. Her dull dark hair had become loosened, and even her habitual tailor-made suit of clerical grey looked in some way different today.

'I'd like to. I won't leave you stranded without someone, of course. Will you think it presumptuous of me if I suggest someone? Do you remember the girl who came to help with the letters after your wedding? Dorothy Blunt? Short, rather plump, about forty?'

'I think I do. I'm going to miss you terribly, Ena. There's no way in which you could stay on, is there? We've got such heaps of room here, and we could easily fix up a suite for you and Paul, a complete flat if you like – or you could have the tower rooms.'

'That's lovely of you, Philippa, and I do appreciate it, but it wouldn't work. For one thing, Paul has to live in Town, and be easily available, and for another – you'd be flying in the face of every sort of tradition if you harboured Paul Kerslik here, in the sacred precincts of Hollmere Abbey!'

'Why—Ena! Fancy *you* saying anything like that! I thought I was the only person who metaphorically and quite privately cocks a snook at anything Hollmere!'

Ena laughed rather shamefacedly.

'I know I ought not to. The family has always been so kind to me ...'

Philippa interrupted her with a short laugh.

'Kind! Working you like a galley slave and paying you as little as possible because of the valuable "perks" which they considered went with it, being allowed to sit in the rooms the family occupy, to dine with the visitors when an extra woman is wanted to balance the table, even to take a hand at bridge when no other fourth can be found? My dear, don't talk to me about the kindness of the Hollmeres where you are concerned. Justin is kind because he could never be anything else to anybody, but I can never fathom where in the Hollmere make-up he got his quality of kindness.'

Ena was looking at her with a speculative and surprised frown and Philippa recovered herself with a mental shake.

'Don't mind me,' she said. 'I'm just having a difficult day. Let's go on about your marriage. I do understand, of course, about it being better for Paul to live in London, though if it were not so, I should keep on nagging until you had promised to live here. What are your plans? Afterwards, I mean? Of course you'll be married from here, and I shall give a reception for you.'

'Oh no, Philippa! That would never do, I assure you,' said Ena, shocked. 'I may as well tell you now that Lady Hollmere discovered my friendship with Paul and taxed me with feeling more than that for him, and when I wouldn't deny it, she was furious and read me a long lecture about upholding the traditions of the Hollmeres and not lowering myself ...'

Again Philippa interrupted her with a laugh, that new laugh of hers, flavoured with something slightly bitter.

'She felt that Justin was lowering the traditions by marrying me, but money made quite a satisfactory prop when it came to the point.'

'Philippa, what's happened to you? Oh, I know losing your father like that was a terrible blow to you and a grief you find it hard to get over – but isn't there something else? Or do you not want me to ask you?'

Philippa looked into the distance unseeingly.

'I don't mind your asking and if there were anyone I could tell, it would be you, Ena,' she said. 'It's always been hard to believe that you're one of the family, and I can only imagine you're far enough away from its core to have escaped the infection. Don't ask me, Ena. Let's go on talking about you. I shall be really upset if you refuse to be married from here. This is your home and we are your people. Paul is a good man and a great artist and there is no reason in the world why you should not marry him nor why the Hollmeres should consider him beneath them. Let me do this for you, Ena. Please.'

'I can't refuse when you put it as a personal affair, Philippa dear,' said Ena sincerely. 'I know Paul will feel honoured, and I have so little to bring him that I am grateful for the chance to show him honour. Heavens, doesn't that sound pompous? Was it said like a Hollmere?'

They laughed together, and Philippa threw herself into the affairs of Ena to find relief, if only temporarily, from the torment of her own private life. She not only arranged the wedding to take place from the Abbey, the actual ceremony in the village church where she herself had been married and the reception in the Great Hall, but she also persuaded Ena and Paul to let her help them with their home. Like nearly all young people marrying, they had despaired of finding a home of their own. They must either live in someone else's house, with other people's furniture, or else they must pay a rent they could not afford for an unfurnished flat, or find a large lump sum which was actually a premium though it might masquerade under the name of 'remainder of lease', 'furniture and fittings', and so on.

Philippa persuaded them, with considerable difficulty, to let her pay such a sum demanded for a charming, small flat in Chelsea whose rent they could afford once the initial bribe had been paid.

'It's partly for myself,' Philippa had told them. I shall have somewhere to stay when I want a night in Town. Justin hates to tear himself away from his beloved pigs and crops even for one night, and it isn't worth opening up Hollmere House every time, and one of the things that are not done, even in this day and age, is for Lady Hollmere to stay in an hotel unaccompanied by her husband or elderly female relative!'

She was, of course, exaggerating a little, because if she wanted to stay in Town in an hotel, she did so, but she knew that it was looked upon with disapproval by old Lady Hollmere, and through her, by Justin.

'Of course, you'll always be welcome,' Ena and Paul had told her warmly.

The wedding, which necessitated opening up the reception rooms at the Abbey and issuing invitations and seeing people again, brought

Philippa out of the solitude into which she had sunk after her father's death. Though there was no open breach between her and her mother, relations were strained and Philippa's visits to The Beeches, where Mrs. Joliman lived alone with the servants, were fewer and more formal than they had been. Soon after her marriage, Philippa had had a path cut through the woods so that a short walk took her directly to her parents' home, and now when she went to see her mother, she found it easier and less embarrassing if she took Trevor with her, wheeling him in his pram. The path took her near enough to the Dower House for it to be possible for old Lady Hollmere to catch sight of them from her windows, and it gave Philippa secret satisfaction to know that the old lady disapproved of her wheeling her own pram. It was one of the many things 'not done' by the bearers of her name. When Philippa took the child to see his paternal grandmother, however, she went in state, driving or being driven along the car road which led to the front door of the Dower House and taking the nurse with her.

Justin was delighted with anything that could help to restore Philippa to something of her former enjoyment of life, and though Lady Hollmere's reactions to the seal of approval of the marriage set upon it by her son were what Philippa and Ena had expected, there was nothing she could do about it. She had to accept it as graciously as she could. The wedding looked like being one of the big, important events of the spring. Philippa found herself adding more and more names to the list which she and Ena were compiling and Ena grew alarmed.

'Paul will be horrified,' she said. 'He's so desperately shy, and all these people – what if he turns tail and can't face it?'

'I shall go early to the church and see to it personally that he doesn't escape,' said Philippa. 'It's a pity you can't be a white bride, Ena, but I suppose your idea of a frock and hat is best.'

'Of course it is. I should look ridiculous at my age, decked out like a young virgin being led to the sacrificial altar!'

Philippa laughed.

'I've often wondered,' she said.

'Whether I'm a virgin? My dear, I am, and I suppose that if it hadn't been for the providential death of Paul's wife, I should have gone to my grave not knowing! It's still wonderful to me that he wants me, that any man would want an old crow like me, but especially Paul.'

'Oh, Ena, I'm going to miss you so much. You're one of the few really human beings at Hollmere. And as for it being wonderful that Paul wants you, haven't you had time to look in the mirror lately? The years have simply dropped from you like leaves in autumn, except that it's spring that's come to you, not autumn. You look—transfigured, and it would not be at all inappropriate for you to be, as you say, decked out in white for the sacrificial altar.'

'Only that it isn't in the least sacrificial,' laughed Ena, her eyes shining, her face faintly flushed. 'If it weren't for all these crowds you're gathering together, I should be able to skip up the aisle towards Paul and the sacrifice in a bound!'

After the marriage, Philippa found she could not, even if she had wanted to do so, retire into her shell of solitude again. Invitations poured in which Justin said they should accept, even though such acceptance meant opening the big, dreary London house, staffing it from the Abbey servants with new additions, spending considerable sums on essential repairs and alterations.

Though it was Justin who had suggested that Philippa should try to widen her interests in this way, he became anxious at the high cost of the work she said must be done.

She brushed aside his anxious calculations.

'What does it matter?' she asked. 'The money's there doing nothing and who knows what the future will bring? If we don't spend it ourselves, the government will find means of taking it away from us, and if we do find that it has not been worth it as far as we are concerned, look how convenient we are making it for the Coal Board, or the Electricity or Gas Boards, or for some Labour Minister to live in!'

He withdrew his objections when he saw her taking an interest in things again, though she surprised him by going to some trouble to retain as much as possible of the original atmosphere of the ugly Edwardian house. The new bathrooms, the improved heating and lighting and plumbing were all cunningly contrived so that they did not war with the heavy furnishings, the sombre draperies, all the relics of many dead generations and a dying age. The only completely drastic changes were in the kitchen and servants' quarters, which she removed from dark basement and draughty attic respectively, and installed a service lift further to save the work of her servants.

Looking at the huge carved pieces of furniture, fingering the hangings of heavy damask and brocade, eyeing the crowded pictures of dead Hollmeres, Philippa could not entirely understand what had prompted her to retain them and let them decide the atmosphere of her London home. Possibly it was with some idea of trying to associate herself more fully with the Hollmeres, to force herself into the pattern so inescapably that she became part of them. If she could act as they did, think as they did, might she not in time feel as they did? Become what she so truly desired she might become, a part of Justin's life, welded to it inseparably? Only by so doing could she hope for peace again.

But she had set herself a task beyond her powers. She could not cast out or even for any length of time forget her aching desire for Fergus, for the comfort of his understanding of her, an understanding which needed no words but was instinctive. It was as if, wandering about in the aloneness of life, she had come upon a friend and companion, had for a little time walked with him hand in hand and had then been torn apart from him and sent into an aloneness so infinitely worse because she had known what it was not to be alone. She knew now that at the first sight of him, the first touch of his hand, each had said to the other: 'You are here at last. You are what I have waited for, I have found you.'

She did not belong to herself any longer. He had possessed her body but that now was almost unimportant. Beyond and within that possession had been the perfect, hitherto undreamed-of possession of her mind. As long as life lasted, without him she would be incomplete.

Summoning all her strength of will, reminding herself fiercely of all the precepts, all the inhibitions of her childhood, of all she had undertaken in marrying Justin, she had kept away from her club though whenever she thought of it (and it was often) the letter which would be lying there from him seemed to burn with an incandescent light, an ever-glowing brightness in the darkness.

Eventually, after some small argument and upset with Justin, an unimportant thing in cause but potent in effect, she took herself off to Town and went into her club, pushed her way unseeing through a small crowd of curious acquaintances, smiling mechanically and returning greetings without realising that she was doing so.

She asked if there were any letters for her.

Some might possibly be addressed to me as Mrs. Breane, she told the girl in the office, trying to make her voice sound casual. 'I sometimes give that name as a refuge from my title,' with a little smile which invited her sympathetic understanding, though the girl did not in the least understand why anyone who could call herself Lady Hollmere should ever want to be addressed as plain Mrs. Breane.

'No, I'm afraid there aren't any, Lady Hollmere,' she said when she had run quick fingers through the little pile of letters from the pigeon-hole labelled 'B'.

Philippa thanked her and walked away, bitterly disappointed and chagrined. It was seven months since she had left Bonavie, and in all that time he had not written to her, had merely accepted what must have seemed to him her decision to end their association. Hadn't he cared enough to try to see her? To try to get her to change her mind? Had he just accepted it like that?

She went round to the flat which was now ready for the Kersliks when they returned from their short honeymoon. She had a key and had undertaken to see to the last-minute arrangements. They would be here later in the day, and Philippa saw that everything was there for their immediate needs until Ena started housekeeping the next day. She had bought flowers and arranged them in some of the new vases, the last of the spring flowers and great bowls of wallflowers, some early roses which had been sent up from the Abbey.

It was a small flat but so soon it would become a home, have that lived-in look which her great house in Mayfair would never have. Ena's work-basket would appear, half-knitted socks for Paul would be lying in a chair, there would be musical scores on the piano which had been Justin's wedding present to them, and sometimes Paul would play his precious violin whilst Ena, who was a good accompanist rather than a musician, would play for him. Philippa closed her eyes and saw the happy, comradely scene, stood outside the happiness and knew it could never in equal measure be hers.

Ena and Paul would probably never have much money. He could not hope to reach the top ranks of world-famous violinists. He would be known to the few, would make up the requisite items in programmes where bigger names reigned. He might possibly become the leader of the orchestra which at present provided him with his regular income. But there would never be any money over, never any to waste on things not strictly useful or necessary. Philippa would gladly have made Ena an allowance, but this had been at once and almost resentfully refused.

'It's lovely of you, but we'll stand on our own feet or topple over together and sit on the edge of the kerb until we can get up again,' she had said, and Philippa had not been able to do more than help them to get the lease of their flat, and slip into it one or two things of her own, which she told Ena cluttered up her rooms at the Abbey.

When the Kersliks returned to take up occupation of the flat and there was nothing more she could do for them, Philippa flung herself with a reckless abandon into the new social life occasioned by the opening of the London house and its varying contacts, contacts which now included the sort of people who form the environment of a rising artist like Paul. To help him, she gave parties at which he played and was a generous donor at the so-called 'charity' performances which included his name.

Lady Hollmere, who had been pleased at first to see Hollmere House open and the Abbey filled with visitors, pursed her lips over some of the parties and some of the guests.

'Your wife seems to have entirely recovered from the death of her father,' she remarked to Justin.

Her reference to Philippa as his wife always indicated displeasure and Justin, meekly amenable over all other things, rose in defence of his wife.

'You mean all this entertaining and going about? I think it is sensible of her. She has by no means forgotten him or really got over his loss. She was very fond of him, you know.'

'Quite extraordinary,' put in Her Ladyship lightly, with a curl of her lip, and Justin knew that there were times when he actually disliked his mother.

'He was her father and she was his only child,' he said. 'She grieves still a great deal over his loss, and all this gay life she is leading is her way of defence against people knowing it. I am glad for her.'

'Well, I am afraid I cannot agree with you. Her name is always in the newspapers, and not always in the sort of company suitable to her position and very seldom, it seems, with her own husband.'

'Things have changed, you know, Mother. What you call our "position" has no real importance now in the country. In fact, it is becoming an embarrassment and a burden and only Philippa's money helps to boost up the Hollmere name for one more generation. As for my not being with her – well, you know how it is. If I were with her all the time, or even much of the time she spends in London, I should have to employ an agent on her money whilst I lived an idle life, and this I am not prepared to do. I like working, and I am improving the property, making it productive and justifying the money Philippa has poured out on it.'

'Then she should spend more time here with you and be in London only at such times as you can be with her,' announced Lady Hollmere finally, her time and the arrogant lift of her head adding silently 'I have spoken'.

Justin did not continue the argument, but for Philippa's sake he made arrangements with Cartwright, his head outside man, so that he could spend a week or two away from home and be with her. Not for the world would he have allowed his mother to know that he himself had suffered a good many pangs at the sudden wildness of Philippa's gaiety and on account of some of the people with whom she shared it.

His personal relations with her had changed since her father's death though neither of them had commented on it or shown any wish to change it. His natural delicacy had at first kept him from intruding on her passionate grief, and only gradually had he realised that, the first anguish of her loss subsiding, their new relationship was so much established that there was no longer any suggestion, tacitly or by word or hint, that she would welcome him. The door between their rooms was never locked, but they had formed a habit of saying good night more or less perfunctorily downstairs, or outside her door. Though he had none of her passionate sex-ardour in his make-up, he was a normal man and would have liked a normal life, unexciting and undemanding, but it was quite beyond his powers to invite what Philippa had ceased to offer. To some extent it worried him. He had realised almost from the first that they were not truly mated and that he could not satisfy her ardent nature, but it was humiliating to him to conclude that he had so far fallen short of her needs and desires that she did not feel it worthwhile to continue their, to her, unsatisfactory sex relationship.

It was perhaps strange that it never occurred to him to wonder whether she had replaced him by a more satisfactory lover, and at a much later date he wondered why it had not occurred to him, except that there was no room in his love for her for suspicion. She was his goddess, and he did not look for the feet of clay.

In London, she had arranged the rooms for the comfort and convenience of both of them. The original main bedroom, vast and high-ceilinged and gloomy, had been reduced to better proportions by cutting off a portion of it to make her bathroom, and the bedroom next to it, formerly the chief guest room, had been treated in the same way to give Justin similar comfort. There was no communicating door, but the rooms had been so arranged that, by turning a third room into a small private sitting-room for herself, and the former huge, dreary bathroom into a dressing-room for Justin, they had now a suite of rooms which could be shut off from the rest of the house by a folding door.

This is very nice. Very clever of you,' he told Philippa.

He had not taken much interest in her plans for the house, secretly chagrined that it should have to be done with her money to which he could add nothing, and this was the first time he had seen the finished effect.

In these times nobody is expected to want any privacy,' said Philippa cheerfully, 'so I have forestalled any attempt to invade ours. When Lady Hollmere saw this, she observed that when she entertained here, guests were invited into her own room to leave their wraps and so on. I particularly liked the "so on" because whatever my guests may think about not bang conducted to the state apartments to leave their mink, they cannot possibly think my provision of a special "so on" attached to the retiring-room downstairs anything but an improvement on the archaic place they had to use up here!'

She rattled on, he knew, to pass the first moment of mutual embarrassment, and he smiled and nodded.

You've done everything beautifully, my dear – but then everything you do is done beautifully.'

It struck her suddenly that Justin was *old*, though in actual years forty was not old for a man, and a number of her men acquaintances were older than that in years but seemed her contemporary in everything that mattered. When she had married him, thirty-five had seemed quite a lot older than twenty-two, but the difference in years had either been covered up by mutual interests or else she had become used to it. Now it struck her forcibly that only a middle-aged man, a man already settling down into an acceptance of life, would have used just that tone to her, would have called her 'my dear' as her father might have done, would have smiled in just that indulgent fashion, approving the activities of a child.

'Justin, you make that sound as if I were still a schoolgirl,' she said unexpectedly.

'Well, sometimes that's what you seem to me to be,' he said.

She had a frightened feeling, as if she were losing her hold on something that she had trusted to sustain her. Impulsively she laid a hand on his arm and then withdrew it and turned her head away and made some irrelevant remark about the colour of the curtains. She had seen the quick response in his eyes, of interest and pleasure, and she knew, hating the knowledge, that she shrank from that response. What was it she really wanted? she asked herself impatiently – and knew the answer. She wanted what most women want in their hearts, the security of a steady, unexciting, reliable husband and the excitement of a gay and ardent and unpredictable lover, and if these two things could be combined in one man, then indeed should her cup be full and running over.

Justin could never be the latter and probably Fergus never the former. In her relationship to her husband there had always been something of the daughter, the child, the young friend; with Fergus, as well as being lover, she was the mother Justin would never require her to be.

It was during the fortnight which Justin had conscientiously and somewhat pompously arranged to spend with her in London that she found herself going up the steps of her club, not to see if there were a letter for her from Fergus but to leave a message for a friend whom she could not locate elsewhere.

The office was momentarily empty, the door wide open as if the girl had only just left it, and Philippa glanced inside for a piece of paper on which to leave a message. Close at hand were the pigeon-holes in which members' letters were placed, and almost unintentionally she put her hand up to the 'B's' and took out the handful of letters, some eight or nine. Suppose that, after all, Fergus had at last written?

There was none for 'Breane', but there were three with typewritten envelopes, two of them with French stamps on them, addressed to 'Mrs. Philippa Browne'.

Her heart missed a beat. Philippa was not a very common name, and it was surely possible that he had taken the name Breane, as pronounced by the one or two inhabitants of Bonavie who had known it, for the more English-sounding Browne, and if he had seen it written, he had noticed the final 'e'. Thinking back, she could not remember that she herself had ever given him her name as Breane.

She heard footsteps on the stairs and slipped the three letters into her bag. If they were not for her, she must return them and think up some sort of excuse. In her mind she felt certain that they were from Fergus. One of them had been posted in England.

At that time of day it was easy to find a quiet corner of the club. She found an unoccupied writing-table and sat down at a desk and laid the three envelopes before her, her heart beating fast.

She picked up a letter-opener and slit open the envelope that bore the earliest date. She knew she had not been mistaken. It was from Fergus and had been written the day after she had left Bonavie, and it was a love-letter that tore at her heart and set her pulses leaping and her whole being craving for him. He suggested in it that her sudden flight had been the smiting of conscience, and he urged her to see him, not to end everything between them so precipitately and without thought.

His second letter, written a week later, was again filled with love and longing for her and with disappointment at not hearing from her. It said that he would be returning shortly to England to do some sort of ground job for a few months, and that he begged her to see him.

The third one, giving an address in Surrey, had been written after a lapse of more than two months, and it was in a different vein, still urging her to see him if only in some public place for a few minutes, but not to insist on ending everything between them without a word. She looked again at the date. It had lain there in that pigeon-hole for nearly five months.

She wished she had not read the letters, which had brought back the past too vividly for her mind to be able to cast it out. She knew now how deeply she had longed to hear from him, how bitter had been the thought that he had mutely accepted her disappearance from his life. She pressed the letters against her heart and her face was flushed and her eyes shining. It was futile to remind herself of Justin, and that he deserved better at her hands. She must see Fergus again, if only, as he said, in a public place and for a few minutes. No consideration of loyalty had any power over the urgency of body and mind for her lover.

The address on the third letter was that of an aerodrome in Surrey, and she took some paper from the rack in front of her and wrote quickly, addressing her letter to him there.

She made no formal opening, unable to be sure that the letter would find him.

PHILIPPA

*I have only just received your three letters, she wrote. If you still
want to contact me, will you write again? And the name is Breane,
not Browne, which accounts for my not having received them. P.*

She hoped the reception clerk would not notice the disappearance of
the letters to Mrs. Philippa Browne and associate her with them, but
she could not help it if she did. She slipped by the office, forgetting
the message she had come there to leave, and hurried to a post-box.
What if, as was more than probable, he had left that address?

But two days later, when she went into the club looking as
nonchalant as she could, the girl in the office smiled at her and took
a letter from the rack.

'The letter you've been expecting has come at last, Lady Hollmere,'
she said, and there it was, addressed this time to Mrs. P. Breane in the
writing she now knew so well.

Philippa took it and put it with a show of indifference into her
pocket.

'Thank you. It's quite unimportant after all this time,' she said and
strolled off to find a place where she could avidly read what Fergus
had written.

My darling,
How criminally absurd of me to have let that happen! I nearly
went out of my mind through not hearing from you and when I
came to England I wonder I wasn't arrested for hanging about a
yeomen's club the way I hung about yours in the hope of seeing
you. I am still in this Godforsaken job, my nose to the ground, but
I must see you. Will you telephone me at the number above? It's
the local pub and more private than the mess. I'll hang around
each evening from seven till ten-thirty until you can ring me there,
and let it be soon if you don't want me to drink myself to death.
My darling – my dearest – everything.
Fergus.

It was a difficult evening for her, as she was giving a dinner-party to
important guests; Lady Hollmere was to be present (and her eyes

never missed one movement nor her ears one syllable from her daughter-in-law), and as the Kersliks would be there as guests, two influential men in the musical world had been asked to meet Paul.

It was not until nearly ten o'clock that she had any opportunity to leave her guests for sufficient time to get a call through to the number Fergus had given her, and in the end she had to ask Ena to cover her.

'Please keep them all talking and all here, if you can, for the next ten minutes,' she whispered. 'I simply must make a telephone call and the only private extension is in my bedroom.'

Ena had watched her during the evening and thought she had never seen her lovelier nor more animated. Her eyes were starry, her whole face illumined by them as if by an inner glow. Laughter came from her and followed her wherever she went. Always a competent and attractive hostess, tonight she had surpassed herself in gay sallies, in quick flashes of wit and retorts so apt that the Very Important guests were charmed and intrigued by her. For the first time since her father's death, she had come fully out of mourning and wore a gown of stiff brocade, amber threaded with gold, which set off to perfection her colouring to which she added little artifice. Her hair was frankly brown when that of most others of her generation was ash blonde, or platinum silver, or gold, brass, red, black, anything but the honest brown of Philippa's. The make-up she used was merely conventional, her own colouring beneath it being that of her vigorous health.

Tonight, witty and gay and surrounded by that aura of happiness which had for so long been missing, she yet contrived to retain that quality which Ena had once described as 'being Lady Hollmere', a mixture of dignity, poise and leisurely watchfulness for the comfort of every guest which made her hospitality something to be sought after and appreciated.

Ena, who loved Philippa second only to Paul, watched her with affectionate concern. Undoubtedly something had happened to bring that gaiety and light-heartedness back, and it seemed reasonable to suppose that it had nothing to do with Justin who was exactly as usual, serious, a little heavy, taking his duties as host with grave earnestness. Ena saw Lady Hollmere watching her daughter-in-law, disapproving of her as she had always done but seldom able to find anything concrete on which to base that disapproval.

'If she can hurt Philippa or spoil Justin's satisfaction with her, she will,' thought Ena anxiously, and her anxiety deepened when Philippa came to her with her whispered request. She wanted to say to her 'Be careful. For heaven's sake, don't slip up, whatever it is,' but that was a thing one could not say to Philippa, and Ena, though she was no longer merely a paid employee and a poor relation, could not bring herself to overstep the boundary.

It took Philippa so long to get her call through that she knew she would be missed downstairs and her absence noted, if not yet commented upon, by both Justin and Lady Hollmere, but her longing to hear Fergus's voice made her defiant, and when at last it came through to her, she felt almost faint with the joy of it.

'Fergus—oh, darling!' she said, and scarcely heard his reply for the beating of her heart and the tumult of her senses.

'When can I see you? Where? Darling, aren't you *there*?' he was asking insistently, and, foolishly, she nodded and put a hand to her throat which ached.

'Yes—yes, of course I'm here,' she said shakily. 'It's just that—that I can hardly speak.'

'I know. Does my voice sound queer too?'

'Yes, queer but still yours. Oh, Fergus, what a fool I was to let that happen! To let you get my name wrongly!'

'I couldn't imagine what had happened. I simply refused for months to believe that you would cut me off like that.'

'It would have been better,' said Philippa, some of the radiance going from her voice now that the first ecstatic moment was over.

'I won't let you say that. I've been in hell all this time without seeing or hearing from you. What do we do next? Where do we go from here? When can I see you?'

'Almost any time or any place,' she told him recklessly.

'Shall I come up to Town or shall we meet somewhere?'

'I'll meet you.'

They arranged a time and place and she put up the receiver and went back to her guests. Her face was flushed and her eyes were shining. Susan Therne, who was there by virtue of having recently become engaged to one of the Very Important guests, a Dr. Raymond Millet, was watching her as she entered the long double drawing-room. It occurred to her mind, ready as usual to look for undercurrents, that Philippa wore the look of having been recently and very satisfactorily kissed.

'By whom?' thought Susan at once, and looked around with lively and spiteful interest to see who was missing, but she could see no one with whom she could associate any such idea.

She had disliked Philippa when they were at school together mainly from jealousy, though she would never have admitted it. Philippa had and was everything she herself so ardently longed to have and to be, lovely to look at, rich and popular. Her jealousy found its outlet in the small, spiteful tortures she devised over Philippa's background and the source of her father's wealth. Then, infuriating her, Philippa unexpectedly turned the tables on her by reappearing in her life, after schooldays were over, as the fiancée of the very man Susan had picked out for herself. Justin had been a friend of her childhood and companion of her girlhood and she had been encouraged by Justin's mother, who had seemed all-powerful where her son was concerned.

That marriage had been galling to Susan in the extreme, especially as she was obliged to be a constant witness to its apparent success and happiness. Tonight there had been a certain somewhat mordant satisfaction in appearing for the first time in public as the future wife of the distinguished scientist, a man of middle age who had somewhat surprisingly been attracted to the girl whose malicious tongue had frightened off men who would otherwise have found her quick wit and the clever way in which she actually exploited her lack of beauty, attractive. Few people could remain unaware of Susan Therne's presence in any company, and there were always a little knot of people, mostly men, about her, enjoying her mischievous and at times slightly salacious talk.

She was as much surprised as anyone at finding herself singled out by Raymond Millet, fifty, a widower with a grown-up, married family, well known for his work and writings on modern scientific theories and likely, people said, to be knighted for them. Though not a wealthy man, he seemed to be comfortably off and Susan at twenty-eight decided she would be doing as well for herself as was now likely.

The thing that surprised her most, however, was that she found herself becoming quite fond of her middle-aged suitor, never inclined to sharpen her claws on him but almost embarrassed at discovering something she had never known was in her make-up, a gentleness and sincerity which made her afraid of herself, so unfamiliar did she appear in her own eyes.

She was not, however, so preoccupied by herself that she had no longer a lively curiosity about Philippa Hollmere, but for the rest of the evening she was quite unable to find any adequate reason for the sudden re-flowering of her beauty and vitality. She could not believe that it had anything to do with Justin, for she had never thought that marriage to be anything but one of mutual convenience, Philippa acquiring Justin's title and position and paying for it with the Jolly Man's money, and, to a secondary degree, by providing Hollmere with an heir. Though she was growing quite fond of her fiancé, she could still be envious of Philippa, both for being Lady Hollmere and also because she would certainly never know the need of money, which was an ever-present worry to Susan. She was deeply in debt to her dressmaker, to as many shops as had been unwise enough to give her credit, and to her book-maker, for she was an inveterate race-goer and a born and seldom successful gambler. She had a few moments' regret that she had not made a friend rather than an enemy of Philippa, whose easy generosity was well known, but it was too late in the day to change that, and the Jolly Man's daughter was the last person in the world to whom she could go for a temporary loan.

Philippa had arranged to meet Fergus the following afternoon, though it had meant the reckless abandonment of several engagements, including spoiling at the last moment a bridge party to which she had long been committed, and excusing herself from dinner at the house of some friends with whom she and Justin were going to the Opera.

He remonstrated mildly when she told him she had to see a sick friend and could not get back until it was time to go to the theatre.

'My dear, it seems rather discourteous to the Alisons,' he said. 'It's their box.'

'I'll make it alright with Lydia,' said Philippa. 'I've just got to run down to see Mary before she goes into hospital. She's one of my very oldest friends. Don't worry. I'll get back in time to dress and meet you at Covent Garden.'

'I can hardly go without you, dear.'

'Oh, Justin, of course you can. Nobody ever minds having an odd man at a party of any sort.'

'Not a staid old married man,' he said with his quiet smile. 'Sure you wouldn't like me to come with you? I wouldn't come in or even let Mary know I was there. I could stay in the car.'

'I wouldn't dream of it,' said Philippa quickly, and left him in a hurry before he could get persistent.

She knew she was doing something unworthy, but she was obsessed to the exclusion of every other consideration by the need to see Fergus again. He was like a fever in her blood, altering all other values, burning her up.

Chapter Ten

Philippa, looking with a frown into her driving mirror, saw that the little cream car was still following her.

How long had it been behind her? She was beginning rather uncomfortably to wonder, for she had been driving slowly and now, thinking back, she decided that it had been there almost immediately after she had started from the small, isolated country inn where she and Fergus Wynton had been staying.

She slowed down and the cream car did the same; going through a small town, she made a complicated digression and even stopped and went into a shop, but when she was on the road again, there was the same car just a little way behind her.

She took fright. This was the fourth time she had gone to Fergus in this way, staying with him at The White Horse, small, snug and tucked away some distance from any main road. It seemed to be patronised only by the few initiated 'regulars' who now recognised them as incipient habitués and would nod and smile.

Wildly happy with a sort of mental intoxication and the perfect satisfaction of her body while she was with Fergus, her present reaction was inevitable. She knew she would never become the hardy, defiant sinner who could lead these two separate lives with no anguish of mind, no self-abasement. She could not give Fergus up; neither could she leave Justin and go openly to her lover as he constantly urged her to do.

'Don't ask that of me, Fergus. I couldn't leave Trevor, and I'd never take him away from Justin.'

She could not leave Justin either, she told herself. However deeply she loved Fergus, and he had become the very core of her being, she could not deal that blow to Justin.

Torn by her loyalties, fully conscious of the publicity towards both the men who loved her, she did not try to excuse herself or condone what she was doing. She lived a day at a time, merely existing between the hours she could spend with Fergus, not all of them at The White Horse. Those were the exceptional red-letter occasions, but in between them they met as frequently as his work and her social duties would allow, though still he did not know who she was, nor that she had other reasons for her reiterated refusal even to consider taking Trevor away from his father and his home, that it was impossible to take the Hollmere heir away as if he were no more than the son of a Mr. and Mrs. Breane. Sometimes Philippa wondered in a panic how it was Fergus never saw her photograph in what he called 'the snob mags', with their pictures and paragraphs almost exclusively concerned with the titled and the rich. The only reason why he did not do so was that he never looked inside the covers of them, though they lay about on the tables in the mess and he heard other men commenting on them. Her deception in that matter had gone on for so long that now she had a morbid fear of his finding out. He had always urged on her the need for them to be utterly honest with each other, believed that they owed that to their love. If he found out now, what else could he believe but that it was on that account she refused to leave Justin and her home?

Her mind was further confused by the knowledge that there actually was an admixture of that in her refusal. In spite of her habit of poking sly fun at the Hollmere traditions and ways, the past five years had inevitably made their mark on her. She had grown accustomed to being Lady Hollmere, Somebody with a capital S, to be flattered and admired and sought after, and few really feminine women could have totally ignored the fascination of such a position, and Philippa was entirely feminine. Fergus was of a totally different nature from Justin. Though she had never told him she was a wealthy woman in her own right, Fergus had guessed it, had once taxed her with it, and she had not denied it.

'Yes. I'm pretty well off,' she admitted. 'I shall never have to worry about money, I suppose. My father left me quite a lot.'

Lest he should ever trace her to the Hollmeres, she had hidden from him as well the identity of her father.

For a few moments he did not reply, and she looked at him.

'What's the matter?' she asked. 'You look fierce.'

'I'm sorry you've got money, though I've guessed that you have. It's almost the only thing I've got against you – that and the fact of Justin and Trevor.'

She laughed.

'Well, does it matter?' she asked.

'Of course it does. Some day you're coming to me, Philippa. I feel it in my bones. Some day you're going to be mine, really mine and all mine – and I shan't want you to have any money by that time.'

She laughed again.

'Darling, you can hardly expect me to do a terrific splash and cover myself in diamonds, wear mink-trimmed pants and what have you, just to get rid of my money – or give it away.'

'Why not?' he asked curtly.

She stared at him.

'Fergus, you're not serious? If ever such a wonderful thing happens that we can really belong, having a little money will make things easier surely?'

He had confided in her that the thought of the future, when the R.A.F. had finished with him (or finished him, he said), worried him a little. What was he going to do then? Live on a very inadequate pension or keep chickens?

'Listen, my sweetest. I've never lived on anyone else, least of all a woman, since I left school, and I'm not likely to change my habits now, or for you. If ever you come to me for keeps, my darling, it'll be for my keeps.'

'But, Fergus dear, if I've got the money?' she protested.

'Keep it for yourself. If ever I've got to marry a rich wife, it won't be to make myself a rich man.'

She had not pursued so unproductive a conversation, but the memory of it had shown her how difficult it would be to show Justin to Fergus with any fairness if she were ever called upon to do it. It would be impossible for Fergus to think anything but hard, contemptuous thoughts of Justin for letting her spend her money on the Hollmere estates, and it was an added reason why she was becoming increasingly anxious for him not to discover who she and Justin really were.

These were some of the thoughts that had been running through her mind when she first saw the cream car and began to suspect that it was trailing her.

When the suspicion had become a certainty in her mind, she waited until she was approaching a town so that people would be within call if the unknown pursuer meant to attack her, and then she pulled in at the side of the road and waited. The driver of the cream car pulled round in front of her, stopped the car and got out.

To her amazement, Philippa saw that it was Susan Therne.

She sat quite still, staring out of the windscreen at her, and then, when Susan stopped beside the driver's window, she turned to face her.

'Hullo, Susan,' she said, making her voice sound as undisturbed as possible. 'What on earth are you doing out here? Broken down or something?'

Susan put her foot on the running-board and rested her hands on the top of the window. The look in her eyes took Philippa back to their schooldays and she almost expected Susan to ask her the price of meat – a question that had been considered an exquisite jest at Leaway.

'No, there's nothing wrong with me for me to worry about,' said Susan with a smile that had a touch of insolence in it, her voice slightly accenting the personal pronoun in each case.

'What is this then? Just a chat?' asked Philippa frostily.

'Yes, just a chat. Shall I get into your car or will you come into mine?'

'I don't quite see the necessity of either. I'm on my way home, so if I can't help you in any way, will you mind if I get on? I'm in rather a hurry.'

Susan's eyes wore a smile of mockery that was almost insolence and Philippa sat up very straight, very much Lady Hollmere.

'In a hurry?' echoed Susan. 'Oh, to get back to Justin, you mean? Before he inquires too closely into where you've been?'

Philippa felt sick. Susan knew – Susan, of all people in the world.

'I have no idea what you mean,' she said coldly.

'Haven't you? I rather think you have – or would you really not mind if I told Justin where you've been?'

'I fail to see what concern of yours it is where I happen to have been,' said Philippa, wondering if she looked as pale as she felt.

She did. Her face looked pinched and grey. Susan could be in no doubt whatever and she followed up her advantage.

I happen to be very fond of Justin,' said Susan. 'In fact, as I am sure you know, we were to all intents and purposes engaged before he got tangled up with you and your money, after which, of course, the poor lamb had no choice. I couldn't have done a thing to keep Hollmere Abbey from falling to bits.'

'Really, Susan, I can't in the least understand why you keep me here discussing these things,' said Philippa, her hands moving on the driving-wheel. 'I repeat that my private life is no concern of yours.'

Susan did not move but continued to stand there, her hands resting on the top of the open window, her fingers tapping out a little tune on the glass whilst her eyes still held Philippa's with that look of malice in them which was so sickeningly familiar, bringing back the past when Susan had been able to make her life so miserable.

'What if I make it my concern, Philippa?' she asked. 'What if you cannot prevent me from doing so?'

'I don't know what you mean,' replied Philippa again, though she knew the net was closing round her. Susan could hurt her, but exactly how?

'Oh, but you do, you know,' said Susan. 'It was a mere chance which delivered you into my hands – you and Wing-Commander Wynton.'

Philippa drew a long, uneven breath and closed her eyes for a second before she opened them to face her enemy again.

'I don't know what you're talking about,' she said, but she knew she had already given herself away.

Susan laughed softly.

You never would give up the game until the whistle had blown, would you? Well, it's blown now, my dear. As I said, it was a mere chance, just one of those things. I was driving back from Meads (that's Dr. Millet's house, you know) on Tuesday, and I had the devil of a thirst on me and stopped to ask a yokel where the nearest pub was. He directed me to The White Horse, and whilst I was having a beer (they have good beer there, don't they?), to my utter astonishment I saw you and your—er—well, you and Wing-Commander Wynton come in. You didn't see me, did you? I was in the corner where there's not much light. But I saw you perfectly, Philippa dear, and judge of my astonishment and interest when I heard the barman address you as Mrs. Wynton! You were obviously staying there, but in order to leave no doubt at all, your—er—friend ordered drinks to be sent up to what he called "our room", at which the man turned to someone inside and gave the order, which was to be sent up to Number Six. I was so much interested and intrigued, my dear, that when I left the bar I went round to the hotel entrance and took the opportunity of looking in the visitors' book. There it was. Number Six. Wing-Commander F. Wynton and wife. So droll! I must say I admire your pluck, Philippa. If I were Lady Hollmere, I'd never have the nerve to go in for anything like that. I'd be too scared of being found out. What a juicy scandal for the newspapers!'

Philippa had let her hands drop from the wheel to her lap, and she sat staring straight out of the windscreen, seeing nothing, hearing only Susan's voice with its mockery and its spite. What could she ever hope from Susan Therne but malice?

'Well?' she asked curtly when Susan paused. 'Why have you told me all this?'

It was futile to deny the thing any longer.

Susan shrugged her shoulders.

'I thought that might be obvious,' she said, taking out a cigarette and lighting it.

'Do you want money?'

'When don't I? And who doesn't – except you, of course, my dear Philippa.'

'And if I don't pay you, you'll take your tale to Justin? Hasn't it occurred to you that he won't believe you?'

'No. I think he will believe me. You see, my dear, you were very careless. You left something there, a head-scarf that is quite unique, made by that firm who boast that they never make two alike.'

'I didn't leave it there, I lost it,' said Philippa, her heart lurching uncomfortably.

'No, you didn't really lose it. I took it,' said Susan calmly. You had no idea, but I had the room opposite yours. I slept there Tuesday night and Wednesday night and most adroitly managed not to let you see me. I took the scarf from your room when you were out, and after you left this morning I gave it to the reception clerk, told her it was Mrs. Wynton's, and suggested that she should keep it until you wrote for it. If Justin should not be inclined to believe my story, I could get him to ring up The White Horse and ask if Mrs. Wynton had left a scarf there. With my help, he could describe it exactly so that there should be no mistake about its being your scarf.'

'And that's what you intend to do?' asked Philippa, trapped. 'I wonder why you've always done your best to harm me, Susan. What have I ever done to you?'

'Only had everything I've ever wanted including Hollmere Abbey, Justin and his title. However, that's finished now and I'm quite fond of Raymond and likely to be happily married to him. The only thing about it is that before I can get married, I need money, a lot of it.'

'How much?' asked Philippa shortly.

'How much is it worth to you to have me keep silent? To let you get your scarf? A thousand pounds?'

Philippa thought rapidly. Though she had a large income, she left the management of it in Justin's hands and he never left more standing to her account than she was likely to need. He thriftily invested it or put it on deposit. A thousand pounds was a large sum for her to find without offering any explanation of it to Justin. Certainly he would not ask her. It was her own money and he would not question her use of it in any way, but the thing would be awkward, embarrassing. She had always been so frank about what she spent. He could not fail to wonder what she had spent a thousand pounds on, and wonder the more when she did not tell him.

Still, it would have to be done.

Have I any guarantee that you won't come back for more? Blackmailers do, I am told,' she said scornfully.

'Do they? I wouldn't know, it's a new line for me, and it wouldn't have occurred to me had this heaven-born chance not been thrown right at me. You haven't any guarantee, of course, and you probably wouldn't think my promise was worth much.'

'No,' said Philippa, icily contemptuous.

'You'll have to trust me, won't you?' Then, after a pause: 'Well? Do I get my thousand? It may relieve your mind in the future if I tell you that I want to get clear of my debts before I marry Raymond, who doesn't believe in debts!' She laughed at the thought of anyone not incurring debts, but Philippa's face did not vary from its look of stony contempt which hid despair. She was in Susan's power and she could see no escape from it.

'You can have the money,' she said curtly.

'Good. I somehow thought I could. In cash?'

'That would cause comment at the bank.'

'Not in these days when most shady transactions, and even a good deal of ordinary business affairs, are done in cash to save income tax. You wouldn't know about that, of course, though, my mind reels at the thought of the amount of tax *you* must pay. I hope the government leaves you the odd thousand now and then, though.'

Philippa's mind had been working rather than listening. Though the fact would not, of course, be divulged outside her bank, she did not like the prospect of arranging to draw such a large sum in cash any more than she liked the thought of her bank manager, who was a personal friend of both her and Justin and who had been a friend of her father as well, speculating on why she was paying this sum to Susan Therne. He knew the long-standing enmity between the two girls and would almost certainly surmise that in some way Susan had a hold over her, an unpleasant idea.

'You must give me a few days,' said Philippa. 'Justin and my bank manager and my solicitor look after my affairs between them and a thing like this has to be arranged.'

'And meanwhile you'll get legal advice and frame me?' suggested Susan unpleasantly.

'If I am to trust you, you will have to trust me,' said Philippa scornfully. 'What I propose to do is to open a fresh account with another bank in another name and I will draw you a cheque on that as soon as it is established.'

'Well, if that's the only way. Be quick about it, though, won't you? Some of the people who were so anxious for me to owe them money are now pressing most unpleasantly for it.'

'I am as anxious as you to finish the business and be rid of the necessity of seeing you,' said Philippa.

'My dear, that won't be easy. Remember that Raymond is a man everybody wants to entertain and when we're married he will certainly not go to houses at which his wife is not welcome, which in your case might cause comment and inquiry. Don't forget that once I've got my thousand I shall have nothing to lose by telling what I know about you.'

'I believe you would even be capable of that,' said Philippa with supreme contempt. Inside her she was frightened. She did believe Susan was capable of that, so why not give up now, at once?

Then she thought of all the other people involved, of the terrible hurt to Justin, of the smear there would always be in Trevor's personal history, of the loss of the child himself.

'You always thought the worst of me, didn't you?' asked Susan lightly. 'My dear Philippa, once I get rid of these debts and am married to Raymond, I shall be a reformed character. You'll see.'

'I hope so for your own sake, and Dr. Millet's. I want to go now. I'll see about the money and let you know.'

'Don't be too long about it or some of these fiends will put the bailiffs in and then Raymond may get to know and you won't be able to be of service to me,' said Susan lightly, released her hold on the car, nodded nonchalantly and strolled back to her own car.

Philippa waited until she had driven off and then followed slowly.

It was a horrible predicament to be in, but she had no choice. Her mind, having accepted the necessity, sought ways and means, and she decided that rather than risk the certainty of at least her solicitor and accountant knowing she was occupied in some private business involving a thousand pounds, she would sell something material that was really hers and did not figure in her accounts.

What?

She thought with sick dismay of the emeralds which her father had given her when Trevor was born, 'something for me first grandchild', he had told her, always fastening on any excuse to give her presents. She was not fond of emeralds, and these were ornate and too flashy for her tastes, large, flawless stones set in gold and diamonds. Joe Joliman retained his faith in gold. No platinum for him, he said. 'Looks too much like silver.' Give him gold and he knew where he was.

So the necklace and the bracelet, the earrings and the brooch and a crescent moon which she was supposed to wear in her hair, were set in heavy gold. Philippa did not like the jewels and had worn them only once and would probably never have worn them again now that the affectionate necessity had gone, but they had been her father's last present to her and he had been so naively pleased with it and it had been her intention to keep them so that someday they could be reset for Trevor's wife, to be given to her as a gift from Joe himself.

Well, Joe would be just as pleased to have got his beloved Philippa out of a scrape, though her mind sheered away in shame from the thought of his being able to know of her relations with Fergus. How disappointed, how disgusted he would have been. That sort of betrayal would have been utterly beyond the comprehension of Joe Joliman.

Justin saw her car as it turned in at the Abbey gates, waved to her and came across the wet grass towards her. Pouring rain during the last few miles had suited her mood better than the fitful summer sunshine.

He had a brush and a pot of white paint in his hand and was dressed in the corduroy-breeches and leggings and open-necked shirt which constituted a uniform when he was at home and in his element. He never referred to the London house as home.

She pulled up and waited for him. She had hoped for a brief respite before she need meet him again. He came to her, smiling and contented now that she was home again, but he did not offer to kiss her.

'I'm very dirty and wet, darling,' he said. 'I won't get into your car like this,' for she had reached across to open the other door for him.

'What are you doing out in the park with a pot of paint?' she asked to make conversation easy.

'Unfortunately marking trees that will have to come down in the winter. I hate doing it. Sorts of them have been there longer than any living man's memory, but they're not safe and I daren't risk their falling in the March winds.'

'It's like cutting off a bit of your own body to part with anything belonging to the Abbey, isn't it?'

He smiled rather sheepishly.

'Yes. But sometimes I think you're getting the same way yourself. Look how indignant you were when I suggested selling the Holbein to pay for the extra plumbing!'

Sue nodded. Perhaps it was true. Perhaps, so insidiously that she had not noticed its approach, the Abbey had taken hold of her so that it had become a part of her, or she a part of it, as if she had been born a Hollmere instead of merely the Jolly Man's daughter artificially grafted on.

'It wasn't necessary to sell anything,' she said.

His brief, grateful smile expressed his appreciation of that.

'Had a nice time?' he asked.

'Yes.'

'Ena alright?'

'Ena? Oh—oh yes, quite all right, thanks.'

'And is the baby more than a rumour?' asked Justin with an indulgent smile.

'They don't know yet, but it's probably only that,' said Philippa, who had been presumed to be spending these three days with the Kersliks. She must remember to ring Ena up as soon as she got to her room, to warn her that she had been supposed to be staying with her and to ask what the doctor had said. She knew she was putting herself in Ena's power, but that in it she was perfectly safe even though she knew Ena was sorry that the Something, about which she only vaguely guessed, was going on.

Better be in Ena's power than in Susan's, she thought with all her sick fears and her wretchedness returning to her. The calm affection of Justin, the beauty of the Abbey parkland about her just touched with the first of autumn's brushes, the sight of the house through the trees, with its serenity, its air of age-old wisdom, its patient acceptance, its immutability – this was her home, her real if only adopted background. Against it, her life had shape and coherence. She was deeply nostalgic for things as they had been before the coming of Fergus. It was as if he had taken up the pattern of her life and it had fallen to bits like a jigsaw puzzle and nothing made sense any more, nor could she find the way to fit the pieces together again.

Justin did not detain her but stood back to let her go in.

'You've just time for your bath and change,' he said, glancing at his watch. Justin lived by his watch. Their hands controlled his every act and thought.

'Aren't you coming in?' asked Philippa, just to say something.

'I'll meet you for cocktails,' he said. 'The Vospers are coming for dinner and bridge. I couldn't avoid it. You know we owe them several meals.'

She nodded, relieved that they were not to be alone. Lee and Mick Vosper were amongst their closest friends. Philippa would have preferred almost anyone to them that evening, however, for the lively American woman's bright eyes and quick mind were observant and missed little that happened to their friends.

On her way upstairs, she called in to see Dorothy Blunt, who had taken Ena's place, to assure herself that nothing needed her urgent attention, and then went on up to the nursery floor.

Just as outside the Abbey she had felt that sense of belonging, of coming into safety after the storm and tempest, so inside the house she felt that peace which her conscience told her she had no right to accept. She paused on the curving, graciously proportioned staircase as she had so often done and looked down. She had always loved to stand here at this time of day, when the late sun streamed in through the great windows of stained glass, the secret of its colours kept inviolate by the age which had produced them, an age of craftsmen, of long weeks and months of toil which the patient hands had loved because by their work they were producing beauty. They had no thought of machinery, of speed, of the soulless, endless repetition of the original design. Here each piece had been evolved with loving care and skill, set in its place as something individual and unique. For generations the sun had poured through as it did now, sending the blues and the reds, the orange and green and purple, over blackened oak, over high carved rails, over dim tapestries and faded rugs, an indissoluble part of the quietness and the peace of history whose strife is long.

Philippa loved it. That was a part of her burden of conscious guilt, her awareness of her betrayal. Each time she returned to the Abbey she experienced this; each time her wild heart and urgent body sent her from it to her lover again.

She sighed, closed her eyes and clenched her hands, for a moment hating herself, and then went on towards the double baize doors which shut off the nursery wing.

Trevor, adorable, naked elf, gave her a shout of welcome from his bath, getting to his feet with a swirl of splashing water, Brownie in the background voicing half-hearted protests. Philippa was glad that it was Brownie. It was evidently one of the free evenings of the child's nurse, and Brownie loved to take over from her.

'Mummy! Mummy!' shrieked the child and Philippa bent down and caught the wet little body up in her arms.

'Your lovely suit, My Lady,' murmured Brownie.

'It doesn't matter,' said Philippa and felt again the indescribable happiness of the clinging arms, the lips pressed ecstatically to her cheek, the child's passionate delight.

At eighteen months Trevor was a sturdy, lovely child, in every way a worthy representative of his race, sturdier and lovelier, she told herself jealously, because of the admixture of her own good, plebeian blood. Physically he was almost entirely a Joliman, but there were many reminders of his Hollmere ancestry. The expression of his rapidly forming features, his movements, the tones of his voice, childish as it still was, his gestures. These were definitely and even absurdly like Justin's, though people told her the child was much more like his Uncle George, and Philippa had seen Lady Hollmere stare at Trevor for a long moment and then suddenly turn away, her usually impassive face working as if behind her eyes were the tears she was too proud to shed.

Brownie, who had culled much information from the rest of the Abbey staff and from her own family, who had lived in Sloworth almost as long as the Hollmeres themselves, had informed her that though he might be a Hollmere to look at, underneath he was all Joliman. No Hollmere (according to Brownie) had ever been so quick to walk and to talk, had acquired his teeth so easily or shown such brilliance of intelligence at the early age of eighteen months.

Whilst Philippa knelt by the bath in order to join in a somewhat complicated game with boats and ducks whose chief object seemed to be much wild splashing, Brownie kept up a commentary in the background on Trevor's amazing accomplishments as if Philippa had been away weeks, even months, instead of two or three days. She had to hear of all the stupendous things Trevor could do, of the new words he had learnt, of the very satisfactory way in which he had greeted his grandmother when she paid him a visit the previous day.

'Just as if he knew who she is, the lamb!' said Brownie admiringly. 'She certainly thinks the world of him, and so she should.'

'Did you take him to see Mother, Brownie?' asked Philippa, raising her voice above the din of protest when she lifted Trevor out of the bath and sat with him on her lap, wrapped in a big, warm towel. 'For goodness' sake, Trevor my beautiful! Even you can't always do what you want. Look, here's Sammy Swan, wanting to know what it's all about,' distracting his attention so that the wail of protest ceased.

'Yes. I took him this morning,' said Brownie.

'How was she?' asked Philippa anxiously.

'Oh, nicely, nicely. Coming round, I think. Wanted to know when you were coming back and where you had gone. I couldn't tell her, of course.' (Brownie's tone was respectfully disapproving of that.) 'I should go over to see her in the morning if I was you, Philippa—My

Lady, that is,' quickly, as they heard footsteps outside and the door-handle turned.

It was Justin, who had quickly washed and changed into his dressing-gown to be in time for the bath ritual.

'Oh, I haven't made it after all,' he said, seeing the child on Philippa's lap.

'Daddy!' shrieked Trevor, pulled his arms away from the restraining towel and bounced up and down with them held out to his father.

Philippa felt a pang which she immediately quelled and surrendered the child to Justin's arms, watching the way they closed about the chubby, adorable body and the way Trevor's lips clung to his father's cheek.

'Nice. Nice,' he said, patting the cheek.

'He means your toilet water, I suppose,' said Philippa.

He's ever so cute about smells – perfume, I should say, My Lord,' said Brownie. 'He simply can't abide bad ones.'

Justin laughed and tickled his son into squirming laughter.

You'll have to get over that, Sunny Jim,' he said, 'or you'll never make a farmer, and a farmer is what you're going to be when you own this place.'

Watching them, aware that the child turned constantly from one to the other as if consciously afraid that the link that joined him to both of them might not hold, Philippa knew that she could never take him from Justin. Whatever sacrifice lay in store for herself, however broken and incomplete her own life, this union must not be allowed to break.

'Here, go to Brownie to be polished off,' said Justin. 'You will be rushed if you don't start dressing soon, my dear,' to Philippa.

'I know,' she said and rose and kissed Trevor, now back in Brownie's arms.

'I could be with you in ten minutes or so, My Lady,' said Brownie hopefully.

'No. Stay with Trevor. Packer's alright,' said Philippa, but there was a tired note in her voice. She would have been glad of Brownie's gentle hands helping her to dress instead of the hard efficiency of the well-trained maid, but she would not take Brownie away from her loving care of Trevor. The boy adored her and he was utterly safe and guarded when she was with him. It was another thing which she had to give up for her secret life with Fergus. Only whilst he was in Brownie's charge was Trevor really safe, she felt, safe from the hundred risks and dangers to which it seems every small child is subjected every hour of his young life in a world too much civilised – danger from cars, danger from electricity, danger from polished floors and slippery baths and pampered dogs and bottled drugs and all the other things which, according to the newspapers, seemed to lie in wait for the curious minds and the active bodies of small children.

No, Brownie must concentrate on Trevor, even if she herself went without those loving hands, the understanding kindness, the sympathy which knew without asking infuriating questions just what she needed.

Brownie gave a little sniff and went on drying Trevor's wriggling little toes.

'That Packer,' she said. 'You're tired and what you want is to have your head and neck rubbed and half an hour's quiet lie down. She'll want that half-hour for dolling you up. I know. Still, have it your own way—My Lady,' adding the last two words with a sudden return to respectful servility as she caught the disapproving look in His Lordship's eyes.

Philippa smiled at her briefly, kissed the top of Trevor's curly head again, and left them.

'Brown is rather too familiar,' observed Justin as they went down the stairs to their own rooms.

'She's known me all my life and sometimes slips back into the old days and ways,' said Philippa lightly. 'Trevor adores her and that's the main thing. She'd lay down her life before she'd let anything happen to him.'

'Yes, that's all very well whilst he is a baby, but don't you think she spoils him? He's got to be able to meet life someday, public school and so on.'

She laughed.

'Justin, really! He isn't two yet. Schools are a long way away and babies aren't babies for long,' with a little sigh. 'I want him to stay a baby as long as he can.'

They had reached the door of her room, and he paused a moment with his hand on the door-handle before he turned it.

'Trevor is not going to be the only baby, is he, darling?' he asked, but he was not looking at her and she knew that, though she was his wife and he was Trevor's father, the question embarrassed him. There flashed into her mind the memory of Fergus and his frank, unashamed love-making which so filled her with rapture that it was hard to count the cost, always to make sure that there could be no tangible sequel to it. Fergus, her lover, was like that, whilst Justin, her husband, felt ashamed if he were obliged to mention their sex-relations and obviously regarded them as the somewhat embarrassing but essential procedure for putting into the world more Hollmeres!

'There's no need to think about that just yet,' she said more curtly than she intended, and went into her room where the efficient Packer stood waiting with that respectful disapproval on her face.

'I have run your bath. My Lady,' she said. 'Will you wear the black lace tonight? It will take less time than any of your ladyship's other dinner gowns.'

Philippa knew that the suggestion conveyed the maid's disapprobation of the short time she had allowed for dressing, especially after a journey.

She nodded indifferently.

'Yes, it will do,' she said, and crossed the room to glance at herself in the mirror. She had not worn a hat for the last few miles in the car, opening the roof to let the wind blow on her head. It might have helped to clear something of the muddled confusion wrought on her mind by Susan Therne. All it had done was tangled her hair so that Packer tut-tutted at it and gave her accusing and, she thought, inquisitive looks.

'I'll have a bath and a massage,' she said more brusquely than she usually spoke.

The maid glanced meaningly at the clock. Philippa ignored it and started to undress.

By the time she was ready for dinner she felt more relaxed, though she would far rather have dined alone in her room and gone to bed. The Vospers were not difficult to entertain, but they wanted to play bridge afterwards. The game, as played by Lee and Mick, was never a serious affair to anyone but Justin, and it was constitutionally impossible for him to take it light-heartedly so that he and Lee won, and Philippa and her partner paid up indifferently. They did not play for high stakes when Justin took a hand.

Still, it passed the evening away and kept Philippa from thinking coherently of Susan Therne until she had gone to bed.

Then, inevitably, the thoughts came.

She must, of course, give Susan what she demanded, thought she knew, with a sick certainty and a dread of the future, that it was useless to expect that this thousand pounds would be the end. She longed for the relief of sharing the burden with Fergus, not the financial burden which was the least of it, but the constant dread of exposure.

She knew she must not tell Fergus, however, for it would mean that she must reveal her real name and all the mixture of reasons why so far she had refused all thought of leaving Justin. She knew, too, that Fergus would feel angry and ashamed that he could not find the blackmail money himself but must leave it to Philippa to find.

Her cursed money, she thought! If she had none, she could not have been involved in this. Then came the unpleasant thought that if she had had none, Justin might not have married her, and she would not have had Trevor, and her life following so different a course without Justin, she would not have met Fergus either.

The next day she took the emeralds from the underground strong room, looked at them with a poignant memory of the pride and delight in her father's eyes when he had given them to her, and shut the cases and did not look at them again even when the jeweller, in some surprise at the request, handled them and examined them for valuation.

'They could be reset very attractively, Lady Hollmere,' he said. 'They are very fine emeralds. We could have designs made for you ...'

'No. I want to sell them. I have so much jewellery,' she said with an air of indifference, and the man said no more, though he went on wondering why the only child and heiress of the Jolly Man should want to sell anything at all.

The value of the emeralds considerably exceeded what Susan Therne had demanded, and Philippa took the money in cash, in a taxi, to a bank where she was not known, and opened an account in the name of Philippa Browne, the first name that occurred to her when she was asked for one. She had not thought of that essential detail.

'I shall be drawing on it quite soon,' she told the bank manager and asked for a cheque-book and left him.

She could have given Susan the money in cash, but she had made no definite arrangement yet for meeting her, and she did not want to carry about with her, or to have within easy access, so large a sum of money. She could only hope she had hidden her identity, though she knew that a bank manager must always be a depository for many secrets which nothing can induce him to divulge.

Susan came to the Abbey the next day, and Philippa, her voice cold and her face contemptuous, handed her the cheque.

'It will probably be simpler to pay it into your bank than to cash it over the counter,' she said.

Susan looked at the signature.

'Philippa Browne,' she said. 'Rather clever that. Thank you, my dear. That will be a great help to me, and I know you won't miss it. That's the son and heir, I take it?' as Brownie, with Trevor in his pushchair, went past the window.

'Yes,' said Philippa shortly.

'I'd go and have a word with him, though babies are not much in my line and I hope to heaven Raymond won't land me with any. Goodbye, Philippa darling, and a thousand thanks!' with a mocking look as she opened the long window and stepped out on the terrace.

Trevor, a friendly child, welcomed her as if she were an old friend and she found herself surprisingly attracted by him. As she had truly said, babies were not in her line.

It was so like Philippa Joliman, she thought with sudden anger, to have this as well. Not only was she Lady Hollmere, with Justin for her husband and the Abbey for her home and all that money, but she must also have this really charming baby to add to her many possessions. How bitterly unfair life could be, she reflected. So intensely had she desired to be Lady Hollmere and mistress of the Abbey that for the moment even her growing affection for Raymond Millet paled. She hated Philippa and, pressing closely to her her handbag in which the cheque lay folded, she was conscious of a diabolical gladness in her power to hurt and to frighten her.

Chapter Eleven

Fergus closed the door very quietly, but Philippa stirred and turned towards him, half opening her eyes.

'Fergus? It's the middle of the night,' she protested sleepily.

He looked at his watch.

'Only quarter past eleven,' he said.

'Feels like middle of night,' she murmured. 'Anything the matter?'

'No, of course not, darling. Go to sleep again,' he said and, without putting on the light, felt his way into his own bed.

Philippa dropped off to sleep again, but when she woke in the morning, she remembered and wondered if it had been a dream.

'Darling, did I dream it, or were you wandering about the hotel in the middle of the night?' she asked.

They were not at The White Horse. Without giving him her reasons she had suggested that they did not go there again, and when he pressed her, said that it was just the sort of place where their presence might be noticed and remembered.

'In London, one can always get lost and feel safe,' she said, and though he would have preferred the peace of the country, he could not argue about what was a comparatively trivial issue.

Yet, though he gave way to her wishes and they went to one of the countless small hotels which surround the West End without being in it, he realised that she was not at ease as she had been at The White Horse.

'I thought I heard something, a noise,' he told her vaguely and she laughed a little.

'Dearest, we're in a London hotel. You don't have to investigate nocturnal noises, surely?'

'No, of course not,' he agreed. 'Perhaps I've caught your restlessness and something of your fear. I wish you weren't so much afraid. Philippa sweetheart. I hate you to suffer anything I can't bear for you.'

'So you try to bear my fears even for me?' she asked wistfully.

He knelt by her bed and put his arms about her.

'Darling, my dearest heart, we could allay those fears if only you would trust me,' he said. 'If you don't feel you could tell Justin, and you won't let me tell him, come away with me, come away now, today, this morning. I've finished my time with the R.A.F., as you know, and though my term is not officially up until the end of this week, there would be no trouble about getting my leave to start now, in the circumstances. I'm not much use to them now that they won't let me fly, and they know as well as I do that I'm only wasting the time until I'm out. Come with me, darling. Let's make a fresh start somewhere, Australia, New Zealand, anywhere. I know you're going to talk about the child again, but darling heart, you can't live in a child's life and his need of you is so short whereas I need you for all my life. And there will be other children ...'

She shook her head and he knew by her face that he was no nearer moving her from her determination not to abandon her child than he had ever been.

'Fergus, darling Fergus, don't let's spoil the short time we have together by talking about the future. You know in your heart that I can never leave Trevor.'

He got up and stood looking down at her. She thought with a catch at her heart that he looked strained and drawn, and wondered if he had got up and wandered about the hotel during the night rather than risk waking her by another of those terror-filled dreams.

'Is that all there is to it?' he asked, an unusual note of acerbity in his voice. 'Are you sure it isn't your husband as well that you can't leave?'

'That's not quite fair,' she said in a low voice and then, as he did not move, she slipped out of bed and linked her arms about his neck, pressing against him, her face filled with remorseful tenderness.

'Darling,' she said, 'you're tired and over-wrought or you couldn't have said that. Did you have dreams last night? Was that what sent you wandering about? Why didn't you wake me? You know I can always soothe and comfort you.'

He put up his hands, unbelievably, to break the linked hold of hers, let her arms drop to her sides and walked over to the dressing-table and began mechanically to brush his hair. Behind him, Philippa stood in shocked surprise, hurt and bewildered but trying to understand. What was there she could say that she had not said? She could do as he urged her, leave Justin, abandon her child, go off to the ends of the earth with him and start a new life, a life which would be hard since she knew he would never allow her to smooth his path with her money. Fiercely independent, he would insist on making their life and environment by his own efforts. Yet she knew that if she had no child, she would go with him, whatever the cost.

The age-old struggle of a woman between her child and her man could, in Philippa's case, have only one ending. Fergus could get along without her. Trevor could not. Or, at least, that was how she saw it. Though the child loved his father and loved Brownie and had a wealth of affection for every person and every animal in his world, it was to his mother he turned in every emergency, to her he looked for approbation, for sympathy, to share his enjoyment, to comfort his woes. She knew that he missed her badly whenever she was away from the Abbey for a few days, and even her ephemeral happiness with Fergus was a little dimmed by the thought of his watching eyes, his constant question 'Where Mummy?' The prospect of seeing him again helped to assuage the pain of parting with Fergus, and he knew it, though he seldom put into words the look in his eyes which reminded her that she was going back to the home where she was loved, whereas he was losing his world when she went.

She watched him for a few moments as he stood, his back to her, automatically brushing his thick, fair hair whose feel her fingers knew so well. Then she came to him and, without touching him again, spoke quietly.

'Fergus, are you feeling that it must end?' she asked gently.

He turned to her and said almost roughly: 'No. No. How can it end?'

'Only in one way, I'm afraid. How can we go on like this, tearing each other and ourselves to pieces every time we have to part? It was my fault. I ought to have left things where they were in April instead of writing to you. I knew even then that it was worse than foolish.'

'So you're tired of it?' he asked with that roughness of speech and manner so foreign to their usual relations.

'What's the matter this morning, Fergus? Why do you talk and look like that? You know perfectly well that my feelings for you haven't changed and never will change, except to grow deeper and stronger. When I suggested that you might like to end it, there was no thought in my mind that you had changed or grown tired of me, so why should you accuse me of it?'

Her voice was still gentle and without hint of anger, and he was passionately contrite at once, his arms about her, pressing her to him with a kind of desperation.

'Darling, forgive me. Forgive me. I'm on edge this morning. I'm worried for you. Perhaps—dearest—dearest ...'

He could not go on, but she finished it for him slowly. 'Perhaps it would be better to end it?'

'It's like death to say so. Philippa, we've been happy, but all the time there has been the knowledge that we must hide it, always watch and be careful, always feel afraid. If I've been afraid, you know that it's been for you because, though it's galling to have to admit it, I can't wean you away from husband, home and duty,' with a bitter little smile. 'I've been forced to the conclusion that you wouldn't be happy with me, so I've got to stop trying to persuade you into it, and—well, it has to be the end, hasn't it, my darling?'

She nodded her head, stood for a moment wordlessly within the close circle of his arms, and then turned away and groped blindly for her dressing-gown.

'I'll dress,' she said indistinctly and went into the adjoining bathroom.

Fergus could not really afford the suites he always insisted on taking for them and she knew it. That was another reason why she felt their association could not continue along these lines, yet what else was there for them? Loving him with an ever-increasing strength the better she grew to know him, their position was the more untenable, impossible as it was not to let it rank as it would to others as a sordid intrigue, a nasty little affair between a married woman still living with her husband and some other man.

She knew it must end and as she bathed she constantly washed the tears from her face, but Fergus saw their traces when, later, they sat at breakfast together in the corner of the dining-room where last night they had dined so gaily.

'I'll take you to Victoria, darling,' he said when they had finished. There had been little talk between them. What was there left to say? It seemed impossible that this could be the end, that she might never see him again after today.

She nodded and rose from the table.

'I can catch the nine-forty,' she said. 'I'll finish off my packing.'

'I've done mine. I'll pay the bill and then send the porter up for the bags. How long will you be?'

'Ten minutes. Fergus—don't come up,' she said, and left him swiftly without looking at him.

When she had closed her suitcase, she went into the corridor to look for the chambermaid. The tipping was the one thing she insisted on doing.

The girl was loitering farther down the corridor, pale-faced and wide-eyed, staring at one of the closed doors.

Philippa called her and she came reluctantly, glancing back over her shoulder as she came.

'Thank you, madam,' she said and then, unable to keep the bursting mind within bounds, she stammered out: 'Oh madam, isn't it awful? Have you heard?'

'Heard what?' asked Philippa.

'Dead. A lady dead down there,' she said, nodding her head in the direction of the closed door down the corridor. 'I'm glad I never found her, though. It was Rose. She took in the tea at 'arpast eight and couldn't get an answer and she went in as it was ordered for 'arpast, and there she was, dead. Rose spoke to her and then touched her and she was stone cold. Awful it musta been. I'm glad it wasn't me.'

'Poor thing,' said Philippa compassionately. 'How dreadful for her, dying alone like that in an hotel room. Didn't anybody know she was ill?'

'She seemed as right as rain last night,' Rose said. 'The manager isn't half wild!'

'Well, I don't suppose the poor thing wanted to die in his hotel,' said Philippa.

'No, but it gives a place a bad name, and having the police here and all.'

'The police? Whatever for?' asked Philippa.

'I d'know. Rose screamed and carried on, and Dr. Brand that lives here came up and now there's two policemen there. I shall have to go, madam, or I'll have Mrs. Tye on me track. Thank you for this, madam,' indicating the tip which she had been holding in her hand.

The porter had not come up for the luggage, so she telephoned to the office.

'I'll send someone up, madam,' said the clerk and he, too, sounded put out. Of course they would all be upset, thought Philippa. Not a nice thing to happen, either for the hotel or for the poor woman.

Downstairs, Fergus had paid the bill and asked for a taxi to be called, but the manager came to speak to him.

'I'm very sorry, sir, but I hope it will not inconvenience you too much to be asked not to leave for a short time?' he asked.

'Oh? Why not?' asked Fergus somewhat testily. Now that the time had come to part with Philippa, he wanted to get it over and not to prolong the anguish of those last minutes.

'There has been an unfortunate occurrence, sir, most unfortunate. As a matter of fact, one of the guests, a lady, has been found dead in her room.'

'Oh dear, I'm sorry to hear that. Most unpleasant for you,' said Fergus. 'I don't see why it should hold me up, though.'

'It's the police, sir,' said the worried manager apologetically. 'They don't want anyone to leave the hotel. Excuse me, will you?' darting forward to intercept with the same apologies another guest who was about to go through the revolving doors.

Fergus stood there uncertainly. It was a maddening thing to have happened. Philippa would be worried sick in case there were any publicity, for of course the intervention of the police could mean only one thing.

Whilst he still stood wondering what to do, the lift doors opened and she came out. He hurried to her and guessed from her face that she knew.

'You've heard?' he asked her.'

'That some woman died in the night here? Along our corridor too. Rather horrible.'

'The police are there.'

'I know. The maid told me. Why are they here?'

'It can only be for one reason, it could not have been a natural death, or that's what they think at present.'

'Fergus! You mean she was—murdered?' she asked, horrified.

'Looks like it. Anyway, we've been asked not to go yet. Oh, not just us. Everybody,' as he saw the look on her face. 'I'm terribly sorry, darling. I know it's going to worry you. They may ask all sorts of questions and we've got to make up our minds what answers we're going to give. What are we going to tell them about you?'

She was very pale. He saw the fear in her eyes, and put a hand under her arm to lead her to a chair in a quiet corner of the hall. It was already filling with guests who were reacting in various ways to the news filtering through, most of them annoyed at having to be held prisoners in the hotel. One of the doormen was on duty, politely but firmly refusing to allow anyone to leave or to enter except the uniformed police, several of whom were passing in and out, soon to be joined by plain-clothes men and with them a photographer with his paraphernalia. Newspaper reporters, with their miraculous olfactory organs, were already arriving, but were not admitted. They had to stand on the pavement outside, watching the comings and goings and glancing up at the windows.

Philippa drew more deeply into the shelter of her corner. She knew, even if Fergus did not, that these were reporters. She had often seen them outside houses where she had been entertained, or at some function where photographs and titbits of gossip might be obtained. Quite possibly they would recognise her.

The beautiful Lady Hollmere. The lovely young mistress of the famous Hollmere Abbey. Lady Hollmere, charming arbiter of up-to-the-minute fashions, wore ...

Almost certainly they would know her, and then what?

The manager was speaking to one and another of his guests, trying to soothe them, and he came to Fergus.

'The police want to ask a few questions, just formalities, of course,' he said. 'If you will come with me, sir, they will see you first so that you can go. I expect you have important matters to attend to,' glancing with respect at the insignia of Fergus's rank.

Philippa rose.

May I go with my husband?' she asked, and Fergus knew from that that she was telling him what their answers were to be. They were to uphold her fictitious name.

'Oh. I think so, madam,' said the manager, and took them both into his private office where a plain-clothes officer sat at the desk, a uniformed man in attendance.

'Wing Commander Wynton and Mrs. Wynton,' said the manager and left them there.

Chief Inspector Wand looked at them, smiled cheerfully and indicated a chair opposite him.

'Do sit down, Mrs. Wynton. Another chair for the Wing Commander, Batten,' he said. 'I won't keep you long, Wing Commander. Just routine. You know what's happened upstairs?'

'That a woman guest was found dead this morning. That's all,' said Fergus with the utmost calmness. 'It's a bad business, of course, but I hope you won't have to detain us long, Inspector. I have to get back to my base and I'd like to take my wife into the West End first. She's doing some shopping.'

'I'll be quite brief. Just your names and addresses. Your occupation I know, of course,' with a smile at Fergus's uniform.

Fergus gave the answers with easy unconcern, Philippa's name as Philippa Wynton, and her address, on a sudden brainwave, as that of the Kersliks in Chelsea. You never knew what line these inquiries might take, and it would not do for it to be discovered at the outset that his 'wife' was not living with him in the block of flats maintained for officers near his aerodrome.

Philippa controlled with an effort the little gasp. She realised at once his reason, and she must go as soon as they were released and explain matters to Ena. It would be a shock to her, of course, and she would disapprove, but she would stand by her.

The inspector compared the address with the one in the hotel visitors' book open before him.

'That isn't what you wrote in the book when you came, Wing Commander,' he said.

'No. I never do write a different address for my wife in hotel registers,' said Fergus easily. 'I never think it looks well to give different addresses for husband and wife. It's because we can't get a home together whilst I'm in Sussex that she has to live elsewhere and we stay in hotels.'

'I see. It's strictly illegal, though, and I should advise you to state the facts as they are another time. I can get in touch with you at that address if I need you, Mrs. Wynton?'

For a brief moment Philippa did not answer. Though she had many times stayed under that name, she had very rarely been addressed by it, and the inspector noted that brief, unexpected hesitation, and the slight colour which crept into her pale cheeks when she said 'Yes.'

There were one or two other questions. Had they seen anyone in their corridor? Had they heard anything unusual in the night? Did they know the dead woman at all?

They both answered the other questions in the negative, but Fergus queried this one.

'We haven't heard her name,' he said.

'It was Therne. Miss Susan Therne,' said the inspector, and this time there was no mistake about Philippa's gasp of utter surprise.

The inspector turned to her swiftly.

'You knew her, Mrs. Wynton?' he asked.

Philippa took tight hold on herself.

'By name, of course,' she said. 'It's quite a well-known name to anyone who reads the society papers and the magazines, or even some advertisements.'

Susan's face, much glamorised by the photographers, appeared from time to time advertising various beauty preparations. They formed welcome additions to her income.

'But you didn't know her personally, Mrs. Wynton?'

Philippa hesitated. It had been such a shock to her that she could not immediately foresee what might happen. Never in her wildest dreams had she supposed that she knew the dead woman, but that it should be Susan Therne of all people!

'I—I may have met her,' she said uncertainly.

'Did you not know she was in the hotel?'

'No.'

'I understand she had dinner in the public dining-room last evening.'

'We did not dine in the hotel,' put in Fergus.

The inspector looked from one to the other and then nodded as if satisfied.

'Well, that will be all, I think,' he said, and they rose.

Philippa could not resist an urgent question.

Inspector, do you mean—you don't really mean that Susan was *murdered*?' she asked incredulously.

He noted again the use of the dead woman's Christian name, though one would have expected someone who 'might have met her' to refer to her as 'Miss Therne'.

'That, of course, is something which must be left to the doctors and the coroner, Mrs. Wynton,' he said.

'But you must think she was or there would not be all this trouble?'

'I'm afraid, Mrs. Wynton, that I am not here to *answer* questions,' said the inspector gravely, and Fergus touched her arm and they went back into the reception hall, where they were allowed to leave when a taxi had been called.

Philippa turned to Fergus, her face still white and her eyes filled with horror.

'Fergus, fancy it being Susan Therne! Somebody I know! Did I give myself away? It was such an awful shock.'

'I don't think so, dear. You told the inspector you knew her, or at least that you'd met her. That would account for it being a bit of a shock.'

She shuddered.

'I did more than just meet her. I knew her very well. We were at school together, and hated each other, and we've always felt the same ever since. She wanted to marry Justin and be ...'

She caught herself up in time. She was just going to say 'and be Lady Hollmere' when she remembered that Fergus did not know her real name.

'Was it alright to give Mrs. Kerslik's address?' he asked.

She nodded.

'Ena will stand by me,' she said, but she shrank back into the corner of the taxi.

She had taken Fergus to see Ena and Paul, and she had to warn them that to him she called herself Mrs. Breane, leaving them to think what they liked about the affair. Now she would have to leave Ena in no doubt.

'I think I'd better go there now right away,' she told Fergus, who had asked the driver to take them to Victoria, and he leaned forward and opened the glass screen to alter the instructions.

'We were going to make this the end,' he said to Philippa in a low voice.

'I know. With this horrible affair about Susan, perhaps we can't,' she said, and there was even a faint relief in her voice.

'May I write to you, Philippa? At Ena's address? Will you write?'

'We may have to keep in touch,' she said, with another little shiver. 'I can't see how we can possibly get involved in it, though, do you? I'm not surprised somebody wanted to murder her. I've wanted to do it a good many times myself. She was a nasty piece of work but I wonder who really did do it? How was she killed, do you know?'

'I don't know. The police managed to keep very close about that. Everybody was asking the same question. Of course it might not have been that at all. She might just have had a heart attack or something, and died.'

Philippa gave a hard little laugh.

'Impossible. She hadn't a heart,' she said. 'Oh, we're here,' as the taxi drew up. 'Don't let's say any goodbyes, Fergus. Just let me get out and give me my bag and—that's all.'

'But you'll write, beloved?'

She nodded speechlessly, did not look at him again or touch him, but took her bag from him and went into the entrance to the flats.

It was not possible to think any longer that she and Fergus were not to meet again. The horrible business about Susan Therne had made another meeting almost inevitable. If the police wanted to ask any more questions, or found out that Fergus was not married and that therefore she was not his wife, they were bound to meet again somehow and somewhere. In prison perhaps, she thought hysterically. Could they put you in prison for writing a false name in a hotel register? She had no idea.

Ena opened the door to her in glad surprise. She had improved almost beyond recognition since the coming of her happiness. Her figure had rounded in the right places and slimmed in the right places, and her plain face wore an expression of contentment which made its blunt nose and large mouth and high cheek-bones of no importance. In her eyes was the light which love had set there, and in her voice was the note of beloved women the world over.

She wore a business-like apron over her dark-red dress and her hands were encased in working gloves.

She laughed apologetically as she pulled them off.

'Isn't it funny to see me taking such care of myself?' she mused. 'Paul is such an idiot about my hands. Says they are my one beauty! I look after them really because I have to play the piano so much now. Do go into the sitting-room, Philippa. I'll be with you in a moment. Shall we have some coffee, or would you rather have tea? Or strong drink?'

'Will it shock you if I ask for a brandy, Ena? Have you any, by the way?' asked Philippa.

'Yes, we've got a drop somewhere. Paul always takes some with him in case he gets the jitters before he goes on the platform at a concert, though I don't think he ever takes it. Yes, here's some. Pour out for yourself, will you? What will you have with it?'

'I'll have it neat,' said Philippa, and Ena looked at her inquiringly.

'There's nothing the matter, is there? You're not ill or anything?' she asked anxiously.

'No, I'm alright but I've had a bit of a shock. I'll tell you in a minute.'

She sat, relaxing a little, in the comfortable, pleasant room which served the Kersliks for sitting-room and dining-room, and, since music was the essence of Paul's daily life, music-room as well. It was a large room, so that one end could accommodate the small grand piano without too greatly subordinating the living space to it. The rest of the flat consisted of bathroom, tiny kitchenette and one small bedroom in addition to that shared by Paul and Ena.

Philippa drank her neat brandy and lit a cigarette, and Ena came back and stirred up the small fire which, whenever there was a nip in the air as on this September morning, she lit for Paul's comfort, he could not practise in a cold room. This morning, she explained to her guest, he had gone out to make some recordings and would not be back until lunchtime.

'Now,' said Ena, putting the cigarettes and the rest of the brandy near them, 'what's it all about?'

'I'm in an unholy mess,' said Philippa without preamble. 'To begin with, here's the shock. Susan Therne is dead.'

'Dead?' echoed Ena. 'What of? It's certainly a shock, but I'm not going into mourning.'

'That isn't the real shock, Ena. They think she was murdered.'

Ena stared at her and gave a low whistle.

'Well, that *is* something! Who by and what for?'

'I don't know. I don't think anybody does yet.'

'Where was she?'

'At the Medway Hotel, near Earls Court.'

'What on earth was she doing there? She's got a flat in London, hasn't she?'

197

'Yes. I don't know what she was doing there, but—you see, Ena, I was there too,' said Philippa, not looking at her.

'Go on,' said Ena. 'I can see there's some more. You're not going to say you saw the business?'

'No, of course not, but—I hate telling you this. I've got to, though. I was there, in the hotel I mean, with—with Fergus Wynton.'

Ena looked into the fire. Philippa's tone had conveyed what it had been meant to convey.

'You can't expect me to feel glad about that, can you?' Ena asked at last, slowly. 'That's the shock, a bigger one than Susan Therne being murdered. I guessed, of course, when you brought him here that you were in love with each other. It was rather obvious. Even Paul who never notices anything could see that and asked me if I thought there was anything serious in it. It seems there was—and is. You haven't left Justin or anything like that?'

'No, and I don't want to. I'll never be able to make you understand. It will sound cheap and rotten to you, but, do believe me, Ena; it isn't. Fergus and I do love each other, sincerely and deeply and—forever, I think. He wants me to leave Justin. He has always wanted that. We both hate the hole-and-corner business it has been, staying in quiet hotels, meeting in out-of-the way places for a stolen hour or two. What we feel for each other isn't a squalid thing like that, just fun and games. It's the real thing.'

'But not real enough to give up being Lady Hollmere?' asked Ena with her uncompromising honesty.

'I know I deserved that, Ena, but it isn't like that. It's not so simple. I could give up that. It's Trevor I can't give up, even for Fergus, and of course it's not possible to take him with me, nor to expect that Justin would let me have him. I couldn't leave Trevor – and in a way I feel the same about Justin. It would hurt him so terribly.'

'You know I'm fond of you, Philippa. Next to Paul, you're more to me than anybody else in the world. I'm sorry, though, that you didn't think of all that, of Trevor and Justin, before you got involved with Fergus. I liked him a lot. I thought he was a fine type and he's quite the sort of man you ought to have married. But you married Justin, and that should be the end of it for you. You know that as well as I do. You're trying to get the best of two worlds, to keep your lover on the quiet and still stay with your husband. You didn't expect me to like it, Philippa, did you?'

'No. I don't like it myself. I'm not a bit proud of it. I say far harder things of myself than ever you could think of. It probably sounds feeble to say this now, but this morning, before we'd heard about Susan, we'd agreed to end it, Fergus and I. We weren't going to see each other again.'

'And now? Has the business of Susan Therne made any difference?'

'I don't know. Probably it hasn't, but I've got so horribly involved in it. The police were in the hotel and we all had to be interviewed by them before we were allowed to leave and as I was there as Mrs. Wynton, I—I stuck it out and—Ena do forgive me, but this is where you come in. Fergus had to give addresses for us both, and of course he couldn't go on giving the one he'd put in the register because they would be certain to find out, if they made any inquiries, that he doesn't live in the flats at the airfield with a wife. So—we gave this address, Ena, yours. I do hope you don't terribly mind. It was all done in such a rush. We had no time to work anything out, and it was better to give a real address than to make one up. Do you mind a lot?'

'Well,' said Ena slowly, 'of course it isn't what I would have chosen to happen, but I do see that you were in a spot, and of course I'll stand by you. You know that. The thing I don't like is helping you to deceive Justin. He's too good for that. He hasn't deserved it of either of us.'

'I know. Do you think it's been all honey and roses for me? But I love Fergus, and when I married Justin, I suppose I was—well, a bit dazzled, Philippa Joliman turning into the Countess of Hollmere and all that. I thought I was Cinderella to Justin's prince, but it didn't work out that way, and when I met Fergus—oh, Ena, you're in love with Paul. Can't you understand? Can't you?'

'Yes, I suppose so. Anyway, it's never any use going over what might have been or trying to pretend that things are not what they are. You think the police might make inquiries about you here? Because you knew Susan Therne? Did you tell them you did?'

'I had to. They asked me point-blank. I didn't tell them that I had cause to hate her like poison, though. I had that much sense.'

'She hated you because you married Justin but why should you hate her?'

'Because she found out about Fergus and me,' said Philippa slowly, 'and she was blackmailing me. She made me pay her a thousand pounds a few weeks ago, and I suppose she had been tracking us down and came to the Medway to get a fresh lot of evidence against me to hold me up for more. She told me she's in debt and that thousand was going to put her in the clear before she married Raymond Millet.'

'She would never stay out of debt,' said Ena. 'Well, she certainly got something when she got a line on you and you're going to be a lot safer and happier now she's dead. Oh!' as a thought suddenly struck her and she put a hand across her lips as if horror lay on them.

Philippa made a wry grimace.

'If the thought crossed your mind that perhaps it was I who killed her, forget it. I might have wanted to, and I can't pretend I'm sorry she's dead, but I didn't have any hand in it.'

'Nor Fergus?' asked Ena coolly.

'He didn't know about the blackmail. Didn't know her either. He still has no idea who I really am but thinks my name is Breane – which it is, in a way, I suppose. There were reporters outside the hotel when we left but I put my handbag up to my face and hurried past them into the taxi and I don't think they saw me. I sincerely hope they didn't because of course if anybody recognised me—well, that'll be that. A nice juicy little bit for their newspapers and curtains for Philippa.'

'They'd be very careful not to slip up,' said Ena. 'Unless for any reason you have to appear at any of the proceedings, the inquest or anything, there seems no reason why it should come out.'

She added to herself that she would not, however, like to be in Philippa's shoes just at the moment.

'Do you think perhaps I'd better stay here for a day or two, Ena? That is, if you don't mind? The police expect to find—Mrs. Wynton here, and Justin thinks I'm here too,' the colour flooding her face.

'You certainly intended me to be in on it one way or another, didn't you?' asked Ena drily. 'Well, I said I'd stand by you and of course I will—and not as if I'm the virtuous woman with an erring sister either!' her tone and smile lightening the atmosphere. 'After all, I don't know what I'd have done myself if I'd met Paul too late. I don't wonder you asked for a spot of brandy. I put some coffee on and I expect it's perked by now, so I'll get it. Then I've got to see to the lunch. Paul has a concert tonight and I always give him a good midday meal when he is going to miss his dinner. We used up our lordly meat ration on Sunday, of course, so I'm going to make a meat pie. Out of the Jolly Man's tins too!'

Philippa smiled and rose to her feet. She felt a little better for sharing her burden, in spite of the dressing-down which she knew was merited. Now there would be no more of it. Ena had said her say. She would not go on saying it.

Paul was delighted to see her, glad that she was going to stay a few days. The two women had agreed to keep him in ignorance of their special knowledge of Susan Therne's death, so they were suitably surprised and impressed when the first notification of it appeared in the early evening papers.

Obviously the reporters had been warned to be reticent about it, for though there was a heading in large type,

SOCIETY GIRL FOUND DEAD IN LONDON HOTEL

there were no details. The short paragraph gave Susan's name and the fact that she was engaged to, and had been expected shortly to marry, the distinguished scientist, Dr. Raymond Millet, but nothing more.

After Paul had gone, Ena going with him because he liked to know she was in the audience, Philippa put a call through to Justin.

'Darling. I hoped you would ring,' he told her. 'I never like to ring the flat in case Paul is in the middle of one of his best efforts or something. How are you?'

'I'm very well, Justin dear,' she said. 'I rang up to ask if you've seen about poor Susan Therne in the papers.'

'Yes, I've just been reading about it. How dreadful! And why on earth should anyone want to murder Susan?'

'It doesn't suggest that it's murder, surely? Not in our evening paper, anyway,' said Philippa, shaken.

'No, nor in ours, but she was perfectly strong and healthy and very happy about her forthcoming marriage to Millet, so what else could it be but murder? She couldn't possibly have wanted to end her own life just now, and she was not the sort to take drugs. You read of such terrible crimes in these lawless days of government by the mob. Nobody is safe. I think it will turn out that she had some of her wedding presents with her, some jewellery perhaps, and that might have been the motive for murder. She would have defended herself.'

'Yes. It might have happened like that,' said Philippa.

'It has upset me quite a lot. I've known her for so long, all her life and most of mine. It's like losing a sister almost. I've been trying to get on to poor Millet, but I understand he went up to Town this morning. The police got on to him and he had to go to identify the body, poor fellow. He's with his sister at Cragg Court. You remember her? Mrs. Ebling. Nice woman. You might like to call, dear? It would be nice if you did, I think, as we knew Susan so well.'

'Yes,' said Philippa without committing herself. Dear Justin. Always the thought for someone else, especially someone in trouble. The last thing she wanted to do, however, was to condole with anyone who might be grieving for Susan Therne.

'Will you be staying in Town for a few more days, dear?' he asked, and she could not miss the meaning in his voice.

'Only a day or two,' she said. 'You don't mind?'

'I always mind when you're away. Don't make it too long, dear.'

'Goodnight. Justin—dear,' her voice wobbling suddenly on the final word. She did not hear his reply. She was groping for the telephone-stand and when she had replaced the receiver she threw herself down on the settee in a passion of tears which she knew were of self-pity – tears because she had betrayed Justin, tears because she would have to part from Fergus, tears because of the terrifying mess she had made of her life, tears because she was frightened of tomorrow.

Chapter Twelve

The next day's paper provided the news that Susan Therne had been strangled to death, and from that moment Philippa was cast headlong into a pit of nameless horrors, for she was visited by the police at Ena's flat and asked searching and repeated questions whose object she could not at first even dimly guess.

'Why do they come here, Ena?' she asked wildly. 'Why do they ask me things? What time we arrived at the hotel, where we had dinner, what time we went to bed, what time we got up, and now a quite impertinent question about why I am staying here instead of living with Fergus at the airfield—as if it were anybody's business but ours! And the questions about Susan, making me admit I've known her quite a long time and asking why at first I merely said I had met her. Ena, I'm frightened. I'm afraid they've found out who I am.'

'My dear, you know you'll be forced to tell them in the end, so why not now?'

'But why should I have to? I hadn't anything to do with the way she died. Surely they don't think I killed her?' but the miserable ironic laughter changed suddenly, faltered and stopped and she stared at Ena.

'Are you thinking what I'm thinking?' she asked at last, as Ena said nothing. 'Are you wondering if—if they think—if they are trying to suspect ...'

She could not finish her sentence and Ena finished it for her quietly.

'Fergus? Yes, I am wondering that. You are too, aren't you?'

'But it's too absurd, too fantastic. He didn't even know her!'

'The police find out a lot of things in a case like this. They may know who you are without your having to tell them and if they have discovered that Susan Therne was blackmailing you ...'

'They couldn't. I took the money from an account which I opened in another name. They could not possibly know I had given her money.'

'What name?'

'Philippa Browne.'

'Why on earth had you to call yourself Philippa? Why not Mary or Jane or Flossie, or anything but your own name?'

'I didn't think about it like that. Besides, I'm not the only Philippa.'

'No, but it isn't a very common name, and if they found that a big sum of money had been paid to Susan by a Philippa Browne, and in the hotel that night, and very near her room, someone called Philippa Wynton was staying, they might have put two and two together.'

'And made it five?' asked Philippa contemptuously. 'Besides, how could they have found out that Philippa Browne had paid money to Susan? She would have cashed that cheque weeks ago.'

'Are you sure she did? Have you had the paid cheque back? Why a cheque too? I thought all these shady deals were done in cash.'

'I couldn't go carting a thousand pounds about in notes,' said Philippa. 'That's the very reason why I opened the account in another name.'

'Why not ring up the bank where you've got that account and ask if the cheque was ever cashed?' suggested Ena.

'It must have been. She was desperate for the money – but I'll do it if you like, just to set your mind at rest,' and she found the number of the bank in the telephone book and rang through.

'This is Philippa Browne speaking,' she said. 'I have an account with you. Will you please tell me if a cheque I drew on the twentieth of August for one thousand pounds, payable to a Miss Therne, has been presented for payment yet?'

The clerk at the other end gave a low, soundless whistle and put his hand over the mouthpiece of the telephone.

'Wade, tell the boss,' he said to a junior standing near him. 'There's an inquiry about that thousand pounds drawn by Philippa Browne to

Susan Therne.' Into the telephone he said politely to Philippa: 'I'm afraid I may have to keep you a moment whilst it is looked up, madam. Will you hold on?'

'Yes, I'll hold on,' said Philippa, and to Ena, 'They've gone to look it up.'

The bank manager put a call through quickly to Scotland Yard and the line was tapped and the mechanism set in motion which would trace the call to the block of flats from which it was made. Then the clerk returned to the telephone.

'No, madam,' he said. 'It has not been presented.'

'Thank you,' said Philippa, drew a troubled breath, and hung up. 'It hasn't, Ena. Why on earth did she keep it? She wanted the money desperately, and an uncashed cheque wasn't much use to her.'

'I can't imagine, unless it was part of some deep-laid scheme to harm you. She hated you, Philippa, for marrying Justin, you know.'

'They were never actually engaged, were they? Once Lady Hollmere mentioned her as if they had been.'

'My dear, no! Justin's never had a thought for any woman in the world but you, and his marriage was the only thing he's ever stood up to his mother about. If it really was so as to be able to hurt you that she kept that cheque, I really don't understand it, because she seemed quite happy about being engaged to Dr. Millet, so she must have got over anything she had felt for Justin.'

The whole truth about that cheque never emerged, though the holding of it uncashed was to prove a very great factor in determining the course of Philippa's life. Susan's actual reason for keeping it so long was a simple one and had no deep-rooted meaning such as Ena would have imputed to it. Knowing herself to be an inveterate spendthrift, Susan had meant to keep it as long as she could without turning it into the cash she might so easily and quickly have frittered or gambled away. She thought that if she staved off her creditors as long as she could, she would cash the cheque just in time to have a grand settlement of her debts prior to her marriage and before she could incur another lot. It was as simple as that. She could not know that she would, in fact, never cash it and that it would remain Philippa's.

Only once during the week she stayed with Ena did Fergus contact Philippa. The telephone rang very late one night and Ena got up to answer it, and then popped her head inside Philippa's room.

'It's for you,' she said. 'Fergus, I think.'

Philippa ran in in her nightdress, shutting the door of the living-room behind her.

'Yes?' she asked, breathlessly.

'You, Philippa?'

'Yes. Oh, Fergus, I'm so glad you've called. I didn't like to. Are you alright?'

'Yes. You?'

'I'm alright, but the police keep coming. I think they know I'm not your wife.'

'They know alright,' he said grimly. 'They've been at me too, though they're not made very welcome here, of course. It was too darned easy for them to find out first go off that I'm not married. What have they been asking you, Philippa?'

'Silly things about times, about that night. And they made me say I knew her quite well. I couldn't help it, and of course they looked at me as if I were a criminal when they got me to admit it, though I can't see what business it is of theirs.'

'Everything's their business, of course, when it's a murder case,' he said grimly. 'Don't tell them anything you don't have to. You need not say anything at all, you know. Darling …'

'What is it, Fergus?' as he paused.

'Darling, don't you think it might be a good idea if you got yourself a lawyer? A good solicitor, I mean?'

'What on earth for? You don't think—Fergus, you can't possibly be suggesting that they think I had anything to do with it?' she asked, aghast.

'No, of course not. But we can't help being a bit involved in it. After all, we were there that night, and in a room on the same floor, and you've admitted now that you knew her whereas at first you—well, you didn't give them that impression, did you?'

'I know. It was silly of me. Fergus, I've got to tell you something. She was blackmailing me.'

'Good Lord! Why didn't you tell me?'

'I didn't want you to know about it. It would have worried you and it didn't matter all that much to me, not the money part of it. I could give it to her.'

'I've not been much use to you, have I?' he asked with that grim tone. 'Anyway, don't tell the police anything, darling, not anything at all, will you? And get that solicitor. Do you know a good, reliable one?'

Yes. Justin's solicitor, Jeffrey Templar. Oh ... breaking off as she realised with a sickening dismay that to go to him, or to any other reputable solicitor, meant making a full revelation of herself.

'Please go to him, darling.'

'Fergus, don't you realise? It means I'll have to tell Justin,' she said miserably.

'Philippa—dearest—I don't think you'll be able to avoid that in any case. I hate saying this to you and I wish with all my heart I were with you instead of on the other end of this beastly wire. You see we're involved in this,' he ended with a desperate rush.

'Just because we had a room on the same floor and I happened to know her?' asked Philippa irritably.

'No. There's something else.'

'Fergus! What else?'

Her voice was shrill with alarm.

'It isn't you who are going to be mixed up in it to start with. I'm the one, and it's going to drag you in as well.'

'You, Fergus? But how can it be? You didn't even know her.'

'I did. Not much, but enough. Darling, I can't talk over the phone and I feel it might be unwise, for you that is, if I come to see you. I'll have to ring off, but I do beg that you will go to a good solicitor and tell him everything.'

'And Justin?'

'I don't think it can be helped. I'd rather have killed myself than get you into this mess, but there's nothing I can do about it now, and if I did kill myself, the mess for you would be even worse.'

'You wouldn't do anything so idiotic?' she asked sharply.

'Of course not. Will you do as I ask, my darling?'

'Oh yes, I suppose so. If I absolutely must,' she said drearily.

'Then—goodnight, my sweet. God bless you,' and he rang off.

In spite of his urgent request, she could not bring herself to take the final step which she felt must inevitably lead to a full confession to Justin, nor had she the courage to return to Hollmere Abbey, though she hungered for a sight of Trevor and knew he must be looking for her and asking for her. Brownie wrote faithfully every few days, assuring her that the child was well, turning the knife in her breast by describing every new trick he was learning, repeating every new word. Was she going to lose him? What would be Justin's reaction to the truth? Though she had felt that she knew her husband through and through, she found that that was not so, for she was quite unable to visualise the scene she must enact with him if he had to know.

And a week later, whilst she was still trying to make up her mind to go to Jeffrey Templar, whom she knew as a kindly, efficient man, her own and Justin's personal friend, the initiative was taken out of her hands in a ruthless and terrifying manner.

Fergus Wynton was arrested on suspicion of murdering Susan Therne.

Philippa was distraught.

'It isn't possible. It just isn't possible. It doesn't make sense!' she cried to Ena.

But of course, in the eyes of the law, it did.

Philippa had not been obliged to attend the inquest, a short affair in which, the medical evidence being clear, a verdict was returned that Susan Therne had been strangled by some person unknown who had twisted a silk stocking round her neck. She was, however, informed by the police that she would be required to attend the preliminary proceedings which would determine whether or not Wing Commander Fergus Wynton should be committed for trial on a charge of murder.

She fled to Jeffrey Templar's office and made immediate and full confession.

'Jeffrey, I'm frantic,' she said at the end of it.

He was a squarely built north-countryman, his small, keen blue eyes observing every detail, his quick, capable mind able to assess and compare values, never jumping to conclusions or accepting anything not abundantly proved.

She had known him only socially before. He was good company, a born raconteur, enjoying his whisky, and his cigars, an excellent host and a much-sought-after guest. Now she was seeing somebody very different facing her across his office desk.

He nodded.

'Yes, you would be,' he said. 'You'll have to tell Justin, you know.'

'Yes. I know,' she said in a low voice. 'Jeffrey, the whole thing is so fantastic. I mean, it's utterly impossible for Fergus to have done such a thing. Why on earth should he, for one thing? He didn't even know she was blackmailing me, and even if he had, he knew I was not short of money.'

'Look. Lady Hollmere ...'

'Not Philippa? Aren't you my friend any more either?' she asked bitterly.

'Of course I am, but at the moment you're my client, and that is the way I shall have to speak to you and refer to you in front of other people,' he said with a momentary relaxation of the gravity of his face. 'Philippa, if you like, at the moment. There can be no two ways about it. You must tell Justin, and when you go into court you must give your real name.'

'Jeffrey, the talk there'll be!' she said, squirming.

'I know. You've got to face it, Philippa. I'll help you all I can, of course, and we'll get the best man we can to advise you ...'

'And Fergus? Jeffrey, he'll need someone.'

'You mean you want to pay for his defence?' he asked gravely.

'I must. He hasn't any money.'

'In this country that never prevents anyone from being able to be defended by the best brains in the land. You must know that.'

'Yes, but there's no need for him to have just anyone,' she said wildly. 'He must have the very best, no matter what it costs.'

'Alright, m'dear, though I think it is unwise of you in the circumstances. I'll get in touch with his solicitor. I presume he will have one by now. We might be able to get Sir Harvey Gawtell for him, and perhaps James Larney for you.'

'Jeffrey, you're not suggesting that I might find myself actually on trial, do you?' she asked, alarmed.

'One can never tell. You see, you *are* involved, Philippa, If there is sufficient evidence to make the police believe that Wynton murdered Miss Therne during the night, and you were with him that night, they might very well and very sensibly conclude that you knew about it, even if you did not actually connive at it. Of course we don't know yet what sort of evidence the police have got against Wynton, but we shall find out and can then begin to combat it. I think you must be prepared for anything that may happen.'

'I agree that *anything* might happen when the police are such fools as to think Fergus capable of murdering anyone,' she said bitterly.

'Don't make any mistake,' said Jeffrey Templar gravely. 'The police of this country are not the ignorant fools they are so often made out to be in detective fiction. They are a very capable, intelligent, *trained* body of men, and they do not act without adequate cause nor jump to unfounded conclusions. If they have arrested Fergus Wynton on suspicion of this murder, you can be quite sure they have very serious and intelligent reasons for doing so. To you he is—a friend whom you cannot conceive capable of any crime. To them he is just a man actuated by the impulses and motives which determine the actions of most of us in any given set of circumstances. We don't know, *you* don't know, what the real circumstances are. It will be our business to find out just as it will be the business of the other side to do so. Now take my advice, Philippa. That's what you came to me for, isn't it? Go back to the Kersliks' now. I'll get in touch with the police and find the proper contact and tell them, for the moment in confidence, who you really are. Then, if they don't want to interview you again at the moment, go down to Sloworth, to the Abbey, and make a clean breast of the whole thing to Justin.'

She quailed.

'Oh, Jeffrey,' she said in a low voice and sat staring at the wall with a bleak look on her face.

He watched her in silence. He was sorry for her, as he was sorry for anyone in trouble, especially a woman. He was one of those rare men who think women should be guarded and cherished and sheltered against everything that could hurt them. Whenever possible, his voice was raised in protest against the conditions of the country in which women work intolerably hard for as many of the twenty-four hours a day as they can possibly keep awake and drag round on their feet, whilst the men clamour for a five-day week and an eight-hour day and expect to do nothing for the rest of their lives but sleep, or sit with their feet up, or hang over a bar. Jeffrey Templar was a passionate advocate of the rights of women, not for the vote only, but for their fair share of leisure and time to enjoy the homes which only they could make homes. He had married young, and in the early days of his struggle to get where he now stood it had been an intolerable hurt to him to see the way the ordinary housewife worked, even then, long before the Second World War had speeded up the inevitable social revolution. He had made it an inflexible rule in those early days, before he could afford to hire help for his wife, that he would never sit down at his ease until she could do the same. When the children came, he shared the new batch of duties, learned with cheerful ease to do everything for them, and many an evening had been spent after the children had gone to bed, Jenny mending and Jeffrey ironing.

The only thing which finally they had not been able to share was his success, for he could never persuade her to go with him to the social functions nor meet the important people brought into his life by his growing reputation and practice. She was an inveterate stay-at-home, and few but his most intimate friends knew her.

Philippa and Justin had been amongst these, and the Templars had on rare occasions spent a weekend at the Abbey when there were no other guests, and the Hollmeres had been entertained in the small suburban house where the Templars had lived for many years and where, although she had had to yield to her husband's insistence about domestic help, Jenny Templar still did her own cooking and went to the shops with a basket over her arm. With their children married, they had slipped back to as near their original position in the home as Jeffrey would allow and the only reason why Jenny kept the daily woman was because otherwise he would have been doing some of the housework and the ironing again rather than let her work longer hours than he did himself.

It was the best marriage Philippa knew, for the Kersliks still had to prove themselves and each other.

As if he had divined the trend of her thoughts, she from sheer need of relief momentarily from her own problems, he broke the silence.

'Would it help you to have a few days with us if you feel you must get away after telling Justin?' he asked. 'Jenny's the best person I know to be with in time of trouble,' with his kind, friendly smile replacing the business-like look of the solicitor again.

'You mean if—if I want somewhere to go after Justin's turned me out?' she asked bleakly.

'My dear child, you misjudge him entirely. Perhaps you always have done?'

'Oh, Jeffrey. I do feel so awful about it. I don't mean only for the terrible trouble Fergus is in because, of course, he will be out of that. I've heard you say that the chances of an innocent man being found guilty of—of murder in this country are almost nil though I suppose it must be so sometimes.'

'Not a chance at all,' he said.

There seemed nothing more to be said, so she did as he told her, went back to Ena's, had an unexpectedly easy interview with the Scotland Yard official who came to see her and did not appear to be at all surprised at discovering that the somewhat mysterious 'Mrs. Wynton' was actually the Countess of Hollmere, and afterwards went down to Sloworth.

Ena had offered to telephone to Justin after she had gone, to tell him she was on her way.

'Don't ask me to tell him anything else, Philippa,' she said. 'That, I'm afraid, is your job.'

'I know,' said Philippa. 'Thank you for everything, Ena.'

At the last minute Ena did an unusual thing, for she was not demonstrative. She put her arms round Philippa and kissed her.

'You know you can come back if you want to, don't you?' she said. 'Paul joins me in that. Come when you like and for as long as you like.'

'I know what you mean,' said Philippa in a low voice. 'Thank you again,' and she went out to the waiting taxi.

'It's all very well for them to say cheerfully that Justin is so wonderful he'll understand,' she thought wretchedly, 'but at the same time Ena does what Jeffrey Templar did. They've both offered me sanctuary after I've told him.'

Justin was at the station to meet her, as she had known he would be – so unchanged, so apparently changeless, in his old, well-cut tweeds, his face wearing the same friendly smile – that it seemed impossible so much should have happened to her and yet left him the same. For one thing, she felt years older, and he looked at her critically after the first smile and his usual calm, friendly kiss on her cheek.

'About time you came home,' he said. 'You look like a ghost, and you're thinner. I shall have a word with Ena when I see her again.'

He had been prepared for something, though he had no idea what it was. When Ena had told him the time of Philippa's train, she had added something she had not intended to say.

'Justin, be prepared to be very kind to her.'

'My dear Ena, when have I ever been anything else to her?' he asked in surprise.

'I know, but this time be specially nice and understanding. She'll need it.'

'Ena, what's happened?'

But she rang off and left him wondering, so that he was still wondering but not actually surprised to see that Philippa looked tired and ill and as nearly plain as was possible. It tore at his heart and he would not have needed Ena's plea to show her even greater tenderness and consideration than usual.

He had driven the car himself and as he was the type of driver to concentrate almost grimly on his job, even on the quiet country roads, they were silent until they reached the Abbey and he had followed Philippa into the house, with a word to Best about the car when he came to get the luggage.

'Come in here, Justin, will you?' she asked, crossing the hall to the door of the little octagonal room which she had turned into a private sitting-room for herself, the one room in the house where no one ever came uninvited, not even Justin, and where she was never disturbed.

Not even telephone calls were put through to her there unless she had specifically asked for them.

He followed her and she shut the door and stood with her back to it, facing him desperately. She must get it over, whatever the cost was going to be.

'Justin, I've got something very dreadful to tell you,' she said, her face losing the last vestige of its colour.

Dear, whatever is it? Do sit down. Is it about yourself? Have you been seeing doctors or ...'

She interrupted him.

'Nothing like that. I'm perfectly well, and I'd rather stand. It's a confession, Justin. I've been unfaithful to you. I've got a lover. I've had one for months, ever since I went to Bonavie last year in fact.'

She turned her head so that she could not look at him, and there was deathly silence in the room. Every little sound from outside was magnified by it, the whirr of the motor-mower, the sound of an aeroplane overhead, the closing of the garage gates after Best had put the car away, the chatter of the birds arranging their winter quarters or discussing flight.

Then Justin moved his hand, and a small brass ornament on the table fell with a little clatter to the ground. He stooped to pick it up and stood with it in his hand, his fingers automatically tracing its outline.

He spoke at last, very quietly.

'Shall we sit down? You'd better tell me about it. It doesn't appear to have made you very happy, by the way.'

'Happy? I didn't know it was possible to be so utterly miserable,' she said, sitting down in the chair he had moved for her.

'Well, I can find comfort in that,' he said, sitting down near her. 'Does it mean that you're not going to leave me?'

'Oh, Justin, don't be kind to me! That I couldn't bear!' she cried.

He even smiled.

'What do you want me to do? Beat you?'

'Yes, if it would do any good, but it won't. Nothing will.'

'We'll see about that. Who is it, by the way? Anyone I know?'

No. I'll come to that. Justin, what have you read about this business of Susan Therne?'

'Susan? Is this a sudden change of subject?' he asked, frowning.

'No. Do you know about that? That a man has been arrested on suspicion of having killed her?'

'Yes. Some man in the Royal Air Force. Philippa, you're not trying to tell me ...?'

She nodded.

'Yes. Fergus Wynton,' she said, and looked away again.

'You mean that he, this Air Force man, is your lover? And that he's charged with the murder of Susan Therne?'

Justin's voice was slow, very quiet, inexpressibly shocked. His face was suddenly tilled and lined with pain. His whole body seemed to shrink with pain.

'Yes,' said Philippa, and for another moment or two there was silence again.

Then Justin spoke.

'I am shocked, naturally,' he said in that slow, quiet voice. 'I am not quite sure why you have decided to tell me, though. What am I supposed to do about it?'

'I haven't told you everything yet. It's all so—awful. You see—I was there that night. I was there with Fergus.'

'You are the woman who has been mentioned in the papers? The one referred to as this man's wife?'

'Yes.'

'I see.'

He got up and walked to the window and stood with his back to her, staring out at the fair vision of his home, so dearly loved, re-established and given back to its former beauty by Philippa's money, poured out lavishly, accepted by him reluctantly and only because it was also her home and would be the home of their son, saved for perhaps two or three generations more.

His home. His inheritance. The inheritance of so many of his name before him, every stone and tree and blade of grass bearing some part in its long, honourable history. In the room where he stood, how many of Philippa's predecessors had sat with their tapestry, their music, their friends, their children, their husbands – all the gracious accompaniments of each changing age making it an individual room just as, for her generation, Philippa had made it hers?

And now she was to be dishonoured, publicly, inevitably, for all the world to see, for people to snigger at and make lewd jokes about. They would laugh at him, too, and say it served him right for selling his barren title and the crumbling ruins of his home for the Jolly Man's wealth.

He thought of Susan, who had always wanted him, lying dead, murdered heaven knew why by the man who was Philippa's secret lover; Lady Hollmere the furtive mistress of a murderer!

He remembered her as he had first seen her, her brown curls blowing beneath her jauntily set cap, her sleeves rolled up as she manoeuvred her boat into position and then the small shriek, the horrified laughter in her face, as she fell overboard, to come up capless, dripping, but still laughing.

He thought of her on their wedding day, so pale and still in all the drift of white, her eyes meeting his for a moment, gravely, sweetly, as she gave him her promise.

He gripped the edge of the window-sill hard and then, master of himself again, he turned back to her and the sight of her as she was at this moment, her head bent, the gay curls a mockery of her sadness, her face drained of colour and of the eager, vitality which had seemed so inseparable a part of her, everything fled from his mind but his love for her and her need of him. For perhaps the first time in their lives, she needed him. Was this a time to fail her?

He crossed the room and put a hand on her shoulder and pressed it with firm fingers, silent still whilst she became aware of the gesture and could understand what it meant.

Then he spoke very quietly.

'Have I still any part of you?' he asked.

She lifted her head with a jerk and looked at him, startled, incredulous.

'Justin, you can ask that? Only that? There's no bitterness in your voice and you don't hate me?'

'How could I? I told you a long time ago that I should love you till I die. I haven't changed.'

'But I have, Justin. I'm not the girl you fell in love with and married.'

'No. You're the mother of my son, Philippa. You're my wife.'

She let her head sink again. The pressure of his hand was too kind to be borne.

'If you were angry, disgusted, if you called me all sorts of names and—and threw me out, Justin,' she said with a quivering attempt at a smile which he found infinitely pitiful, 'I think I could bear it better. Your heavenly kindness makes me—feel so despicable. Don't be so kind to me. I can't bear it.'

'Well, I've told you I'll beat you if it would make you feel any better, though I shouldn't really know how to set about it, and I don't think I should make such a success of it. I don't think it's beating you want. It's kindness and love you want, Philippa, and those are easy things for me to give you.'

She gave a gulping sob and let her cheek rest against his hand for a moment. She could find nothing to say. For the moment her mind felt blank. The only thoughts in it were of unimportant small things – that the gardener had made a good job of the lawn, that she must order the new rose trees before the winter, that the colour of the curtains exactly matched the flowers that someone (Brownie?) had put in the window.

'I think you're very tired,' he said. 'Why not go to bed and I'll send some dinner up to you? It's too late to go up to Trevor in any case.'

'Yes. I wasn't going up,' she said drearily. 'I think I will go to bed. Have you got any of those tablets you got for me after Daddy died?'

'I expect so. I have certainly never needed anything to make me sleep,' he said with a smile which gave no hint of the effort it cost him. 'Have your dinner first, and I'll look for them.'

She made a gesture of agreement and rose from the chair. He opened the door for her but she did not look at him as she passed him.

It was an effort to eat a few mouthfuls of the food he sent up to her – carefully chosen to tempt her – some clear soup, thin slices of breast of chicken with the cleverly cooked vegetables which were always plentiful in their own gardens, a pear glazed and filled with whipped cream and chopped nuts, her favourite sweet which she knew the cook had prepared specially for her. Justin had sent up a small flask of Orvieto, again her favourite wine, for her to drink with it, and she drank it thirstily though she ate little.

Packer came in to take the tray.

'You have not eaten very much, My Lady,' she said with an air of concern which might or might not be sincere. Philippa felt she never knew with Packer, and she wished Brownie had come instead.

'I'm not hungry,' she said. 'Give me my cigarette-case from my bag, and my lighter, please.'

The maid did so. Philippa could feel her looking at her though she herself did not return the look.

What if she knows already? Philippa thought. How she will enjoy it. How they'll all enjoy it!

'Nothing else I can do for you, My Lady?'

'No. Nothing. Turn out the lights as you go out. The lamp will be enough for me.'

A little later, Justin tapped at the door and came in. It was a long time since he had been in her room. He hesitated a moment and then closed the door softly and came across to the bed.

'I've brought you the tablets, dear,' he said, and put them down on the table beside her.

'Only two?' she asked with a little smile. 'Afraid to let me have the bottle?'

'A little, yes,' he said. 'I thought you might be unhappy enough to do something very foolish, and I should never have forgiven myself.'

'It might be the best way out,' she said, crushing out the stub of her cigarette and swallowing the two sleeping pills with a drink of the water he had brought her.

'I couldn't conceive of a worse way,' he said. 'It would be the coward's way, and you've never been a coward, Philippa.'

'I could be one now. I hate life and myself.'

'And me?'

She managed a shadowy smile and slid her hand into his as he sat on the edge of her bed.

'Nobody could hate you, Justin,' she said.

'I'd have liked you to feel a slightly warmer sentiment, but I'll try to content myself with what I can get,' he said, smiling down at her.

She looked like a forlorn, unhappy child, he thought, sitting propped up by her pillows, no make-up on her face, and around her head the blue ribbon which she had tied there automatically, because she always did it, to keep the hair from getting into her eyes if she turned on the pillow during the night. The frail transparency of the white nylon nightdress, a sophisticated, seductive garment, gave her rather the look of that child dressed up than the actual owner of the gown. It fell away softly from the curve of her breast and as he found himself looking at it, it rose sharply with her half-uttered sob. Her eyes were dry and she had herself under complete control. She hated 'scenes' and was not going to treat him to one, but that sob had welled up from within her and it caught at his heart.

He had come to her room determined to let her set the pace of their present relations, but at that sob, at the childish appeal of her, at the bewildered, hurt look in her eyes which she did not know was there, his determination failed.

He leaned down and picked her up in his arms and cradled her against his breast, at first with the feeling that he held in his arms a child to be comforted but soon being made aware by the response of his body that he held the beloved woman.

Drowsy with the unaccustomed drug its insidious comfort seeping through her to dull her bran, and give her body the lethargy which at last relaxed her overstrung nerves, she lay in his arms, scarcely aware of it, except that the bliss of feeling nothing, knowing nothing, needing nothing, had come back to her after all the anguish and restlessness. Justin looked down at her in the light of the shaded lamp which cast a rosy glow over her, touching her cheeks and intensifying the shadow of her eyelashes beneath her closed lids, lying like the bloom of a pearl over her throat, her shoulders, her breasts beneath the revealing transparency which offered them seductively to his seeking gaze.

He had never seen her like this before, lethargic and unresponsive in his arms, and even when he bent his head and his lips pushed aside the fragile stuff of her gown, she scarcely stirred, half-opening her eyes and closing them again, an incoherent murmur of contentment coming from her lips. He felt the excitement rising in him. In all their love-making, she had been so eager to meet his kisses and his touch, the strong life within her seeking, consciously or instinctively, to compel his own. However much he despised himself, told himself he was unnatural, inhuman, a freak of manhood, this ardour of hers had cooled rather than provoked his own. His blood, thinned by what was almost inter-breeding by the Hollmeres, had chosen moments like those to cool because he was not sufficiently the hunter, or because the prey was too easy, rushing to him rather than away from him. He had tried to analyse that but could not. He had only known that he had failed her, time after time, until at last he had been relieved, and she apparently content, that their relations had practically ceased and for almost a year now he had not touched her.

She stirred again, lay back in an unconsciously provocative posture, smiled again without opening her eyes.

'Stay with me,' she murmured. 'Don't leave me.'

She was not even aware that she had spoken. She only knew vaguely that she was in blissful comfort, her body in warm, enfolding arms, her mind empty of any other thought. If there were thought at all, it was that she was in her lover's arms but she did not speak his name.

Justin could not speak. She had come back to him. He refused to let himself remember anything but that, or to let his brain tell his clamorous body that another man had held her like this, that her lovely body had known the embraces of a lover that was not himself.

'Philippa,' he whispered thickly. 'Philippa, my darling, my love, my beautiful.'

Presently he lay relaxed, drowsy, utterly contented beside her and Philippa slept and woke hours later cramped and chilled, the lamp still burning and Justin sleeping beside her.

Her mind cleared slowly but with only vague memory. Her lips curled a little in distaste. She had been doped, of course, but she would not have denied him. He should not have wanted her, she felt with that faint nausea, not after what she had told him, not when he knew that she had taken a lover and was worthless.

What were men made of, after all? Was a woman's mind of no account to them if her body was slim and straight and desirable, her features made in a certain mould? Didn't it matter what they were like inside?

She felt an utter revulsion from that side of her nature. That, after all, was the thing that had caught and chained Fergus to her and she to him, that ephemeral, unimportant thing in which the women of the street traded.

She drew herself from the flaccid hold of Justin's arms and went to her bathroom and lay in the hot, scented water, trying to find a relief and comfort for her mind to match that of her rested body. It was beyond her powers. All the sick misery of the past fortnight swept upon her again and she rested her aching forehead against the cold rim of the bath and longed to find oblivion. If only Justin had given her the bottle instead of doling out those two tablets, she could find it. He had called upon her courage, but she had none.

Yet she must go on. Life when you are twenty-seven is not to be ended merely by the wishful thought.

Chapter Thirteen

The public revelation that Lady Hollmere was the mysterious 'woman in the case' when the first hearing of the charge against Fergus Wynton was heard produced the sensation of a dull season, and not even the newspapers, with their blazoned headings in large type, could out-do the repetition of her name on the lips of her friends.

Popular and flattered as she had been, Philippa had had many unconfessed enemies from envy and jealousy, and those who had professed the greatest friendship and admiration for her now enjoyed thoroughly the opportunity to say to one another: 'My dear, what could you expect? Look who she was!'

Philippa kept her head high. Her demeanour in the crowded courtroom, and afterwards, would not have disgraced a French aristocrat walking up the steps of the guillotine. No one, not even Justin, was allowed to catch a glimpse of the hell in which she was living, the horror, the fear.

The proceedings were a terrifying revelation to her of facts of which she had never dreamed, and for the first time she realised that Fergus was in actual danger, that his arrest was not the idiotic mistake of some jaundiced official out for a victim, no matter who.

Trying to shield her as she had tried to shield him, Fergus had kept from her the fact that Susan Therne had also been blackmailing him, though the sums she had demanded had been judiciously smaller than the large sum she had extracted from Joe Joliman's daughter. The last ten pounds he had given her before that ill-fated night was to have been the last, of course.

'I'm not really out for your blood, Fergus,' she had told him when he handed it over. 'If I could get along without this sort of thing, heaven knows I would, but I can't. I'll let you alone from now on, though, cross my heart!' and he had actually believed her until he had met her, face to face, in the foyer of the Medway.

The look on her face showed him that it was no surprise to her, and his heart sank. He had been a fool, of course, to believe her. His only desire at that moment was to keep her from Philippa. Susan, extracting the small sums from him, had amused herself by keeping Philippa's secret so that he had remained unaware of her real name and identity until they had been revealed to him, with stunning effect, by his solicitor.

'Where can we talk?' Susan had said when she met him in the foyer.

'We can't talk anywhere here,' he told her, looking round nervously for Philippa, whom he had left in their room a few minutes earlier. He was trying to get seats for them for an evening show at the theatre agency in the foyer. He had his wallet open, and Susan's greedy eyes had fastened on it. He put it quickly into his pocket, but not until she had seen that it was well stuffed with notes. He had drawn out as much as he could to buy Philippa a present the next day, a jewelled evening bag which she had seen and liked and on which he had secretly paid a deposit until he had been able to amass enough to complete the purchase. Susan's depredations had infuriatingly delayed the gathering together of the fifty-odd pounds that he required, but at last it was there in his wallet.

And she had seen it.

'I don't want to talk to you,' he replied curtly to her question.

'Oh, you'd better, you know. I do see your point, though. By such a lucky chance, my room is quite near yours.' (There was no mistaking the malicious glint in her smile. Of course she had contrived that.) 'Come along and see me. Not too early, of course. Say about eleven? That won't interrupt your night too much, I hope?' with another of her fiendish grins.

'What about your own reputation?' he snarled.

'Oh, but Fergus dear, you'll take care of that, won't you?' she asked lightly. 'Number eighteen and—bring your wallet with you, darling.'

She had sailed away, confident that he would obey her.

'It doesn't matter about the seats,' he said to the clerk who had taken considerable trouble to get the offer of them, and he walked away.

All that came out in detail at the hearing, and it was indisputable that he had been in Susan Therne's room that night. The maid had cleaned the bedroom basin when she had gone to turn down the bed at nine o'clock and in the morning Fergus Wynton's finger-prints had been found on it, and on other parts of the room and on both sides of the door-handle.

Philippa herself, ever since his arrest, had not been able to rid her mind of the frightening memory of having wakened after an early sleep to find him coming back into the room with no very clear explanation of why he should have gone out of it. They had a connecting bathroom and toilet. He told her he thought he had 'heard something', but even then she had thought it odd of him to want to investigate a noise in an hotel at eleven o'clock at night.

Was it then he had been in Susan Therne's room? And the time of her death was put between ten o'clock and one o'clock.

There was more. The police had found a motive. They knew that Susan had been blackmailing him. She had written a note which she had intended to have sent to him, but as she had run into him in the foyer, the note had been found in her bag.

Come along and see me (she had written). I'm in 18. About eleven. Bring something with you.

It had not been addressed to him, but they had found his fingerprints and they had also found an uncashed cheque for a thousand pounds in Susan's handbag, the signature on the cheque being that of Philippa Browne – and the woman who was not Fergus Wynton's wife was also named Philippa, and when the call to the bank, asking if the cheque had yet been cashed, was traced to the address given to the police by the *soi-disant* Philippa Wynton, the rest had been easy.

The motive, in the eyes of the law, had been greatly increased by the discovery that the woman Fergus Wynton was trying to shield was the Countess of Hollmere, a woman to whom it was much more than ordinarily important that she should not be discovered.

Fergus told his own version of it without any deviation however many times he had to tell it, but his patience, never a strong point, was exhausted and his temper worn thin by the time he faced his accusers publicly, and he did not make a good impression.

For one thing, nobody believed that until these proceedings began to take shape, he had not known who Philippa was. It was too fantastically improbable, though she herself confirmed his story, standing white-faced, icily composed, in the witness-box. Her dignified self-possession gave no indication that she was in the pillory, hating and shrinking from the curious eyes of her 'friends' who were jammed together like sardines in a tin in their determination to watch her degradation.

According to Fergus, he had gone at Susan Therne's bidding to her room, getting there about ten past eleven and leaving again at quarter past. He had left her well and very much alive and counting out the notes which he had taken from his wallet and flung on the table before he left her.

'How can you be so sure of the time, Wing Commander?' had been one of the smooth questions put to him.

'Because when I got back to my own room, my—Phil— Lady Hollmere woke and asked me.'

Philippa's heart, still acutely alive through its anguish, ached for him and the hideous agony through which he himself was passing. It was the first time she had heard him use her own name. It seemed to put her at an incredible distance from all this. That had not been Lady Hollmere snuggled up in his bed, but Philippa – just Philippa who had loved and belonged to him.

His reply produced a ripple of pleased enjoyment amongst the spectators round the arena.

'My dear, how awful! Fancy his actually having to *say* that about her,' and the claws had worked in and out of the velvet sheaths and their owners had purred happily.

He did not know how his fingerprints had got all over the room, he said. He would have thought he had been standing still without touching anything, but he had been worried, angry. He must have leaned back against the washbasin if fingerprints had been on it, must have walked into the room and touched things.

There was no evidence that anyone else had been in Susan's room. He had, he said, left the notes, nearly fifty pounds on the table and walked out, closing the door behind him. Susan had been in her dressing-gown. He did not know whether she had been in her pyjamas or not. The gown was of the house-coat style, zipped from neck to hem. She had been standing by the table picking up the notes when he left her.

It was slender evidence, but two of the essentials were beyond doubt, the motive and the opportunity, and minute inquiry seemed to make it impossible that anyone other than the hotel guests and the staff could have gone to Room Eighteen entirely unobserved after eleven o'clock at night. It was a very quiet hotel, and there were very few guests, and the night porter had not left the reception desk, right inside the entrance doors, until he had been relieved at seven o'clock the next morning.

Fergus was committed for trial, and the harpies gathered up their furs and their handbags and chattered their way out of the courtroom in happy anticipation of more pleasure to come when the law had tightened its grip on Philippa Hollmere's lover (my dear, quite a fascinating type!) and had examined all its nuts and bolts and the links in its chain.

Philippa was stunned. She had never for one moment believed that this could happen. It seemed so entirely beyond doubt that he was telling the truth. Surely even people who did not know him must have realised that it would be quite impossible for him to murder anyone, tie a stocking round a woman's neck and twist it until she had ceased to struggle, and then to take the stocking off, throw it on the floor and calmly walk away. The idea was so fantastic that she went away from the courtroom in a daze, scarcely able to believe that she was awake and not imprisoned in some dreadful nightmare.

Justin took her elbow and firmly led her across the pavement, his face expressionless, his step firm and unhurried, between the lines of curious sightseers to whom he and Philippa were part of the exhibition. Through all the growing horror of the inquiry, she had been aware of him, coming into the court-room with her and Jeffrey Templar and the Q.C., James Larney, whose thin, bitter-mouthed face was familiar to all readers of the popular Press. He had been briefed for the Crown or for the defence at very many famous trials, and it was not surprising that he should be representing Lady Hollmere in this one, though she was not as yet one of the principals in the case. Philippa had quailed at the first sight of the crowded room, its small capacity bringing the spectators so close to those who had business there that Philippa brushed against some of her own acquaintances as she pushed through the lane made for her by the clerk of the court. She had heard the little ripple of whispering talk that greeted the appearance of Justin. Whatever they had expected, it was obviously not that he would stand solidly by her, would treat her, speak to her, look at her, as if it were a matter of no consequence to him that her infidelity was being thus cried to the world. No one had ever seen his face wearing its present hard look, but the hardness was not for Philippa. Whenever he met her eyes, he smiled and now, when it was over and the bigger drama would presently follow, his hand held her arm firmly and his attitude was solicitous and affectionate as he waved Best aside and himself stood holding the door of his car open for her.

Inside the car, she lay back, shrinking into as small a space as possible, her face grey with pain and fatigue. Ever since the arrest of Fergus and her confession to Justin, they had been staying quietly in two or three rooms at Hollmere House, at home to no one except Jeffrey Templar and Philippa's counsel, who had frequently been a guest there and paid her the unusual courtesy of going to see her there instead of requiring her to meet him at his chambers or at the solicitor's. Justin had spoken to him briefly as they left the court-room.

'Come along to dinner if you feel like it,' he said.

'Thanks. I will,' said the counsel, nodding at Philippa and showing no sign of being in any way disturbed by the result of the inquiry of the magistrate's court. There was no reason why he should be. It was going quite well for him. If Philippa turned into an even more important factor at the trial, as she might very well do, as accessary before or after the fact or both, his own position would be very much enhanced. In any case the affair was one of the most sensational ones of the year because of the social position of the people concerned, and it might well take him a good step nearer to becoming Mr. Justice Larney. Philippa's youth and beauty, and Hollmere's position, would give him an unparalleled opportunity for displaying his particular brand of rhetorical eloquence and his undoubted ability would for once have a worthy backcloth.

Philippa had at last begun to realise that she might be drawn even more closely into this case than she was at present, but she would not allow her apprehension to become apparent. Justin, obviously anxious, came to her room for a few moments when she went to bed, fussily trying to show her his affectionate concern, asking at least to be allowed to send Brownie to her.

'Thank you, Justin,' she said wearily, hiding her exasperated irritation. 'I don't want either her or Packer. I just want to be alone. You're terribly sweet to me but—I'm better left alone.'

To her surprise and a mingling of relief and shame, her mother came to her with an offer of help and assurance of support.

'Thank you, Mother. I do appreciate your coming,' she said, 'but there is nothing anybody can do. I've got myself into this mess and I'm not going to drag everybody else into it. I suppose I shall get out of it somehow.'

Mrs. Joliman, living the lonely, enclosed existence which she had chosen after her husband's death, had learned of the disastrous affair first through the newspapers. It had shocked her to the soul. She had seemed already to have met and sustained the worst that life could do to her in taking away her beloved Joe, but now she reeled from yet another blow. She shut herself in her bedroom with all the morning newspapers (she did not read the evening papers or she would have known of it the night before) and read every word of the scant, careful paragraphs that told her this incredible and shattering thing. Her mind reeled, almost refusing to believe that this should happen to the Jolimans! God-fearing, good-living people to whom all this wealth had come through no crooked dealing but only through Joe's perception and cleverness and the dreadful chances of the two world wars. Ella Joliman had never wanted the wealth, never really appreciated the change in her position, though she had conscientiously and loyally done her best to live up to it for her Joe's sake, had dressed expensively and worn furs and jewels and silly hats because it had pleased him to see her like that. Since his death, she had been able to be herself again, plain Ella Joliman, looking after her own home, doing her own work, though everything now seemed pointless and useless.

But if Philippa were in trouble, bad trouble at that, it was by her side that her mother should be if that was where she could give any help or support.

Yet even there, it seemed, there was no need of her.

'It's lovely of you. Mother, and I shall never forget it,' said Philippa gratefully, 'but Justin thinks we should be in London, so we're going to stay in a room or two at Hollmere House and—and well, just wait, I suppose,' and she turned away, her face white and sick-looking, from the look in her mother's eyes.

'Goodness knows I don't want to make things worse for you,' said Mrs. Joliman, 'but 'owever could you a'come to do it, dearie? Brought up like you were, always with nice friends and married to anybody like his lordship …'

Philippa made a helpless gesture with her hands, her face still averted.

'I know. I know,' she said in a low voice. 'There's nothing I can say, nothing anybody would understand. I'm sorry—I'm so sorry, Mum, to have brought this on you. You'd better leave me alone to—to wallow in it. I shan't blame you. Nobody could.'

'You know very well I'd never do that. I'm your mother, dearie, and that's how I'll always be, and if you want me, or if I can do anything— well, I'm here all the time. I can only hope that when it's all over – you know what I mean – whatever 'appens, *whatever*, Philippa, you'll keep to Justin. He's a good man. He's deserved better of you. The only thing I'm glad about is that your dear father didn't live to see this day.'

There was nothing Philippa could say. She just stood there, her eyes hot and dry with the tears she could no longer shed, her throat aching, her mind a desolation, and Mrs. Joliman went heavily away.

Philippa and Justin went up to London, Justin with his head high, with a proud, cold face and frosty eyes that defied any look or curiosity or pity they met. Since they had reopened Hollmere House, they had kept a skeleton staff there. An elderly couple who were pensioners of the Hollmeres, retired when old Lady Hollmere left the Abbey, had come thankfully out of their retirement to take up a position as housekeeper and butler in the London house, servants being brought from the Abbey when Hollmere House was opened for a round of entertaining. Now, with no suggestion of any sort of function, the Lees managed with only one woman, so that the house was almost empty and very quiet.

'You ought to have this lit early in the evening,' said Justin, stooping to put a match to the gas-fire in Philippa's room the first night they were there. 'It's much too cold for you in here. Don't start to undress until it's warmed up a bit, dear. Why not come down again for a few minutes by the library fire?'

They were using the library as both sitting- and dining-room in preference to the larger rooms.

'I really don't care whether I'm cold or not,' said Philippa drearily.

'Well, sit here for a bit anyway,' he said with determined cheerfulness, pulling an armchair close to the warmth for her.

She did so with an air of weary indifference and rested her cheek on her hand.

'You're very good to me, Justin. I can't think why,' she said. 'I know how utterly beastly it is for you. How long do they take? When—when ...'

'I don't know, dear. I think it depends how much work there is to do on the case. I asked Larney but he shrugged off the question in the way he has. I don't like the man, but he's about the best you could have.'

'You're quite sure Sir Harvey Gawtell will be able to do everything humanly possible for—for him?' she asked, at the last moment unable to speak Fergus's name.

A spasm of pain crossed his face. She was still thinking of him, he thought bitterly.

'I'm quite sure of it,' was all he said.

'He'll be alright, won't he?' she asked next.

'I wouldn't know that,' he said, 'though I did not think the case was by any means tied up and sealed. After all, there are some loose ends. You heard Larney say that Wynton went up the stairs of the hotel and into—his room without being seen, and though it would not seem possible to go from the door downstairs to the lift without being seen from the reception desk, it is quite possible to reach the foot of the stairs unnoticed. Sir Harvey will make a point of that. Also one of the notes may turn up. The prosecution say, of course, that Wynton took them back himself after he had killed Susan, but if anyone could get to the room from the outside without being seen, he could also have left by the same route, or even by the fire-escape, without being seen, and robbery might have been the motive, after all.'

She shivered.

'Do you really think anybody would *murder* anyone for fifty pounds?' she asked. It was a trifling sum to her, but surely too small for anyone to kill for.

'No. Actually I don't. I think myself that what the defence will work on is to try to find someone else who had a motive for wanting to get rid of Susan. I must admit that amongst all the shocks I have had over this case, not the least of them has been discovering that she was a blackmailer.'

'You think Fergus and I were not the only ones?'

'I think it quite likely that you were not. Her affairs were in a mess, and apart from her debts she seems to have been spending considerably more than her known means would allow. That odd business of her not encashing your cheque in itself suggests that she had other sources of income to be able to keep it without cashing it.'

She was silent, her thoughts running along that new line of thought, wondering, hoping, praying that this would prove to be the solution of the mystery of Susan Therne's death, for her complete faith in Fergus never wavered. She believed utterly in the truth of his own explanation of how he came to be in Susan's room that night. She felt that she, out of all the people in the world, was in a position to be sure of that, for he had come back to her and shared again with her the rapturous delight of their love-making, and what man on earth could come straight from murdering one woman to making passionate love to another? He had been worried. She had realised that without knowing the cause. Now she understood it, but the worry had been through the constant threat held over him by Susan and because he had been forced to give her the money he had saved for Philippa's evening bag. It had certainly not been because he had just killed her.

She rose from her chair with a sigh.

'I might as well go to bed,' she said. 'Can I have some of my pills?'

'I've brought them,' he said. 'I'm not very keen on your taking this stuff, but you must have sleep and I don't think you'll sleep without it. Dear—I'm very sorry for you. You know that, don't you?'

'You're being very good to me, Justin, and I'm terribly sorry for all I've brought on you. You don't deserve any of it. You ought never to have married me.'

'I should have missed the best thing I've ever had in life if I hadn't,' he said. 'When all this is over …'

She interrupted him swiftly.

'That's been in my mind too. It's there all the time. Justin, I haven't got the courage to ask you not to stand by me now, but when it's over – whatever happens – we can't go on together. No, please let me speak. I've known all day I've got to say this to you. I can't go on taking all this from you, letting you stand up for me and endure what today must have cost you, and then just throw it all back at you. Don't stand by me anymore, Justin. Let me go. Leave me to whatever is in store for me. Save what you can of your name and your reputation and— forget me. You can divorce me and marry someone else, someone of your own kind, not—not a meat man's daughter!' breaking off with a little hysterical, bitter laugh.

After his one attempt to interrupt her, he had stood silently listening to her, but now he spoke with quiet finality.

You are talking nonsense, Philippa, and you know it. You know I shall never let you go, as you call it, and as for divorcing you – that I should never do, in any circumstances at all, even if it were possible.'

'Of course it's possible. I've admitted before the whole world the terms on which I was with Fergus.'

He shook his head and smiled with sad eyes.

'No, my dear. You don't know the English law. If I had wanted to divorce you, I should not have kept you with me nor come back here with you today. I have what they call 'condoned' it by being here with you, so that in law your offence against the marriage has been wiped out. Not that it makes any difference to me. As I say, nothing would ever induce me to divorce you, not even if Wynton goes free and you want to marry him.'

She flinched.

'I don't. I shan't,' she said. 'I've had enough of men, of all that side of life. Look what it's brought us to! No, Justin, it won't matter to me whether you divorce me or not, but it ought to matter to you, and if by letting you look after me like this I have made it impossible for you to get a divorce, then somehow, sometime, I must—make it possible again,' with a little shudder of distaste.

'Don't talk nonsense. For one thing, I shall never let you go, Philippa. You're my wife and how about Trevor? You wouldn't suggest taking him away if you left me?'

'No, she said bleakly. 'I couldn't do that. He belongs to you, to the Abbey. It's his heritage. I wouldn't try to take him from you. He'll get over it in time and when he is old enough to know about me, he'll be glad I left him.'

'You're talking arrant nonsense, my dear, because you're overwrought and over-tired. Take these. I'll get you some water. Then get into bed quickly and go to sleep.'

They remained in London a few days, and then they went back to the Abbey, Philippa no longer cared where she went nor what she did. One pair of staring eyes was no worse than another, and she knew that Justin would be happier working than trying to kill the long hours in London, since they no longer cared to go into any public place to be recognised and stared at.

At first a few of their friends and acquaintances called or telephoned when they had returned to the Abbey. After all, since apparently Justin did not intend to divorce her, eventually life would have to be taken up again there, and few people could afford to ignore or be ignored by the Hollmeres. They denied themselves to everyone, however, so that gradually calls and callers ceased and they were left to themselves. Their only visitor now was Ella Joliman, who walked along the private path between her house and the Abbey most days and who was very popular in the nursery. Lady Hollmere never came and on the only occasion when Philippa and she met face to face in the village the older woman looked at her icily and looked away again.

Philippa flushed and kept her head high. She knew that the tale of it would fly round the village like wildfire, but she was past caring.

She did not know whether or not she would have been allowed to see Fergus, but she made no attempt to do so. She was deeply sorry for him and angry that he should be placed in a position which she felt to be utterly unjustifiable, but something seemed to have died within her. It seemed that she had spoken the truth when she had told Justin that she had finished with men, that there was nothing left in her of all the emotion and the passions and desires which had brought them to this pass. All she asked now was to be able to cut herself adrift from all that now constituted her life and to try to make a fresh one, how or where or what sort of life she did not yet know. She had nerved herself to let Trevor go, resolved that this was the best thing she could do for him. Without her, he would become altogether a Hollmere, brought up and schooled and trained in their traditions, but with her always in his life he would never be able to escape the cloud which would hang over him until, in time, he would learn the truth about her and despise and hate her for blotting the fair page of his young life.

She said no more to Justin about leaving him, but withdrew into herself with the least possible contact with him, attending to such duties in the household as she had from the first undertaken but taking no active interest in anything outside them.

And then Jeffrey Templar came down to them with news which completely altered the circumstances.

Philippa had gone to bed with a headache. She had not been well for some days, Justin told him anxiously, but she refused to see a doctor and said it was only a passing ailment.

'She's been under a terrible strain, of course,' said Justin. 'I shall be thankful when it is all over, whichever way it goes. What'll you have, Templar? Whisky? Gin? Rum? Beer?'

'The house of plenty,' said the solicitor. 'Whisky, whilst I've got the chance, I think,' and when he was settled with his drink, he gave his news.

'Perhaps it's as well I can give it to you alone first. I don't know how you'll feel about it, or how Philippa will feel, but Wynton is going to get off, and pretty soon.'

'But the trial? It isn't to be for some months yet, or so I understood.'

'Some new facts have come to light, and actually, though I must ask you to respect this as a confidence until you see it in the newspapers, they have found the man who killed Susan Therne.'

'So it wasn't Wynton?'

'Quite definitely not. The poor chap, a man named Frederik Hovener, gassed himself last night and has left a full confession. The police were on his track and would have got him. They traced some of the notes to him, the ones Wynton left in Susan Therne's room, and also a diamond ring of a somewhat unusual design which has been identified as hers and which some people she was out with that afternoon testified that she was wearing. She had been blackmailing the poor devil and driven him nearly out of his wits. He'd seen her in the afternoon and had followed her, not he said with any special purpose but because he was making up his mind to talk to her and try to get her to set him free. It seems she had some letters of his which he did not want his wife to see letters to him from a doctor who had been treating him for syphilis before he married her. He hung about near the hotel until midnight and then slipped in and up the stairs without the night porter seeing him.'

Justin nodded.

'That was what Larney said Sir Harvey would try to press,' he said. 'And this man killed her?'

'Yes. She refused to give him or to let him buy the letters, and in a sudden rage of frustration he took her by the throat and finally strangled her in the way we know. The poor devil went mad for the moment, as I imagine any of us might have done in the circumstances, and she had a cruel tongue. He didn't realise he had killed her at first. He thought he had only done enough to keep her quiet. He searched her handbag for his letters and found them. He also found the fifty pounds Wynton had given her, and the diamond ring, and he took the lot as part retribution for what he had suffered at her hands and what he had then accepted as inevitable. It must have been a shock to him to read in the newspapers that she was dead. By the way, he left by the fire-escape.'

'Why were there none of his finger-prints?' asked Justin.

'That's another part of the story. He wasn't an altogether desirable character, though until Susan Therne got hold of him he was trying to run straight. He had done two or three prison stretches for burglary, and he had actually made up his mind that the only way he could get money for Susan Therne without letting his wife know was to steal it. Seeing her go into the Medway Hotel, which is not a flashy hotel but one where people of substance often stay when they want to be quiet, the thought struck him that he might do a job there if he did not have any luck with Susan Therne, and he went in equipped and wearing gloves. After he had lost his temper so thoroughly as to attack her, he knew he could not hope for mercy from her, so he did not stop to break into any of the rooms. He took the fifty pounds and the ring and cleared out by way of the fire-escape and went home. It was only the slip-up with the notes that betrayed him, though he says in his last letter that he could not, in any case, have let another man swing for him. Well, we shall never know whether that would have been so or not. The police were well on his track. He had been foolish enough to pawn the ring, of which nothing had been said in the papers though a description of it had been given by Dr. Millet, who had given it to her and noticed it was not amongst the things found on her or in her room though it was one she always wore in addition to the engagement ring which was still on her finger. When the friends of the afternoon were found and gave the information that she had been wearing it then, all the likely jewellers and pawnbrokers were circularised and it duly turned up. Almost at the same time, Mrs. Hovener had come upon the fifty pounds, had thought her husband was pulling a fast one on her by having this private hoard, and had thought to pay him back by spending some of it on a new carpet she wanted. So I think they would have got him in any case, and the way he chose has certainly proved the best way for Fergus Wynton.'

'Have they released him?' asked Justin, neither his face nor his manner betraying what he felt about this turn of events.

'No, though of course that is only a matter of routine now. As he was committed for trial by the magistrate's court, the case will have to be heard, but Sir Harvey is certain to apply at once for bail, if he has not already done so, and will press for an immediate hearing. It will be purely formal, the prosecution offering no evidence, and the case will be dismissed.'

'I see,' said Justin thoughtfully. 'And then what, I wonder?'

Jeffrey Templar did not answer. There was nothing he could say and the question had been merely rhetorical with no reply expected.

'Will you tell Philippa, or shall I?' he asked, after a long pause.

'I will,' said Justin. 'My grateful thanks to you, Jeffrey. You've been a great help and comfort to us both.'

The solicitor rose.

'And will be again any time you or she wants me,' he said.

'I may as well tell you, in case you are wondering just when that time will be, that I have no intention of trying to divorce Philippa. I know, of course, that I couldn't, as things are at present, but in any case I should not want to do so.'

'What if she wants it, Justin? Wynton will be free, you know, and without a stain on his character other than the affair with her, which isn't exactly a criminal one.'

'She doesn't want it.'

'Good. I think that is sensible of her, and of you, if I may say so. Half the divorces in this country, or any other for the matter of that, need not take place if only people would see things in their right proportions and not set off one bit of foolishness against years of companionship and affection. To my way of thinking, the only real justification for divorce is if the two are hopelessly incompatible and simply cannot get on together however much they try. That isn't so with you and Philippa— – but go easy with her for a bit, Justin.'

'I am very much in love with my wife,' said Justin stiffly, and his friend and solicitor nodded amicably and took his leave.

But Philippa, though intensely relieved at the turn of events, steadfastly refused to alter her decision.

'I'm going to do what I said I would, Justin. I'm going away,' she said, her voice expressionless, all her emotions spent. 'Mother is coming with me. We are going to Wales, to a place of which we both have memories of many years ago when—we were all happy. I may buy a little house there. I don't know. At the moment we haven't got any further than that.'

'Very well. If that is what you're determined to do, I won't try to stop you. It might even be a good thing. It will give you an opportunity of getting back to normal after all this stress. Only one thing, Philippa. You're not going with Wynton?'

She gave an impatient sigh.

'No. I thought you understood. I don't want either of you, or any man, ever again. As you say, it will be an opportunity to get back to normal, but I don't know what normal is yet. All I do know is that it will contain no man in the world. To put it crudely, I've had men in a big way and I've had enough.'

She went without goodbyes, slipping quietly out of the house one morning before even Trevor was awake, steeling herself not to go to him, not even to listen at the foot of the nursery stairs for his morning song which would have torn at her heart and possibly shaken her determination.

She had left her own car, with her luggage in it, at The Beeches the night before, and she walked for the last time through the field path to find her mother ready and waiting.

'I've packed a picnic lunch and put it in the car in case we feel peckish but don't want to stop for a proper meal,' said Mrs. Joliman, 'but you'd better have some coffee and a bit of toast before we start. I don't suppose you've had anything, have you?'

'No. Nobody was up.'

Her mother grunted disapprovingly.

'Don't know what servants are coming to nowadays,' she said. 'Why, when I was girl it would have been more than me place was worth not to be down by six – and we never got to bed till past eleven neither, and one half-day a month and Sunday evenings if we spent them going to church. And we thought ourselves well off with five bob a week, all found, too.'

Philippa managed a smile. She knew that these reminiscences, which she had heard so many times before, were being told to fill in the gap through which they had to pass, the gap between the life that was ending and the one now beginning for both of them.

'Everything has to change, Mum,' she said with that dreary little smile. 'The only thing that it seems has to go on is life, just the elementals.'

'Dunno about elements,' grumbled her mother. 'Sounds like the stuff I used to rub your father's back with when he got the lumbago. Anyway, it's coffee I'm thinking about now, and you must eat something.'

Philippa drank the hot coffee thirstily but she could not eat anything, and when they had finished she carried the used dishes out to the kitchen and left them beside the sink. Since her husband's death, Ella Joliman had gone back to as near an approach as she could to the hard, simple life of their early married years. She had gradually got rid of the servants Joe had made her keep, shutting up many of the rooms, and had done the work herself with the help of a village girl who came in for an hour or two every morning. Vera would not be arriving for some time, and she had a key to the back door. Mrs. Joliman had told her she was going away, would be leaving early the next morning, and did not know when she would be back, and she had paid Vera and told her she need not come after today until she heard.

Ella had also written to her one friend, Mrs. Tagger, to ask her to keep an eye on the house after she had left. Mrs. Tagger would not get the letter until this morning's post, so that there would be no farewells or expostulations.

At the last minute, standing at the door of the car, Ella Joliman looked back at her home, with its memories and its love and its happiness and its abiding sorrow, and Philippa caught the look in her eyes.

She touched her mother's hand.

'Sorry, Mum,' she said in a low voice. 'I seem fated to make a mess of the lives of everybody I care for most. I ought not to have dragged you into this.'

But the moment was over and Ella got into the car.

'Don't talk rubbish. Where would I be if not with my only child when she's in trouble, I'd like to know? Let's start, my dear, though I wish you'd had a bite to eat. It's a cold morning and you'll feel faint on the way with nothing inside you.'

Philippa started the car.

'I'll be alright. I've been feeling a bit squeamish the last few days, not that I wonder at it, but I shall pick up again now that I've taken a definite step.'

But when they had gone a few miles from Sloworth, working towards the Great West Road that would take them most of the way to their destination, she pulled up outside a chemist's shop. A boy was taking down the shutters and he told her that yes, the shop was open and the chemist was inside.

'I'm going to get something for this sick feeling I've still got,' she said and went inside.

The chemist gave her bicarbonate of soda in a tumbler, and she took the rest of the packet with her.

Bicarbonate of soda for a breaking heart! she thought derisively, getting back into the car, but as the morning wore on, she certainly felt better, tired and unhappy but physically better.

She had decided that it was too long a drive for her mother to do in one day, so they stayed the night at a country hotel and the next morning, when she got out of bed to take the tray of tea from the maid, she set it down quickly and sat down again, her head bent.

Mrs. Joliman looked up sharply from the other bed.

'What's the matter?' she asked.

'I feel so sick again,' said Philippa.

'Do you know what I think's the matter with you?' asked her mother slowly.

'Oh, I'm just over-tired—gone to bits,' said Philippa, a long shudder passing through her. 'I'll be alright soon.'

'Yes. In a few months. Aren't you going to have a baby, Phil?'

Philippa looked up with a start and a stare of incredulity. Then, as it slowly dawned on her, she said in a startled whisper: 'Yes. Yes, I believe I am. Oh, Mum!' and she threw herself face downwards on the bed and wept long, bitter tears. This was all she needed! Just this.

Her mother comforted her, holding her as if she were a child again, saying nothing until the storm of tears had subsided. Then she spoke in her quiet, sensible way.

'The best thing to do now is to get back into bed,' she said, 'and we'll have a doctor in and make sure. Then, if he says it's that, I'll speak to Justin on the telephone ...'

'No,' said Philippa sharply. 'No, Mum. That's over and I'm not starting it again, ever.'

'Phil, it's his right to know. It's the right of the baby too. You can't just take it away like this and rob it of its father before it's even born.'

Philippa gave her a strange look.

'How do you know—who is its father?' she asked, and her mother flinched and took her arms away and stood up, looking down at her with grieved eyes.

'That's dreadful,' she said.

'I know. Everything about me has been dreadful for so long that one more thing doesn't make much difference to me,' said Philippa wearily. 'But, Mum, I'm not going to hold you to it. If you want to go ...'

'Hush, child. Where would I want to be but with you now you're in even more trouble than we knew?'

'Oh, Mum, what am I to have all the things nobody deserved less? You—and Justin ...'

If Mrs. Joliman was thinking that she did not include Fergus Wynton, she did not say so but busied herself pouring out the tea, bringing a cup to Philippa, persuading her to drink it and to eat the biscuits in spite of recurring attacks of nausea which she assured her daughter would pass.

'I know you weren't sick with Trevor,' she said, 'but the second one is often different. I was that sick with you that I felt my very heart would come up, but it generally goes after the first month or two, and it doesn't last longer than just first thing in the morning. Dress as soon as you feel like it and then try to get some breakfast inside you, and when you're over this we'll get on our way so as to get to Llantydd before dark. Do you think you'll remember the way once we leave the main roads? It was a long time ago.'

'Yes, I think I shall remember, but if it's getting late, we'd better find somewhere to stay the night. We'll go through Cardigan in case. It won't be much out of our way and we shall find hotels there.'

But once the sickness had passed and her mind had accepted the alarming fact of her pregnancy, Philippa made good headway and decided to push straight on and trust to her memory when she had to take the small by-roads leading to the Welsh coast and to the tiny fishing village of Llantydd so poignantly remembered from her childhood. It had represented heaven to her then; now she hoped it would prove a haven.

There was grateful comfort in the discovery that nothing seemed to have changed, that they could recognise the small landmarks which had been there, just as they were now, fifteen years ago. This quiet, remote countryside, much of it incapable of cultivation and too rough for the making of main roads without disproportionate expense, had not changed as her own southern England had changed and expanded, and when they had climbed the last hill, she stopped the car at the top to look down. A little cry of joy mingled with the sadness of the years between at sight of Llantydd, still the same straggle of stone cottages, the tiny quay, the small fishing-boats, their sails furled, rocking gently on the almost motionless sea in the setting sun.

'Oh, Mum, it's just the same,' said Philippa, and when her mother did not reply, she looked at her to see the slow, heavy tears running down her cheeks.

'Perhaps we ought not to have come,' said Philippa, slipping her hand into her mother's. 'It's going to be too sad for you,' but Ella shook her head, smiled and wiped the tears away.

'Nonsense. I wanted to come. I'm just having a moment's foolishness. Joe loved this place. I think perhaps I may feel he's here with us. Perhaps he is,' with a sigh which Philippa knew was for the hopes, so high, so undefeatable but so far so entirely unfulfilled, of getting into touch with her beloved dead through the spiritualistic mediums which she so assiduously consulted. Philippa, with her very recent past, had no desire to hear, were it possible to do so, what her father might have to say to her and about her.

They had decided to stop at the village stores, which was also the post-office and almost everything else, to ask to be directed to probable rooms to let, but as everything seemed so unchanged, Philippa suggested that they go first to the cottage where they used to stay. But when they found it, a rough-walled, sturdy little house facing the sea, they were disappointed to see it shuttered and obviously empty, the garden overgrown, the gate swinging on one hinge, even the white scut of a rabbit whisking over the garden at the back, which had become a field again.

'Oh well, I suppose it was too much to expect,' said Philippa. 'Let's go back to the shop and ask.'

The girl who was looking after the shop was a stranger to them, but then she must have been a baby in a pram, or perhaps not even born, fifteen years ago. She found it difficult to understand what they wanted, and at last called to her mother, explaining to her in her native, lilting Welsh her difficulty, and the woman came in, drying her hands.

'Mrs. Owen! Do you remember me?' asked Mrs. Joliman, and after another and closer look, the two women almost embraced.

'It's Mrs. Joliman. Well, well! Indeed to goodness!' and they laughed again, though tears were not far from Mrs. Joliman again, for the last phrase was one which Joe had so often used, teasingly, to this same Mrs. Owen, pretending that by using it he was able to speak Welsh. Mrs. Owen had remembered.

They told her what they wanted, comfortable, clean rooms for a few weeks, or whilst they looked round for a place of their own, and mentioned that Bryn Cottage where they had hoped to stay, seemed deserted.

'Oh yes. Mrs. Lloyd, poor soul, didn't have the heart to stop on after the night of that terrible storm when her man and her boy Lewis were drowned. You remember Lewis? She went away—oh, might be four years ago now. If you want somewhere, go along to Morgan the milk's and say I sent you. Mrs. Morgan is a nice body and now her

Daisy's gone off to London in a fine situation, she'll have an empty room. Come and see me tomorrow, mind.'

They promised, found the house of Morgan the milk, and Mrs. Morgan welcomed them gladly. She could give them her best bedroom and the parlour for as long as they liked to stay.

The youngest Morgan, a boy of about eleven, carried in their luggage and showed them where they could put the car under cover, in an old shed no longer used to house the cows, and by the time Philippa had put it away, she found her mother already unpacking.

In a day or two it was almost as if they had lived there for years, so easy it was to pick up the threads, though most of the people they remembered seemed to have grown so much older than they themselves felt. That feeling was more acute with Philippa because of her youth than with the older woman or perhaps it was that after the excitement of the first few days, her own problems crowded back into her mind to set her apart from these hard-living Welsh folk whose difficulties seemed so much more simple, the chief amongst them being the primitive struggle to keep alive and sheltered, fed and clothed, and always fearing the sea which they lived.

Beyond once more asking her whether she did not feel she ought at least to tell Justin of the expected child, Philippa's mother made no attempt to interfere with her chosen way.

'Mother dear,' said Philippa, 'I feel I am doing the only possible thing. I could not subject him and Trevor to the beastliness of having to live me down. You know how it would have been if I had stayed and brazened it out. It would have been quite impossible for Trevor not someday to learn the facts about me, and I would rather he grew up without me so that, when he finds out, it won't matter so much. And if I told Justin about the baby, he would find some way of forcing me to go back to him. You know something though not all about the Hollmere family pride, and it would gall him unspeakably to know that somewhere there was a Hollmere child living outside the family. And—he would never be quite sure. I don't know how he would get me back, but he would. He's weak in many ways, which is perhaps why I did what I did and went off the rails with Fergus, but when he does make up his mind, nothing shifts him until he has got his own way. He'd get me back and look at my position then. People would say that he took me back only because of the child—and they wouldn't know either whether I went back to him because the child was his, or to give Fergus's child the Hollmere name. Please, Mum, leave it like this,' and Mrs. Joliman had done so.

She was finding Philippa greatly changed and knew that the girl was haunted by the thought of the havoc she had made of other lives beside her own, though they did not again speak of it, and Fergus Wynton's name never crossed their lips.

Philippa felt as if inside her was a pit filled with unspeakable desolation and decay, shaming her, offending her high pride in herself and respect for her own integrity. She tried to keep herself from resenting the child within her, the innocent victim of her love for Fergus, for although in her own mind she was satisfied that the child was Justin's, in different circumstances there would have been no question of her having left him and condemned the child to the sort of life she by herself would make for it.

But the very fact that other people, her mother, Justin, Fergus, and all the vultures who had gathered about her to enjoy her downfall and dissolution, would never be sure which man had fathered this child, that very fact made her feel unspeakably degraded. That she, Philippa, Countess of Hollmere, should have descended to that! She loathed herself but could never draw away from herself as she would have done from a woman of the streets.

Outwardly, though she was quiet and seemed to have forgotten how to laugh, she lived the life of apparent serenity which she had come to this remote Welsh village to find. After staying a week or two with Mrs. Morgan, they discussed the possibility of trying to buy, or to rent, Bryn Cottage, and they were able to trace Mrs. Lloyd who was easily persuaded to sell.

It was even more dilapidated inside than out but the repair and modernising of the little house, in so far as the available public services would allow, kept Philippa occupied and raised her spirits considerably.

Not without a good deal of difficulty, she had been able to persuade Justin to respect her wishes in the matter of her name, since she had no intention of hiding herself from him but had told him where she was going. She was, therefore, known as Mrs. Breane and in that name she bought the house and there in due course came her first letter from her husband, a calm, unemotional letter which began *My dear Philippa* and ended *Your affectionate husband, Justin.* He gave her the small items of news from the Abbey and from Sloworth, describing the effect of some of the redecorating which had been put in hand and to her choice before all the trouble began. He spoke of it as if it would not be long before she saw it for herself.

You will be pleased, I think, that you chose the blue instead of the green in the Long Drawing-room, he said, and in another place: The new housemaid, Annie, wants to get married, but I am hoping she will wait a bit. I should not be much good at engaging a new one.

Philippa folded the letter and put it away, giving her mother the various items of local news in which she would be interested but saying nothing about his obvious belief that their separation was only a passing phase. She wrote to him to tell him of the new house, making it as clear as she could that this was where she intended to live and evincing no interest whatsoever in the news he had detailed to her. She realised that she must leave it to time to convince him that she was not going back to him.

She tried not to think of Fergus and when something brought him suddenly and vividly to her mind, she thrust out the thought determinedly. He belonged to the part of her life which she wanted to forget and must forget if she were to make anything of this new life. She was kept busy by Mrs. Joliman's firm refusal to employ any resident domestic help.

'I like my kitchen to myself,' she said. 'Mrs. Morgan says she can spare her Gwen to come along once a week or so to do the floors but it'll be a real treat to me to get my hands on my own things again, specially if we decide to send for the china and stuff from The Beeches, and our own linen.'

So when they moved into Bryn Cottage, early in the new year, they found plenty to do, and though Mrs. Joliman would not let Philippa get down on the floor with brush and pan, or carry coal for the fires, or hang out their weekly wash, she learned how to do a great many things which all her life had been done for her, and found a certain satisfaction in doing them.

At first it seemed as if Mrs. Joliman had found a new lease of life in the pleasure she took in working in her own house again, but after a time Philippa found herself watching her mother rather anxiously, noticing that she sat down more often and for longer periods, went to bed earlier and was not so anxious to get up at crack of dawn, even though it meant that Philippa got up and raked the fire into a glow again and made their early tea.

Then on a day of early April, a day that was a gift of the gods, with clear, pale skies, warm sunshine and the lightest possible, flower-scented breeze. Philippa sat outside with her sewing whilst her mother went into the little market town five miles away, getting a lift there and back with the carrier since Philippa was now finding it uncomfortable to drive the car.

The child was due in two months' time and she was heavy and easily tired, though after the early sickness had passed she had felt as well as any healthy young creature should feel in pregnancy.

Bryn Cottage was surrounded on all four sides by its rambling, untidy garden, untidy in spite of the sporadic attentions of Evans the carrier, and the side which Philippa and her mother liked best was the one which faced the gap between the hills with only a side peep at the sea. It was sheltered and sunny, and today it was as nearly perfect as anything in nature could be. Bees hummed busily in and out of the tangle of spring flowers, and in a tree nearby two birds were discussing the housing problem which, for them, was so easily and satisfactorily solved without the need to fill in any forms, or ask anyone's permission or pay for any of the freely given materials.

Happy birds who know no better!

She heard a step on the concrete path that led to the back door.

'Is that you, Mr. Morgan?' she called. 'I've left a jug out for the milk.'

But it was not 'Morgan the milk' who came round the corner of the house and stood for a moment looking at her, waiting for her to see him, his heart in his eyes.

It was Fergus Wynton.

Chapter Fourteen

Philippa, subconsciously aware of being watched though she had not heard the footsteps come round to the side of the house, turned her head – and remained motionless, one hand on the arm of the cane chair, her needlework dropping from the other, her face turned towards him.

'Fergus,' she said in an almost inaudible whisper. 'Fergus !'

He came to her and knelt by the side of her chair and took her hands in his and looked deeply into her eyes.

'Am I welcome? Do you want me, my darling?' he asked, and at once the woman turned to stone became flesh and blood again, rosy flesh, swiftly flowing blood.

Instead of an answer in words, she took her hands from his and framed his face in them, looked long and sweetly at it and then put her mouth to his with an infinite, hungering tenderness.

'Always. Always,' she said, and knew that in all these months she had been deceiving herself – or no, only pretending that she was deceived. She had been waiting for him, she knew now, had known that he would come, though she had never wondered how he would find her.

Another step sounded on the path.

'That really is Morgan,' she said. 'I must see if he has any eggs now you're here,' and she rose from her chair, steadying herself for a moment with her hand on his arm, and then went across the grass and to the back of the house.

He watched her slow step, her ungainly figure, and as realisation came to him, his face flushed with the wonder and the delight of it. And he had so nearly not come! Had so nearly allowed himself to be persuaded that she did not want to see him, that she had said definitely that she wanted to be left alone.

He was standing by the chair when she came back, and she saw at once that he was aware of her condition. For the moment, in the sudden delight of his appearance, she had forgotten. She stood still, her breath coming quickly, one hand at her throat, wondering what to say, what he would say.

He came to her swiftly then and gathered her into his arms and held her with such tender care for her that she gave a shaky laugh.

'I'm not all that breakable,' she said.

'Philippa – didn't you mean to tell me? Would you have let anything so wonderful happen without my knowing anything about it? Did you really mean to keep it to yourself and not give me any share in it? Oh, Philippa, my beloved, my dear love, my—wife,' and he kissed her as if to shake the thirst of all these weary, empty, desperate months of their parting.

Philippa's mind reeled. How could she tell him? What could she say? Whatever must be said, she could not say it now, in this first poignant hour of being together again. Later. There would be time later. He would never understand. He had never been married. He would not be able to reconstruct that scene even if she tried to show it to him, to make him see Justin's kindness, his care of her though she had so greatly injured him; the unexciting normality of their being in her bedroom, Justin sitting on the side of the bed talking to her, trying to comfort her as if she, and not he, were the injured one; the sleeping pills which were so strong that they made her drowsy and in a dream-like state so quickly; the confused idea she had had that it was Fergus with her.

No, he would not understand. He would merely accept the fact that she had turned in her hour of anguish to the one who had every right to comfort her, every right to be there with her, in her room, in her bed, every right to be the father of her child.

She could not tell him, not now, not just yet. She must have today, this one day. After that she would tell him – and he would go away – and after that nothing else.

'How soon, darling?' he asked when he had released her and with the same exaggerated care led her back to her chair and settled her in it and himself at her feet.

'Not long now. June,' she said.

He chuckled.

'I still can't think how it happened, but it's very obvious it did. Oh, darling, supposing ...'

She leaned forward and put her fingers over his lips. 'Not that. Never speak of it my dearest. We suffered too much.'

'I know. All right. Shall we agree never to speak of it?'

She nodded and they gave her a moment's silence to that memory before they put it away from their lips even if it could never be erased from their minds.

'Fergus, how on earth did you find me?' she asked then.

'Justin told me.'

She stared at him.

'*Justin* told you? But—how—why—Fergus, you're not just being funny?'

'I assure you it was not a bit funny, but as I didn't know how else to get hold of you, I had to ask him.'

'And he told you? Just like that?'

'Just like that. I went down there to see you, not knowing you had gone. I had tried to telephone you but I always got put off by tales about your being out, or resting, or something, so I went down.'

'To the Abbey?'

'Yes. It made me feel—very queer to see where you lived, Philippa, though I'd been obliged to get over the horrible discovery of who you really were. That shook me, I can tell you! I met Justin outside. Somehow I knew who he was, though he didn't look a bit what I would have imagined a lord to look like.'

She nodded.

'I know. Old tweed coat and leggings and hat like a limpet,' she said.

'I walked up to him and couldn't think how to begin when I'd got there, so I just said "I'm Fergus Wynton," and he said "Yes, I know who you are," and then I remembered that of course he had seen me in that beastly court-room, though I was in such a state that I didn't see anybody but the old magistrate – and you, of course, my dearest dear.'

'We agreed not to talk of that,' she said.

'Alright. Sorry. Well, I thought he would have gone all haughty and asked me what I wanted before he summoned his grooms or whatever they are to throw me to the lions, or into the pond or the dungeons. He didn't. All he said was "You'd better come in," and so in we went. He even offered me a drink, but though I wanted it desperately, I couldn't have taken it from him. He waited, so I just asked him straight out where you were.'

'And he told you?' she asked, feeling that she had fallen flat on her face.

'Well, not just like that. We argued a bit, with gathering heat on my part because I am not an aristocrat trained for the stake, but with perfect and unmoving calm on his.'

She nodded. She could visualise it so well.

'Then,' went on Fergus, 'when I told him that in spite of him, whatever he did or didn't do, I should never stop looking until I found you, and that when I did find you I should give you your free and unhampered choice between him and myself, he got my point, saw that I was presuming to rate my sense of fairness to you higher than his, and told me where to find you.'

'Yes, that would get under his guard,' murmured Philippa.

'He added something I ought to tell you, though. He added that in no circumstances at all would he ever divorce you.'

They were silent for a little while.

'Did you realise that?' he asked then.

'He told me so, yes.'

'And you don't think—this—would make any difference?' with a meaning glance at her figure.

'I don't know,' she said slowly and painfully.

Fergus seemed to be accepting it as he had always accepted her, as if she could dissociate herself at will from everything in her life which did not include him, Fergus. How could she ever convey to him any idea of that bond which still held her to Justin? Not the merely legal bond, but the bond of their shared life, the home they had made together, all the little things which had made up the quiet, unexciting happiness which has nothing to do with sex and passion?

She loved Fergus with her whole heart and was completed by him, and yet part of her would always be with Justin.

'Well, if he didn't set you free to marry me, he'd be a skunk, and I don't think he is a skunk. He's stiff and formal and very much his lordship, but underneath all that, I think he's a decent sort. In fact, for the first time, darling, I've begun to realise why you felt you couldn't leave him, and now I've got to ask, for both our sakes — have you the smallest feeling left for him, Philippa?'

She hesitated, torn between her loyalties and her love.

'That's too difficult,' she said at last. 'He's my husband, Fergus. We've been in the closest possible relationship, but if you mean do I love him — no. No, I don't, Fergus.'

He had watched the changing, anxious thoughtfulness of her face, so tell-tale always, so revealing to eyes that loved her, and he knew with a sinking of his heart that, whilst she spoke the truth when she said she did not love her husband, there would always be something in her memory which he, Fergus, could not claim or touch. The mysterious, unique linking of mind and body which is marriage can never be entirely severed. What if for Philippa, always, Justin would hold a place in her heart?

He had to accept it.

'And you don't hanker after being a grand lady anymore?' he asked her with a smile.

She was glad of the lessened tension and smiled back.

'No. It was fun in a way being My Lady, but it palled on me. I don't belong to that world.'

'Good. Then you raise no objection to my going back to him and telling him what your choice is and asking him to divorce you so that we can marry? Darling honey, I want you so desperately for my wife, especially now that you're like this.'

She drew her brows together, hesitating.

'I think it would be better for me to ask him that,' she said.

'You can't go to him,' said Fergus quickly, so quickly that she had to smile.

'Like this? Almost the old picture of returning through the snow with a bundle in a shawl to the ancestral home? No, my dear, I wasn't going to suggest that. I'll write.'

'You'll tell him about the baby?' he asked urgently.

'That's the focal point,' she said non-committally.

Mrs. Joliman came back, getting down stiffly from the carrier's van with her basket and parcels, to find them still out there though it was getting cold.

Fergus hastened to her to take her heavy basket.

'Mrs. Joliman, I'm ...'

'Alright. I know who you are, Fergus Wynton,' she said grimly. 'I don't know how long you've bin here but you should know better than leave her out to get cold. Go in, Philippa – and put a coat or something on, but stay indoors.'

Fergus liked the valiant old woman, for old woman she seemed to be, for all her lack of an old woman's years. The first sight of her had shocked him. He remembered dimly that he had seen her in the court-room beside Philippa, but he had not thought her so lined and drawn nor having so little vigour. She almost tottered as she went up the path, even though he had taken all her parcels from her and she had nothing to carry but her handbag.

Philippa had the kettle boiling on the trivet by the small fire which they kept burning, but it was Fergus who insisted on getting the tea whilst the two women sat in their chairs and told him where to find everything. It was an odd situation, he thought, one which he had never anticipated, the frail old woman who seemed to him to be on the verge of an illness, and Philippa rendered almost stationary by the burden of her coming maternity. It gave him a feeling of responsibility, of belonging, which he had never known before, and when after the meal Mrs. Joliman went upstairs to take off the hat and coat she had so far not removed, he spoke of it to Philippa.

'Darling, I've got to do something about you. I'm not going back, not tonight anyway. I've come out of the R.A.F., as of course you've seen, and I haven't made any plans yet. I was waiting until I had found you. I don't know what the chances are of getting anything to do in Wales, though they're building all sorts of new factories and must be always wanting people. For the moment, though, I must stay near you, and as soon as possible we'll get married. How long do these things take nowadays? I'm told they've speeded up the ridiculous interval between the two parts of the divorce, but even so I doubt if we can get married before June.'

'I'm sure we can't,' she said. 'I shall be alright, though.'

'But you'd rather I was somewhere near you, wouldn't you?'

'Of course I would, but—Fergus dear, you mustn't make your life revolve round me or in any way dependent on where I am. To be honest with you, I don't think Justin will ever divorce me. When he makes up his mind, nothing changes it, and when I left him he was very definite. He said he never would.'

Fergus frowned unhappily.

'So then—what do we do?' he asked. 'I'm not going to let you go again, ever. I can be as stubborn as my lord high Hollmere, you know. By the way, do the people round about here know who you are?'

'No. I'm known as Mrs. Breane, and I suppose they regard me as a widow − or those who are charitably minded do. The rest probably regard me as a woman who's slipped up and who has come here to hide her guilt.'

'I hate you being in such a position. Philippa …'

'Yes?'

'Darling, even if he won't divorce you, you won't drive me away, will you? Especially not now?'

She drew a deep breath.

'Don't ask me to make any more plans yet, Fergus. At the moment I can't see beyond June and I don't want to.'

'But you will write to Justin?'

'Yes. Soon.'

He took his leave, and as Mrs. Joliman had not come downstairs again he left a message for her. He had found a room, he said, for the night, in one of the cottages, and he would look in in the morning.

Philippa knew that his appearance in the village, directly and obviously connected with her, must cause comment and conjecture and told him so the next day.

'Fergus, please go away,' she said. 'Can't you see what it must look like to the people here? Me obviously pregnant and with so far no man to account for it? Then you appear?'

'Then let me stay actually with you, darling – the husband returned from the wars, or darkest Africa or Siberia or somewhere.'

'No, Fergus,' she said in a low voice.

'No way at all in which I could stay without hurting you?' She shook her head.

'It isn't just because of the people here. It's my mother. She has stood by me in circumstances which are absolutely anathema to her, my running away from Justin, giving up all that she's been so proud for me to have, and then finding out that I'm going to have a baby – and now you turning up again. She has buoyed herself up all the time with the belief, whether she really does believe it or not, that this is Justin's child. If you came to live here – well, what could she think?'

'You've got yourself to consider, your life, mine too. She's had hers and her happiness with the one man she loved and married. Dearest, isn't it the turn of the next generation?' he urged her, but she would not be persuaded and later on that day he left Llantydd, but would not go further than Cardigan in case she needed him.

'I shall have to get a job,' he said, 'but there should be some there and I could get to you in a very short time.'

He told her how she could contact him there.

'You're quite sure you've made all the necessary arrangements about yourself?' he asked again anxiously.

'Absolutely. I shall go into the nursing home in plenty of time so as not to be jolting over these roads at the last minute.'

She had arranged to go into Cardigan to have the baby.

He left her with obvious reluctance, and after he had gone life had become empty again.

Mrs. Joliman grumbled a little.

'Why did he have to come and upset you when you were getting on alright without him?' she asked. 'I hope you told him to keep himself to himself now, and I wish to goodness you'd let me write to his lordship,' always preferring to refer to her son-in-law in the way she would have done had Philippa not brought him into the family.

'Please don't do any such thing, Mum dear,' said Philippa with that quiet air of authority which she had acquired during her marriage and which always reduced her mother to acquiescence.

She wrote to Fergus and begged him not to come.

I really mean it when I ask to be left alone, she told him. I feel I have been battered about so much by my emotions over the past eighteen months or so that I can't be bothered with any man at all about me, not even you, Fergus dear, and for a week he stayed away.

Then one evening, when Philippa was sitting in her favourite part of the garden waiting for her mother, who had gone in to fetch some needlework, it began to dawn on her that Mrs. Joliman had been gone a long time, and she called to her.

'What on earth are you doing? For heaven's sake, no more dusting and polishing for today!' for in spite of Philippa's protests, her mother spent hours every day keeping the little house as bright and shining as a new pin.

When there was no answer, she rose reluctantly, having reached the stage when every movement was an effort, and went into the house.

She found her mother crumpled up and unconscious on the floor of the kitchen, breathing in noisy gasps. With a tremendous effort, she turned her over and saw that her face was drawn into a hideous, convulsive grin, the eyes rolled up and sightless and the mouth open.

Philippa pulled herself upright again and hung on to the table whilst she controlled her own difficult breathing and shaking limbs. Then she went to the door and looked frantically down the road, little more than a path, to the village. They had not yet succeeded in getting a telephone, though it had been promised, and they were cut off from other houses by their large garden and the stretch of cliff between it and the next house.

There was no one in sight, and she stumbled along the path taking such care as she could, in her distress, not to fall, and was in an almost fainting condition by the time she reached the gate of the nearest cottage, where mercifully she could see old Mrs. Williams at the window.

The old lady did not understand any English, but she called to her young granddaughter, realising that 'Mrs. Breane' was in distress, and Bessie came running out.

'Can you use the telephone, Bessie?' asked Philippa, gasping and white-faced.

The child nodded, wide-eyed.

'Then please telephone to these numbers. At the first, ask Dr. Morrison to come at once, and at the second leave a message to ask Mr. Wynton to come. Here is some money and hurry—hurry, please, won't you?'

The child, scared but pleased to be of such importance to 'the English lady', went running off, the money held tightly in her hand, and Philippa dragged herself back to Bryn Cottage to find the condition of her mother unchanged. All she could do for her was to wedge a thin pillow beneath her head and cover her with a blanket. It was a warm evening and the kitchen fire was alight, but Mrs. Joliman was lying on the stone floor.

When the doctor came, he was surprised to find that his patient was the mother and not the daughter, and he glanced at Philippa sharply.

'You haven't been lifting her, or trying to, have you?' he asked.

'Only to try to keep her warm,' said Philippa.

'Do you feel alright yourself?'

'Oh yes—yes. Please see to my mother,' she said impatiently, and in spite of the doctor's fears for her, she had to give him some help in lifting Mrs. Joliman from the floor and carrying her to the couch in the living-room.

'There is nothing very much to be done but keep her warm,' he said, when they had made her as comfortable as possible. 'I've got something I can give her if we can get her to swallow it, and I must leave her as I'm on my way to another urgent case. Little Bessie Williams caught me just as I was leaving. I'll come back later unless it's very late, and I'll try to send a woman from the village.'

'Come however late it is, Dr. Morrison,' said Philippa. 'I couldn't possibly go to bed and leave her.'

'You've got to look after yourself, you know,' he said with a frown. 'Sure you're alright? No pains or discomfort?'

'I'm alright. I've still got six weeks to go, you know.'

'Well, be careful. No lifting or straining. I'll get someone to come to you,' but either he forgot to send someone or the woman decided not to come (they looked askance at her now because of her husbandless condition); no one came near her until, in the early hours of the morning, the door opened to admit Fergus.

Philippa rose from her chair and threw herself into his arms.

'Oh, Fergus, thank God you've come! I'm getting so frightened,' and when they had stood looking down at Mrs. Joliman, whose condition seemed not to have altered, Philippa suddenly let his hand go and dropped into a chair. The relief of having him here was almost too much for her.

'Seems to me you're the one that needs looking after,' he said. 'You sit there whilst I make up the fire, and finish trying to give the old lady that broth, and then I'm going to put you to bed and you're going to stay there.'

She was too tired to protest but left herself meekly in his hands and at length, comforted by the warmth and ease and the certainty that her mother would be well looked after, she fell into the deep sleep of exhaustion from which she did not wake until the afternoon sun was streaking in through her western window.

She sat up with a jerk and immediately lay down again, full understanding sweeping over her.

The sharp pain in her back was a labour pain. She could not mistake it and she lay there, worried and helpless. Of all times to have a premature baby!

She could hear Fergus moving about in the rooms below and presently he came as softly as was possible up the creaking old staircase and paused outside her door. She called his name, and he came in, his face grave and anxious.

Before she could speak, another pain shot through her and she writhed, her face in the pillow.

'Darling, what is it?' he asked in alarm. 'It isn't ...?'

She nodded.

'I'm afraid so,' she said when she could speak again. 'How's Mother?'

'About the same. The doctor came early this morning, but there was nothing he could do. We put her to bed in the other room, and managed to get her to swallow some brandy and something he brought. But what about you? I'd better get the ambulance or a car or something—and the doctor again.'

'I don't want to leave Mother,' said Philippa faintly.

'I'll look after her. What a curse this is without a telephone. Will you be alright whilst I go down to the post office—or get someone else to do it if I meet anyone who can speak English?'

She nodded, but felt terrified once his footsteps had died away, and got out of bed to drag herself across to the other bedroom where her mother lay, red-faced, unfamiliar, breathing stertorously but making no other movement. She stood there for some time looking at her and then, torn again and more fiercely by her pain, managed to get back to her room and fall across the bed.

When Trevor had been born, she had been surrounded by every sort of comfort and care and up-to-date knowledge so that after the very beginning of her labour she had been scarcely conscious of pain. Now she was to know all of it, for by the time Fergus returned she was in an advanced state of labour and there could, she knew, be no question of taking her all those rough miles in any sort of conveyance to Cardigan.

If he were frightened or nervous, he did not show it. There was nothing more he could do for Mrs. Joliman, so he devoted himself entirely to Philippa, who could tell him no more than she knew herself, and the mother is usually the last person to know what is going on at childbirth.

'I hope the doctor comes in time,' she said weakly in between the spasms of frightful pain.

'So do I, but if he doesn't, we shall manage,' he told her comfortingly. 'If animals and savages can cope with it, surely we can? And there's going to be something rather good about us bringing our child into the world entirely on your own. Will you be alright if I just have a look at your mother?'

'Yes—nurse,' whispered Philippa with the ghost of a smile.

'Atta girl,' he said.

Philippa lay there exhausted, bathed in sweat, feeling that she was being torn in two. Vaguely in her mind was the thought that this was Justin's child Fergus was helping her to deliver, but gradually she was beginning to accept her lover's claim to it – and anyway, what did it matter at this moment whose it was, since it was undoubtedly hers?

The child was still unborn when the doctor came, but he saw at once that there was no question of moving her.

Surely it will be any minute now?' asked Fergus anxiously.

The doctor had shown no surprise in finding a strange man there. In fact, he seemed to have accepted him without question as having a right to be there, since he said once: 'You can't look after them both. I don't know why Mrs. Evans didn't come, but I'll see that someone else comes to look after your mother-in-law. There's not much to do for her, poor soul.'

But Fergus repeated his insistent question.

'But Philippa? Is the baby likely to be long now?'

'Difficult to say. Five or six hours probably.'

Fergus was aghast.

'Five or six hours? Like this? But she won't be able to stand it!'

'Oh, it's wonderful what women can stand,' said the doctor, who was of the complacent school of men, even some medical men amongst them, who hold that as child-bearing is a natural function, no artificial relief is needed to help the mother to bear her pain. Such men should bear just one child. It would be enough.

'Can't you give her something? Or give me something for her?' urged Fergus as the doctor showed signs of leaving again.

'Not possible, I'm afraid,' he said. 'Only qualified persons are allowed to give chloroform. Besides, if you gave it, she would stop struggling to free the child from the womb, and you couldn't do anything to help and the child and probably the mother would die.'

'But you can't leave a woman to bear this!' cried Fergus, almost beside himself. 'You don't know who she is ...'

'My dear young man, even if she were the Queen, she would still have to bear her own children,' said the doctor comfortably. 'She will be quite alright. She is young and strong and this is a completely natural function. I'll look in in an hour or two's time.'

'And you'll send a woman along?'

'Yes, yes,' said the doctor, but again no one came near Bryn Cottage and he began to realise that what Philippa had said was right, and they were being ostracised by the devout, chapel-going community of the little village.

What she had not told him was that the previous week the middle-aged pastor of the chapel, a gaunt ascetic with wild eyes and a fiery Welsh tongue, had climbed the hill to visit, her and had warned her that unless she repented, she would assuredly be cast into the eternal fire. She had told him politely that she did not believe in his sort of God nor in the eternal fire, and had been so completely unmoved by his gesticulating eloquence that at last he had left her, warning her of all that would undoubtedly happen to her unless she repented in sackcloth and ashes before it was too late.

He had referred to her 'child of sin', which she thought somewhat indelicate since the child was still within her womb.

'How do you know it is a child of sin?' she asked him.

He had waved the question aside.

'Everybody in the village knows that it is, woman,' he told her and left her.

It seemed that they did, for no one came to help her in her extremity and Fergus moved between the two rooms and up and down stairs, tireless, efficient, cheerful, giving no sign of the anxiety that tormented him.

Eventually, however, spurred on either by Dr. Morrison or by the desire to be in that superior position which could satisfy the gossiping curiosity of the village, a Mrs. Cuddey arrived to help – a short, round, middle-aged woman with an air of bustling importance and a flow of almost unintelligible English.

Philippa was by this time too exhausted to care what happened to her and voices came to her only vaguely.

When Mrs. Cuddey stumped into the house without knocking at the door, Fergus was stirring over the fire some soup from a tin.

He looked up with infinite relief. Mrs. Joliman seemed no better and Philippa was, or so it appeared to him, desperately ill.

He explained the position to Mrs. Cuddey, who nodded (having understood very little, he realised later), took off her coat and put on a business-like apron which considerably cheered him.

'The soup is for both of them, I thought,' said Fergus, lifting the pot from the fire and pouring the contents into two cups on the table.

'I'll take this up to …' she began importantly, lifting one of them.

'You go to Mrs. Joliman and make her quite comfortable and then you can stay all the time with—my wife,' said Fergus, looking her straight in the eye.

'Oh. That will be Mrs. Breane?' asked Mrs. Cuddey.

'Mrs. Wynton,' said Fergus firmly.

'I came to look after Mrs. Breane, look,' she objected.

'Mrs. Wynton,' repeated Fergus firmly. 'Mrs. Joliman is her mother.'

A new, sharp sound came from Philippa, and they both left the soup on the table and ran upstairs. Though she was curious, disapproving and inclined to disbelieve Fergus's translation of Mrs. Breane into Mrs. Wynton, the woman was capable and experienced, and to his infinite relief, Fergus resigned Philippa to her hands, hanging about on the stairs after he had attended to Mrs. Joliman, ready for any service required of him.

And shortly afterwards, Philippa's daughter was born.

Mrs. Cuddey called him, and when he instantly appeared she thrust into his arms, bundled up in a towel, the hideous red thing covered with yellowish slime which had caused all this agony of body and mind. From the noise, it appeared to be an angry kitten.

'Wipe its face whilst I see to her,' she said as his arms closed automatically round the yelling bundle.

'Is she going to be alright?' he asked, looking at the inert figure on the bed, its twisting, writhing agony stilled.

'Yes, yes,' said the woman impatiently and turned from him.

Terrified lest he drop the thing in his arms, he laid it down on a chair and steadied it with his bent knee whilst he gingerly cleaned the worst of the mucus from the tightly screwed-up features almost obliterated by the open, squalling mouth. His ears were trying to hear any sounds from the other side of the room that might break through the baby's raucous yelling and he was relieved when at last Mrs. Cuddey came to take the baby from him, soothing it instantly by the close enfolding of her arms and giving him a look which showed her contempt for his sex and especially for him as a specimen of it.

He went across to the bed, where Philippa now lay as white as the pillow, her eyes closed, her hair in tight, wet curls.

'Darling,' he said in agony, for she seemed like one dead.

Her eyes opened for an instant and she smiled.

He dropped on his knees by the bed and laid his forehead against her hand.

'Beloved, you must never go through that again, never,' he whispered brokenly. 'I can never forgive myself. Are you going to be alright?'

'Alright,' she murmured. The baby—is it—alright?'

'I think so. It made enough noise. I'll ask her what it is.'

Mrs. Cuddey, who had taken care to lose nothing of the conversation which would be so valuable in village gossip later, did not need the question.

'A little girl,' she said, 'and of course she's alright. She's beautiful.'

Fergus grimaced and Philippa opened her eyes again and saw and smiled.

'I expect she looks hideous,' she whispered.

'Absolutely beautiful,' lied Fergus. 'Do you want anything, sweetheart? Are you comfortable?'

'By comparison, yes,' she said, and then they heard the doctor coming up the stairs and Fergus was bundled out again, this time told to go downstairs and make some tea.

He thought about the three of them upstairs, Philippa, her daughter and her mother, three helpless females and all now his! It was an odd, disconcerting thought, though at the same time he exulted in it. Philippa could not leave him now. She had borne his child and he had owned it publicly, taken Philippa for his wife in the sight of this tiny village community. She was irrevocably his, and the hideous, mewing thing in the towel was his, and the inert, unconscious figure in the second bedroom was also his. For the first time since his mother had died, he had a family tie again. With the coming of this child, he was no longer the solitary being he had always felt himself to be. The child was his, he told himself exultantly, his kin, his actual blood, and neither Philippa nor the child could ever leave him again.

Mrs. Cuddey came down, a covered pail in her hand.

'How is my wife?' he asked her.

'She'll do, and the baby's strong though it's too soon, the doctor says. Make the tea and I'll carry it up when I've thrown this away,' and she bustled out into the yard at the back of the house.

Chapter Fifteen

'I seem, then, to have failed,' said Fergus bitterly, his eyes narrowed into hatred.

'Completely,' said Justin, his composure concealing the tumult of his thoughts as he had been trained from infancy by the code of his social class to conceal his emotions.

The three years since Philippa had left him had taken their toll of her husband and at forty-four he looked more than middle-aged. His greying hair was thin and his frame had shrunk. There was no lustre in his eyes and no expression in his voice. He seemed a man from whom the reason for living had gone, and who lived only because he had not physically died.

At first Fergus had been shocked and sorry for him, and had not been without a consciousness of guilt, but now every other feeling had been swallowed up in angry disappointment, for he had come, at long last with Philippa's consent, to ask Justin to divorce her.

'It's sheer, rank selfishness,' said Fergus. 'You know, you must know, that Philippa will never return to you.'

'I retain my own views on that, Mr. Wynton,' said Justin stiffly.

They were in the library at Hollmere Abbey and unconsciously the beautiful old house with its age-old history, its atmosphere of indestructibility in an age when everything else that was old had been, or was being, swept away, had made its mark on Fergus. In spite of the years of happiness he and Philippa had spent together, he was feeling for the first time since their reunion that there was something of her that he did not possess. Something must have remained and been held by the life she had lived there, a life foreign to his nature and inconceivable by his imagination. He could never actually have

266

believed that she might be called back by anything inside or outside her to the Abbey and the man who was, after all and indisputably, her husband, and yet he felt it to be impossible for this place not to have retained some hold on anyone who had once lived in it.

He had had a shock, too, when he had by chance seen Trevor going out of the house with his nurse, for the child was very much like his mother, with the same curly brown hair, the same wide-apart grey eyes, and a quick movement of the head when he saw Fergus that instantly recalled Philippa.

He had spoken to him on impulse.

'Hullo,' he said. 'You're Trevor, aren't you?'

The child smiled engagingly, planted his sturdy little body before him and prepared for conversation.

'Yes, and I'm nearly five,' he said. 'I don't know who you are. Have you come to stay here?'

Fergus hesitated, not caring to give his name to the pleasant-looking but obviously efficient girl looking at them.

'No, I'm not going to stay. I have just called to see your father.'

'I like you,' said Trevor. 'Will you have tea with me when I come back? I'm going out on my bicycle but I shall be back soon.'

'That's very kind of you, but I don't think I shall be able to stay,' said Fergus.

'Oh—well. Alright,' said Trevor resignedly. 'Goodbye. I'm sorry you can't stay.'

They shook hands solemnly, and the child went off with his nurse whilst Fergus was admitted to the house.

The episode had shaken him. It was the start of the definite association in his mind with Philippa herself, not as she had been linked with it before merely by being Justin's legal wife.

'It's difficult to understand you, Lord Hollmere,' he said now, when Justin had coldly refused to believe that Philippa was irrevocably lost to him. 'It's now three years since Philippa left you. We have lived together as man and wife for almost the whole of that time. She is known as Mrs. Wynton and she has a child who is my daughter and who is, of course, registered in my name. We are perfectly happy together and Philippa is entirely in agreement with me in wanting you to set her free so that we can be legally married. Why can't you accept the inevitable and be fair to her?'

Justin's face was an expressionless mask.

'Has either of you ever been fair to me?' he asked.

'No, perhaps not, but there is our child, who at least has had no hand in this and who does not deserve to be punished.'

'You seem to have forgotten that there is also a child of mine, Mr. Wynton, who has suffered and will suffer from his mother's desertion of him. Has he done anything for which to be punished? And you spoke just now of my selfishness in refusing to divorce my wife. I see no evidence of unselfishness in any action of the past or the present on the part of either you or Lady Hollmere.'

'It's all part of your ridiculous childishness to refer to her as Lady Hollmere when she is no longer anything of the kind,' snapped Fergus.

'But you are wrong, Mr. Wynton. She will always be my wife and therefore share my title,' said Justin with the infuriating calmness which he had never relaxed for a moment during the interview. 'Need we prolong this conversation? Believe me, it will not get you anywhere.'

'You are determined to make Philippa suffer to the end of her life, or yours, for having preferred another man to you?'

'I have not the slightest wish that she should suffer anything at all. She is perfectly free to return to me whenever she wishes, and nothing will ever be said to her by me, or shown in any way by look or deed, which would savour of blame. She would come back to me as my honoured and—loved wife, the mistress of this house, as if she had never left it. I hope you will tell her that, Mr. Wynton.'

Fergus stared at him for another moment or two, baffled, impotent. Then he turned on his heel and flung himself out of the room, pushed past the butler who stood waiting in the hall and wrestled angrily with the complicated antiquity of the handle of the door.

'Allow me, sir,' said the butler behind him, and Fergus had to stand aside to allow the thing to be done for him.

Outside, the taxi which had brought him from Sloworth station was waiting, and he flung himself into it, to sit hunched up in the corner, frustrated and bitter.

It had taken him a long time to get Philippa to agree to his going personally to ask Justin to divorce her. He had not been able to understand her reluctance, since she had told him almost passionately, and he had believed her, that that reluctance had had nothing to do with her right to call herself Lady Hollmere if she wished, nor with any thought of the dignity of her former life. She seemed completely happy.

Mrs. Joliman had never recovered from the stroke which had paralysed her, though for some months she had had her mind restored without a corresponding recovery of her body, which remained helpless. During those months Fergus had remained at Bryn Cottage, having established himself there so completely that by the time Philippa was up and about again, there seemed no point in trying to break the new system of life.

Even Mrs. Joliman, at first distrustful of Fergus and averse to his being there, had chanted her opinion of him and before she died, when little Valerie was six months old, she had a long talk with him in which she told him she would die happy if only he were able to marry Philippa and 'make an honest woman of her'. She also told him that she was leaving him the small amount of money which, under her husband's will, was all that she could leave away from Philippa, who would now inherit the whole of the Jolly Man wealth.

'You should have something for yourself, Fergus,' she had said, but in the end her death had come before the new will could be signed, so Fergus found himself with his own narrow means made still narrower by the fact that he had not worked for six months, in the unenviable position of being, as he put it rather bitterly to Philippa, 'living on the bounty of a wealthy woman I can't even marry'.

He had a small pension because of the injuries he had sustained which had made him unfit as a pilot, but it was a mere pittance, and his only likely means of making a living was in an aircraft factory, where his knowledge and experience, added to the training he had been receiving before he had given it up to be with Philippa, might be of service.

After Mrs. Joliman's death, they had discussed the position, and Philippa had been obliged to agree with him that it would be intolerable for him to live on her money. There was no work for him anywhere near Llantydd, even if the thought of remaining where they were ostracised and stared at and gossiped about could be borne.

Eventually he got a reasonably good job in an aircraft factory in the midlands, and Philippa sold Bryn Cottage and they moved into one of the small new houses which were being made available to the married technicians who could not otherwise be employed.

The size of the house, its tiny rooms which would accommodate only small, not very comfortable furniture, and the unfamiliarity of her surroundings and of people who seemed to her almost an alien race, suspicious of her and sowing suspicion of themselves – all these things made it difficult for Philippa to settle down, but she tackled the situation with all her old courage, aided by her sense of humour and her love for Fergus.

Though she could, of course, have made her life so much more comfortably materially, she was determined not to do so. She had had the experience of living with Justin in circumstances which had made and kept and widened a gulf between them. It had been a matter of complete indifference to her that it was her money which repaired and restored their home and very largely maintained it. She had never known the lack of money and its usefulness was as easy and familiar as the air she breathed and therefore she thought no more of it. But she realised more now than even she had done then that it had been a source of constant pain to Justin, a barb in his flesh, poisoned and always malignant. She felt that it might have destroyed their peace even without the tragedy which had overtaken them. With this gained knowledge of men (and Fergus, she felt, was not very different in that respect from Justin), she would not risk it happening again. So she maintained the home on the money Fergus gave her, working with her own hands and asserting cheerfully that she liked it, and if she spent her own money on things for their mutual comfort, she carefully hid the fact from him.

Sometimes she wondered how long this state of things would last. She would certainly get tired of the monotonous round, the daily chores which she had learned for the first time to do when she and her mother had lived at Bryn Cottage, but she had reached a stage when she wanted to live in the moment and not to try to see ahead.

She accepted with little comment the information that Justin had refused unequivocally to give her a divorce.

'I didn't think he would,' was all she said in a low voice, and let Fergus rave on about the selfishness, the stupidity, the unreasonableness which kept her legally tied to a man who must know he had no hope of making the bond anything else.

Philippa had nothing to say and finally the invective ceased and he came across the room to her and sat beside her, an arm about her, his cheek pressed against hers.

'You're so silent about it,' he said. 'Don't you really mind, beloved?'

'Yes, I do. I want with all my heart to be your wife, my darling, but I know him and I felt certain he would not change his mind. Don't let's worry about it, Fergus. It doesn't really matter, does it? We won't talk about it or think about it anymore. Look, I've got to the armhole of your sweater,' holding up her knitting. 'Doesn't it look a bit short?'

'Try it against me,' he said, accepting her change of subject.

But later she referred to it indirectly, unable any longer to keep back the question of her hungry heart, that had never ceased to ache.

'Fergus, did you see or hear anything of—Trevor?' she asked, not looking at him.

'Yes. As a matter of fact, I saw him,' he said reluctantly.

He knew he had far more reason to be jealous of the child than of the husband. In his secret heart, he had always resented the boy even though Philippa had left him and never spoke of him.

She looked up, her face flushing a little.

'Oh, Fergus, did you? How did he look? Has he grown? But of course he has. He was only a baby when I—when I saw him last,' her voice and her eyes lowered again. She was pleating her dress in folds as she spoke, her fingers nervously seeking some sort of action.

'He looked extremely well and seemed perfectly happy,' said Fergus. 'He was with a young woman, his nurse I suppose. A very pleasant girl.'

'What was he doing?'

'Just leaving the house. He told me he was going to ride on his bicycle.'

'Trevor riding a bicycle!' and she got up precipitately and left him and he could hear her moving about in the room above, the room where Valerie was sleeping. She had gone, he knew, to try to console herself with one child for the loss of the other, but he had had to accept the knowledge that, devoted mother though she was to Valerie, this second child would never quite fill the void where her first-born had been, the child she had deserted.

When she came down again, she was outwardly serene, her work basket in her hand and a small garment of Valerie's over her arm.

They smiled at each other.

'I've got over it,' she said. 'I'm not going to make a thing about not mentioning Trevor. If I keep it all shut up inside me, I shall make it too important in my life. I've chosen my way and I don't regret it — and I've got Valerie.'

'You don't know the relief it is to me to have you say that you don't regret it, darling,' he said. 'I've never been so happy in my life as I am here with you — not that I can say I really love my work!' with a chuckle.

'You want to be up again, I know, but even if it's selfish of me, I am glad you can't fly any more. I should never have a minute's peace if I thought you were up. Now you can tell me without my being silly what you thought of Trevor. It's the best way for me to face it, and you know that for his sake I shall never try to make myself known to him. What does he look like?'

'He looks absurdly like you, same hair and eyes, same way of moving. Much too pretty for a boy but he will probably grow out of that. I've often wished Valerie were more like you, but I can never see the slightest resemblance in her to either of us, can you? She must be a throw-back to our ancestors.'

'I didn't know mine,' laughed Philippa, but she busied herself threading her needle so as not to look at him as she spoke.

She knew, with increasing certainty, that Valerie was going to look like old Lady Hollmere, that as she lost the baby contours of her face, she was revealing more and more the high cheek-bones, the thin, aquiline nose, the determined chin of the old aristocrat who, beyond any doubt, was her grandmother. Valerie would be entirely Hollmere, and the secret knowledge made her heart ache, for she had wanted Fergus's child and she knew now that she would never bear him one. Something had gone wrong when this child had been born, but she could never bring herself to tell Fergus. The more sure she became that Valerie was not his, the more desperately she hoped he would never discover the fact.

'Well, whether she's like either of us or not, she's a darling,' said Fergus happily, 'and I wouldn't change one thing about her now that I've accepted her unlikeness to you. I'm going to see about taking out an insurance policy, if I can, to provide for her education. I've been making enquiries. I want her to have the best, and though I know I shall have to let you do something to help there, with costs rising so terrifically, I'm not going to let you have all your own way, Mrs. Wynton,' kissing the top of her bent head.

Philippa smiled at him.

'Fancy talking of her education!' she said. 'Oh, Fergus, I want to keep her a baby as long as I can. They grow away so fast.'

'We'll have others, my darling.'

'Perhaps,' she said quietly.

A few days later, as she came back from shopping, with Valerie in her pram, Mrs. Carling, who came in occasionally to help her, was at the door to meet her.

'I was watching for you, m'm,' she said. 'There's a gentleman waiting to see you. I put him in the living-room and gave him the papers to look at. He came just after you went out, but he said he'd wait.'

'Thank you, Mrs. Carling. Take Valerie's things off for me, will you?' and Philippa went into the living-room, thinking it was probably the man from the Electricity Board to see about some points which were to be put in.

She stopped short in the doorway and then walked slowly into the room and closed the door behind her.

'This is very unexpected, Justin,' she said as calmly a she could.

He had risen when she came in.

'But not too great a shock, I hope? How are you, Philippa?'

'I am very well. Please sit down,' she said, taking a chair near the door.

He must have taken stock of her surroundings, the small house exactly like all the others in the road, the narrow front gate and patch of garden before the front door, and inside it the tiny boxlike hall with the steep staircase from it, and the small crowded room into which he had been left to await Philippa, a room much lived-in, her work basket overflowing on the table, a child's toys on the floor.

He looked round again, meaningly.

'Do you like this sort of thing, Philippa?' he asked.

'I am perfectly happy here, Justin,' she said steadily. 'Is that what you have come to find out?'

'Yes. I want your happiness, my dear. I have always wanted it and tried to give it to you, though not, I am afraid, with much success since you are happier away from me. You know that Fergus Wynton came to see me the other day?'

'Yes.'

'Did you send him to me?'

'No. I should not do that. You ought to know me well enough not to believe I should send someone else to do a difficult thing rather than do it myself.'

'But you knew he was coming?'

'Yes.'

'And that he was going to ask me to set you free so that he could marry you?'

'Yes.'

'Then you know that I refused?'

'Yes.'

'But you were not surprised that I refused?'

'No.'

'Could you be a little less monosyllabic? You are making it very difficult for me, Philippa.'

'I'm sorry, Justin, but I did not seek this interview and forgive me if I say I am not pleased with it. There's nothing to gain by it. Please accept that.'

'You told me before you left me that you wanted neither me nor this man nor any other man. Yet I find you have been living with him for a long time, two years I think he said, and that you have a child by him. I was astonished at that. You were always honest, Philippa. You deceived me with this man, but you did not deny the association and I could have sworn you were honest with me when you told me you did not want him. I believed you and let you go.'

Her head went up. There were bright spots of colour in her cheeks.

'You could not have prevented me, Justin. I was honest with you, though, when I said I wanted neither you nor Fergus. Then—well, you yourself gave him my address. Why did you do that, I wonder?'

'Because I intended to be quite fair to you, Philippa. Also because I was convinced that you did not want him and—well, I would not stoop to any sort of deceit with you. I felt then, as I still feel in spite of everything – in spite of *everything*, Philippa – that you will come back to me. I could only be sure of you, satisfied that it was not merely an impulse, if I gave you every opportunity of considering it. I should have felt I was giving myself an unfair advantage if I kept you hidden from him.'

She was silent. As he had so often done before, and quite unintentionally she knew, he was making her feel small in her own eyes. In a similar position, she would not have given the address of her beloved to her rival as Justin had done.

'I don't know if I made a mistake,' he went on as she did not reply. 'Perhaps I did, though I prefer to think not. I admit that it was a great surprise to me, a shock I might almost say, when I learned that you were living with Fergus Wynton and that, moreover, you have a child by him.'

'You make me feel very small, Justin,' she said in a low voice.

'I am not intending to do so. I merely want to get at the complete truth. Do you really love this man, Philippa?'

'With all my heart.'

'And you want me to divorce you so that you can marry him?'

'Yes.'

He was silent for a moment, and in that moment Fate took a hand again in Philippa's life.

Valerie, escaping laughingly from Mrs. Carling, flung open the door of the living-room and ran to her mother with shouts of glee.

'Carly not cat' Val,' she shrieked in delight and held fast to Philippa's dress when Mrs. Carling came in filled with apologies.

'I'm so sorry, m'm,' she said. 'The little monkey was too quick for me. Come along, Valerie lovey. Come and see what Carly's got for you.'

'Yes, run along with Carly, darling,' said Philippa. 'Mummy's busy just now,' and she gently disengaged the clinging fingers.

Valerie let go, but she stood facing Justin gravely.

' 'Oo you, mans?' she asked.

'I—I am not quite—sure,' he said slowly, and Philippa could not look at him.

Gently she pushed the child towards Mrs. Carling.

'Run along, darling,' she said, and Valerie trotted away, but with a backward glance at Justin as she went.

When the door had closed on her, he spoke curtly.

'Why did you not tell me?'

'Tell you what, Justin?' she asked, trying to brave it out though she knew it was useless.

'That the child is mine. Don't try to deny it. It is quite obvious. Why couldn't you have told me, Philippa?'

'For one thing, I thought you would not have believed it.'

'Possibly,' he agreed. 'Does Wynton know?'

'No. It has never occurred to him. He doesn't know your family, and she is not very much like you.'

He got up and walked about the room, his head bent, his hands behind him, his brow furrowed with painful thoughts. Philippa sat motionless, unable to imagine what was likely to happen next. The fear that Fergus might return to find him here made her feel sick with apprehension. She felt she had had enough crises in her life, and that the one thing she wanted, simple enough surely, would never be hers. That thing was peace.

She broke in on his thoughts.

'Justin, I do beg of you to let things alone. No possible good or happiness can come to any of us by trying to alter them. I know I have no right to ask anything of you, especially happiness, but I *am* happy with Fergus, and he is devoted to Valerie, and all we ask is to be let alone. Please, Justin, let me go out of your life.'

But she saw from the tightening of his lips and the look in his eyes that he had made up his mind and her heart sank. She knew she could do nothing against the obstinacy of a naturally weak man, and behind him were all the generations of Hollmeres who were accustomed to fight to keep their own.

'Surely you realise that you are asking me to surrender my own child to another man?' he asked.

'She can be nothing to you since until a few minutes ago you did not even know that you had another child. Besides—I left you Trevor,' her voice catching on the name.

'You had no choice,' he said. 'I should and could have claimed him.'

'You can't claim Valerie. She has been registered in Fergus's name. Oh, Justin, don't let's take a child's life and tear it to pieces because of our own inability to arrange our own lives. You have Trevor; let me have Valerie.'

'May I remind you that you also have this man and I am without you, Philippa?'

She made a helpless gesture.

'Justin, what's the use of all this? It's not getting us anywhere. What can either of us gain by it? You told me a little while ago that what you want is my happiness, and asked me if I want you to set me free to marry Fergus.'

'I still want your happiness and always shall, but at the time I spoke of divorcing you I did not know of the existence of my second child. That makes a great deal of difference, and your contention that I cannot care about her because I have only just learned of her existence is wrong. I am responsible for her being in the world. I accept that responsibility now that I am aware of its existence.'

She stared at him in consternation.

'Justin, you cannot possibly suggest that you will try to take Valerie from me?' she asked.

'No. What I suggest is that you both return to me, and to your son.'

'I cannot leave Fergus and it would be too cruel to take Valerie from him even if I could.'

'Very well. I cannot, of course, compel you to do so. The only thing I can do is to leave the way open so that you can come back to me, with the child of course, at any time you feel the wish to do so.'

'Please be very sure that I shall remain with the man I truly and deeply love, Justin,' she said in a low voice.

He rose from his chair.

'Very well. I must leave it at that. But I am sorry, Philippa, very sorry. I shall always hope and believe that you will turn to me again. This man is not worth your love. Some day that will prove itself, I feel sure.'

'You have no right to say that,' she said hotly. 'You scarcely know him.'

'No, but I have my own opinion of the type of man who will seduce another man's wife and eventually get her away from him.'

'I was as much to blame as Fergus for that,' she said.

He shrugged his shoulders.

'We will leave it at that. By the way, I brought these pictures of Trevor which I thought you might like to have, and also a brochure which I had prepared about Hollmere Abbey,' laying a packet down on the table. 'You need not, of course, return them. I had copies made especially for you.'

'Thank you,' she said mechanically.

He picked up his hat and then, with an impulsive gesture foreign to his nature, he laid it down again, came to her and took her unresponsive hands in his.

'Philippa—Philippa, my darling,' he said in a tone totally different from the one he had used throughout the interview, a tone that was gentle, affectionate, sad. 'I am going because you don't want me to stay and because I do desire above everything else in the world your happiness. I don't believe it will lay ultimately with this man. I believe you will return to me, and I want you to know that you will find no reproaches, no recriminations, nothing but my deep, sincere and everlasting love.'

She could not answer but stood there, her hands supine in his. Nothing he had ever said to her had power to touch her as these words did. She had injured him deeply, and he had suffered both privately and publicly on her account, and yet it had not altered one iota of his love for her, the love that had left her unsatisfied so that she had turned from it to that of Fergus Wynton, a good love, she knew, but would Fergus ever have been capable of forgiving her so much wrong? Of returning after so great an injury to offer her an unchanged, unchanging love?

She drew her hands from his and turned her head away.

'You make me so ashamed, Justin,' she said shakily.

He hesitated for a moment and then took up his hat again.

'Goodbye, my dear,' he said, and left her standing there.

Chapter Sixteen

Philippa did not know how long she stood there after Justin had left her, but she was disturbed at length by Mrs. Carling, who came in apologetically to ask if she should put Valerie to bed.

'No, I'll do it, thank you, Mrs. Carling,' she said. 'I'm afraid you've stayed late.'

'Never mind, love. That's O.K.,' said Mrs. Carling cheerfully, and Philippa thought 'Shades of Hollmere Abbey!' She wondered if the social revolution would ever actually reach old Lady Hollmere, who up to the time Philippa left Sloworth had contrived to keep herself aloof from it, attended by the few old servants who had gone with her to the Dower House and to whom she was still the Great Lady. Philippa thought of the shock it would be to her if circumstances ever forced her to travel on a London bus, where the conductor would almost certainly call her 'dear' or 'ducks' or even 'my girl', or if she were left helpless on a railway platform where a porter might hail her as 'mate'. Philippa herself could never understand why any personal form of address in buses or on stations was necessary. She had long ceased to expect to be called 'madam', since the new ruling class obviously thought this term used to a woman savoured of subservience rather than the mere courtesy due to an unknown woman. It always passed her comprehension, however, why any sobriquet at all was necessary when she asked for a bus ticket.

She accepted Mrs. Carling's cheery *camaraderie* without comment as the trend of the age.

She went upstairs to the diminutive bathroom with Valerie, who always looked for a final riot in the bath with Fergus when he came in, but tonight he had not appeared by the time Philippa carried the child, clean and pink and sweet, to her own room.

'It looks as though somebody kept Daddy late tonight, darling,' she said, kissing her. 'I'll give him a big hug and kiss for you when he comes in,' and the child, tired and sleepy at last, snuggled down drowsily.

But when Philippa went down into the living-room, she found Fergus there, standing by the table and looking at something in his hand. A few loose photographs lay on the surface of the table and she remembered, with a feeling of annoyance at her carelessness, that she had left there the packet of which Justin had spoken.

Well, there was no help for it now and she came to him and linked her arm with his and turned her face for his kiss.

'You can guess who's been here,' she said.

He did not respond to her inviting gesture but remained staring at a photograph in his hand, a strange expression on his face.

'What is it, darling?' she asked, and, unbelievingly, he released her arm from his and tapped with his finger at the photograph.

'This,' he said. 'I don't need to ask who it is. He's been here, has he?'

'Yes. This afternoon. He left those, but I haven't looked at them yet.'

He put the photograph into her hand and she stared at it. It was a snapshot of Justin with his mother and his son, and, as so often happens with photographs, a resemblance between two people is brought out strikingly. In this case, baby though Valerie still was at two years old, it was impossible for anyone not to see the likeness between her and old Lady Hollmere. There were the eyes with slightly uneven brows above them, the nose already taking shape in Valerie's face, the way in which her hair grew in a 'widow's peak' above the wide, rather high forehead.

Philippa stood looking at the photograph. What was there for her to say? How could she possibly deny it?

'Well?' asked Fergus in a tone she had never heard from him before.

'Well what?' returned Philippa as lightly as she could, laying the photograph down on the table.

'Don't tell me I am imagining it because of course I am not. This woman is most obviously of the same blood as Valerie,' tapping Lady Hollmere's pictured face with his forefinger. 'There is, of course, only one possible explanation of it. Valerie is his child.'

Philippa could not find anything to say. She felt frozen. Nothing would ever make him understand. The stark facts, without extenuating circumstances, were hideous to him. She had left her husband and, after swearing to her lover that there was no physical relationship any longer, had found herself with his child. When her lover turned up again, she had seized on the chance of saddling him with the responsibility for the child that was not his and since then, knowing, as she must do, that the child was Justin's, she had let him live in his fool's paradise.

All this flashed through her mind with the incalculable speed of thought whilst Fergus stood looking at her and waiting for her to speak, his face unfamiliar and frightening in its anger.

'Well?' Again that uncompromising monosyllable.

'I don't know what to say,' she said in a low voice.

'I am not surprised at that. What a laugh you've had at me all this time, haven't you?'

His voice was savagely bitter.

'No, Fergus. It isn't quite as you think. I've never wanted to laugh at you. I'm utterly humiliated. You must realise that I never meant you to know this.'

He gave a short, hard laugh.

'Certainly I realise that you didn't mean me to know. You'd have foisted off another man's child on me for the rest of my life and let me drool over her, refusing in the meantime to have another.'

'I've never refused, Fergus. I can't have another. It's a physical impossibility because of something or other that went wrong at Valerie's birth.'

'So you have deceived me even in that?'

'You're being very unfair, Fergus. As for my having, as you say, foisted another man's child on you – could you have felt any different about Valerie had she been your own? Has there been any actual difference?'

'That's not the point. The point is that she is not mine, and now that I know it she will never seem to me to be mine anymore. There is also the knowledge that—that it was possible for him to have fathered this child. That hurts abominably. It makes *you* into someone I've never known. Oh, I know, if you're going to look at it from one angle, I have no right to mind. He's your husband and I'm not. But what has been between you and me, Philippa, was outside any merely legal status. You've been my wife to me and always would have been ...'

'Would have been? Would have been, Fergus?' She caught him up on the phrase which struck her like a physical blow. 'You can't mean that this is going to make any difference to the way we are to each other? Have these two years counted for nothing? Don't you know that there is no other man in the world for me and never could be? That all I want is for Justin to make it possible for me to marry you?'

His look made her feel paralysed, numbed almost beyond the power to feel anymore. Her world had crumbled to pieces. There was no longer any solid ground beneath her feet.

'You haven't told me yet what he came for,' he said coldly.

'To make sure I was happy and really wanted the divorce, he said.'

'And now? Was he sufficiently reassured?'

'He saw Valerie, guessed the truth about her and—refused the divorce,' she said.

She was horrified to see that he did not believe her.

'It's a big lure, that house and the title and everything, and presumably both your children,' he sneered.

'Fergus, you can't know what you're saying! You could not possibly believe that anything, *anything*, could take me back to him?'

'I don't know. You see, I don't know you anymore. The woman I thought you were could not possibly have had a child by any other man but me. It is an utter impossibility for me to have made love to any other woman but you. We're different. That's all.'

'I don't suppose I can make you understand, darling,' she said brokenly, 'but that night – everything was so confused, so muddled. I had to tell him about us. It was all to come out at the court proceedings. I had to tell him. He was—unbelievably kind to me. I think only one husband in a million, or a million million, would have been like that. He did not reproach me. It was like a death blow to him, but he stood up to it and he tried to comfort me.'

'How admirably he succeeded!' broke in Fergus with bitter scorn.

'I can't say anything else,' she said in a low, helpless voice. 'I'm defeated. If you can't understand, or won't, what is there left for us? Are you going to leave me?'

'I don't know what I'm going to do. I must get out of here until I've thought. I'm stifled,' and he went out of the room and out of the house.

She heard the door bang behind him and listened until his footsteps had died away. Then she sat down at the table and rested her head on her hands. Her anguish was too deep for tears. Dry-eyed she sat there and lost all count of time.

Fergus walked automatically towards the great factory to which, every day, his steps took him. He did not even know where he was going until he found himself halted by the great iron gates which in the daytime stood open but which were now closed and locked, a night guard on-duty in his little hut.

The man came out and Fergus showed his pass.

'I want to look again at a job that was finished today,' he said, making up an excuse at random, and though the man looked curiously at the set, strained expression on his face, he made no comment but unlocked the gate, locking it again after Fergus had passed through.

The factory was turning out a new aeroplane that was still on the 'secret' list, and it was quite true that one had been finished that day. Fergus, in his capacity as a technical adviser, had gone all over the engine and the controls before it had been run into position to await the next day's trials. On paper, the thing would fly, and if nothing on the paper was wrong, the next day it really would fly.

It was a small thing compared with the enormous planes of commerce and the great bombing planes, a two-seater scout capable of terrific speed and manoeuvrability, a lovely thing in the eyes of a pilot, slender, graceful, giving little impression of its terrific potential.

There was high octane spirit in it, enough for the first short trials in which it would merely lift and drop again. Still in a state of dreamlike trance, a trance of anger and misery and despair, he climbed into the cockpit and felt the familiar controls under his hands. It was like coming home after years of exile.

He sat there and looked at the instrument panel, automatically taking note of this and that, his mind registering what he saw without being actually conscious of it.

He was thinking of Philippa – Philippa whom he had adored and loved beyond belief, had trusted so implicitly – Philippa who had betrayed him, gone back to her husband and let him take her lightly and uncaringly – Philippa who had known that the child he himself had helped into the world was not his, but who had let him think so all this time.

And Valerie – little, sweet, adorable Valerie, who was not his at all but Justin Hollmere's – Justin who had been to see Philippa that day and had told her he would not set her free – and Philippa must have acquiesced – perhaps would go back sooner or later to being Lady Hollmere again …

Almost without knowing it, his hands and feet began to work automatically. There were no holding blocks. He himself had helped to design the method of a quick getaway. He knew all there was to know about the plane, which was in many ways revolutionary – all, that is, except whether it would fly.

The man who had opened the gates for him heard the sound of a plane starting up and came out of his hut to stand for a moment in perplexity, straining his eyes, trying to see through the darkness of the moonless night.

What the blazes …? The chap had one of the special passes which enabled him to have access to anything without question, even the private testing grounds, but he might have said if he intended to take a ship up.

Presently he saw it, a dim shape against the night sky, with no lights showing. It rose almost vertically and then was lost to sight. The man returned to his hut and his frying-pan of sausages. He heard the note of the engine change to a steady whirr, then it broke and began to thud. Then, as he stood with the pan in his hand, the thuds stopped and there was an eerie silence – and then the crash.

He dropped his pan and ran out, rushing automatically towards the box which contained the alarm which would bring an ambulance.

Fergus Wynton was still conscious when they extricated him, twisted and crumpled and broken, from the wreckage of the plane.

'Don't try to talk, old man,' said the doctor who had come with the ambulance.

They were lifting him with infinite care on to the stretcher.

'Not—plane,' he said, though every breath was an agony. 'My fault—not plane ...'

'Alright,' the doctor reassured him. 'You can tell us all about it later.'

'Not plane. Plane—good,' insisted Fergus. 'All—my ...'

'Yes, old chap. Later,' said the doctor again.

But there was no 'later' for Fergus.

Philippa stood looking down at what had been the man she loved. Something of herself, perhaps of all herself that mattered, lay there with him, dead.

Not knowing how poignant, how terribly barbed their words would be, they had told her of what he had managed to say before he died, of the loyalty and faith in his work which had made him struggle to justify, before he died, the work in which he and others had put so much work and hope.

'He wanted to make it quite clear to all of us, Mrs. Wynton, that the crash was not due to any fault in the plane. We shall never know what happened. Of course he may have blacked out. He had not been in the air for a long time ...'

She had turned away, her hand over her eyes as if to shut out the sight of her mind's picture.

'Yes—yes—I understand,' she said.

But did she? Would she ever be able to understand? Ever know whether he had died intentionally? Had chosen that way out, unable to face life any more since she, who had been his heaven and his hope, had so deeply injured him?

She would never know.

She had to talk of all the necessary arrangements, though everybody tried to help her. They had all liked Fergus. His death was a personal grief to them.

But it was over at last and there was nothing more to do, nothing more to say.

She went home to face life again, to face Valerie who wailed constantly for 'Daddy' and who could be no more consoled by Mrs. Carling's talk of angels and heaven than by her mother's wordless, tearless embraces.

It was on the day of the funeral that she came back to find Justin pacing to and fro on the pavement, waiting for her. Mrs. Carling had taken Valerie off for the day, and the house was empty.

Philippa stopped, looking at him with eyes that seemed to him like the eyes of the dead, blank and sightless.

'May I come in for a moment or two?' he asked.

Without speaking, she unlocked the door and he followed her into the living-room in which Mrs. Carling had drawn the curtains.

Philippa went to them and pulled them back. She wanted no parade or panoply of grief. She did not even wear mourning, thereby somewhat scandalising her neighbours.

'I have only just learnt from the papers what has happened,' said Justin. 'I am sorry, my dear. That is all I have really come to say.'

'Thank you,' she said quietly, and sat down and waited with complete composure and no interest to anything he might have to say.

'I don't want to make this difficult for you,' he said after an uncomfortable pause. 'I can only ask you to believe me when I say I am sorry.'

'I do believe you,' she said in the same unemotional tone.

'Also—Philippa, everything is just the same, exactly as it was when we met the other day. I love you very much.'

'Thank you, Justin.'

'Philippa—was it my fault?'

Her answer came in a quick, desperate rush.

'Your fault? Fergus's death? No. No, I don't think so. Perhaps I am beginning to believe that what is to be, will be. All the time I have known that it could not last, that we were stealing something – from life, from each other, from—you. It had to end.'

Her words had a sound of winter in them, bleak, frozen. The whole of her was like that, no longer fully alive, not even caring to become alive again.

He rose and laid a hand gently, timidly almost, on her arm.

'That had to end perhaps, but not everything, not life for you, or happiness,' he said.

'Happiness?'

Her smile was bitter.

'Yes, happiness. This thing will pass, my dear, as mercifully everything passes. You said yourself that you have known it could not last. But I believe that you will find happiness again. I shall never cease to believe that and to hope for it. I think that someday you will come back to me, Philippa.'

She did not respond to his gesture nor look at him. Her head was bent. He could not see her eyes.

'I don't know,' she said. 'At the moment there is nothing for me anywhere. That hurts you. It must do. I'm past caring, Justin. Perhaps I died with—him.'

She knew that at last she was near to tears, the tears she had not been able to shed.

But that must not be yet. Not until Justin had gone. Not until she was alone again with her grief.

He stood looking at her, powerless to help. Then he lifted her hand and kissed it.

'I love you very much, Philippa. I shall always love you,' he said and quietly he left her.

She sat motionless until she heard the outer door close. Then, on a sudden, inexplicable impulse, she rose and went to the window to watch him go.

Justin.

Justin.

Was this the end?

Give Back Yesterday

Helena Clurey has it all – a devoted husband, money and family. She is happy and secure, but her apparent contentment is about to be shattered by a voice from the past. Mistress she may have been, but that is not the way it is put to her: 'you were not my mistress - you were, and are, my wife.'

The Weir House

Philip wants to marry Eve. It is her way out - he is rich, not too old, and has been in love for years – but not a man she can accept. He has even secretly funded her lifestyle, such that it is. Eve feels trapped. Unlike her friend Marcia, who cheerfully accepts an 'ordinary' life without complaint, Eve has known better and wants better. A chance encounter then changesthings – Lewis Belamie pays her to act as his fiancée for a week. Adventure, ambition, and disappointment all follow after she journeys to Cornwall with him, where she eventually nearly dies after what appears to be a suicide attempt because of a marriage that has seemingly failed. However, the mysterious and mocking Felix really does love her. Just who is he; how does Eve end up with him; and what part does 'The Weir House' play in her life? Has Eve's restlessness and relentless search for stability ended?

Through Many Waters

Jeff has got himself into a mess. It is, on the face of it, a classic scenario. He has a settled relationship with one woman, but loves another. What is he to do? It is now necessary to face reality, rather than continually making excuses to himself, but can he face the unpalatable truth? Then something beyond his influence intervenes and once again decisions have to be made. But in the end it is not Jeff that decides.

Misadventure

Olive Heriot and Hugh Manning had been in love for years, but marriage had been out of the question because of the intervention of Olive's mother. Now, at last, she was of age and due to gain her inheritance and be free to choose. A dinner party had been arranged at the Heriot's home, 'The Hermitage' and Hugh expects to be able to announce their engagement. Things start to change after a gruesomely realistic game entitled 'murder', which relies on someone drawing the Knave of Spades after cards are dealt. Tragedy strikes and other relationships are tested and consummated – but is this all real, or imagined?

Printed in Great Britain
by Amazon

35994851R00169